Regency Reputations

Regency Reputations:

Ransleigh Rogues

JULIA JUSTISS

MILLS & BOON

First Published in Great Britain 2022
By Mills & Boon, an imprint of HarperCollins*Publishers*
1 London Bridge Street, London, SE1 9GF

www.harpercollins.co.uk

HarperCollins*Publishers*
1st Floor, Watermarque Building,
Ringsend Road, Dublin 4, Ireland

REGENCY REPUTATIONS: RANSLEIGH ROGUES © 2022
Harlequin Enterprises ULC

The Rake to Rescue Her © 2015 Janet Justiss
The Rake to Reveal Her © 2015 Janet Justiss

ISBN: 978-0-263-30462-6

MIX
Paper from
responsible sources
FSC™ C007454

THE RAKE TO
RESCUE HER

To the Evelettes:

You've hugged me, cried with me, and been there for me every step of the way on the long twilight journey of the last two years.

I love you guys!

Chapter One

It was *her.*

Shock rocked him like the blast of air from a passing cannonball. Struck numb in its wake, Alastair Ransleigh, late of His Majesty's First Dragoons, stared at the tall, dark-haired woman approaching from the other side of Bath's expansive Sidney Gardens.

Even as his disbelieving mind told him it couldn't be her, he knew on some level deeper than reason that it *was* Diana. No other woman had that graceful, lilting step, as if dancing as she walked.

Heart thundering, he exhaled a great gasping breath, still unable to move or tear his gaze from her.

So had she glided into the room the day he'd first met her, bringing a draught of spring air and enchantment into the Oxford study where the callow collegian he'd once been had gone to consult her father, a noted scholar.

Memory swooped down and sank in vicious claws. *Just so he'd watched her, delirious with delight, as she walked into the Coddingfords' ballroom eight and a half years ago. Awaited her signal to approach, so her father might announce their engagement to the assembled guests.*

Instead, she'd given her arm to the older man who had followed her in. The Duke of Graveston, he'd belatedly recognised. The man who then announced that Diana was to marry him.

A sudden impact at knee level nearly knocked him over. 'Uncle Alastair!' his six-year-old nephew Robbie shrieked, hugging him around the legs while simultaneously jumping up and down. 'When did you get here? Are you staying long? Please say you are! Can you take me to get Sally Lunn cakes? And my friend, too?'

Jolted back to the present, Alastair returned the hug before setting the child at arm's length with hands that weren't quite steady. Fighting off the compulsion to look back across the gardens, he made himself focus on Robbie.

'I've only just arrived, and I'm not sure how long I'll stay. Your mama told me you'd gone to the Gardens with Nurse, so I decided to fetch you. Yes, we'll get cakes. Where's your friend?'

Still distracted, he followed his nephew's pointing finger towards a boy about Robbie's age, dressed neatly in nankeens and jacket. The child looked up at him shyly, the dark hair curling over his forehead shadowing his blue, blue eyes.

Diana's eyes.

With another paralysing shock, he realised that Robbie's friend must be her son.

The son that should have been his.

Pain as sharp as acid scalded his gut, followed by a wave of revulsion. Buy the boy cake? He'd as soon give sustenance to a viper!

Shocked by the ferocity of his reaction, he hauled himself under control. Whatever had occurred between himself and Diana was no fault of this innocent child.

It was the suddenness of it, seeing her again after so long with no warning, no time to armour himself against a revival of the anguish of their bitter parting. The humiliation of it, he thought, feeling his face redden.

Certain there must be some mistake, he'd run to her. Desperate to have her deny it, or at the very least, affirm the truth to his face, he'd shouted after her as the Duke warned him off and swept her away. Never once as he followed them did she glance at him before his cousins dragged him, still shouting, out of the ballroom...

Hurt pierced him, nearly as sharp as on that night he remembered with such grisly clarity. An instant later, revitalising anger finally scoured away the pain.

Ridiculous to expend so much thought or emotion on the woman, he told himself, sucking in a deep, calming breath. She'd certainly proved herself unworthy of it. He'd got over her years ago.

Though, he thought sardonically, this unexpected explosion of emotion suggested he hadn't banished the incident quite as effectively as he'd thought. He *had*, however, mastered a salutary lesson on the perfidy of females. They could be lovely, sometimes entertaining, and quite useful for the purpose for which their luscious bodies had been designed, but they were cold-hearted, devious, and focused on their own self-interest.

So, after that night, he had treated them as temporary companions to be enjoyed, but never trusted. And never again allowed close enough to touch his heart.

So he would treat Diana now, with cordial detachment.

His equilibrium restored, he allowed himself to glance across the park. Yes, she was still approaching. Any moment now, she would notice him, draw close enough to recognise him.

Would a blush of shame or embarrassment tint those

cheeks, as well it should? Or would she brazen it out, cool and calm as if she hadn't deceived, betrayed and humiliated him before half of London's most elite Society?

Despite himself, Alastair tensed as she halted on the far side of the pathway, holding his breath as he awaited her reaction.

When at last she turned her eyes towards them, her gaze focused only on the boy. 'Mannington,' she called in a soft, lilting voice.

The familiar tones sent shivers over his skin before penetrating to the marrow, where they resonated in a hundred stabbing echoes of memory.

'Please, Mama, may I go for cakes?' the boy asked her as Alastair battled the effect. 'My new friend, Robbie, invited me.'

'Another time, perhaps. Come along, now.' She crooked a finger, beckoning to the lad, her glance passing from the boy to Robbie to Alastair. After meeting his eyes for an instant, without a flicker of recognition, she gave him a slight nod, then turned away and began walking off.

Sighing, the boy looked back at Robbie. 'Will you come again tomorrow? Maybe I can go then.'

'Yes, I'll come,' Robbie replied as the child trotted after his mother. Grabbing the arm of the boy's maid, who was tucking a ball away in her apron, his nephew asked, 'You'll bring him, won't you?'

The girl smiled at Robbie. 'If I can, young master. Though little notice as Her Grace takes of the poor boy, don't see that it would make a ha'penny's difference to her whether he was in the house or not. I'd better get on.' Gently extricating her hand from Robbie's grip, she hurried off after her charge.

Alastair checked the immediate impulse to follow her, announce himself to Diana, and force a reaction.

Surely he hadn't changed that much from the eager young dreamer who'd thrown heart and soul at her feet, vowing to love her for ever! As she had vowed back to him, barely a week before she gave her hand to an older, wealthier man of high rank.

Had he been merely a convenient dupe, his open devotion a goad to prod a more prestigious suitor into coming up to snuff? He'd never known.

Sudden fury coursed through him again that the sight of her, the mere sound of her voice, could churn up an anguish he'd thought finally buried. Ah, how he *hated* her! Or more precisely, hated what she could still do to him.

Since the night she'd betrayed him, he'd had scores of women and years of soldiering. He'd thrown himself into the most desperate part of the battle, determined to burn the memory of loving her out of his brain.

While she seemed, now as then, entirely indifferent.

Mechanically he gave his nephew a hand, walking beside him while the lad chattered on about his friend and his pony and the fine set of lead soldiers waiting for them in the nursery, where they could replay all the battles in which Uncle Alastair had fought. It required nearly the whole of the steep uphill walk from Sidney Gardens across the river back to his sister's townhouse in the Royal Crescent for him to finally banish Diana's image.

Damn, but she'd been even lovelier than he remembered.

Sending Robbie up to the nursery with a promise to join him later for an engagement with lead soldiers, Alastair turned over his hat and cane to his sister's butler. He'd placed boot on step to follow his nephew up the stairs when Simms halted him.

'Lady Guildford requested that you join her in the

morning room immediately upon your return, Mr Rans-leigh, if that is possible.'

Alastair paused, debating. He'd hoped, before meeting his all-too-perceptive sister, to return to the solitude of the pretty guest chamber to which he'd been shown upon his arrival early this morning, where he might finish piecing back together the shards of composure shattered by his unexpected encounter with Diana. But failing to respond to Jane's summons might elicit just the sort of heightened interest that he wished to avoid.

With a sigh, he nodded. 'Very well. You needn't announce me; I'll find my way in.'

Moments later he stepped into a back parlour flooded with mid-morning sunlight. 'Alastair!' his sister exclaimed with delight, jumping up from the sofa to meet him for a hug. 'I'm sorry I was so occupied when you arrived this morning! Though if I'd had any inkling you were coming, I would have had all in readiness,' she added, a tinge of reproof in her tone.

'Do you mean to scold me for showing up unannounced, as Mama always does?' he teased.

'Of course not! I assume you're not here for some assignation, else you'd not come to stay with me.'

'Assignation?' he said with a laugh. 'You'll make me blush, sister mine! And what would a proper matron like you know about assignations?'

'Nothing whatever, of course, other that you're rumoured to have many of them,' Jane retorted, her face flushing.

'You shouldn't listen to gossip,' Alastair said loftily. 'But let me assure you, if I did have an "assignation" in mind, I'd choose a more convenient and discreet location than Bath to set up a mistress.'

'It pains me that you've become so cynical. If only

you'd become acquainted with any of the lovely, accomplished and well-bred girls I've suggested, you'd find that not all women are interested only in title and position.'

'Of course not. You married Viscount Guildford out of overwhelming passion, the kind you'd have me write about,' he said sardonically.

Her flush deepened. 'Just because a match is suitable, doesn't mean there can't be love involved.'

'Oh, I'm a great believer in love! Indulge in it as often as I can. But I could hardly make one of your exemplary virgins my mistress,' he said, then held up a hand as Jane's eyes widened and she began to sputter a reply. 'Pax, Jane! Let's not brangle. I came to see you and Robbie, of course, and I do hope I'm welcome.'

'Always!' she said with a sigh, to his relief letting the uncomfortable topic go. He loved his sister and his mother dearly, but the succession of women with whom he'd been involved since his break with Diana—with their attempted claims on his time, his purse or his name— had only strengthened his decision never again to offer his heart or hand.

Jane looped her arm with his, leading him to a seat beside her on the sofa. 'Of course you may come and go as you wish! But if the ladies in your life would prefer to prepare a proper welcome and perhaps cosset you a bit, you must forgive us. We waited too many long anxious years while you were in the army, not sure you would ever make it back.'

'But I did, and I wager you find me as annoying as ever,' Alastair pronounced, dropping a kiss on the top of her head. 'So, was it my unannounced visit that I've been summoned to answer for? I thought, with Guildford off in London toiling away for some Parliamentary committee, you'd be delighted to have me break the tedium of marking time in Bath while your papa-in-law takes the waters. How is the Earl, by the way?'

'Better. I do think the waters are helping his dyspepsia. And I can't complain about being in Bath. It may not be the premier resort it once was, before Prinny made Brighton more fashionable, but it still offers a quite tolcrable number of diversions.'

'So which of my misdeeds required this urgent meeting?'

To his surprise, despite his teasing tone, his sister's face instantly sobered. 'Nothing you've done, as well you know, but I do need to make you aware of a…complication, one of some import. I'm not sure exactly how to begin…'

Brow creased, Jane gazed warily at his face, and instinctively he stiffened. 'Yes?'

'It's…'

Though Alastair would have sworn he neither moved a millimetre nor altered his expression in the slightest, Jane's eyes widened and she gasped. 'You've already seen her! You have, haven't you?'

Damn and blast! He was likely now in for the very sort of inquisition he'd heartily wished to avoid. 'If you mean Diana—the Duchess of Graveston, that is—yes, I have. At any rate, I believe it was her, though we didn't speak, so I'm not completely sure. It has been years, after all,' he added, trying for his calmest, most uninterested tone. 'A lady who looked like I remember her came to Sidney Gardens when I went after Robbie, to fetch her s-son.' Inwardly cursing that he'd stumbled over the word, Alastair cleared his throat.

Distress creased his sister's forehead. 'I'm so sorry you encountered her! I just this morning discovered her presence myself, and intended to warn you straight away so you might…prepare yourself. *That woman*, too, has only just arrived, or so Hetty Greenlaw reported when she called on me this morning.' Her tone turning to annoyance, Jane continued. 'Knowing of my "close connection to a distressing incident involving my maternal family", she felt it her duty to warn me that the Duchess was in Bath—the old tattle-tale. Doubtless agog to report to all her cronies exactly how I took the news!'

'With disinterested disdain, I'll wager,' Alastair said, eager to encourage this diversion from the subject at hand.

'Naturally. As if I would give someone as odious as that scandalmonger any inkling of my true feelings on the matter. But,' she said, her gaze focusing back on his face, 'I'm more concerned with *your* reaction.'

Alastair shrugged. 'How should I react? Goodness, Jane, that attachment was dead and buried years ago.'

Her perceptive eyes searched his face. 'Was it, Alastair?'

Damn it, he had to look away first, his face colouring. 'Of course.'

'You needn't see her, or even acknowledge her existence. Her whole appearance here is most irregular—we only received word of the Duke's passing two days ago! No one has any idea why she would leave Graveston Court so quickly after his death, or come to Bath, of all places. With, I understand, almost no servants or baggage. I highly doubt a woman as young and beautiful as Diana means to set up court as a dowager! If she's angling to remarry, she won't do her chances any good, flouting convention by appearing in public so scandalously soon after her husband's death! Although if she did, I'd at least have the satisfaction of being able to cut her.'

'That might not be feasible. Robbie has struck up a friendship with her son,' he informed her, making himself say the word again without flinching. 'He invited the boy to meet him again in the gardens tomorrow.' Alastair smiled, hoping it didn't appear as a grimace. 'So I can take them both for cakes.'

If he hadn't been still so unsettled himself, Alastair would have laughed at the look of horror that passed over his sister's face as the difficulty of the situation registered.

'I shall come up with some way to fob off Robbie,' Jane said. 'It's unthinkable for you to be manoeuvred into associating with her.'

Recalling the strength of his nephew's single-mindedness when fixed on an objective—so like his mama's iron will—Alastair raised a sceptical eyebrow. 'If you can succeed in distracting the boy who chattered all the way home from the Gardens about his new friend, I'll be surprised. Besides, if Diana goes about in Society, I'm bound to encounter her from time to time.'

'You don't mean you'll chance seeing her again?' his sister returned incredulously. 'Oh, Alastair, don't risk it!'

'Risk? Come now, Jane, this all happened years ago. No need to enact a Cheltenham tragedy.'

Pressing her lips together, Jane shook her head, tears sheening her eyes. 'I know you say you're over her, and I only pray God it's true. But I'll never forget—no one who cares about you ever could—how absolutely and completely *bouleversé* you were. The wonderful poetry you wrote in homage to her wit, her beauty, her grace, her liveliness! The fact that you haven't written a line since she jilted you.'

'The army was hardly a place for producing boyish truck about eternal love,' Alastair said, dismissing his former passion with practised scorn. Besides, poetry and his love for Diana had been so intimately intertwined, he'd not been able to continue one without the other. 'One matures, Jane, and moves on.'

'Does one? Have you? I'd be more inclined to believe it if you had ever shown any interest in another *eligible* woman. Do you truly believe all women to be perfidious? Or is it what I fear—that your poet's soul, struck more deeply by emotion than an ordinary man's, cannot imagine loving anyone but her?'

'Don't be ridiculous,' he said stiffly, compelled to deny her suspicion. 'I told you, that childish infatuation was crushed by events years ago.'

'I hope so! But even if, praise God, you *are* over her, I shall never forgive her for the agony and embarrassment she caused you. Nor can I forgive the fact that her betrayal turned a carefree, optimistic, joyous young man almost overnight into a bitter, angry recluse who shunned Society and did his utmost to get himself killed in battle.'

To his considerable alarm, Jane, normally the most stoic of sisters, burst into tears. Unsure what to do to stem the tide, he pulled her into a hug. 'There, there, now, that's a bit excessive, don't you think? Are you increasing again? It's not like you to be so missish.'

His bracing words had the desired effect, and she pushed him away. 'Missish! How dare you accuse me of that! And, no, I'm not increasing. It's beastly of you to take me to task when I'm simply concerned about you.'

'You know I appreciate that concern,' he said quietly.

She took an agitated turn about the room before coming back to face him. 'Have you any idea what it was like for your friends, your family—witnessing the depths of your pain, fearing for your sanity, your very life? Hearing the stories that came back to us from the Peninsula?

You volunteering to lead every "forlorn hope", always throwing yourself into the worst of the battle, defying death, uncaring of whether or not you survived.'

'But I did survive,' he replied. *Far too many worthy men had not, though, while he came through every battle untouched. 'Angry Alastair's luck' the troops had called it. He'd discouraged the talk and turned away the eager volunteers for his command who listened to it since that famous luck never seemed to extend to the men around him.*

'Please tell me you will not see her,' Jane said, pulling him back to the present.

'I certainly won't seek her out. But with Robbie having befriended her son, I imagine I won't be able to avoid her entirely.'

'I must think of some way to discourage the friendship. I really don't want my son to take up with any offspring of hers. He's probably as poisonous as she is!'

'Come now, Jane, listen to yourself! You can't seriously hold the poor child accountable for the failings of his mother,' Alastair protested, uncomfortably aware that, initially, he'd done just that.

'He's the spawn of the devil, whatever you say,' Jane flung back. 'You don't know all the things that have been said about her! I never mentioned her when I wrote you, feeling you'd been hurt enough, but there were always rumours swirling. How she defied the Duke in public, showing no deference to his friends or family. Turned her back on her own friends, too, once she became his Duchess—the few who remained after she jilted you. They say she became so unmanageable the Duke had to remove her to his country estate. I know she's not been in London in all the years since my marriage. I've even heard that, as soon as the Duke fell seriously ill, she took

herself off to Bath, refusing to nurse him or even to remain to see him properly buried!'

'Enough, Jane. I've no interest in gossip, nor have
I any intention of being more than politely civil to the
woman, if and when the need arises. So you see, there's
nothing to upset yourself about.'

At that moment, a discreet knock sounded and the
housekeeper appeared, bearing news of some minor disaster in the kitchen that required her mistress's immediate attention. After giving his sister another quick hug,
Alastair gently pushed her towards the door. 'I'll be fine.
Go re-establish order in your domain.'

After Jane had followed the housekeeper out, Alastair
walked back to his room, trapped by his still-unsettled
thoughts. It was sad, really, that the girl he remembered
being so vivacious, a magnet who drew people to her,
had, if what Jane reported was true, ended up a recluse
hidden away in the country, the subject of speculation
and rumour.

Did she deserve it? Had she duped him, cleverly encouraging his infatuation so he might trumpet her beauty
to the world in fulsome poetry, drawing to her the attention of wealthier, more prestigious suitors? Whether or
not she'd deliberately led him on, she *had* obsessed him
completely, inducing him to lay his foolish, naive, adoring heart at her feet.

He ought to thank her for having burned out of him
early so unrealistic an expectation as eternal love. Still,
something of that long-ago heartbreak vibrated up from
deep within, the pain sharp enough to make him clench
his teeth.

As before, anger followed. He would offer her nothing except perhaps a well-deserved snub.

Though even as he thought it, his heart whispered that he lied.

Chapter Two

Entering the modest lodgings in Laura Place she'd hired two days previous, her son and his nursery maid trailing obediently behind her, Diana, Dowager Duchess of Graveston, mounted the stairs to the sitting room. 'You may take Mannington to the nursery to rest now,' she told the girl as she handed her bonnet and cloak to the maid-of-all-work.

'Will you come up for tea later, Mama?' the child asked, looking up at her, hope shining in his eyes.

'Perhaps. Run along now.' Inured to the disappointment on the boy's face, she turned away and walked to the sideboard by the window, removing her gloves and placing them precisely on the centre of the chest. Only after the softly closing door confirmed she was alone, did she release a long, slow breath.

She should have hugged Mannington. He would have clung to her, probably. Like any little boy, he needed a mama he could cling to. And she *could* hug him now, without having to worry over the consequences—for him or for her.

Could she find her way back to how it had once been? A memory bubbled up: the awe and tenderness she'd felt as she held her newborn son, a miracle regardless of her feelings about his father.

The father who, little by little, had forced her to bury all affection for her child.

She remembered what had happened later that first day, Graveston standing over the bed as she held the infant to her breast. Plucking him away, telling her he'd summon a wet nurse, as a duchess did not suckle her own child. He'd cut off her arguments against it, informing her that if she meant to be difficult, he'd have a wet nurse found from among one of his tenant farmers and send the child away.

So she'd turned his feedings over to a wet nurse, consoling herself that she could still watch him in his cradle.

A week later, she'd returned to her rooms to find the cradle gone. The child belonged in the nursery wing, Graveston told her when she'd protested. It wasn't fitting for a woman as lowly born as the wet nurse to spend time in the Duchess's suite. If she insisted on having the child with her, he'd end up hungry, waiting for his supper while he was dispatched to the servant's quarters.

Of course, she hadn't wanted her son to go hungry. Or to have his balls taken away, as Graveston had done months later when she'd tarried in the nursery, rolling them to him, and been late for dinner.

Though for the first and only time in their marriage, she had tried to please her husband, nothing she did was enough. The day she'd learned her toddler son had been beaten because their laughter, as she played with him in the garden under the library window, had disturbed the Duke, she'd realised the only way she could protect him was to avoid him.

And the only way she could do that was to harden her

heart against him as thoroughly as she'd hardened herself to every other instinct save endurance.

She remembered the final incident, when having noticed, as he noticed everything, that she'd had little to do with the boy of late, Graveston threatened to have the child whipped again when she'd not worn the new dress he'd ordered for her to dinner. He'd watched her with the intensity of an owl honing in on a mouse as she shrugged and told him to do as he liked with his son.

She'd lost her meal and been unable to eat for three days until she'd known for certain that, no longer believing the boy a tool to control her, he'd left the child alone.

Only then had she known he was *safe*.

She sighed again. Having worked so hard to banish all affection, she'd not yet figured out how to re-animate the long-repressed instincts to mother her child. Now that he was older, it didn't help that she couldn't look at the dark hair curling over his brow or the square-jawed face without seeing Graveston reflected in them.

With a shudder, she repressed her husband's image.

Her *late* husband, she reminded herself. That liberation was so recent, she still had trouble believing she was finally free.

Living under his rule *had* perfected her mask of imperturbability, though. Lifting her eyes to the mirror over the sideboard, she studied the pale, calm, expressionless countenance staring back at her. Despite unexpectedly encountering Alastair Ransleigh after all these years, she'd not gasped, or trembled, or felt heat flame her face. No, she was quite sure the shock that had rocked her from head to toe had been undetectable in her outward appearance and manner.

The shock had almost been enough to pry free, from the vault deep within where she'd locked them away, some images from that halcyon spring they'd met and fallen in love. Had she truly once been unreserved, adoring him with wholehearted abandon, thrilling to his presence, ravenous for his touch? She winced, the memories still too painful to bear examining.

She took a deep breath and held it until the ache subsided. Sealing her mind against the possibility of allowing any more memories to escape, she turned her mind to the more practical implications of their unexpected meeting.

She supposed she should have expected to run into him eventually, but not this soon—or here. What was Alastair doing in Bath? His family home, Barton Abbey, was in Devon, and though he'd also inherited properties elsewhere, what she'd gleaned from news accounts and the little gossip that reached Graveston Court indicated that he'd spent most of his time since returning from the army either at his principal seat or in London.

Would she have fled to Bath, had she known he was here? She'd had to go somewhere, quickly, as soon as Graveston's remains had been laid to rest, somewhere she could live more cheaply and attract less notice than in London, but fashionable enough to attract excellent solicitors. Go while the servants were in turmoil, uncertain what to do now that their powerful master was no longer issuing orders, and before Blankford, her husband's eldest son and heir, had time to travel back to Graveston from hunting in Scotland.

What would she do if the new Duke, not content with claiming his old home, was bent on retribution against the woman he blamed for his mother's death and his father's estrangement? What if he pursued her here?

Putting aside a question for which she had no answer, Diana turned her mind back to Alastair. What was she to do about *him*?

She wouldn't remember how many years it had taken to lock his image, their love, and the dreams she'd cherished for the future into a place so deep within her that no trace of them ever escaped. All she had left of him was the pledge, if and when it was ever possible, to tell him why she'd spurned him without a word to marry Graveston.

She might well have that opportunity tomorrow if she accompanied Mannington to the park, where he hoped to encounter his new friend again. Should she take it?

Of course, the other boy might not come back, and if he did, Alastair might not accompany him. So rattled had she been by Alastair's unexpected appearance, she'd not even caught the boy's surname, though he must be some connection of Alastair's. Even his own son, perhaps.

That Alastair Ransleigh had managed to disturb her so deeply argued for avoiding him. The process of locking away all emotion and reaction, of practising before her mirror until she'd perfected the art of letting nothing show in her face, had been arduous and difficult. She wasn't sure how to reverse it, or even if she wanted to. Should that barrier of detachment ever be breached, whatever was left of her might crack like an eggshell.

As if in warning, despite her control, one memory from her marriage surfaced. The hope that she might some day speak to Alastair again had been the only thing that had kept her from succumbing to despair, or heeding the insidious whisper in the night that urged her to creep through the sleeping house to the parapets of Graveston Court and free herself in one great leap of defiance. Besides, though Alastair had almost certainly expunged her from his heart and mind years ago, in fairness, she owed him an explanation for that nightmare night of humiliation.

Very well, she thought, nodding to herself in the mirror. She would accompany her son to the park, and if Alastair did appear, she would approach him. He might well give her the cut direct, or slap her face, but if he allowed her to speak, she would fulfil her vow and tell him the story.

At the thought of seeing him again, a tiny flicker of anticipation bubbled up from deep within. Holding her breath and squeezing her eyes tightly shut, she stifled it.

Having awakened before dawn to pace his room until daylight, Alastair chose to avoid breakfast, knowing he wouldn't be able to hide his agitation from his eagle-eyed sister. When mid-morning finally came, Alastair set out from the Crescent, his exuberant nephew in tow.

Much as he'd tried to tell himself this was just another day, a trip to the park with Robbie like any other, he failed miserably at keeping his mind from drifting always back, like a lodestone to the north, to the possibility of seeing Diana again—a possibility that flooded him with contradictory emotions.

The defiant need to confront her and force a reaction, and curiosity over what that reaction might be, warred with the desire to cut her completely. Overlaying all was a smouldering anger that she had the power to so effectively penetrate his defences that he'd been required to employ every bit of his self-control to keep the memories at bay—a task he'd not fared so well at while half-conscious. He'd slept poorly, waking time and again to scattered bits of images he'd hastily blotted out before trying to sleep again.

Fatigued and irritable, he tried to focus on Robbie's eager chatter, which alternated between enthusiastic praise of the horse his uncle had ridden to Bath, a wheedling plea to be allowed to sit on said horse, and anticipation at meeting his new friend again.

'The boy may not be able to come today,' Alastair said, the warning as much for his own benefit as for Robbie's. 'You may have to settle for just the company of your dull old uncle.'

'Uncle Alastair, you're never dull! And you will let me ride Fury when we get back home, won't you? We can still stop for cakes, can't we? And I'm sure James will come again. His nurse promised!'

'Did she, now?' Alastair raised a sceptical eyebrow, amused out of his agitation by the ease with which his nephew turned a possibility into a certainty, simply because he wished it. How wonderful to possess such innocence!

But then, maybe it wasn't. He'd had his innocence torched out of him by one splendid fireball of humiliation.

Whatever reply Robbie made faded in his ears as they entered Sidney Gardens—and Alastair saw her. Shock pulsated from his toes to his ears, and once again, for a moment, he couldn't breathe.

Dressed modestly all in black—at least her critics couldn't fault her there—Diana sat on a bench, as her son tossed his ball to the nursemaid on a nearby verge of grass. While Alastair worked to slow his pulse and settle his breathing, Robbie, with a delighted shout, ran ahead to meet his friend.

Now was the moment, and with a sense of panic, Alastair realised he still wasn't sure what he wanted. If Diana turned to him, should he speak with her? Ignore her? If she did not acknowledge him, should he go right up to her and force his presence on her?

Before he could settle on a course of action, with a

grace that sent a shudder of memory and longing through him, Diana rose from the bench—and approached *him*.

'Mr Ransleigh,' she said as she dipped a curtsy to his stiff bow. 'Might I claim a moment of your time?'

A reply sprang without thought to his lips. 'Do you think you deserve that?'

'I am sure I do not,' she replied, the serenity of her countenance untroubled by his hostile words. 'However, I vowed if I were ever given a chance, I would explain to you what happened eight years ago.'

The violet scent she'd always worn invaded his senses. Unconsciously, he looked down, into eyes as arrestingly blue as he remembered from the day they first captivated him. No lines marred the softness of her skin, and the few dark curls escaping from under her bonnet made him recall how he'd loved combing his fingers through those thick, sable locks. Desire—powerful, potent, unstoppable—rose up to choke him.

He had to get away. 'Do you really think, after all this time, that I care what happened?' he spat out. 'Good day, Duchess.' Pivoting on one boot, he paced away from her down the gravelled path.

He heard the crunch of her footsteps following behind him. Torn between a surge of triumph that this time, *she* was pursuing *him*, and a need to escape before he lost what little control he had left, he could barely make sense of her words.

'Although I may not deserve to be heard, since you are a gentleman, Mr Ransleigh, I know you will allow me to speak. Infamous as I am, it's best that I do so here, now, out of sight and earshot of any gossips.'

'I have never paid any attention to gossips,' Alastair flung back, turning to face her. She halted a step away, and he couldn't help noticing the flush in her cheeks, the rapid breathing that caused her bosom to rise and fall beneath the modest pelisse—as if she were recovering from a round of passion.

Desire flared again, thick in his blood, pounding in his ears. Curse it, why must the Almighty be so cruel as to leave him still so strongly attracted to this woman?

But what she said was true—if she was determined to speak with him, it was far better here than at some ball or musicale or—worse yet—a social function at which Jane was also present. 'Very well, say what you must.'

'Walk with me, then.'

In truth, some tiny honest particle of his brain admitted, he wasn't sure he could have turned away. Curiosity and lust pulled him to her, stronger than reason, common sense, or his normal highly developed sense of self-preservation.

Despite the volatile mix of anger, confusion, pain and desire coursing through him, he also noted that, though she asked him to walk with her, she did not offer him her arm.

Not that it mattered. So intensely conscious was he of her body a foot from his, he could almost hear her breaths and feel the pulse in her veins.

'I met the Duke of Graveston at one of the first balls of my debut Season,' she began. 'He asked me to dance and accorded me polite interest, but I thought nothing of it. He was older, married, and I had eyes for only one man.'

Her words struck him to the core, despite the fact that she said them simply, unemotionally, as if stating a fact of mild interest. Swallowing hard, he forced his attention back to her narrative, the next few words of which he'd already missed.

'…began seeing him at home, visiting Papa. They had similar scientific interests, Papa said when I asked him.

It wasn't until some months later that I learned just what those "interests" truly were. By that time, the Duke's wife had died. To my astonishment, he proposed to me. I politely refused, telling him that my heart and hand had already been pledged to another. He…laughed. And told me that he was certain I would change my mind after I carefully measured the advantages of becoming his Duchess against marrying a young man of no title who was still dependent upon his father.'

Though they walked side by side, Alastair noticed Diana seemed increasingly detached, as if, transported to some other place and time, she was no longer even conscious of his presence. 'He returned a week later, asked me again, and received the same answer. In fact, I urged him to look elsewhere for a bride, as, though I was fully aware of the honour of his offer, it did not and would never interest me. He said that was regrettable, but he had chosen me for his wife, and marry him I would.'

Alastair had to laugh at that fantastic statement. 'Are you truly trying to persuade me that he "gave you no choice"? That horse won't run! This isn't the Middle Ages—a girl can't be forced into marriage.'

She nodded, still not looking at him. 'So I thought. But I was wrong. You see, those "visits" to Papa hadn't just been spent in scientific discourse. They'd also been gaming together—a pleasant match among friends, Papa later called it when I taxed him about it. But the Duke was a very skilful player, and Papa was not. When I refused again to marry him, he produced vouchers Papa had signed—vouchers worth thousands of pounds. Unless I married him, he said, he would call them in. Of course, there was no possible way Papa could have repaid such a sum. He would be sent to debtors' prison, the Duke said. How long did I think, with his delicate health, he would last in Newgate? At first, I was certain the Duke was joking. He soon convinced me he was not. He warned that if I said a word about this to my father, he would have him clapped in prison, regardless of what I did. I didn't dare call his bluff.'

Scarcely about to credit anyone capable of perpetrating such a Byzantine scheme, Alastair retorted, 'Why did you not come to me, then? True, I'd not yet inherited, but I could have persuaded my father to advance me a sum, and borrowed more on my expectations.'

'He threatened to ruin you, too, if I gave you even a hint of what he intended.'

'Ruin me? How?' Alastair replied derisively. '*I* was never a gamester, and though I was certainly no saint at university, I'd done nothing serious enough to dishonour my name, no matter how the facts might be distorted.'

She paused a moment, as if to say more, then shook her head. 'This would have.'

'No, it's all preposterous!' Alastair burst out. 'Graveston did have a sinister presence about him, but I can't believe he convinced you he would do what he threatened.'

She turned to give him a sad smile. 'Do you remember my little spaniel, Ribbons?'

'The black-and-white one with the ears that trailed in the wind?'

'Like ribbons, yes. After the Duke revealed his intentions, he gave me a day to think it over. When he returned the next day, he asked me how my dog was. I'd not seen Ribbons that morning, and when I looked, I found him—dead. The Duke merely smiled, and told me as his Duchess, I could have as many dogs as I liked.'

Despite himself, Alastair felt the implication of those words like a blow to the stomach.

She continued, 'As you know, we were a small household—just Cook and two maids and a man-of-all-work, all of whom had been with us for years. I questioned each one, and they all swore they'd seen—or done—nothing unusual. I realised then, if the Duke could bribe one of my own household to harm an innocent dog, or infiltrate someone who would, he was perfectly capable of forcing Papa into prison and ruining you. That the only thing to prevent him extracting retribution upon the people I loved would be for me to marry him. His final requirement in leaving you both unharmed was to never tell either of you the truth. You must both believe I married him of my own free will.'

Struggling to decide whether to accept the story she'd just told, Alastair shook his head. 'It's…it's unthinkable that someone would act in such a fashion.'

'Very true. Another reason why the Duke didn't worry about my confiding in anyone but you or Papa. Who *would* believe such a story?'

'Well, I don't,' Alastair retorted, making up his mind. Feeling both betrayed and disgusted that she would try to fob off on him such a Banbury tale, he said, 'Besides, do you really think your apology now makes any difference to me? Frankly, I would respect you more if you just admitted the truth—that the lure of a duchess's coronet outweighed whatever I could offer you.'

She turned to him, for a long moment silently studying his face. 'I have told you the truth. I cannot make you believe it, of course. But I did want you to know that it was not for any lack in you that I wed another man.'

'I never thought it was.'

'I don't expect your respect. I'm rather certain you despise me, and I can't blame you. Nor is there anything I could ever do to make up to you for the embarrassment and humiliation of the Coddingford ball.'

The words exited his lips before he was even aware he meant to speak. 'Well, since I'm currently between mistresses, you could fulfil that role until I tire of you.'

Aghast, he waited for her to gasp with outrage or slap his face. To his astonishment, after staring at him for another moment, she said, 'Very well. Make the arrangements and send me word. Fifteen Laura Place.'

Before Alastair could respond, two small boys pelted up from behind them, one grabbing his hand. 'Can we go for cakes now, Uncle Alastair?' Robbie asked. 'James and I are powerful hungry.'

'Yes, Mama, may I go today?' Diana's son asked her.

'Today you may go,' his mother responded. While the two boys whooped and slapped each other's backs, without another glance at Alastair, Diana turned and walked away.

Stunned, incredulous—and incredibly tempted—Alastair gazed after her until the turn in the pathway took her from view.

Chapter Three

After admonishing the boys that the hoydenish behaviour allowed in the park would not be tolerated in an establishment that served cakes, Alastair shepherded his young charges and Lord James Mannington's nursemaid across Pulteney Bridge, down High Street, around the Abbey and into the bakery off North Parade that served the famous buns. In a mechanical daze, he ordered cakes for the boys and the blushing maid, dismissing with a distracted wave her protest that he need not include her in the treat.

It was good that both boys had learned their manners well—or that the presence of the nursemaid restrained them. For with his mind whirling like a child's top, he could not afterwards recall a single thing they'd said or done at the shop.

Melted butter congealing on the bun set before him, Alastair went over again and again in his mind the exchange between himself and Diana—particularly the last bit, when he, incredibly, had offered her carte blanche and she, even more incredibly, had accepted.

If he'd had more time after that fraught final exchange, he probably would have retracted the hasty words, perhaps covering the naked need they'd revealed by delivering the stinging response that he'd only been joking, for Diana did not meet the minimum standards for beauty, wit and charm that he required of a mistress.

Instead, he'd done nothing, standing mute as a statue while she walked away.

Regardless of how he felt over her former treatment, he should be ashamed of himself for tendering such an insulting offer. To a dowager duchess, no less, who now outranked him on the social scale by several large leaps! As soon as he arrived back at his room at the Crescent, he should write her a note of apology, recanting the offer.

And yet… For the first time, he admitted to himself what meeting Diana again had made only too painfully clear. Despite the bold assertion to the contrary he'd given his sister, he had never really got over losing her. Every woman he'd met since had been measured against her and found lacking; every mistress he'd bedded had been physically reminiscent of her, unconsciously chosen to blot her out of his mind and senses.

None ever had.

Since Diana *had* accepted his offer, maybe he should go through with it. After all, there was no way the real woman could measure up to the romantic vision his youthful, poetic soul had once idolised…especially after how she'd treated him. Marrying a duke to 'save' him? What kind of dupe did she take him to be?

Maybe possessing her now would finally burn out of him the pain and yearning that had haunted him so long.

Like a thief lured into a dwelling through an unlocked window, now that his mind had tumbled on to the possibility of an affair, he couldn't keep himself from exploring it further. The desire she so readily evoked, banked rather than extinguished, raged back into flame.

Anticipation, excitement and eagerness boiled in his blood, and only by reminding himself that two young innocents and their virginal nursemaid sat mere feet away, was he able to restrain his mind from picturing himself possessing her.

He'd do it, then. Unless Diana sent a note rescinding her acceptance, he *would* go through with it.

After sending her son and the maid home in a sedan chair, Alastair hurried the now-sleepy Robbie up to the heights of the Crescent. As soon as he'd dispatched the boy back to the nursery, he descended the stairs at a run, bent on finding the most exclusive leasing office he could.

It was imperative to find just the right property for their rendezvous—in a location elegant enough for the purpose, but well-enough hidden that the ever-vigilant Jane was unlikely to discover it.

An hour later, the bargain concluded, he was escorted out by the beaming proprietor, whom he'd paid double his usual fee for his silence and to obtain possession of the property immediately. Holding the key to a fine townhouse in Green Park Buildings, a respectable address but one well to the west of the most fashionable streets, Alastair set off back to the Crescent.

He'd wait one night, to see if a note arrived from Diana, reneging on her initial acceptance. If he did not hear from her by tomorrow, he'd send *her* a note, arranging to meet after supper that night.

Excitement shivered and danced in his blood, sparkled in his mind. He couldn't remember ever being this consumed by anticipation.

An exalted state that was sure to end in disillusion, once he became better acquainted with the real Diana. Which was exactly what he wanted.

The sooner the affair began, the sooner it would be over—and he would be free of her at last.

In the evening of the following day, Diana sat at her dressing table, a note in hand. As she glanced at her name inscribed in Alastair's bold script, another memory pierced her chest like an arrow.

How many times during their courtship had she opened just such a note, finding within a beautiful verse in honour of her? Praising her wit, her virtue, her loveliness.

How unworthy of them she'd felt.

How unworthy of them she'd proved.

This current missive could hardly be more different. Instead of elegantly penned lines of clever metaphors, similes, and alliteration, there wasn't even a complete sentence. Merely an address and a time—this evening, nine o'clock.

Despite her hard-won self-control, uneasiness and something more, something dangerously like anticipation, stirred within her. Stifling it, she debated again, as she had off and on since receiving the summons this morning, whether or not to dispatch a last-minute refusal of his shocking offer.

It was risky, allowing him to be near her. Graveston had possessed the power to restrict her activities and movements, to hurt her physically, but had never been able to touch her soul—a failure that had maddened him and represented her only victory in their battlefield sham of a marriage. Alastair Ransleigh would never touch her in anger...but it was the touch of tenderness, the touch of a man she'd once desired above all else, that threatened her in a way the Duke had never managed, despite his relentless cruelty.

She'd certainly have to be on guard, lest he get close

enough to threaten her emotional reserve. Still… Once, she'd been so happy with Alastair. Might giving herself to him bring her a glimpse of that long-vanished happiness?

But then, she was reading much too much into this. The insulting nature of Alastair's offer was proof he despised her.

Would it have made any difference, had she explained just how the Duke intended to destroy him? Probably not, she concluded. He hadn't even believed the Duke's threat of debtors' prison for Papa, and what the Duke had promised for Alastair had been far more outrageous.

No, there wasn't any question of warmth or affection between them. She'd humiliated him before all of Society, abused his trust, and like any man, he wanted retribution. She was fair enough to think he deserved it.

Not that yielding her body would prove much of a humiliation for her, not after years of submission to a man who believed he had the right to use her whenever and however he pleased. Whatever his reasons for proposing the liaison, giving herself up to Alastair would be an improvement over the subjugation of her marriage. Alastair, at least, she'd always admired and respected.

In any event, the arrangement probably wouldn't last long. Once Ransleigh had his fill of her, he'd cast her aside, leaving her free to…do what with the rest of her life?

Frowning, she dropped the note on the dressing table and rose to take a restless turn about the room. Alastair Ransleigh's sudden reappearance had distracted her from focusing on how to deal with Lord Blankford, a matter of far more importance.

There was a chance Blankford might simply ignore her and Mannington. With a sigh, she quickly dismissed that foolish hope. Her husband's eldest son had been raised to believe that a duke's desires were paramount, and that he could manipulate, reward or smite all lesser beings with impunity. It was highly unlikely, given how closely the character of the heir mirrored that of the sire, that the injury he believed she'd committed against him and his mother would go unpunished.

At the very least, he would try to take Mannington away from her. Even if he didn't have evil designs upon the child, she wouldn't allow a dog, much less a little boy, to grow up under the influence of such a man. She might not, up until now, have proved herself much of a mother, but she would do everything in her power to prevent her innocent son's character from being distorted by the same despicable standards held by his father and elder brother.

Even as she thought it, she shook her head. How could she, whom her husband had methodically isolated from any friends and family, prevail against one of the highest-ranked men in England?

Putting aside, for the moment, that unanswerable question, then what? Even if she managed to protect her son from Blankford, Mannington needed more than rescue from evil influences to grow into the confident, compassionate, honourable man she'd like him to be.

She first needed to re-establish some sort of normal, motherly link with the boy—something she'd been forced to avoid while Graveston lived. Now that she need no longer fear showing him affection, how was she to retrieve, from the abyss into which she'd buried it, the natural bond between a mother and her child? That she'd hated the man who sired him was not Mannington's fault. Like every child, to grow and thrive he needed love—of which, until now, he'd received precious little.

For the first time in many years, she allowed herself to think about her own childhood—a time so idyllic and distant that it seemed to belong to another person, or another life. Despite losing his wife in childbirth at an early age, Papa had managed to submerge his own grief and create a home filled with love, security, joy and laughter. How had he done so?

Settling back on the dressing-table bench, she stared at her image in the mirror, digging through the bits of memory.

They'd certainly not had the material advantages available to a duke. As a younger son from a minor branch of a prominent family, no objection had been posed to Papa pursuing a career as an Oxford tutor, nor of his marrying for love a gentleman's daughter of great beauty and small dowry. After Mama's death, they'd taken rooms close to the university, where he might more easily mentor his students and pursue his own botanical studies. As both Mama and Papa had no other close kin, it had always been just the two of them.

She'd learned her letters at his knee, studied her lessons in his office, painted and played piano for him in the adjacent studio. Picnics beside the river turned into treasure hunts, often enlivened by games of hide-and-seek, as she helped Papa search for rare plants. Every day ended with him reading to her, or telling her a bedtime story. Later, as his eyesight began to fail and his health grew more frail, she had read to him.

First thing, then, she ticked off on one finger, she'd need to spend more time with Mannington….*James*, she corrected herself. No longer a tool of the Duke to control her, but simply a child. *Her son.*

A frisson of long-suppressed tenderness vibrated deep within her, as barely discernible as the scent of a newly opening rose.

Having deliberately avoided him since he'd been a toddler, she wasn't sure where to start. Other than accompanying him to the park, what did one do with a young boy?

Perhaps she could start by reading to him at bedtime. All children liked being read to, didn't they? If he enjoyed the interaction, his happiness should warm her, too, and begin the difficult process of dismantling the barriers she'd put in place to stifle any feeling towards him.

But the creation of a true home meant more than just spending time with him. Her father had not been nearly as prominent or powerful as her husband, but he'd been an enthusiastic, optimistic man who inspired love and admiration in everyone with whom he came into contact. Even students not especially interested in botany grew to appreciate the natural universe whose wonders he unfolded to them.

He'd exuded an infectious joy in life, in every little detail of living, from lauding the warmth of the fire on a cold evening, to savouring tea and cakes with her in the afternoon, to the enthusiasm with which he read to her, altering his voice to play all the parts from Shakespeare, or emoting the sonnets with an understanding that brought the beauty of the words and the depth of their meaning to life. He'd loved being a scholar, never losing his excitement at finding and recording in meticulous drawings all the plants he collected.

She could almost hear his voice, telling her how everything fit together in the natural world, with all having its place. She, too, had been designed with particular talents and abilities, her contributions unique, irreplaceable, and a necessary part to the whole.

She swallowed hard and her eyes stung. She hadn't remembered that bit of encouragement for years. Did she have a place and a purpose? Having lost first Alastair and then her father, was there something more for her than mere survival?

She could start by saving her son from Blankford. She could try her best to unlock her feelings and love him again. She could attempt to create the kind of home he deserved, that every child deserved, where he was wanted, appreciated, nourished.

The last would be a stretch. She wasn't her father, or even a pale echo of him. Once, another lifetime ago, she'd been a fearless girl who loved with all her heart and met life with reckless passion...

But how could she, who had forgotten what joy was, offer that to a child she might not find her way back to loving?

Sighing, she raised an eyebrow at the image in the mirror. The reflection staring back at her, the only friend and ally she'd had during the hellish years of her marriage, merely looked back, returning no answers.

She'd just have to try harder, she told the image. Once Alastair Ransleigh finished with her, she could close the book of her past and begin a new volume, with James.

Pray God she'd have enough time to figure it out before Blankford made his move.

But first, tonight, she must begin repaying the debt she owed Alastair. Her hands trembling ever so slightly, she rang for the maid and began to dress.

Chapter Four

Alastair paused in his pacing of the parlour of the small townhouse he'd rented, listening to the mantel clock strike three-quarters past eight. Unless she'd changed her previous habit of promptness, in another fifteen minutes, Diana would be here.

His pulses leapt as a surge of anticipation and desire rushed through him. Too impatient to sit, he took another turn about the room, then set off on yet another tour of the premises.

He'd arrived at eight, wanting to ensure everything was as he'd ordered. The new staff dispatched by the agency, all with impeccable references, had done their jobs perfectly. The immaculate house gleamed, every wooden surface and silver object polished to a soft glow in the candlelight. Taking the stairs, he inspected the sitting room adjoining the bedroom, nodding dismissal to the maid who'd just finished setting out a cold buffet. In the bedroom itself, a decanter of wine stood on the bedside table, and two glasses reflected the flames of the lit candles on the mantel above.

Wine to lend courage to him—or to her? he wondered with a wry grin. Maybe for consolation, if the joke was on him and Diana simply did not show up.

Which would, he admitted, be a justifiable rebuke for his ungentlemanly behaviour.

Even as he thought it, he heard the click of the front door opening, and a murmur of voices as the new man-servant admitted a visitor.

So she had come after all.

Alastair descended the stairs nearly at a run.

'I've shown the, ah, lady into the parlour,' the servant told him. 'Will you be needing anything else, sir?'

'Nothing more tonight, Marston. Thank you.'

Expression impassive, the servant bowed and headed off towards the service stairs. Alastair wondered, not for the first time, what the handful of employees thought of their new situation—and how much they'd been told when the agency he'd consulted had hired them. Certainly upon arrival, if not before, they would have realised they were being called upon to staff the love nest of some wealthy man's *chère-amie*. He'd not been able to glean from the behaviour of Marston, the cook or the maid whether they disapproved or were indifferent to the situation.

To tell the truth, he felt a bit uncomfortable. In his previous liaisons, after hiring a house, he'd simply given the lady of the moment the funds to bring or hire her own staff—and had never given the servants' opinions a thought. But this was *Diana*—and how she was regarded by the staff, he realised suddenly, did matter to him.

Rather ridiculous that he was concerned she be treated like a lady, when he'd set up this whole endeavour to humiliate her.

No, not to humiliate—simply to slake his desire for her, so that he might achieve the indifference that seemed to come so easily to her. So he could get over her and get on with his life, as she so obviously had.

Heartbeat accelerating, Alastair walked into the parlour.

A lady stood at the hearth with her back to him, enveloped in a black cape with the hood drawn up over her hair. Very discreet, Alastair thought, glad that she was evidently as concerned as he that this liaison be kept secret.

She turned towards him, and the visceral reaction she'd always evoked flooded him immediately, speeding his pulses, drying his mouth, filling him with desire and gladness.

'Good evening, Alastair,' she said. 'Where would you like me?'

Something almost like…disappointment tempered his enthusiasm. So there'd be no illusion of polite conversation first—just a proceeding straight to the matter at hand. She'd always been honest and direct, Alastair remembered.

Which was just as well. She wasn't here to revive an old relationship, but to bury the long-dead corpse of one.

'Come,' he said, motioning to the hallway.

Obediently she exited the parlour, brushing past him in a cloud of violet scent that instantly revived his lust and determination. She mounted the stairs, pausing at the top until he indicated the correct bedchamber.

He let her precede him into the room, already so taut with arousal that his hands were sweating and his breath uneven. In one fluid movement, she swept off her cloak and cast it in a shimmer of satin on to the chair beside the bed, then turned to him, waiting.

He scanned her hungrily. The full swell of bosom, the graceful curve of neck and cheek, the dusky curls gleaming brightly in the firelight, the lush pout of a mouth…the eyes staring sightlessly ahead of her, the face as devoid of expression as a statue. As if she were bored, waiting for the episode to be over.

While he stood, barely able to breathe, gut churning with eagerness and longing.

Sudden fury consumed him. But before he could sort through his wildly varying impulses—send her away or seduce her into feeling something—she sank to her knees before him and calmly unbuttoned his trouser flap. Wrapping her hands around his swollen length, she guided him into her mouth.

Shocked that she would play the courtesan so unresistingly, he opened his lips to tell her to stop…but at the touch of the exquisite softness of her tongue, moving over and around his throbbing member, thought dissolved into pure sensation. Gasping, he fisted his hands in her hair, every fibre of his being focused on the delicious friction of her mouth and tongue as she pushed him deep within, withdrew to suckle the sensitive tip, laved it with her tongue and took him deep again. Passion built with unprecedented swiftness until mere moments later, he climaxed in a rush so dizzying and intense he nearly lost consciousness.

Staggering backward, he collapsed on the bed, his heart trying to beat its way out of his chest. Dazed, he dimly noted Diana rising and walking noiselessly over to the washbasin on the bureau.

Sometime later, his heart finally settled back into its normal rhythm and enough rational thought returned that he recognised what had just transpired. He'd meant to slake his lust, not use her like a doxy—or bolt straight to conclusion, like a callow youth with his first woman.

Shame and embarrassment filled him. Looking around, he found Diana sitting silently in the chair, gazing into the fire, her cloak wrapped around her.

'I'm sorry. I hadn't meant for that to be an exclusive experience,' he said. 'I assure you, I can do much better.'

And he meant to. Of the many things that had attracted him to Diana during their courtship, one that had drawn him most strongly was her passion. She'd gloried in his kisses, giving herself to him with wild abandon, guiding his hands to her breasts, moulding her hands over his erection. He might not be able to love her again or truly forgive her, but they could at least have the honesty of pleasure between them.

'It doesn't matter,' she said.

'It does to me,' he replied, and held out his hand.

This time, he vowed as she took it, he would undress her slowly, as he'd dreamed of doing so many times. Kiss and caress each bit of skin revealed. Use all the considerable skill he'd amassed over nearly a decade of pleasuring women to give her the same intense release she'd just given him.

'I didn't hire you a lady's maid,' he said, turning her so he could begin unlacing the ties at the back of her bodice. 'I shall perform that function myself.'

She didn't reply, which was just as well, for as the ties loosened, the bare nape of her neck so distracted him he'd not have comprehended her words anyway. Unable to resist, he bent to kiss her.

That intoxicating violet scent wrapped around him again as he tasted her skin. Desire returning in a rush, he slid his hands into her hair, winnowing out the pins with his fingers until the heavy mass fell to her shoulders and cascaded down her back. Wrapping his hands in the thick lengths, he pulled her closer, moving his lips from her neck to the shell of her ear.

Already fully erect again, he parted the hair and pulled it forward over her breasts, unveiling the pins and lacing that secured bodice and skirt. Making quick work of those, he peeled off the top and nudged her to step out of the skirt, then guided her to the bed.

Seating her on the edge, he tilted up her head and took her mouth, moving his lips slowly, gently over their silken surface as he dispensed with her stays. At the pressure of his tongue, she parted her lips, allowing him entry to the softness within.

While he licked and suckled, he moved his hands to cup her breasts, full and ripe under the thin linen of her chemise. His breathing unsteady now, he thrust a pillow behind her and urged her back against it, then slid the chemise up, baring her from ankle to waist.

Going to his knees, he slowly rolled down her stockings, kissing and licking the soft skin of her knees, calves, ankles, toes, then moving in a slow ascent back up to her thighs. Urging those apart, he kissed his way slowly higher, while his hands moulded and caressed her hips and derrière.

By now, he was more than ready to enter her and find consummation again. But wanting this time to give maximum pleasure to her, holding himself under tight control, he moved his mouth closer and closer to her centre as he slid a finger over and around the nether lips. Another bolt of lust struck him as he found her moist and ready.

Unable to wait any longer, he moved his mouth to her core, parting the curls to run his tongue along the plump little nub nested within. But though his own breathing was by now erratic, Diana did not, as he'd expected, grip his back or wrap her legs around his shoulders. She didn't arch into him, her body picking up the ancient rhythm leading to fulfilment. Eyes tightly closed, she simply lay against the pillow, her face tense, her hands fisted.

Perhaps she'd been schooled that an uninhibited response was unladylike—he'd have to re-educate her about that. Or perhaps complete possession was necessary to trigger her reaction—he was certainly ready!

Murmuring, his hands gentle and caressing, he moved on to the bed and straddled her parted thighs, positioning himself over her. Kissing her, he lowered himself, slowly penetrating her.

He thought she flinched, and halted. But as he pressed carefully downward, her body greeted him in hot, slick warmth. Thrilled, he pushed deeper into the soft, yielding depths, until he'd sheathed himself completely.

Sweat broke out on his brow and his rigid arms trembled as he stilled deep within her, battling the urge to thrust and withdraw, thrust and withdraw in wild rhythm to reach the pinnacle that shimmered just out of reach.

But though her body was obviously primed to receive him, Diana did not moan, or tilt her hips to pull him deeper…or move at all; she lay, eyes still closed, passively beneath him.

Knowing that even remaining motionless, he'd not be able to stave off his own climax much longer, and wanting desperately to bring Diana with him on that journey to ecstasy and back, Alastair wondered what to try next.

Granted, his previous amours had all been experienced, or at least enthusiastic participants. Almost, he was ready to withdraw completely—except that despite her self-control, her body didn't lie. The peaked nipples and liquid heat within told him that she wasn't unreceptive. The tightly closed eyes, clenched fists and rigid posture told him she was exerting all her will to resist responding.

Well, he'd see about that. Slowly he began moving in her, rocking deep, caressing the little nub with every stroke, then bending to suckle the taut nipples.

But though he was soon riding the razor's edge, trying to stave off climax, Diana remained stiffly unmoving. Desperate, he redoubled his efforts.

Only to have her place a hand on his sweaty chest. 'Go ahead, finish now,' she said, her eyes still closed. And rocked her hips to force him deeper.

He wasn't sure he could have resisted much longer anyway. But as she finally moved beneath him, the dyke of his control broke and wave after wave of pleasure crested, washing over him with a force that robbed him of breath and consciousness.

Suddenly aware that his weight must be crushing her, he rolled to the side and up on the pillow.

'May I wash now?' she asked, not meeting his gaze.

Too passion-drugged for coherent thought, he simply nodded. And watched as she slid off the bed, walked to the bureau, and calmly plied the sponge and linen towelling, then turned to face him, still naked.

Despite the perplexing episode that had just transpired between them, she was still so lovely, still called so strongly to some uncontrollable something deep within him, that all he wanted was to pull her back into bed and love her again.

'May I dress now? Or do you require…more tonight?'

That prosaic question dashed whatever remained of his sensual haze, unleashing a boiling cauldron of emotions. Disappointment. Puzzlement. Curiosity. Embarrassment. Anger.

No previous experience had prepared him to deal with an outcome like this. But he'd not take her again tonight, much as he wanted to, not until he'd had time to figure out what had happened and what to do about it.

'That will be all for now,' he said curtly, the dismissal eroding what little remained of the euphoria. She nodded, seeming entirely untroubled by the cold, transactional nature of the interlude.

In silence he dressed her. 'Have Marston summon you a chair,' he said at last, when the final tape had been tied, the pins replaced and her hair, much too thick for his fumbling attempts to recreate a coiffure, had been thrust under her bonnet.

'Will you require me tomorrow?' she asked, still not meeting his eyes.

'I'll send you a note. You'll make yourself available?'

'As you wish. Goodnight, then, Alastair.'

With a nod, she exited the chamber.

Alastair listened until her footsteps faded down the stairs. Then, with an oath, he poured himself a glass of wine and downed it in one swallow.

What the hell had just happened?

Chapter Five

Frustration boiled up, and Alastair had to exert all his self-control to keep from hurling the unoffending wine glass into the hearth, just for the satisfaction of hearing it smash.

Had Diana been secretly laughing at him, mocking his all-too-evident desire with her ability to resist him?

Oh, how things had changed! After their engagement, she'd tantalised him, trying to drive him wild enough to overcome his refusal to take her before they were wed. He'd insisted she deserved better than some furtive, hurried coupling in the library or garden, where her father or a servant might at any moment interrupt. When they finally tasted consummation, he wanted them to be able to love each other freely, at length and at leisure.

This time, he had been eager and she'd been…indifferent.

If he'd not had numerous ladies testify to his expertise as a lover, he'd have been unmanned by her total lack of response.

But that wasn't quite right, he corrected himself. Her *body* had responded; of that, he was certain. But for some reason, she'd refused to allow herself to experience pleasure.

To punish him for coercing her into this, so he might not revel in her satisfaction at his hands?

He didn't think so. She'd exhibited no triumph at having resisted his skill; there'd been nothing of gloating superiority in her being able to render him helpless with pleasure, while refusing to allow him to do the same for her.

Besides, though he might have had the bad taste to propose the liaison, he'd done nothing to force her into accepting. As she certainly knew, were she to have refused the offer, he would have left it at that.

Instead, it was almost as if she had withdrawn entirely, not permitting herself to experience pleasure.

How had the passionate girl he remembered come to this?

Was this startling transformation her late husband's fault? For the first time he began to doubt his certainty that the account she'd given him of her marriage was a complete, or at least exaggerated, fabrication.

A sympathy he did not want to feel welled up in the wake of that doubt.

Stifling it, he jumped up and began to pace. There had to be some way to penetrate that wall of resistance. Break through to reach the body trembling for completion, and bring it to satisfaction.

If she'd been repulsed by him, or truly unresponsive, he would have, regretfully, dismissed her tonight. Instead, there'd been an intriguing disconnect between her will and her body's arousal.

He'd hoped a few episodes would be enough to set him free of her. But he knew now with certainty that he could never let her go until he'd *reached* her, coaxed forth the response simmering beneath the surface, until she cried and shuddered in his arms with all the passion he'd not allowed himself to taste all those years ago.

How best to tempt her?

Pouring another glass of wine, he set himself to consider it.

Dismissing the sedan chair, Diana let herself into the townhouse and crept up to her chamber on legs that were still not steady. Summoning the maid to help her out of the gown—mercifully, the girl made no comment on hair that looked like an escapee from Bedlam had arranged it—she then dismissed her.

Sleep was out of the question. With her body still humming with awareness and her hard-won calm in tatters, she settled into the chair before the hearth, heart racing as she tried to determine what to do next.

Oh, she had been so right to fear letting Alastair Ransleigh get close to her! She'd thought, after eight years of fulfilling a man's desires in whatever way demanded of her while mentally distancing herself from the activity, she would be able to service Alastair with detachment.

And so she had…but just barely.

The process had been much easier with the Duke, who had no interest in her physical satisfaction. In fact, he'd mentioned on several occasions that he thought it demeaning for a man to have a wife who disported herself in the bedchamber like a harlot; such behaviour was for strumpets, not for the high-born woman chosen for the honour of breeding the offspring of a lord.

Given his opinion, she might have been tempted to 'disport' herself on occasion, had it not meant lengthening the time she had to suffer his touch. As it was, she slowly perfected the ability to wall herself off from what was happening to her. Viewing actions, even as she performed them, as if she were a spectator observing them from afar had allowed her to tolerate the bedchamber requirements of her role.

But Alastair was not the Duke she hated. And hard as she tried to block out what he was doing, ignoring it had proved impossible. Alastair's touch had been more veneration than violation, and it had taken every iota of self-control she'd developed over eight miserable years to keep herself from responding.

He'd always had the power to move her. She'd not allowed herself to remember that. Once she was irrevocably married, it would have been a cruelty beyond endurance to recall the joy of being caressed by a man whose touch thrilled her, while being forced to submit to intimacies with a man she loathed.

She'd given herself up to Alastair completely that halcyon summer, eager for him to possess her, arguing against waiting until after the wedding for them to become lovers.

She smiled wistfully. Would it have made any difference, had she not been a virgin when the Duke sought her out?

Probably not. He'd regarded her as a treasure like the Maidens of the Parthenon, and like them, she'd have been collected even if 'damaged'. He'd merely have constructed an inescapable cage to prevent any lapses after marriage, and waited to bed her until he was sure she was not carrying another man's child.

And simply disposed of the evidence, if she had been.

But that was neither here nor there, she told herself, pulling her focus back to the present. The problem was how to deal with Alastair Ransleigh *now*.

Perhaps if she *had* remembered how quickly and deeply Alastair affected her, she'd have armoured herself better to resist him. After this evening, she no longer suffered from that dangerous ignorance. So what was she to do to avoid another near-disaster?

Forbidding herself to react had simply not been effective. Especially since, unlike the Duke, he'd clearly *wanted* her to respond. Wanted to give her pleasure… as a gift?

Or was that to be the form of his revenge: making her respond to him, making her burn for his touch, then abandoning her, as she had abandoned him? Would he not be satisfied until he'd succeeded in doing so?

Could he succeed?

She didn't *want* to feel anything. Not passion, not desire, not longing, not affection. Overcoming the forces ranged against her, doing what she could to safeguard the boy unlucky enough to be her son, would require all the strength she could muster. A wounded bird marshalling all her efforts to lead the predator away from her nest, she couldn't afford to bleed away any of her limited energy in resisting Alastair Ransleigh.

His reappearance was a complication she didn't need.

She could simply not see him again. Send him a note saying she'd changed her mind. Follow the instincts for self-preservation that were screaming at her to run. Unlike the Duke, who had ignored her refusals, she knew with utmost certainty that if she sent such a message, Alastair would let her go.

But that would be taking the coward's way out. All these years, she'd promised herself that if she ever had the chance, she would do what she could to make amends to him. Reneging on their agreement and bolting at the first sign of peril would snuff out what little honour she had left, like a downpour swamping a candle.

Deep within, beneath the roiling mix of shock, dismay,

and frustrated desire, a small voice from the past she'd shut away whispered that she *couldn't* let him go. Not yet.

She shut her ears to it. She'd made him a promise, that was all, and honour demanded she keep it. However difficult it proved, however long it took, she would endure, as she always had.

Decision made, she walked over to the dressing table, seated herself on the bench, and regarded her image in the mirror. The forehead was puckered with concern; with fingers she refused to let tremble, she gently smoothed the skin there, beside her eyes, around her mouth, until the woman in the glass looked once again calm and expressionless.

She took a deep breath and held it, held it, held it until she couldn't any longer. Blowing it out, she took another lungful of air, wiping her mind free of anything but the passage of air in and out, the rhythmic ticking of the mantel clock throbbing in her ears.

Over and over she repeated the familiar ritual. Anxiety, foreboding, and worry gradually diminished until all emotion vanished into the nothingness of complete detachment.

She *was* the lady in the glass—a shadow of a real woman, a trick of light and mirrors, untouchable.

Only then did she rise and walk to her bed...squelching the tiny, stubborn bit of warmth that stirred within her at the thought that tomorrow, she would see Alastair again.

The following evening after dinner, Diana paced the parlour restlessly. Without the Duke's overbearing presence to impose a structure on her days, she was finding herself at a loss for what to do.

Long ago, in another life, she'd enjoyed reading, but

she'd had no books to bring with her. It might be…pleasant to resume that activity, or do some needlework.

She should visit the shops and look for a book or embroidery silks. Though she needed to carefully hoard her limited coin against her uncertain future, she could spare enough for a book, couldn't she?

She had gone out today, visiting the park with Mannington—*James*. It was still a surprise, discovering how…*liberating* it was to leave the house and walk about freely, with no possibility of being recalled, lectured, or punished.

And she'd followed through on her resolution to try reaching out to her son. Haltingly, she'd talked to him, even thrown him his ball, to the astonishment of his nursemaid.

She should go up to the nursery and offer to read to him now.

Her cautious mind immediately retreated from the suggestion. Soon she must leave to meet Alastair, and she'd need all the mental and emotional defences she could summon. Having bottled up any tentative reactions after the walk to the park, she didn't dare breach the calm she'd re-established by approaching her son again.

But putting her son's needs on hold, now that it was no longer necessary to do so to protect him from his father, was just another form of the same cowardice that made her desperate to avoid Alastair Ransleigh, she admonished herself.

Mannington had suffered through six years without a mother worthy of the name. She wasn't sure she could ever become one, but she should at least try.

To do so, she'd need to loosen the stranglehold she'd imposed over her emotions. She'd grown so adept at stifling any feelings, she wasn't sure how to allow some to emerge, without the risk that all the rage, desolation and misery she'd bottled up for years might rush out in an ungovernable flood that could sweep her into madness.

Still, finding her way back to loving a boy whose face so forcefully reminded her of his father was likely to be a long process. He needed her to begin now.

Resolutely, she made her way to the nursery.

She opened the door to find her son in his nightgown, rearranging a few lead soldiers near the hearth. The nursemaid looked up, startled, from where she was turning down the boy's bed.

'Did you need something, my lady?' Minnie asked.

'I…I thought I would read Mannington a story.'

Something derisive flashed in the girl's eyes. 'I'm sure that's not necessary, my lady. The lad's nearly ready for bed, and I can tuck him—'

'Would you really read me a story, Mama?' James interrupted, hope in his tone and astonishment on his face, as if she'd just offered to reach out and capture the moon that hung in the sky outside his window.

'If you'd like…James,' she replied, his given name still coming awkwardly to her tongue.

His eyes brightening, he abandoned the soldiers and ran over to her. 'Would you, please? I'd like it ever so much!'

'Could you fetch me a book?' she asked the maid, who was still regarding her with suspicion—as if she had evil designs on the boy, Diana thought with mild amusement.

She couldn't blame the girl for her scepticism. Minnie had been James's nurse for four years, and never before had his mother appeared at his nursery door with such a request.

How many stories had Papa read her by the time she'd reached the age of six? she wondered. Hundreds.

'A book, my lady?' Minnie said at last. 'Don't have any, your ladyship. I—I don't know how to read.'

Diana had abandoned books years ago, and never thought to see that her son had access to them. 'I see. Well, perhaps we can purchase one tomorrow. Shall we say tomorrow night, then, James?'

His face falling, he reached out as she turned to leave and clutched her hand. 'Can't you stay, Mama? You could pretend to read.'

A tiny flicker of humour bubbled up. 'Very well, I'll stay. But I can do better than pretend. I'll tell you a story. That will be all, Minnie. I can tuck him in.'

Still looking dubious and more than a little alarmed, the maid sketched her a curtsy. 'As you please, ma'am. But I'll be right near, if he—if either of you need anything. Goodnight, young master.'

'G'night, Minnie,' the boy called, then ran to hop in his bed. 'See, I'm ready, Mama. Can you begin?'

At first, she'd had no idea what to say, but in a flash, it came to her. Now that it *was* safe, he should learn about his family—*her* family.

'Shall I tell you about your grandfather? My father, whom you never met. He was a great scholar, and collected plants. One day, when I was about your age, he took me to the river to look for a very special plant…'

And so she related one of the escapades she'd shared with her father, hunting for marsh irises outside Oxford. She'd slipped and fallen into the stream, and while scolding her for carelessness, Papa had slipped and fallen in, too. He'd emerged laughing and dripping. Then he'd wrapped her up in his coat and carried her home for tea by a hot fire.

James was asleep by the time she finished the tale. Looking at his small, softly breathing form, she felt a stirring of…something. Tucking the covers more securely around his shoulders, she slipped from the room.

That had not been so very hard, as long as she avoided looking at the forehead and jaw so reminiscent of…*him*. She did not want to spoil the mild warmth she'd felt by even thinking the name. It had been almost like recapturing some of the sweetness of her own long-ago childhood, when she'd felt safe and cherished.

Regardless of whether or not she could revive her own emotions, she would do her best to give her son that security.

As she returned to the parlour, the clock struck half-past eight. Apprehension flared in her gut.

Walking to the mirror, she began breathing methodically, until she'd achieved a state of detachment.

She'd do better tonight, she reassured her image. Alastair Ransleigh had shown himself even more susceptible to her touch than she was to his. She had only to begin at once, to use his sighs and gasps to gauge what ministrations affected him the most, and continue them with all the vigour and imagination she could devise until he was so sated by pleasure, he had neither thought nor strength to attempt touching her. Then take her leave, before he recovered.

She would do that tonight, and for however many nights she must until, inevitably, he became bored with her and ready to move to the next conquest.

Her vow to him fulfilled, she could then concentrate fully on reaching out to James—and decide how best to protect him.

But now, there was Alastair. Giving her impassive image one last look, Diana rose to summon a sedan chair.

Chapter Six

W̲ithout her mirror friend to reassure her, Diana had lost a bit of her self-assurance by the time she reached the rendezvous. She arrived before the hour specified, hoping to go up to the bedchamber and ready herself, but the impassive servant who admitted her indicated that Mr Ransleigh was already in residence, and would join her in the parlour.

She damped down an initial flicker of alarm as she followed the man into that reception area. The bedchamber would have been easier, allowing her to implement her plan immediately.

Perhaps their sojourn in the parlour was meant to maintain some veneer of propriety for the servants' sakes, though since there could be no doubt of the purpose for which she, and this house, had been procured, it seemed rather a superfluous effort. No lady worthy the name would ever meet a single gentleman at his abode, day or night.

Before she could consider the matter further, the door opened and Alastair walked in.

She sucked in a breath, struck by a wave of attraction and longing. He'd always had a commanding presence, his tall, broad-shouldered figure standing out from the others, even as a young collegian. Time had magnified the sense of assurance with which he carried himself, the air of command reinforcing it doubtless a result of his years with the army and his current role as manager of the large estate he'd inherited.

The dark hair was still swept back carelessly off his brow—she couldn't imagine the impatient Alastair she'd known ever becoming a dandy, taking time over his appearance—and the skin of his face was a deep bronze, a result of much time in the saddle under the hot Peninsular sun, she assumed.

The most notable change between the young collegian she'd loved and the man standing before her was the network of tiny lines beside his eyes—and the coldness in their dark-blue depths that once had blazed with warmth, energy and optimism.

For that chill, she was undoubtedly much responsible.

Suddenly realising she'd been staring, she dropped her gaze. 'Good evening, Alastair. Shall we proceed upstairs?'

'No need to rush off,' he returned. 'Let me pour you some wine.'

She almost blurted that she'd just as soon get straight to it. Clamping her teeth on the words, she nodded before calmly saying, 'As you wish.'

So they were to have civility tonight. She could manage that, and bide her time. Especially since, if he meant this to give the appearance of a cordial call, he was unlikely to try to seduce her in the downstairs parlour.

Slow, easy breaths, she told herself, accepting the glass of wine he offered, taking a tiny sip—and waiting. She might not force the issue, but she certainly didn't mean to draw out this nerve-fraying delay by initiating a conversation.

'I brought you something,' he said, startling her as he broke the silence. He walked to the sideboard to collect a package and offered it to her. 'I hope you'll like it.'

'Brought me something?' she echoed, surprised and vaguely uncomfortable. 'You don't need to get me anything.'

'Nevertheless, I did,' he replied. 'Go ahead, open it.'

She accepted the parcel, willing her heartbeat to slow. *'I've brought you something...'* How many times during their courtship had he said that, his blue eyes fixed on her as he offered a bunch of flowers, a book he thought she'd enjoy, a new poem rolled up and secured by a pretty ribbon?

Breathe in, breathe out. Aware her hands were trembling, she fumbled to unwrap the parcel. And found within an elegant wooden box containing a sketchbook, a set of brushes and an assortment of watercolours.

'I understand you came to Bath in a hurry, and might not have had time to pack any supplies,' he offered by way of explanation. 'I know how much you hate to be without your sketchbook and paints.'

So unaccustomed was she to having anyone give a thought to her desires, she found herself at a complete loss for words. While she tried to think of something appropriate to reply, Alastair said, 'Perhaps you could paint me something.'

'You are...very kind. But I'm sure I couldn't produce anything worth looking at. I...I haven't touched a brush in years.'

His eyes widened in surprise. 'You don't paint any more? Why did you stop? Not lack of time, surely! I should think, in a duke's establishment, there would have been plenty of servants to see to the housekeeping and care for the child.'

Unprepared and not good at dissembling, she fumbled for a reply. 'Paints were…not always available.'

'What, was the Duke too miserly to provide them?' he asked, a sarcastic edge to his voice.

Not wanting to explain, she said, 'Something like that.'

Caught off balance, her guard down, the memory swooped out before she could prevent it.

One of the first afternoons at Graveston Court, despondent after having been summoned to the Duke's bed the night before, she'd taken refuge in one of the north-facing rooms and set up her easel. Trying to shut out her misery, she focused her mind on capturing the delicate hues of the sunlit daisies in the garden outside.

She had no idea how long she worked, lighting candles when the natural light faded, but when a housemaid found her, the girl had been frantic, insisting she come at once and dress, as she was already late for dinner.

The Duke said nothing when she arrived, merely looking pointedly at the mantel clock. But when she returned to the room the next day to resume her work, easel, paints and all had disappeared.

She'd asked the housekeeper about them, and was referred to the Duke. Who told her that when she could appear at dinner on time and properly attired, he might consider restoring them to her.

She'd never painted again.

She looked up to see Alastair regarding her quizzically. Frustration and alarm tightened her chest.

She couldn't allow him to start speculating about her! He could be as tenacious as a terrier with a rat, and she didn't think she could fend off persistent enquiries without further arousing his curiosity.

She must regain control of this situation immediately.

'I'll just put them back in the box. I'm sure you can return them,' she said, giving him a determined smile. 'Shall we go upstairs now?'

To her further frustration, he shook his head. 'There's no need to hurry. We have all evening. I thought we'd chat first.'

She had to work hard to keep her expression impassive. 'Chat' was the last thing she wanted.

She should give him a flirtatious look, try to entice him, but she couldn't remember how. 'I thought you would be...impatient,' she said, a little desperately, trying to bring his mind back to the physical.

'Oh, I am. But delay just heightens anticipation, making the fulfilment all the more satisfying. Now, my sister said you've spent most of the last few years in the country. What did you do there, if you didn't paint? Although in such a grand manor house, I expect there was an excellent library. Did you re-read the classics, or more modern works?'

Once again, she struggled to find an innocuous reply. 'I...wasn't much given to reading.'

And once again, his eyebrows winged upward. 'But you always loved to read. Was the library inferior?'

Her chest was getting so tight, it was difficult to breathe. 'N-no, the library was, ah, was quite good.'

'Then why did you not avail yourself of it?'

Oh, why would he not just leave it be? 'I didn't always have access to it,' she ground out.

'Not have access? But you were mistress of the household. I can't imagine you letting some old fright of a housekeeper deny you books!'

'It wasn't the housekeeper,' she blurted.

He was silent so long, she thought perhaps he'd finally taken note of her obvious reluctance and dropped the matter. Until he said quietly, 'Your husband denied you books?'

Oh, why had she never learned to tell a convincing lie? 'Yes,' she snapped, irritated with him for his persistence, with herself for not being able to come up with a plausible story to deflect him. 'Whenever I displeased him. And I displeased him constantly.'

Setting down her wine glass with a clatter, she reached over to seize his hand. 'Please, can we have no more of this? I'd like to go upstairs now.'

Though he continued to regard her with an expression entirely too penetrating for her comfort, he nodded and set down his own glass. 'Far be it for me to deny an eager lady.'

He had no idea how eager, she thought, light-headed with relief as he followed her up the stairs. Eager not for caresses, but to pleasure him and be gone before he could tug out of her any more ugly secrets from her marriage.

At the chamber door, she took his hand and led him to the bed. 'Let me make you more comfortable,' she said, urging him to sit, then attacking his cravat. The sooner she got to bare skin, the closer she'd be to seducing— and escaping—him.

But though he let her unwind the cloth and toss it aside, when she started on the buttons of his coat, he stayed her hands and pulled her to sit beside him on the bed. Tilting her head up to face him, he asked, 'Did he take away your paints, too, when you did not please him?'

Caught off guard again, she couldn't seem to come up with anything but the truth. 'Yes.'

'How long have you been without books and paints?'

She pulled her chin from his fingers, not wanting to meet his gaze. 'A long time.'

'And piano?'

Ah, how she'd missed her music! *She'd hung on the longest to that, sneaking out in the depths of the night, like a burglar who's discovered where the valuable jewels are hidden. In the smaller music room, a location far removed from the servants' quarters and the main rooms, she'd played softly, in darkness or in moonlight...until that last, terrible night.*

She jerked her mind free of the memories. 'I'm not the woman you once knew, Alastair.'

Gently he recaptured her chin and made her look up at him. 'Aren't you?'

He lowered his mouth to hers, barely brushing her lips, his touch butterfly-light. This time, it was she who levered his lips apart with her tongue, then stroked at the wet warmth within.

With a growl deep in his throat, he responded immediately, seizing her shoulders and deepening the kiss. She wriggled her trapped hands down his chest and stomach until she could reach the buttons of his trouser flap, then struggled to open them against the erection that stretched the cloth taut. Finally working two buttons free, she slipped a hand inside, caressing down his length to the silky tip and back.

When he gasped, she broke the kiss, pushed herself off the bed and knelt before him. Before he could countermand her, she quickly popped the other buttons, grasped his member in both hands and took him into her mouth.

With him now beyond words, she ran her lips and tongue over every surface, listening carefully for his responses, deepening her touch or increasing friction when he gasped or thrust against her. Having catalogued his most sensitive areas, she focused on them, sucking, nipping and laving gently, then harder, then gently again, trying to stave off and intensify his climax.

It seemed she had done well, for some moments later he cried out, his nails biting into her shoulders through the fabric of her gown as he reached his peak, shuddering.

Not until he sagged back on to the bed did she gently disengage. Noting that he seemed for the moment insensate, she walked over to the washbasin to refresh herself, planning how she would next attempt to satisfy him.

Undress him, stimulate him, straddle him, she thought, ticking off in her mind the techniques that might leave him most sated. She damped down the shivers of feeling sparking at her breasts and between her thighs as she envisaged pleasuring him.

Pleasuring *him*, she rebuked her stirring senses. This had nothing to do with her.

Hands at her shoulders startled her. 'Come back to bed,' he whispered, nuzzling her neck.

Obediently she turned and allowed him to guide her over. 'Let me undress you first,' she urged.

'Only if I can then return the favour.'

Get him naked and she might avoid that. Murmuring a non-committal response, she turned to seat him at the bedside.

Swiftly, she removed his jacket and waistcoat, then pulled the shirt over his head. And caught her breath, as any woman would, for he was so beautifully made.

Strong arms and shoulders gleamed in the candlelight. The muscles of his chest tensed as she ran a finger over them, down the taut belly to the edge of his trousers, then back up and over the scar that circled one shoulder.

'Sabre slash,' he answered her unspoken question. 'Doesn't hurt any more.'

'Where?' she asked, curious in spite of herself.

'Badajoz.'

She'd read accounts in the newspapers about the battle. Not yet retired from Society, she'd also heard he'd entered the fortress city first, leading the van of the 'forlorn hope' through the breach the engineers had blasted into the walls. Her heart, not yet armoured against him, had swelled with fear at his recklessness, with joy that he'd been spared.

Denying the heat building within her, she ran her tongue along the scarred ridge of flesh, feeling him gasp and flinch under her touch. Encouraged by his response, she kissed lower while her hands caressed the lines of muscle and sinew.

Concentrate on him, she urged herself as her fingers tingled and the tension within her coiled tighter.

She suspended her kisses to strip off his boots, socks and trousers, then urged him down on the bed, pressing him back against the pillows. But when she lifted her skirts to follow him, intending to straddle the erection that sprang up boldly before her, he stopped her.

'My turn.'

She made a murmur of inarticulate protest, but, ignoring it, he stood and turned her so he might access the fastenings of her gown. Not wanting to provoke a dispute by refusing, she allowed him to proceed.

She'd just have to resist as best she could—and resist she would, she promised herself.

Stiffening, she suffered him to unfasten her bodice and skirt, tightening her jaw as he began to caress her breasts through the linen of her chemise. He cupped them in his big hands, dragged his thumbs over the nipples until they peaked, each swipe sparking a flash of sensation that shot right to her core.

Her control already unravelling, she jumped when he

hooked a finger at the hem of the chemise and dragged it up, letting cool air flow over the hot, damp place between her legs. Gently he pushed her to the bed, kissing her with insistent, drugging kisses that stole her breath.

Her pulse grew unsteadier still as she struggled to resist the tide of sensation hammering at her. She bit down on her lip to keep herself from rubbing against him when his finger insinuated itself between her thighs, bit down even harder when he slid that finger up to caress the nub at her centre. Her arms ached from holding herself rigid.

Then he slipped that finger inside her, evoking a sensation so intense, she had to hold her breath until she almost lost consciousness to battle down a response.

He bent to kiss her again, suckling her tongue in rhythm to the stroking finger. Everything within her seemed to be melting, building towards some precipice she was desperate to reach.

If she couldn't stop him before she got there, she'd come apart.

Frantic, she broke the kiss, rolled on to the bed and pulled at his hips, urging him over her. 'Now!' she gasped.

Mercifully, he must have thought she was ready to finish. At once, he plunged within, filling her, which was better—or maybe worse. Rocking urgently against him—this time, she simply couldn't remain motionless—she sought to bring him to fulfilment, before the sensations he was unleashing drove her mad.

In deep, penetrating thrusts he drove to the core of her, possessing her through every inch of her body. *So the two become one flesh*, flashed through her disjointed mind.

Never. Never one. Not now. Chance. Once. Lost.

Thoughts disintegrating to chaotic bits, she despaired

of holding out any longer, when, buried deep within her, Alastair went rigid and cried out. A few moments later, he collapsed on her, then rolled with her to his side.

Heart hammering a crazy rhythm in her chest, she tried to steady her breathing. *Please, let him fall asleep now, as he had the night before.* Any illusions of courage abandoned, she would steal out as soon as his relaxed body and steady breathing told her he was beyond consciousness.

She couldn't withstand a repetition of that assault on her senses.

With him limp beside her, she wriggled free of his entrapping arm. Silently, she threw on her skirt and fixed the pins of her bodice as best she could—thank heavens for the all-concealing cloak! She was groping for her shoes, ready to tiptoe out, when a hand reached out and grabbed her wrist.

She jumped, startled by his touch. Desperate to escape, she attempted a smile. 'I'm sorry. I didn't mean to wake you. I'm afraid I must…must get home. Right now. My son. I'll…I'll meet you again. T-tomorrow?'

Sweet heavens, she was stuttering, her control a shambles. She had to get away.

'He denied you passion, too, didn't he?'

Unable, unwilling to answer, she stared at him, her eyes begging him for the mercy of release.

'Why won't you let me give you pleasure?'

'Why would you want to?' she shot back, anguish loosening the hold over her tongue.

His lazy eyes widened. 'You can't believe I'd try to hurt you?'

'You have no reason to be kind. Please, Alastair, I'll come tomorrow, I promise, but no more tonight.'

She was trembling now, light-headed with sensations

denied, torn between her body's eagerness for what he offered and her need to resist. If she didn't get out soon, the battle might rip her in two, right here in bedchamber.

She nearly let out a sob when he let go of her wrist. 'Very well. I would never keep you against your will. But…tomorrow?'

She nodded, her head bobbing back and forth like a child's toy. This had been bad, much worse than she'd anticipated. But with twenty-four hours of calm reflection, away from his disturbing presence, she could figure out anything. 'Yes, tomorrow.'

'Goodnight, then, Diana.'

Whirling around, she headed towards the door. She could feel the heat of his gaze on her back as she scurried, like a mouse racing from the cat, out of the room and down the stairs.

After Diana's abrupt departure, Alastair stared at the open doorway. Her effect on him had not been lessened after the first possession yesterday. In fact, with the enthusiasm of her ministrations, his climax tonight had been even more intense. So intense, his mind was still not functioning properly, or else he'd not have let her go so easily.

Instead, disturbed and disbelieving, he would have coaxed her to stay and questioned her further.

It was hard to credit that she'd truly been deprived of books and supplies. But years of gauging the veracity of men's accounts from their tone and manner as they related them, a skill essential to an officer in an army at war, argued that what she'd revealed was the truth.

What kind of man would take away what most delighted his wife, only because she'd displeased him?

The same kind who would force her into marriage

by threatening her father with debtors' prison and her fiancé with ruin?

When she'd first related to him the reasons behind her marriage, he'd rejected the story with contemptuous disbelief. But from the bits he'd just pried from her, it was just possible that her tall tale might be true.

Another memory surfaced: once during their courtship, he'd read her a piece of effulgent, adjective-laden verse, then waited expectantly for her reaction. After a few moments, her lips opening and closing as she sought a response, she'd blurted, 'Oh, Alastair, that was awful!' After a moment of outrage, he'd laughed and admitted that it was overwritten.

He'd teased her that she'd have to marry him rather than some dandy of the *ton*, for as impossible as she found it to prevaricate, she'd never be fashionable. She'd readily agreed, confessing that her mind went completely blank when faced with constructing a polite evasion to mask her real thoughts, especially if pressed by her questioner.

As he had pressed her tonight.

What was he to make of what she'd revealed…and what she'd left out?

Puzzlement and something more than curiosity stirred in him. Something like compassion, and a concern he didn't want to feel.

All he'd hoped for tonight was to have the gift he'd offered relax Diana enough to finally break the hold she was maintaining over her response to him. Still, he had to admit, he'd enjoyed looking for something to tempt her.

He'd always loved giving her gifts. She'd accepted even the simplest with joy, appreciative of the care he had taken in choosing them. He'd been delighted when he hit upon the idea of the paints, sure she would find them impossible to resist. He'd spent a good deal of time looking for the finest pigments and brushes available.

Instead of accepting the supplies with the pleasure he'd envisaged, she'd put them back in the box and recommended he return them.

He tried once again to take in the incomprehensible notion that a girl of her ability no longer painted.

Well, he'd not be returning them. It was a travesty for an artist of her skill to give up the brush, almost an insult to the father from whom she'd inherited her talent.

He'd have to try tempting her with them again.

Which reminded him of her shocking response to his offer to give her pleasure. Though he'd been stung when she'd seemed suspicious of his reasons, he had to concede her instincts hadn't been all that far off the mark.

He hadn't entered this affair for her benefit. Not that he'd precisely *wanted* to hurt her. Indeed, given how indifferent she'd appeared to him the last few times they met, he'd not considered it possible to injure her. He had, however, wanted to reach her and force a response.

He still wanted that. Every instinct he possessed told him that tonight, he'd come a hair's breadth close to sweeping her beyond control. Next time, he was convinced, he would bring her all the way to completion.

But now, he wanted more than physical surrender.

Not just her body had responded to him. He'd caught her staring at him when he entered the parlour tonight; unaware he was inspecting her closely as well, she'd not been wearing the impassive mask behind which she normally retreated. In her unguarded expression, he'd read wonder, attraction, and a vulnerability completely at odds with the controlled, emotionless woman she tried to appear.

Had she truly been coerced into marriage? What had

the Duke done to turn the vibrant girl he'd known into a woman who turned an indifferent face to the world, who seemed desperate to maintain a rigid self-control?

Now, he knew he couldn't walk away from her until he uncovered the whole truth about Diana.

Chapter Seven

Having fled Green Park Buildings without waiting for a footman to call her a sedan chair, Diana quickly traversed the dark streets, keeping herself into the shadows. Arrived safely at Laura Place, grateful for the enveloping cloak that had allowed her to travel with her gown not fully fastened and to be able to remove it without having to wake up a maid, she crept up to her bedchamber. Knowing she was too distraught to think rationally or worry over what Annie would think of this sudden ability to get herself out of her gown without assistance, she'd shed her garments, thrown on her night rail and wrapped herself, trembling, in the bedclothes.

With her dissatisfied body humming and her mind racing in panicked indecision, she slept poorly.

Diana woke early, hardly more rested than when she'd laid her head on the pillow. But the last hour before dawn was the only time she'd have alone to think before the household was stirring.

Escaping Alastair and his too-persistent questions last night had been the most temporary of solutions. She was still bound to return to him tonight, where she was likely to face even more pointed enquiries.

She could just tell him everything, rather than waiting for him to trick and dig it from her. But, with Graveston having methodically isolated her from everyone she'd known, she'd lost the knack of making confidences. Besides, how could she revisit those scenes of misery and despair, without the risk that some of the ugly emotions she'd worked so hard to bury might escape the pit into which she'd thrust them?

She was free of that place now, of *him*. She didn't *want* to remember any of it.

She could still send Alastair a note, breaking off all contact.

The possibility tantalised. With no Alastair Ransleigh to challenge her control and distract her thoughts, she could bend all her energies into preparing herself to counter the move from Blankford she knew would soon be coming.

At the cost, of course, of whatever honour she had left.

She tried to talk herself out of that conviction; after all, 'honour' was a concept invented by the same gentlemen who wrote the laws allowing husbands to beat wives with impunity, assume control of all their assets and property to use or waste as they chose—and take away their children.

She tried to convince herself, but it wouldn't wash; she was too much her father's daughter. The idea that a pledge once given must be followed through, that a wrong done must if at all possible be righted, were precepts ingrained in her from earliest childhood.

But hard upon the swell of despair brought by that thought, a new, much more promising possibility occurred to her. One that set her needy senses racing.

Why not give Alastair what he wanted? What he truly wanted, which wasn't the sordid details of her marriage, or some sloppy flood of emotion, but her physical surrender. If she allowed herself to respond to him, the nights at Green Park Buildings could be pleasant for them both, rather than exercises in frustration, as she tried to resist his touch. After inciting her to passion, he would be too satisfied and replete for conversation.

Excitement feathered through her, dissipating the lingering fatigue. She'd burned and hungered for his touch during their courtship days, eager for the feel of complete possession. What a dolt she was being, to have been offered that and refused it!

Even better, passion would possess her completely, too, eliminating any thought or emotion beyond the physical. No frustration and anxiety, nor any need either to armour herself against a revival of the love for him she'd buried deep, where its loss could no longer hurt her. There'd be only a firestorm of sensation and then the peace of fulfilment.

Best of all, she knew she could do this. Resisting his touch had been an exhausting, nerve-fraying battle of will. Letting go of that control, her secrets and emotions securely hidden, would be sweet as slipping between silken sheets.

Perhaps some day, when she'd learned to love her son again and figured out how to keep him safe, she might risk remembering the joy of that long-ago spring with Alastair. Their attachment had lacked only physical fulfilment to make it complete. If she claimed that now, in that far-away future she might merge the two memories into one shining, jewelled brilliance of a recollection—the image of a perfect love to sustain her the rest of her days.

She *would* do it.

Energised, she leapt from the bed and went to ring for the maid. Instead of dreading the dusk tonight, now she was almost eager to see the sun set.

On the other side of Bath, having also slept badly and thus not wanting to face his perspicacious sister, Alastair elected to breakfast in his room. Sipping his second cup of coffee, he was feeling more like a rational human being when a footman brought in his correspondence.

Idly he flipped through it, then halted at a gilt-edged note. Disquiet stirred when he read the card: Lady Randolph, who before her marriage had been one of Diana's bosom-bows, had for some inexplicable reason invited him to tea.

Lady Randolph being the same Miss Mary Ellington whom, in the near insanity of his rage and grief after Diana's stunning rejection, he'd subjected to a most improper, most insulting offer of carte blanche.

He felt his face redden at the memory. Luckily for him, the offended lady had merely slapped his face and sent him on his way with the tongue-lashing he deserved. Had she revealed his dishonourable proposal to her brother, he probably would have been shot before ever making it to his regiment.

Mary Ellington had gone on to make a good match to a viscount's son with political aspirations, and, by Jane's account, was now a happily married wife with a quiverful of children.

He'd neither spoken to nor seen her since that disgraceful afternoon. Why would she invite him to tea?

He debated sending a polite refusal, but given the colossal insult to which he'd subjected her on their last meeting, decided that he owed it to the lady to appear in her drawing room long enough to apologise.

Hopefully, Jane's assessment was accurate, and she wasn't now a bored wife, looking to take him up on that long-ago offer. Though if she were, he could sidestep it, a manoeuvre with which he'd had a fair amount of practice.

One didn't earn a reputation as a man who disdained marriage and preferred pleasant, short-term liaisons without attracting the interest of Society matrons long on available time and short on commitment to their marriage vows. Particularly, he thought cynically, when the potential lover possessed a deep purse she might try slipping a hand into.

With Diana waiting for him, he certainly wasn't interested in another mistress.

But Mary Ellington had also been Diana's closest female friend. Might she have some insight into what had happened to the girl he'd once loved?

With a sigh, he tossed the card back on the tray and rang for another cup of coffee. It appeared he was going to have tea with the chaste virgin he'd once propositioned.

More anxious than he'd like to be, Alastair presented himself at the appointed hour at another elegant townhouse on the Circus. Shown by the butler into a salon, he had only a few moments to wait until his hostess arrived.

'Mr Ransleigh, thank you for coming to see me on such little notice,' she said, nodding to his bow. 'Let me pour you some tea.'

Seating himself where she indicated, Alastair held on to his patience over the next few minutes as they exchanged the conventional cordialities.

Finally, he said, 'If you intend to take me to task over my inexcusable behaviour the last time we met, let me relieve you of the obligation. I behaved despicably, for which I am truly sorry. I do hope you've forgiven me.'

She looked startled for a moment, then laughed. 'Oh, that! No, your, ah, regrettable behaviour then has nothing to do with my reasons for asking you to come today. Or at least, not directly. Besides, we all knew that you weren't yourself, that soon after the…break with Diana.'

That being unanswerable, he merely nodded. 'What did you want with me, then?'

She sighed. 'I'm not quite sure how to begin. Let's just say that I'm…aware you have recently seen Diana.'

Inwardly cursing, Alastair struggled to keep a smile on his lips. Blast! Did everyone in Bath know he'd encountered Diana?

When he said nothing, she continued. 'Please hear me out, for what I'm about to say, you could with justification point out, is none of my business. But knowing Diana so well years ago, I felt it important that you know it.'

Hoping what she revealed might shed light on Diana's situation, but wanting to say nothing that might hint of the renewed relationship between them, he'd not decided what to reply when his hostess forged on.

'I know how deeply Diana wounded you. It would be entirely understandable if you wished to seek some sort of…retribution, especially as she is now in the city without benefit of husband or anyone else to protect her.'

Nettled, he rose. 'Are you suggesting, madam, that I would seek to harm her?'

'No! Not at all!' she protested, waving him back to his seat. 'Only asking, if you should be required to have any dealings with her, that you…treat her gently.'

At his raised eyebrow, she rushed on. 'The manner in which she jilted you was inexcusable, but though she may have captured a duke, save for the son finally granted her, it appears she had little joy of her prize. You may have heard that after her marriage, Diana ignored all those who knew her before she became a duchess.'

'Jane told me as much.'

'So it appeared, but it wasn't true. I was as aghast as anyone after she broke your engagement—and in so shocking a fashion! Though normally, one could believe that a duke's offer of marriage would be preferred over one from a mere mister, Diana had never been interested in social advancement. I truly believed she was as besotted by you as you appeared to be by her. After the hasty marriage, I was curious, of course, but also worried about her happiness. The Duke of Graveston was known to be a cold, forbidding, unapproachable man. So I called on her…and was told the Duchess did not wish to receive me. Then, or at any time in future. I was shocked, and hurt, of course.'

'I can imagine.' *Having received just the same treatment.*

'As I was walking back to my carriage—I'd told the coachman to circle the square, as I didn't intend to remain long—Diana ran up to me. Speaking all in a rush, she told me she'd seen my arrival from a window, slipped out the kitchen door and come through the mews to catch me. The Duke had decreed that since her former friends were not of suitable rank—I'd not yet married Randolph—she was no longer permitted to associate with them. Saying she must return before her absence was discovered, she gave me her love and said goodbye. I—I didn't know what to make of it at the time, but I do know she never received any of her other friends, either.'

'"No longer permitted"?' Alastair echoed. 'Could a husband enforce such a stipulation? Or was that a convenient excuse?'

Lady Randolph shook her head. 'I don't know. I didn't

see her again until years later, after Randolph won a seat in Parliament, and we were invited to a political dinner hosted by the Duke. There had already been rumours that the match was a most—unusual—one, and I was quite anxious to have a chance to speak with Diana again.'

She paused, looking troubled. 'Did you speak with her?' he prompted, impatient for her to continue.

She started a little, as if she'd been lost in memory. 'No, for reasons I will soon make apparent. The Duke came down after the guests had assembled, but as the hour grew later, Diana still had not appeared. Finally, just after the butler announced dinner was to be served, she suddenly arrived at the doorway through which the guests must pass to reach the dining room. She wore a striking white-silk gown with a very low décolletage, but neither gloves nor jewels. Instead, circling her neck and wrists were...bruises, the ones beneath each ear clearly fingerprints. In the shocked silence, she walked up to the Duke, and as if nothing out of the ordinary had occurred, said she was ready to go in to dinner.'

'What did the Duke do?'

Lady Randolph laughed shortly. 'What could he do? I'm told he seldom exhibits any emotion, but those near him said his face reddened. Without a word, he offered his arm—and ignoring it, she walked beside him into the dining room. It was the most magnificent bit of defiance I've ever witnessed.'

It was all Alastair could do to guard his expression. To hear of any woman abused would have aroused his anger and pity—but Diana! Sickened, furious, he struggled to find a comment that expressed a degree of outrage appropriate for a former fiancé—rather than a man once again involved with the woman in question.

Giving him a sympathetic look, his hostess continued. 'I know what a shock that news must be, even for one who no longer has any warm feelings for Diana. It's simply wicked, what a wife can suffer without any legal remedy, and makes me daily grateful for my Randolph! Sadly, I've known several poor souls whose husbands treated them…ungently, and without exception they tried to hide the abuse, were embarrassed by it. And afraid. Whereas Diana flaunted the Duke's lack of control for all his world to see, embarrassing *him*. With utter disregard for how he might make her pay for it later.'

The thought chilled him. He'd seen no evidence of current bruises—but her husband might have been ill for months, for all he knew. Had she suffered his hand raised against her through all her marriage?

'As soon as dinner concluded,' Lady Randolph continued, 'the Duke took her arm and escorted her upstairs, saying she was feeling "indisposed", then returned to his guests.' She shuddered. 'I hesitate even to imagine what must have happened later. In any event, it was the last time I saw her. Soon afterward, the Duke took her to Graveston Court, and though he returned to London for Parliament and occasionally entertained there, she never again accompanied him. I heard from guests who dined with them before her banishment that she always conversed freely at table, giving no deference to the Duke or his opinions, pointing out discrepancies as she saw them in his arguments or those of his Parliamentary supporters.'

'Not an ideal political wife,' Alastair observed, before his own words came out of memory like a stiletto to the chest: *You shall have to marry me, rather than some dandy of the* ton, *for as impossible as you find it to prevaricate, you'll never be fashionable.*

Anguish twisted in his gut. Never fashionable. Never appreciated.

Never safe.

'Quite frankly, after what I'd seen and heard, I'm rather surprised she outlived him—but ever so glad! Despite what the malicious are saying about her in Bath, I intend to seek her out and offer her friendship.'

To his surprise, Lady Randolph seized his hands and looked up at him earnestly. 'Diana made a terrible decision that summer so many years ago. But whatever advantage she thought to gain, she's paid a dear price for it. Paid enough, I think. I just ask that you have pity, and if you can't forgive her, at least don't add to her sufferings.'

'I can assure you, I have no intention of doing that.'

Releasing him, she sat back. 'Thank you! Since you are a man of honour—most of the time,' she added with a smile and a pointed look, 'I am satisfied.'

Taking his leave a few minutes later, Alastair scarcely recalled what had been said during the rest of his visit, so preoccupied had he been by what Lady Randolph had revealed—and with not betraying by some comment or expression his full reaction to the information she'd conveyed.

Once free of her restraining presence, though, electing to walk back to his sister's townhouse so he might think uninterrupted, he methodically reviewed her recitation, looking for bits and pieces that fit with what he'd learned himself.

Lady Randolph's account seemed to confirm Diana's assertion that she had never confided to anyone else the account she'd given him of being coerced into marriage. Of course, as he'd told her and she'd readily admitted, the story beggared belief. Even her dearest friend thought it was the temptation of marrying into the highest rank of Society that had, in the end, induced her to abandon him.

Had it been?

His certainty about that, already shaken, wavered further as he allowed himself to recall more about the Diana he'd known. The Diana who, without question, would never lie. The Diana who, even now, could not come up with a plausible evasion.

Equally without question, the girl she'd been would have been capable of sacrificing her own happiness to save those she loved.

A girl who, heedless of her own safety, had had the courage to publicly defy a duke.

Suddenly he recalled her confusion when he'd offered her the paints. The confusion of someone who had received so little for so many years, she no longer knew how to respond to a gift.

The confusion of one who only knew what it was like to have what she loved taken away.

Feeling sick inside, Alastair halted at the street corner, mopping his face with a trembling hand. Had he been wrong all this time, wallowing in self-righteous indignation over her supposed betrayal?

Common sense rejected that conclusion, and yet… Like snow silently accumulating on a windowsill, the doubts that had begun creeping in to trouble his assumptions over what she'd done, and why, redoubled.

He had to know the truth.

Little by little, he promised himself as he resumed his walk, with a tenderness and concern she apparently had not been shown for years, he would coax her to tell it to him.

But before that, he'd need to get a pianoforte delivered to Green Park Buildings.

Chapter Eight

After a session before the mirror to restore her calm—
only in the bedchamber could she permit herself any
emotion—Diana arrived at the townhouse in Green Park
Buildings. So great was her nervous anticipation she'd
had to exercise great self-control not to arrive very early,
so she might have time to position herself before Alastair
arrived.

She'd filled some of the waiting time reading to James.
During a walk down Milsom Street this morning, they
found a picture book of soldiers. She'd enjoyed reading
to him, and he seemed to like it, too. The interlude had
been…pleasant. Perhaps she would be able to revive the
tenderness she'd once felt for him.

Precisely at the agreed hour, she knocked at the door
of Alastair's townhouse. The same expressionless man-
servant—having been spied on by her husband's retainers
for so long, she was inured to expressionless servants—
showed her into the parlour where, this time, Alastair
waited to greet her.

Swallowing hard over a renewed attack of nerves, she
made herself walk calmly over to him. He rose, and when
he angled her chin up for a kiss, she let him.

Feathering her eyes closed, she opened herself to sensation. The soft pressure of his lips brushing against hers was gentle, sweet, and sensual, setting all the nerves of her mouth tingling. When he broke the kiss, she was disappointed—and eager for more.

'I brought you a little something,' he said with a smile, motioning across the room.

So preoccupied was she by this bold new venture of responsiveness, she'd noticed nothing in the chamber but Alastair. Following the direction of his hand, she uttered a gasp. 'Alastair! That's hardly "little"—it's a pianoforte!'

He grinned at her, and a sharp stab of…something struck the barrier she'd erected to restrain her emotions, already shaken by his kindness in remembering how much she loved music. As he stood smiling, the harsh, cynical edge to his expression gone, he looked like the boyish young man she'd once given her heart to.

Good she was about to sweep all thought away with passion, else he might tempt her too much.

'Play for me.'

'I haven't played in years!' she protested. 'I'd likely sour milk and set all the cats on the street to squalling.'

He chuckled. 'I'll risk it. If it's been that long, all the more reason to begin again immediately. It's like riding a horse—you never truly forget.'

'Who told you that?' she asked, swallowing a laugh. 'Certainly no one who played well! Daily practice is essential to remain truly proficient.'

'And you were wonderfully proficient. There might be a few cobwebs to brush off, but I wager that won't take long. So, play for me…please.'

She wanted to refuse, get right to bedroom matters; straying on to the topic of music could bring the dangerous possibility of more prying. But even from across the room, she could tell the pianoforte was a beautiful instrument—trust Alastair to choose only the best. She'd missed music almost as much as she'd missed Alastair, the love for it, like her love for him, suppressed but never extinguished.

'Very well,' she capitulated. 'But you might want to leave the room. I expect I shall be dreadful.'

He merely smiled and gestured towards the instrument. Eagerness bubbled out before she could restrain it as she ran her fingers experimentally along the keys. As the bright tones issued forth, her much-denied, atrophied heart gave a feeble pang.

And so she played, slowly at first, then faster, with more assurance. During her clandestine midnight forays at Graveston, before the instrument had been taken away, she'd memorised many of her favourite works, not wishing to risk leaving sheet music about. She found her fingers returning to one piece after another.

Soon she lost herself in the music. Time ceased to matter, and when the final movement ended and she lifted her hands from the keyboard, she wasn't sure how long she'd been playing.

She looked around to see Alastair in a wing chair by the fire, wine glass in hand, watching her.

Contrition seized her. 'I'm sorry. I...I lost track of the time. So sorry to keep you waiting.'

'Not at all. That was lovely. I've missed hearing you play.'

He looked as surprised as she was by that remark. Not sure what to respond, she rose and came over to him. Now to put her plan into effect before he could initiate any more conversational delays.

'You should have a reward for your patience.' She leaned down to kiss him, her tongue outlining the edge of his lips.

With a murmur, he set down his glass, pulled her into his lap, and deepened the kiss. This time, she let herself respond to the warmth and heat of him, opening to him, fencing back as they tangled tongues, the soft moist heat stoking the passion rising within her.

She brought his hand to her breast, and he caressed her through the material of her gown and stays. Luscious sensation sparkled and shot through her body, setting off a throbbing at her centre as she envisaged how much more acutely she would feel his touch, once his clothes and hers were removed. Revelling in his caress, she rubbed herself against him.

He broke the kiss, his eyes blazing and his breathing unsteady. 'Upstairs, now,' he urged, setting her on her feet.

Before he led her off, she turned to him and tilted her mouth up for another kiss. When he obliged, sweeping his tongue in to possess hers, she wrapped an arm around him and inserted her other hand between their two bodies, massaging the hardness pressed against her.

'More of that later,' she promised, before taking his hand to tug him towards the door.

Wrapping an arm around her, he caressed her bottom as they walked up the stairs. Once in the bedchamber, she whirled around, offering him access to pins and tapes, which he dispensed of quickly, unpeeling her bodice and helping her step out of her gown. She lifted her hands to let him strip the chemise over her head and stood before him, clad only in garters and stockings.

He ran his gaze slowly over her, from chin to toes. 'Lovely,' he murmured.

Kissing him, she unfastened his trouser buttons and urged the garment down, then pushed him to sit back on the bed. As soon as he'd balanced there, she climbed on his lap, straddling him, then wrapped her legs around his back and guided herself down to enclose his swollen member.

Ah, how good he felt, slick hot steel caressing her inner chamber for all his length. Sighing, she leaned back, offering up her naked breasts. Cupping her bottom to secure her, he bent to them, rolling the hard nipples between his teeth, nipping and suckling.

The sensation was exquisite, every sweep of his tongue and nip of his teeth intensifying the throbbing pressure building deep within her, where his member stretched and pulled and teased. Feeling the urgent need for more movement, she began rocking into him, savouring the friction as she pulled almost free, then sank down on him again.

Pressure built and built, lifting her again towards the precipice she'd sensed the night before, driving her to intensify her efforts. If she could just force him deeper, rub against him harder...

Suddenly, in a rush of sensation unlike anything she'd ever experienced, the pressure released in a flow of tingling, throbbing delight. She felt she was soaring, flying above all pain and misery and memory, for long, brilliant minutes before settling softly back to earth.

Boneless, she sagged against Alastair, who simply held her, kissing the dampness of her forehead and her ears. His silence was just as well, for her scattered thoughts were too incoherent for speech.

'Thank you,' he whispered at last.

Surprised, her eyes started open. 'Shouldn't I be thanking you? Especially since...' She rocked her hips around the still-hard member still inside her.

'All in good time. Thank you for letting go, giving me the gift of your pleasure.'

'Isn't it time for you to give me the gift of yours?'

'Gladly.' He smiled against her lips before kissing her.

She wanted to finish undressing him, but he wouldn't hear of it. Rising, still almost fully clad, he slid back to the pillows and lay back, holding her in place astride him.

'What would please you most?' she asked disjointedly, hardly able to formulate the sentence for the pressure of him moving inside her, creating little eddies of pleasure.

'Watching you again, as you ride me. But first, this.'

He pulled her close, kissing her—throat, shoulders, silky skin of inner arms, down to her breasts. Though he'd pleasured them before, he began again, even more slowly, a meticulous caress of every surface, licking the pebbly nipples as he massaged the full softness.

By now, her core was throbbing again, too. Murmuring encouragement, he lay back, urging her to move on him. Balanced better on the bed, she could spread her knees wider and take him deeper still. The thrust of his hardness along the whole of her passage, from the depths to the tight nub at the peak, elicited a whole new range of sensations.

Faster and faster she moved, each stroke tightening the coil of pressure until at last, in a splendid blaze of pleasure, they flew over the crest together.

For a while afterwards, they both drifted in somnolent contentment. When at last she rose back to full consciousness, she found herself beside him, his arm wrapped around her, her head pillowed on his shoulder.

A wave of wonder and delight washed through her. How many times had she dreamed of waking like this?

And this time, she had no need to thrust away or bottle up the thought.

Instead, she nestled closer. 'Must I go now?'

'Go?' he echoed. 'Heavens, no, my sweet. We've just begun.'

Her eyes widened at that. 'Just begun?' she repeated cautiously.

Laughing, Alastair rolled out of the bed, swiftly stripped off his clothes, walked over to pour them a glass of wine and brought it back, while she admired his magnificent nakedness.

'Here, drink up. We've hours yet.'

After taking a long sip, she let herself smile. 'That's excellent.'

He chuckled and took back the glass. 'Let me show you how excellent,' he murmured. Smoothing his hands down over her belly, he nudged her legs apart and moved his clever, wicked mouth to that needy place between her thighs.

Slowly Diana emerged from the heavy mantle of sleep, like a sea creature rising from the deep. Her body felt languid, replete with a humming satisfaction. When she finally forced her eyelids open, she saw a dearly beloved visage, smiling at her.

What marvellous dream was this? A sense of wonder escaping before she could cage it, she raised a hand to trace the face from forehead to lips. 'Alastair?' she whispered.

As if his name had evoked it, consciousness returned in a rush, accompanied by a paralysing stab of fear. 'Alastair! You must—I must get away. At once! He mustn't find us!'

As she frantically pulled at the bedclothes, desperate to flee, he stilled her hands. 'Stop, Diana! It's all right. Your husband is dead. He'll never hurt you again.'

The room seemed to swirl around her dizzily. 'He's... gone?' she repeated, trying to focus her muzzy senses.

'Yes. He's gone, and I'm here.'

She struggled to pull herself free from the iron grip of another world. After a moment of frantic concentration, reality began to fall into place. Graveston's death. Coming to Bath. Meeting Alastair again. The bargain.

The luxuriant somnolence of her body clashed with the agitation of emotions still out of control. Responding to the imperative to reel them in, she pushed at the arm he'd wrapped around her.

'Please, I need…I need to sit.' Detaching herself, she slid away and off the bed, looking around wildly for the dressing table. Spying it in the corner, she hurried over, and heedless of her nakedness and his keen observing eyes, seated herself before the glass. The forehead of the face reflected back to her was creased with anxiety, the eyes feral.

With a trembling hand, she smoothed away the lines and began the ritual breathing. *Long slow inhale, hold, hold, exhale.* Applying every bit of mind and will, she forced back the anxiety and buried the panic, until finally the countenance staring back at her was expressionless and calm.

Only then did she turn to Alastair. He was still looking at her with concern—no wonder, after witnessing that performance! Better distract him quickly, before he could begin questioning.

'I'm so sorry!' She managed a smile. 'I can't recall when I last slept so deeply, I awoke with no idea where I was.'

Though his eyes still looked troubled, mercifully, he did not press her. 'Passion satisfied can do that.'

She smiled in earnest. 'What a wondrous gift! I had no idea such feelings existed. Thank you.'

'I should point out, the gift was mutual. Thank you, too.'

Suddenly she noticed that, though the candles had guttered out, a dim light illuminated the chamber. Her relief at recalling that Graveston was gone and she was in Bath abruptly dissipated.

'Goodness, what hour is it?'

'Just past dawn.'

Shocked that she'd slept so long, Diana hopped off the bench and began gathering up her garments. 'I must get back at once, before the servants begin to stir.'

'I'll summon you a chair.'

'No, I'll walk—it's light enough now, someone might notice the chair.'

'I appreciate your efforts at discretion, but it's not yet full daylight and you shouldn't be out on the streets alone,' he countered. 'I'll escort you.'

'What kind of discretion would that be? No, you mustn't be seen by anyone in the house. The servants can't be trusted not to gossip.'

With a sigh, he came over to help her. 'I'm much better at removing these than putting them back on,' he said as he fitted the gown over her chemise and began pinning. 'Why so worried about gossip? I thought you'd brought with you only a few trusted retainers.'

She leaned back against him as he secured the garment. 'All were hired here but Minnie, James's nursemaid, and she's loyal only to him. The servants at Graveston Court obeyed their master and no one else. Not that I blame them. Had any of them shown sympathy or allegiance to me, they would have been turned out at once without a character.'

'So you truly had no one.'

Deciding, after a moment's hesitation, to ignore the question, she sat to roll on her stockings and slip her feet into her slippers, then stood and twirled before him. 'All put to rights, am I?'

'Sadly, yes. I prefer you in the natural state.'

'Wouldn't give one much chance of slipping through the streets unnoticed, you must allow.' Feeling somehow shyer now in her garments than she had while naked before him in the languid aftermath of loving, she glanced up as she tied on her cloak. 'Will you…want me again tonight?'

The smouldering look he returned sent a little thrill through her. 'You know I will.'

'Then I shall be here.' Stepping towards the door, she paused to look back over her shoulder. 'Alastair, I—I really do thank you. Last night was…magnificent.'

A twinkle in his eyes, he walked over to capture her chin and give her a kiss, long and slow and full of promise. 'Just wait until tonight.'

Warmth bubbled up, and this time, she didn't try to stop it. 'Tonight,' she whispered, parting his lips to delve into his mouth and deliver her promise in return.

Maintaining her vigilance as she slipped through the empty streets, her only fellow travellers a few returning revellers and the last of the night-soil men rattling off with their carts, Diana arrived home to find the kitchen still dark but for the banked embers in the fireplace.

Grateful not to have to manufacture an excuse for appearing downstairs at so odd an hour, she padded softly up to the privacy of her chamber.

As long as she came and went alone, she didn't worry too much about any gossip the staff might exchange about her movements. The servants had already been instructed that she planned to go out most evenings and would let herself back in, so except for the maid who assisted her with dressing, they need not wait up for her. Though she supposed that directive might be unusual, the permission to end their long day when they chose, without having their rest depend upon the vagaries of their employer's social schedule, was attractive enough, none had questioned it.

Once safely within her chamber, Diana seated herself in the chair before her own banked chamber fire. In a moment, she'd strip off the cloak and lie down on her bed, telling the maid when she came later in that she'd been so weary after returning, she hadn't bothered to ring for her. Now, for the next few moments, she could let down her guard and recall the events of the night.

How wonderful it had been to no longer fight against Alastair's insidious attraction! How exciting to respond freely to his touch, to let passion sweep her away to a satisfaction more powerful and complete than she'd imagined possible. She'd suspected loving Alastair would be magical, but words couldn't begin to describe the all-encompassing power and grandeur of it.

The warmth she'd felt earlier bubbled up again, expanding until it filled her with a sense of peace she hadn't experienced since long ago, in that other life.

Home, safe, content, she slept, to awake later feeling energised. The well-being stayed with her through the morning and well into the afternoon. Until, returning from a walk to the park with James and Minnie, the maid informed her as she entered the house that a solicitor was waiting in the parlour to see her.

Chapter Nine

Dread struck her like a fist to the gut. Surely Blankford couldn't be moving against her this quickly! She'd expected it to take at least a fortnight for him to pack up and decamp to Graveston Court after the news of his father's demise reached him, and some time after that for him to trace where she'd fled.

But she couldn't imagine any other reason a solicitor would be asking for her, here in Bath, barely a week after her arrival.

Whoever it was, she must meet him now. With no more time to prepare, she didn't have the luxury of panic. Pummelling down the fear, she told the maid to announce her.

The man who rose to greet her as she entered the parlour was the image of what one would expect of a peer's solicitor: old, sober of demeanour, garbed in expensive, well-tailored but not ostentatious garments.

'Good afternoon, Your Grace. I'm Feral, solicitor to Lord Blankford—the new Duke of Graveston, that is,' he said, confirming her fears. 'I've brought a letter from his Grace, vouching for my identity and authorising me to collect the boy.'

Though she knew exactly what he meant, she repeated blankly, 'Collect the boy?'

'Lord James Mannington, the late Duke's son by his second marriage to you. The new Duke wishes the boy brought back to Graveston Court—where he can be reared as befits his station,' he added, with a disparaging glance around the modest room.

Anger overlay the fear, sharpening every sense. *Delay, expostulate, distract.* She widened her eyes, gave him an incredulous look. 'You've come to take away my son?'

The solicitor had the grace to look discomfited. 'He'll be well cared for, I assure—'

'My husband dead barely a fortnight, and you want to strip me of my son?!' she interrupted, letting her voice rise to a distraught crescendo. 'No, I cannot bear it!'

Closing her eyes, Diana fell in a dramatic faint to the floor.

'Your Grace!' Feral exclaimed, looking down at her.

From her position on the carpet, Diana remained unresponsive. At length the solicitor grew more concerned and rang the bell to summon assistance.

The maid looked in, gasped and ran back off, then returned with the entire household staff. Several minutes passed as they bustled about, Annie chafing her hands while Cook waved a vinaigrette under her nose and Smithers, the manservant, helped the two females lift Diana off the floor.

During those minutes, she schemed furiously, examining and discarding several courses of action until she hit upon one with the greatest likelihood of success.

'Some tea to restore you, my lady?' Cook asked after she had been propped on the sofa.

'Yes. And I suppose I must offer some to Mr Feral, even though he has come to take away my child.'

Diana doubted she'd earned much sympathy from the staff during her brief stay, but all of them were charmed by James, and the idea of stripping a boy from his mama did not sit well. Though none of the servants were ill trained enough to display overt hostility, the gazes they turned towards the solicitor were distinctly chilly.

'As you wish, my lady,' Cook said, returning to her domain.

'Shall I remain until you have fully recovered?' Annie asked, stationing herself protectively between Diana and her guest.

Her point made, and her visitor now looking distinctly uncomfortable—and as rattled as Diana had hoped—she said, 'No, Annie, you may go. Nothing else Mr Feral says or does could wound me more than he already has.'

As soon as the servants exited, Feral turned to her with an exasperated look. 'Indeed, Your Grace, that was hardly necessary! You'd think I was attempting to send the boy to a workhouse, rather than return him to a life of ease in the home of his birth!'

Pushing away from the pillows, she dropped the guise of distraught mother and switched to imperious aristocrat, a role which, after watching her husband, she could play to perfection.

'How dare you, a solicitor, son of a tradesman no doubt, presume to tell me what to do?' she cried. 'My son remains with me.'

As she'd hoped, the change in demeanour took the solicitor by surprise. Years of serving an employer who would have tolerated nothing less than complete deference and absolute obedience had him stuttering an apology.

'I meant no disrespect, Your Grace. But—'

'But you thought you could simply march into this house, my retreat from grief, and order me about?'

That might have been a bit much, for the solicitor, his expression wary, said, 'Though I have every appreciation for a widow's grief, Your Grace, I must point out it was common knowledge that you and the late Duke... did not live harmoniously together.'

'We did live together, however, which is more than can be said for my late husband and his heir, who, long before his father's death, had broken off all relations between them. Yet now you have the effrontery to assure me that this man, who hasn't set foot inside Graveston Court for years, who refused ever to speak to me, will take good care of my son?'

'Surely you don't mean to suggest the Duke would not treat the boy kindly!' the solicitor objected.

She merely raised her eyebrows. 'I believe he will treat Mannington—and everyone else—in whatever way he chooses. I have no intention of abandoning my son to the vagaries of his half-brother's humours. Besides, there is no need for Mannington to be reared at Graveston; he's not the new heir, or even the heir presumptive. Blankford married two years ago, I'm told, and already has a son and heir.'

'The existence of an heir has no bearing on the Duke's wish that his half-brother be raised in a ducal establishment.'

'Even if Mannington were the heir,' she continued, ignoring him, 'until he's old enough to be sent to school, a child should remain with his mother.'

'If a case for custody were brought forward, the Court of Chancery would likely decide in favour of the Duke,' the solicitor shot back, obviously already prepared for that argument.

Before she could put forth any more objections, he said in a softer tone, 'Your Grace, though I sympathise with a mother's eagerness to hold on to her child, you might as well resign yourself. As you should know from association with your late husband, when a Duke of Graveston desires something, he gets it.'

Nothing he could have said would have enraged her more. Welcoming a fury that helped her submerge a desperation too close to the surface, she snapped, 'He will not get my son. I fear you've made a long journey to no purpose. Good day to you, Mr Feral.'

Before he could respond, Diana rose and swept from the room.

Her heart thudding in her chest, Diana instructed Smithers—who'd been loitering outside the door—to escort the visitor out, then paused in the doorway to the kitchens, concealed by the overhanging stairs.

As theatre, it had been an adequate performance, but would it be enough? Would Feral leave, or charge up to the nursery and attempt to remove Mannington by force?

If it came to that, she hoped the staff would assist her, though she wasn't sure she could count on them.

To her relief, a few moments later, Mr Feral, his manner distinctly aggrieved, exited the parlour and paced to the front door, trailed closely by Smithers.

Light-headed with a relief that made her dizzy, she sagged back against the door frame. The first skirmish went to her, but she knew that small victory had won her only a brief respite. At worst, after pondering the matter, Mr Feral might well return and try to carry out Blankford's order by force. Even in the best case—Feral electing to leave her alone and return to the Duke for further instructions—within a week or so she'd face a renewed assault.

Surely Fate wouldn't be so cruel as to strip James from

her now, as she was just beginning to know him again! No, she simply must find some way to prevent it.

Blankford would be furious that she hadn't capitulated to his demand, and was sure to summon every tool of law and influence to exact his will in the next round.

If it did come to that, would a Court of Chancery uphold her right to keep James until he went to university? She had no idea what provisions her husband had made for his second son in the event of his death. Although Blankford had received the title, all the entailed land and the bulk of the assets of the estate, there had probably been something left for James, with trustees named to oversee the assets until he came of age. Her legal position would be weaker still if Blankford had been named one of those trustees—though given the bitterness of the break between her husband and his heir, she doubted the Duke would have appointed him as one.

If Blankford were not a trustee, would that make retaining custody of James easier? She scanned her mind, trying to dredge up what little she knew about how the affairs of wealthy minors were settled under law. But she quickly abandoned the effort. A mere woman, she'd never be allowed to argue the case anyway. She'd chosen Bath over London as her refuge not only because she could live here more cheaply, but also because, as a town still frequented by the fashionable, she might find a solicitor skilled and clever enough to outwit a duke.

The unexpected appearance of Alastair Ransleigh had deflected her from setting out to find such a person as soon as they had settled in. She'd have to begin the search at once, and to hire the best, she'd need additional funds.

However, much as she'd tried to prepare herself for this eventuality, she couldn't repress a shiver as she assessed the odds against her.

You really think you can defeat the Duke? a mocking little voice whispered in her ear. The panic she'd controlled during the interview with the lawyer bubbled up, threatening to escape.

She gave herself a mental shake. No, she would not think about losing James…Graveston's son, yes, but *hers*, too. That way lay madness. With a control perfected through long bitter years, she forced her mind instead back to planning.

She'd obtain funds, consult a lawyer of her own, and find some way to block the Duke's access to James. Thank heavens, tonight she would see Alastair. Perhaps the peace she'd found in his arms last night might ease, for a few hours at least, the fear that still tightened her chest and laboured her breathing.

She simply couldn't give in to it. Once again, she had someone to protect. Whatever it took, she intended that this time, the Duke of Graveston would not have his way.

Meanwhile, Alastair had spent most of the day at Green Park Buildings. After Diana's departure, he'd silently trailed her as she traversed empty dawn streets just stirring to life. Satisfied that she'd made it safely back to her lodgings, he'd returned to the little townhouse ravenous, downed a hefty breakfast of sirloin and ale, then retreated back to the bedchamber they'd shared to refresh himself after a night of great delight and little sleep.

Dust motes danced in the afternoon sunlight when he awoke later. An enormous sense of well-being pervading him, he stretched lazily, running through his mind several of the delicious episodes from last night's loving.

Diana moving under him, over him, pulling his face to her breasts, crying out as he thrust into her, had been intoxicating beyond his wildest imagining. As he'd sensed the first time he touched her, the woman she'd become more than fulfilled the promise of passion in the girl he'd once loved.

Perhaps desire would diminish over time, but thus far, each meeting with her left him more enchanted. The mere thought of touching her, kissing her, tasting her was so arousing he could scarcely wait until evening. Already he was hard and aching, needy and impatient.

But it was more than just the rapture of the physical. When she awakened beside him, rosy with sleep and satisfaction, the unguarded expression of joy and wonder as she recognised him had pierced the barrier he'd erected to armour himself against her and gone straight to the heart. The awe and tenderness with which she'd traced his face and whispered his name had weakened still further the barricades restraining the tender feelings for her that, unable to fully exterminate, he'd buried deep.

She'd gazed at him as if he were her most precious dream.

As she had once been his.

His euphoria dimmed a bit. Allowing her to touch his emotions again wasn't wise and could end badly. He'd entered this affair to purge himself of her, not to fall under the spell of a woman much more complex than the straightforward lass he'd loved. The mere thought of the devastation he'd suffered when she'd abandoned him all those years ago made him suck in a painful breath.

Well, it wouldn't come to that—not this time. He might want to penetrate all her secrets, but he'd not risk his heart imagining they had a future.

And what of her secrets? 'I'm not the girl I once was,' she had told him.

That much was certainly true. She was instead a woman who had, he was reluctantly beginning to believe, suffered isolation, hardship and abuse. If he fully accepted the truth of her account, she'd endured all that to protect her father—and him.

He recalled how frantic she'd become at the thought of the danger their being together placed him in, before he convinced her that her husband was dead.

Then there was that odd ritual at the mirror, during which, she fought her way from distress back to calm.

Alone.

So you had no one, the comment came back to him—a statement she'd neither affirmed nor denied. He recalled Lady Randolph's description of how she'd been isolated from all her former friends.

Isolated, abused—but defiant.

Pity and admiration filled him in equal measure. And despite the danger of letting her touch his emotions, he couldn't beat back the warmth he'd felt at seeing her glow of contentment when she'd awakened in his arms. Couldn't help the need building within him to penetrate the impassive mask and bring that expression to her face again, in the full light of day.

He couldn't give her back the eight years she'd lost, erase the suffering she'd endured, or resurrect the innocent, carefree girl she'd once been. But before they parted, he vowed to do whatever he could to convince her she was truly free to take up all the activities she'd been denied—painting, reading, music—and embrace life fully.

As he thought of that future, a small voice deep within whispered that she must share that new life with *him*.

Ruthlessly, he silenced it.

He was no longer a starry-eyed young man, confident that the future would arrange itself as he wished. In the dangerous matter of Diana, he would move one cautious step at a time, holding the reins on his feelings with as tight a grip as he could manage.

He'd need that knack immediately, for it was past time for him to return to Jane's. Though he had the run of his sister's house and might come and go as he pleased, his absence for an entire day would not have gone unnoticed. The all-too-observant Jane would be curious where he'd been, and he'd have to manufacture an unreadable expression to prevent her from teasing out of him that he was seeing Diana again.

The mere thought of the storm of scolding and possible hysterics that admission would unleash made him shudder.

It would be more prudent to time his return for when his sister was occupied with other matters. Though he did appreciate her genuine concern for his welfare, the matter of Diana was too complicated—and Jane's animosity towards Diana too deep—to be quickly and easily explained.

He hadn't yet brought Jane a hostess gift. Perhaps he'd stop by the jewellers and pick up a trinket to surprise her—and hopefully distract her from any pointed questioning over the curious absences of her brother.

Chapter Ten

Accordingly, an hour later, after a brief stop to bathe and change at the Crescent, Alastair was strolling down Bond Street, bound for the jeweller recommended by his sister's butler. Jane loved flowers; an intricate silver vase or epergne for her table should delight her enough to give him a few days' grace from scrutiny.

Just as he turned the corner, a woman exited the shop. The black cape that swathed her, hiding her face under the overhanging hood, instantly recalled Diana and the delights they had recently shared. He was smiling at the memory when, an instant later, something about the retreating figure made him realise the woman was, in fact, Diana.

A shockingly intense gladness filling him, Alastair set off after her. But by the time he reached the corner, the lady had disappeared. With a disappointed sigh, he turned back towards the shop.

Just as well he'd missed her. Anything he said or did with her on a public street would set tongues wagging. Though he didn't think he was known to any of the pedestrians now passing by him, he'd not noticed any acquaintances in the park the first day he met Diana, either, and word of that encounter had begun circulating immediately.

Besides, he'd rather savour seeing her tonight, when he could undress her, caress by caress. Warmed by that thought, he entered the jeweller's establishment.

Taking one look at him, the junior clerk who greeted him sent at once for the owner. Though he tried to extinguish his curiosity, after that gentleman had shown him several fine silver pieces, one of which he selected for his sister, he couldn't help asking casually whether the lady who'd just left the shop had purchased something similar, so beautifully wrought were the vases.

'I'm afraid she was selling, rather than buying,' the owner replied with a sigh—before his eyes lit. 'I bought from her a particularly nice pearl necklace. Truly, the piece is so fine, I don't think I'll have it for long. A vase is a charming gift, but ladies often prefer a more…personal item. Might your sister be interested in such a necklace?'

Jane might not, but Alastair certainly was. 'Please, do show it to me,' he replied, his curiosity tweaked even further.

Why would Diana be selling jewellery? Whatever the reason, he knew at once he would buy the necklace back.

Beaming, the jeweller disappeared, returning a moment later with a long double-twisted strand of perfectly matched pearls.

For a moment, shock displaced curiosity, as Alastair recognised the necklace. One of the few mementos Diana had of her mother, who'd died giving her birth, the pearls had been a gift to her from her father on her sixteenth birthday. She'd mentioned several times how special it was to her. He couldn't imagine why she would part with it.

Glad he'd encountered the jeweller before the piece had been shown to some other customer, he said, 'You are right. It's exquisite. I shall take that, too.'

Purchases completed, he picked up the wrapped parcel containing the vase and tucked the velvet case with the pearls in his pocket. He'd give Jane the vase just before guests arrived for dinner, leaving them only a short time for conversation, then slip away when her party left for the theatre.

Already impatient to see Diana again, he was now even more eager for the day to fade into evening. He'd present her with the pearls immediately—and try to discover what circumstance could possibly have induced her to part with something that held such dear memories of her long-dead mother.

Alastair arrived at the rendezvous even earlier than the previous nights, then paced the parlour until Diana arrived. Though he'd intended to return the pearls to her immediately, the intensity of the kiss she gave him in greeting fired his simmering desire at once to irresistible need. Almost ravenous enough to take her right then and there, he restrained himself, barely, hurrying her to the bedchamber moments after she stepped in the door.

She seemed as ravenous as he was, kissing him urgently while she tugged at his neckcloth and made short work of the buttons of his trouser flap. Pushing him back to sit on the bed, she lifted her skirts and straddled him, guided him deep and rocked against him, driving them both to their peak within moments.

The next loving was nearly as swift, clothing scattered as it was removed in haste. Then after another, languid cherishing they both drifted into the sleep of the satiated.

Awaking sometime later with Diana tucked in his arms, Alastair smiled as he surveyed the chamber: candles burned low in their sconces, her gown tossed on the back of a chair, her stockings on the bedside table, his neckcloth flung into a corner. Sated for now, he knew that after they consumed the cold collation he'd had set out for them, he'd want her again.

He couldn't seem to get enough of her. Underlying desire, this odd sense of impending loss throbbed in his head like a ticking clock, as if the hours they had together would be limited this time, as they had been before, by some malevolent fate.

Nonsense, he told himself, shaking off the feeling. Eight years ago, they had both been young, still susceptible to the demands of Society and dependent upon others for their support. With him the master of his own estate, she a widow, they now controlled their own destinies, alone and together.

At that encouraging thought, Diana stirred in his arms. Waking, she opened sleepy blue eyes—those beautiful, mesmerising, intense blue eyes—and smiled at him.

Ignoring the wise intention to proceed with caution, his heart leapt with gladness.

Placing a kiss on her forehead, he eased her up against the pillows. 'I'm famished. There's refreshment in the next room.'

He wrapped her in his banyan, donned another, and escorted her to the sitting room, where a fire glowed on the hearth and a simple meal awaited. Though she sipped her wine and accepted bread and cheese, something in the set of her body and the guarded expression of her face suggested an underlying tension.

In a rush, he remembered the necklace. She might well be troubled by whatever had made her part with that once-cherished memento.

'I've got something for you,' he said, hopping up to find his breeches and extract the velvet pouch from the pocket.

'What, more gifts? You really don't have to get me things.'

'I like to get you things—especially when you have such delightful ways of appreciating them.'

'Ever calculating,' she said with a smile. 'Ingenious Alastair.'

His mouth dried and for a moment, he couldn't speak. *Ingenious Alastair...* Diana had coined the nickname, and taken up by his cousins, it had stuck.

It was only one of those she'd devised, her favourite in the game they played, he praising her in verse, she describing him in different moods and circumstances: Adulating Alastair, Adamant Alastair, Eccentric Alastair. He'd joked that she would run out of adjectives, and she'd assured him she had an endless trove of them, enough to last all the years they'd spend together.

He refocused his gaze on Diana. From the stark expression on her face, he knew she was remembering, too—the lost years, the unrealised promise.

'I've brought you something,' he repeated, breaking the mood. He held out the pouch.

Uncertain—the wounded look still in her eyes—she took it from him and extracted the pearls. Colour came and went in her cheeks before she looked back up at him. 'How did you get these?'

'I happened to stop by the jeweller right after he purchased them. Thinking me a likely customer, he showed them to me. I knew at once they must be yours, and bought them back. Why on earth would you sell your mother's pearls?'

The subtle agitation he'd noticed in her earlier intensified. At first he thought she'd simply refuse to answer, but after obvious struggle, she said, 'I was short of funds. I must consult a solicitor about a matter I'd hoped to delay until…until later, but changing circumstances make the need to settle it urgent.'

'Short of funds?' he tossed back, his tone sharpened by a bitterness he'd not quite mastered. 'I find it hard to believe a duke's widow would be less than amply provided for. Graveston was exceedingly wealthy. I should think the settlements would have left you very well off.'

She shook her head. 'In the haste of the wedding, I don't believe settlements were ever drawn up.'

Alastair frowned. 'It would have been exceedingly careless of your father to neglect doing that.'

'You must remember, the Duke possessed a large number of my father's vowels. If the Duke assured him settlements were unnecessary, he was not in a position to press the issue.'

'In the absence of settlements, you're still entitled to the dower. Though much of the estate, like my own, is probably tied up in land, your right to a third of it should provide more than sufficient funds to meet whatever needs you have.'

'Perhaps. Except for the fact that the new Duke despises me. Any claims I might make against the estate, whether entitled to them or not, he would do his utmost to disapprove or delay. And I can't afford to delay.'

'What is it you must do that is so imperative, you would sell your mother's pearls to accomplish it?'

She opened her lips, closed them. With short, jerky movements, she set down her wine glass and leapt up. 'I…I must go. It's late, and I cannot stay the night this time.'

Everything about her radiated distress. His concern intensifying, Alastair caught her arm. 'What is it, Diana? You can tell me. Surely you know I wouldn't break a confidence.'

Eyes wide, she stared up at him, her breathing quickening, then cast a glance through the open door, towards the dressing table.

'Talk to me,' Alastair urged, following the direction of her gaze. 'I think I can be at least as much help as a mirror.'

She snapped her gaze back to him and pulled her arm free. 'You don't understand! I…I can't talk to you. I can't confide in anyone. I don't know how any more.'

'We used to talk easily, about everything. We can do so again. Won't you trust me?'

The urgency of her expression became tinged with sadness. 'Even if I could, you won't be here for long. Why should you? This…trouble has nothing to do with you. I'll have to face it alone. I should prepare for it alone. After all, I've had years of practice.'

For a moment, he had nothing to reply. She was right; he hadn't planned for this to be more than a temporary liaison, initially one restricted only to the physical. He'd not yet resolved the conflicting desires pulling at him to embrace her, or to escape before she drew him in more deeply.

'That may be so,' he said at last. 'But you're no longer forced to be alone. You can fashion a life for yourself now, the life *you* want, with friends and allies and advocates. There's no danger to them any more for helping you. If you're going to be confronting the Duke, you'll need allies.'

In her face, he could read the hesitation, the conflict between the urge to speak and the habit of withdrawal. Pressing, he continued, 'If there's something threatening you, a friend would want to help.'

Her eyes widened, and he knew he'd scored a hit.

'A threat. Yes.' She took a shuddering breath. 'You are

right. When battling a duke, one should enlist all the allies one can muster.'

'So tell me.'

To his intense satisfaction, at length, she nodded. 'Very well. There is a threat—but not to me.'

Anxious to have her begin before she changed her mind and fled, he urged her back to her seat. 'What sort of threat?' he prompted, pouring more wine and handing it to her.

'Blankford's—the new Duke's—solicitor called on me today. I'm not sure how he traced me so quickly, but I anticipated the demand. He wants to take my son back to live at Graveston Court.'

'Were you not planning to return at some point to the Dower House at Graveston anyway?'

A look of revulsion passing over her face, she shook her head. 'I'll never willingly set foot on the estate again. Nor do I want my son there. I've told you how the Duke coerced me into wedding him. His heir was raised with the same beliefs—that he possesses ultimate power and the right to do whatever he pleases with it, heedless of the desires of anyone else. Even if I didn't fear for James, I wouldn't want my son reared under the influence of such a man.'

Alastair raised an eyebrow. 'Fear for him? Is he frail?'

'No, but he might be in danger. You may remember I told you that when Graveston—the late Duke—first paid me attention, his wife was still living. Before I could become too uncomfortable with his unusual regard, it ceased, and he struck up a friendship with Papa. Guileless as he was, Papa welcomed anyone who seemed interested in the botanical studies that consumed him. Within the year, the Duke's wife died and, using the debts Papa had accumulated, he forced me to wed him.'

A frown on her forehead, Diana leapt up and began to pace, as if the agitation within was too strong for her to remain still. 'I was…rather oblivious of my surroundings after being brought to Graveston Court, only dimly aware of the quarrels between my husband and his heir. Blankford had not previously acknowledged my existence or exchanged a word with me, but the day he broke with his father and left Graveston for good, he tracked me down in the garden. He accused me of having bewitched the Duke, obsessing him so that he drove his first wife to her death and lost interest in his only son and heir. He warned me that he'd outlive his father, and when he inherited, he would exact vengeance for himself and his mother.'

'Troubling words, but he was younger then, hot-headed as young men often are. Are you sure he still bears such enmity?'

'He is his father's son. In the coldness of his absolute will, Graveston spent almost a year setting up the trap to force me to wed. Blankford would be fully capable of nurturing his hatred for five years. He wants to deny me access to James to punish me, of course. But why would he have any interest in nurturing the son of the woman he holds responsible for the death of his mother and the break with his father? I cannot trust his intentions.'

'You really believe he might harm the boy? I have to say, that seems…excessive.'

'So was Graveston's poisoning my dog and threatening to ruin my father,' she flashed back. 'For men of their stamp, the lives of others are of no importance. Only their will matters.'

Alastair still thought it highly unlikely the new Duke, however arrogant and wilful, would go so far as to harm a child. But quite obviously, *Diana* believed it. And that was enough for him.

'I sold the pearls, the most valuable of the jewels I possess, to obtain funds to hire the best solicitor I can find,' she continued. 'One who can build a case for retaining custody of James that will prevail against the Duke's claim in a Court of Chancery.'

'Preparing such a case is likely to be a lengthy endeavour—which will cost you far more than the value of a string of pearls. I already have an excellent solicitor on retainer. Why not let him look into it? As you already admitted, if you contest the Duke on this, he'll likely do everything legally possible to delay or tie up whatever you're entitled to as dower, so you need to conserve the assets you have with you. Unless you have substantial cash reserves on hand?'

'I wouldn't have sold the necklace if that were so,' she admitted.

'Then let me find out what I can,' he urged.

She frowned. 'As much as I appreciate your offer, I…I really ought not to accept it. The battle will likely be ugly as well as expensive. The Duke will not forgive anyone who takes my part, and I don't want you dragged into it.'

'I'm not a callow collegian any more, Diana. I can hold my own. Besides, you need to utilise every resource you can muster to protect your son.'

'To protect James,' she repeated with a sigh. 'Very well, let your solicitor look into it. I've been a poor enough mother thus far, I cannot afford to turn away help, hard as it is to accept.'

'You, a poor mother? That, I can't imagine.'

She laughed shortly. 'Do you remember the paints? The books? The music? Everything that might affect me was utilised by the Duke to try to force a reaction or keep me under control. A child was just one more tool. The only way to protect him was to be indifferent to him… whatever the Duke said or threatened.'

Her voice faded. 'To my shame, as the years went on, I didn't have to struggle so hard to be indifferent. Not nearly as hard as I should have. Every time I looked at James, I saw…his father.'

'Truly? I knew the first time *I* saw him that he must be *your* son. He has your eyes.'

Startled, Diana looked back up at him. 'You think he has…something of me?'

'Absolutely! Have you never noticed?'

She shook her head. 'I am trying to do better, now that I can. But after years forcing down and bottling up and restraining emotion, I…I'm afraid I'll never find my way back to loving him.'

Alastair thought of how he doted upon his nephew, how easy and affectionate the relationship was between Robbie and Jane. A pang of compassion shook him, that the honest, open, loving Diana he'd known could have been brought to shut out her own son.

The late Duke of Graveston had much to answer for.

'Just let him love you,' he said, thinking of how Robbie had inveigled himself into Alastair's heart. 'In time, you will find yourself responding.'

Diana smiled sadly. 'I hope so. Now I really must go. How long do you think it will take for your solicitor to have an answer? If Feral—Graveston's man—left Bath today, he could reach the Court by week's end. Which means Graveston could make some new demand within a fortnight, if not sooner.'

'I could summon Reynolds, but it would be faster for me to call upon him in London. If I leave tomorrow, I should be able to return with some word in six or seven days, so you have time to prepare before the Duke can make another move.'

She nodded. 'I would like that.' Swallowing hard, she said softly, 'How can I thank you? Or ever repay you?'

'Protecting a child is payment enough. As for thanks…' He gave her a wicked grin. 'When I return from London, I'm sure I can think of something.'

She managed a wan smile. While normally he would have tried to persuade her to stay longer, now that he was aware of the worry consuming her over the safety of her son, he made no attempt to seduce as he helped her track down and slip on her garments. When she was clothed again, her hair tidied as best they could manage and the concealing cloak in place, he pulled her close. To his delight, after a moment of hesitation, she clung to him.

Though he didn't regret his offer to go to London, it meant probably a week or more until he would see her again. Already he felt bereft, and with her pressed against him, his body protested the abstinence about to be forced upon it.

'Try not to worry too much,' he told her as he released her at last.

'I'll try. I'll try with James, too.'

He kissed the tip of her nose, still reluctant to let her go. 'I'll miss you,' he admitted.

'Then come back quickly.'

With that, she walked from the room.

Alastair followed her through the bedchamber to the stairs, listening to the soft footfalls as she descended and the murmur of voices in the entry below where Marston, as previously arranged, waited to engage a chair to carry her safely home.

Once the last echoes faded, he returned to the sitting

room, threw himself in a chair, poured another glass of wine, and reviewed what he'd just committed himself to doing.

It did not represent him easing the reins restraining his feelings, he assured the cautious voice in his head. Any man of honour would step in to assure the safety of a child.

It did indicate, however, that sometime over the course of their renewed association, he had come to accept as true the explanation she'd given him for breaking their engagement to marry the Duke.

Drawing back from considering the full implications of that transformation, he turned his mind instead to considering what Diana had told him about her relationship with the new Duke and her fears for her son's safety.

Though he still thought Diana's long, bitter association with her husband and his heir caused her to exaggerate the son's ruthlessness and enmity, he had to admit he was curious how well she'd been provided for. If there truly were no settlements outlining the exact arrangements for her support if widowed, it represented a grievous failure of his responsibilities on the part of her father.

But it was also true that the professor had been a completely unworldly man, a scholar absorbed in his studies. If he had come to view the Duke as a friend and colleague, he might well have been satisfied with just a verbal assurance that his daughter would be well taken care of in the event of her husband's demise. Particularly as, in the absence of some formal agreement, she would have the dower to a very wealthy estate.

He'd have to confer with his solicitor on this matter, but he didn't see how the new Duke could deny rights guaranteed under English law. He had to admit, though, that being entitled to something and effectively claiming it could be quite different matters, especially if a personage with the power and resources of a duke set his mind to making it as time-consuming and difficult as possible.

But all of that was for his legal counsel to discover. What warmed him now, as much as the satisfaction of his well-pleasured body, was the fact that he'd managed to persuade Diana to confide in him.

Since encountering her again, he'd been accumulating evidence in mites and snippets of what her married life had been: her at first rejected account of her marriage, the episodes described by Lady Randolph, the information he'd teased out of her about the removal of her paints and books. But aside from that single moment upon awakening yesterday, when she'd looked at him with awe and tenderness, she'd maintained emotionally aloof.

Regrettable as it was that she'd found herself in such a vulnerable position, Alastair had to admit he was almost—glad of it. Without such an imminent threat to her son, she might have continued keeping him at arm's length indefinitely.

Instead, with some persistence, tonight he'd managed to breach the wall of impassivity she'd erected to disguise her thoughts and feelings, giving him the clearest-yet glimpse into her life. It wrung his heart to realise how difficult it had been for her to force herself to reach out to him, emphasising even further how isolated and alone she'd become.

Still, the concern, independence and initiative she'd exhibited in seeking to shelter her child not only called out his strongest protective instincts, they also gave him enticing glimpses of the girl he'd once known, now more mature, stronger and seasoned by the loss and suffering she'd survived.

Having disarmed her defences to the point of eliciting those revelations, he was more determined than ever to complete the job. To release the Diana still not free of the mask, persuade her it was now safe to step out of isolation and encourage her to claim the life that awaited her.

Only after he'd arranged for her and her son's protection and coaxed her out of the shadows, would he turn his attention to their possible future. And decide whether to try winning her anew, or let her go before it was too late for him to walk away.

Chapter Eleven

Several days after Alastair's departure, Diana restlessly paced her parlour. Rain had kept her from a walk with James this morning, and with the resulting mud and wet, it was probably best not to attempt to walk this afternoon.

She was finding it harder and harder to force down her worry, bottle up concern over the future, and present an impassive face to the staff. Even sessions before the mirror were failing her.

Would talking with Alastair again help? She'd felt calmer after returning from their last rendezvous. She told herself it was not missing him that further complicated her tangle of thoughts.

He certainly had been effective at stirring up her feelings. Which meant it would be better to avoid him, once he ended their bargain. Since she'd started seeing him, dribs and drabs of emotion had been leaching out, each leak further weakening the dykes she'd erected to contain them.

Perhaps one day she would be able to ease those restraints, release the anguish and the memories in slow, manageable bits and at length, be free of them.

But now was not that time.

She'd thought if she relaxed just enough to permit

Alastair to reach her physically, she'd be able to distract him with passion and escape more intense scrutiny.

Instead, after only two meetings, he'd managed to unearth her most shameful secret and her deepest worry.

In her defence, only the imperative to do whatever she could to protect James had pushed her to reveal the situation. In the wake of that confession, she'd careened from horror that she'd divulged the dilemma to him, shame over admitting her failings with her son, and relief that she would not have to contest the Duke alone. Embracing Alastair without reservation before she left him, she'd felt…safe. That concerned her.

It had been wise to elicit the aid of anyone willing to help her in her battle with the Duke—that much she owed to James. But to assume that Alastair Ransleigh or anyone else would stand by her was foolish. Not only foolish, it put James's safety at risk to depend upon support that could disappear as unexpectedly as the whim to offer it.

Alastair hadn't denied it when she'd stated that he'd only be around a short time. He'd pledged to have a solicitor spell out the legal parameters of the threat she faced. She could not expect him, nor had he offered, to involve himself beyond that point. She must prepare herself to enter the struggle and deal with its consequences alone.

She began to consider what she would do if the solicitor returned an unfavourable assessment of her ability to retain custody of James.

Allowing him to go to Graveston was out of the question. She would flee England before she'd permit that. With the war finally over, they might be able to settle in some small rural village in France. Her French was impeccable—Papa had seen to that; she could give lessons in English, piano, watercolours.

Except how was she to obtain a position without references? The amounts she could obtain from selling her few remaining jewels would support them for a time, but even in the depressed economy of a war-ravaged area, they wouldn't be able to live on them for ever.

She had no other assets besides that small store of jewellery, inherited from her father's mother. Not grand enough that the Duke had permitted her to wear any of it, nor valuable enough for him to bother selling the pieces, she'd been able to secrete them away. She'd left all of the ornate and valuable jewels presented to her by the Duke at Graveston Court, wanting nothing that reminded her of her life as Graveston's Duchess.

What would she do if they exhausted her small store of assets?

Coming up with no answers, exasperated with pacing, she decided to go visit James. She felt a slight smile curving her lips. As Alastair had predicted, her son was always glad to see her.

'Let him love you,' Alastair had advised. She'd been trying that, not forcing her emotions, simply chatting with him, asking about his interests and responding to his answers.

He particularly loved getting outdoors, but that wasn't wise today. Suddenly, she remembered something else she might try. The morning after Alastair had given her back the pearls, a package arrived containing the box of watercolours and the sketchbook she'd told him to return. Not knowing from which establishment he'd obtained them, she had kept them.

On impulse, she gathered the supplies from her wardrobe and continued to the nursery.

As she entered, James was listlessly pushing a soldier around on the floor before the hearth, a picture of boredom. When he turned to see her, his small face lit up and he jumped to his feet. At that expression of gladness, Diana felt herself warm.

'Mama! Can we go to the park? It's not raining any more.'

'That's true, but I fear it is still very wet.' Giving the nursemaid a nod, she walked over to seat herself at the table before the fire, setting down the package. James hurried over to perch on the bench beside her. 'Just think how cross Minnie would be if she had to soak out of your breeches all the dirt you would surely get on them, jumping in and out of puddles.'

His face fell. 'I promise I won't go in puddles.'

He looked so earnest, she had to laugh. 'I know you would try to be good, but heavens, how could anyone resist discovering how deep the puddles are, or seeing how high the water splashes when one jumps in them? I know I cannot, and Annie would be even crosser than Minnie if she had to press the mud out of my skirts. No, I've brought something else for us.'

His crestfallen look dissolved in curiosity. 'In that package? May I open it?'

'You may.'

He made quick work of the wrappings, unlatched the box and drew out a brush. 'How soft it is!' he exclaimed, drawing the bristles across his hand. 'It's awfully little for scrubbing, though.'

'It's not for scrubbing. It's for painting. Those little dishes contain watercolours. Minnie, would you pour some water in that bowl and get James something he can use as a smock? A nightshirt will do.'

Though it had been years since she'd prepared paints, she fell back into the familiar pattern immediately, blending into the dishes some of the paint with water from the bowl brought by the nursery maid. By the time the girl had James's nightshirt over his head to protect his clothing, Diana had half-a-dozen colours prepared for his inspection.

'Which colours do you like the best?'

'Red and blue,' he pointed out promptly. 'What do we do now?'

'We decide what we want to paint.'

James looked around quickly. 'My soldier!'

'Good choice. Let's sit him on the table so we can see him better. First, we'll make an outline of his body, then fill in with the colours.'

She showed James how to dip his brush in the paint, then stroke the brush across the sketchpad. She expected that after a few minutes of meticulous work he would get bored with the process, but he did not, continuing with rapt attention under her direction and suggestions until he'd completed a creditable soldier in a bright-red coat and blue trousers.

'That's very good!' she said approvingly, surprised that it was true. Even more surprised that, with his head bent and a rapt expression on his face, James reminded her of her father, recording in deft brushstrokes the details of one of the plants he'd discovered.

Another wash of heat warmed her within. Perhaps Alastair was right. Perhaps there was more of her—and her father—in the boy than she'd thought.

Vastly pleased with his work, James was delighted when she set it above the mantel. 'There, you'll be able to see it from your bed and admire it as you eat your supper.'

'Look at my painting, Minnie!' he cried to the nurse, who, to Diana's mild amusement, hovered nearby whenever Diana visited her son. Though the girl seemed to have somewhat relaxed her vigilance, Diana sensed Minnie still didn't entirely trust her mistress's sudden, un-precedented interest in her charge.

'That's wonderful fine, young master,' the maid an-swered, a deep affection in her tone. 'A right handsome soldier you've drawn.'

'Mama, will you make one, too?'

'If it would please you.'

'Oh, yes! I'd love having something from you, some-thing to keep.'

The artless words pricked her again, reminding her how little she'd offered her son since she'd forced her-self to turn away from him as a toddler. True, she'd had a compelling reason for withdrawing from him—but no more. Silently she renewed her vow to do better.

'What kind of picture do you want?'

'Another soldier.'

'Very well.' Taking the brush from him, she deftly created a replica of the toy soldier. James looked over her shoulder as she painted, seeming entirely absorbed.

When she finished, he gave a little sigh of awe. 'Oh, Mama, that's wonderful! He looks just like my soldier. Will you put him on the mantel next to mine, so they can keep each other company?'

'Of course.'

After she'd arranged the two pictures side by side and stepped back, James clapped his hands with delight. 'It's like having more soldiers for my army! Only maybe bet-ter, 'cause you and me made them together. Thank you, Mama!'

Jumping up, he ran over and wrapped his arms around her.

Still not accustomed to hugs, she started—then slowly wrapped her arms around him as well. From deep within, an impulse welled up to pull him nearer, hold him tighter.

Immediately she resisted it…until she realised that she didn't have to restrain herself any longer.

Let him love you. You'll find yourself responding.

Hearing Alastair's words echo in her ears, she hugged James tighter, pressing her face against his soft dark hair. An aching warmth curled around her heart.

As much as she owed Alastair Ransleigh for his efforts to keep her son safe, she owed him even more for this.

Meanwhile, in the London office of his solicitor, Mr Reynolds, Alastair explained his need for some information regarding settlements.

A smile creased the older man's face. 'Dare I hope that means you expect a momentous occasion in the near future? Let me offer my congratulations!'

Startled at first, Alastair had to laugh. 'I'm afraid not. A close family friend was recently widowed. Her father is now deceased, and she is not aware if settlements were ever drawn up.'

'Are the circumstances not specified in her late husband's will?'

'The circumstances are rather…complicated. What would normally be set up?'

'Normally, the dowry or portion brought into the marriage by the bride is guaranteed to her as an annuity in the event of the husband's death. If a specific sum is not mentioned, usually she is deeded some property as her jointure, the income and rents from which are intended to support her after the husband's death, when his estate passes to his heir.'

'In the absence of settlements, she would be entitled to a dower?'

'Yes, to one-third of the property and assets of the estate. Which, for a wealthy man, could be quite considerable, hence the desire for settlements to simplify the process and limit the annuity to a specific sum.'

'If dower rights were invoked, how would the widow obtain the assets?'

'The local sheriff's court would have the handling of it.'

That was what Alastair had feared. 'And if there were… ill feelings between the heir and the widow?'

Mr Reynolds sent him a questioning look. 'Would this heir be a man of high rank?'

'The highest.'

The solicitor gave him a thin smile. 'Then obtaining her due could be difficult. The local sheriff would, understandably, be reluctant to antagonise a man of wealth and influence in the community. Your widow would require a strong solicitor and a prominent advocate to ensure the heir was compelled to recognise her rights.'

Alastair nodded. 'Thank you, Mr Reynolds. I appreciate your expertise.'

'If I can assist you further, please let me know. The poor widow is entitled to her due.'

'She is indeed,' Alastair agreed. 'I will certainly call upon you again if circumstances require it.'

'Always a pleasure to serve you,' Mr Reynolds said with another smile as he ushered Alastair to the door.

As he paced the street to summon a hackney, Alastair mulled over what he should do next.

Would the new Duke really make problems for Diana? How much of her suspicion and foreboding were the results of her miserable existence as his father's wife? Would the mature Blankford have outgrown his youthful resentment?

There was only one sure way to find out.

He'd just have to make a trip to Graveston Court.

Chapter Twelve

Several days later, Alastair passed through the entry gates and rode down a long, tree-bordered lane. Around one bend, set like a jewel against the hill behind it, its long columned facade reflected by a symmetrical pond before it, stood the huge Palladian mansion that was Graveston Court.

After turning his mount over to a waiting lackey, he was admitted by a grim-faced butler, ushered through the marbled entrance down a corridor flanked with what appeared to be Grecian antiquities, and shown into a beautifully appointed parlour. The Duke would be informed of his arrival, the butler intoned before bowing himself out.

So this was the prison in which Diana had been trapped for so many years, Alastair thought. He paced the room, whose arched windows, flanked by gold brocade drapery, echoed the Palladian influences evident in the mansion's facade. More antiquities—vases embellished with Greek battle scenes, Roman busts and bas-relief carvings—were set on pedestals or artfully arranged on shelves.

The scale was oppressively overwhelming, everything about the room and its opulent furnishings designed to dazzle the visitor and intimidate him with a sense of his insignificance, compared to the wealth and rank of his host.

At length, losing interest in examining the various treasures, Alastair took a seat on the lavishly embellished gold sofa, and waited. And waited. And waited some more, his anger beginning to smoulder.

Of course, he had arrived without notice and the new Duke would have many pressing matters to attend to, taking over the reins of such a large estate. However, leaving him tapping his fingers this long, without an offer of refreshment or any other courtesy, was, Alastair felt sure, a deliberate insult.

Any deference to rank Alastair might once have felt had long since been dissipated by the refusal of his uncle, the Earl of Swynford, to support his younger son, Alastair's cousin and best friend, after the scandal that had embroiled Max at the Congress of Vienna. A deference already worn thin by his army service, where experience and ability was worth far more in battle than rank or title, and his own previous dealings with a Duke of Graveston.

So he was not feeling particularly amiable when the Duke finally deigned to make an appearance.

After exchanging the obligatory bows and greetings, the Duke said, 'So, Mr Ransleigh, to what do I owe the honour of this visit?''

The sly smile accompanying those words gave Alastair the distinct impression that the Duke knew exactly who he was and why he was here.

Which shouldn't come as a surprise. In order for Graveston's solicitor to have found Diana so quickly, the new Duke must have had his own spies hidden among the household at Graveston, some of whom had trailed her when she fled to Bath after her husband's death. If those informers remained in the city to watch her, they would have already sent word to the Duke about his relationship with the widow.

If the Duke wished to be coy, not revealing what he already knew, he could play along, thought Alastair, his irritation building. 'As a friend of the Dowager Duchess, I wished to approach you about a family matter. Gentleman to gentleman, without recourse to involving the sheriff or the courts.'

'Gentleman to gentleman,' the Duke repeated, raising an ironic eyebrow. 'Do proceed.'

'The Dowager, naturally distraught over the death of her husband, needed time away to compose herself. She seemed to doubt that you would agree to provide her with the support and assistance to which she is entitled as your father's widow.'

The Duke's smirk of a smile compressed to a thin line. 'I'm surprised the doxy is intelligent enough to understand that. Support *her*?' His raised voice had a derisive ring. 'She left Graveston Court voluntarily; let her support herself. I'm sure she wheedled enough baubles out of my father to keep herself in furs, gowns and sweetmeats for the rest of her life.'

'Nonetheless,' Alastair countered, holding on to his temper, 'she's still entitled to her dower.'

The Duke's eyebrows lifted again. 'She can certainly apply for it. Any claims submitted on that account will be referred to my solicitor.'

'She was your late father's legal wife. Your man might obstruct, harass and delay such a petition, but in the end, the law will see she gets what she's entitled to.'

The Duke laughed outright. 'Oh, I certainly hope she gets what she deserves! My father's legal wife—ha! Only think, he set aside my mother, who lived only to please him, for *her*. And what an ideal duchess she made! Incapable of running the household. Contradicting my father in front of his guests. Disputing the gentlemen's opinions and ignoring the ladies, to whose company she should have directed her attention and remarks. Well, he had little enough joy of her. Just the one brat, after eight years of marriage.'

While Alastair bottled up his mounting ire and disgust, Graveston continued. 'Ah yes, the brat. I shall very much enjoy helping him discover what it's like being the son of a displaced mother!' He smiled, anger glittering in his eyes. 'I'll enjoy even more having *her* know he's experiencing that delight, and she's responsible.'

Diana had warned him, but he hadn't believed it. 'You would punish a child?' Alastair asked incredulously, revolted.

Graveston shrugged. 'Not punish. Just…instil in him a proper recognition of his place. He'll survive. I did. It will make a man of him.'

A man like you? he thought. *No wonder Diana wants to keep her son away.*

'He's a Mannington brat, for all that, even if he is half *hers*. Perhaps we can beat that out of him. One can try.' He smiled again, as if relishing the prospect. 'He will need to be trained to his role—to serve my son and heir. Which brings me back to a matter more important than the spurious claims of my father's former *wife*. Since you seem to be on such good terms with her, perhaps you'll inform her if she does not return the boy voluntarily, and soon, I shall have the Court of Chancery order it.'

'She would appeal such a demand. You can't know for sure they would rule in your favour.'

'Can I not? When the head of an ancient, venerable family of vast resources magnanimously offers to support a half-brother, even though he's the spawn of a nobody?

Worse than a nobody, a woman whose odd and irregular behaviour forced her husband to banish her from Society. Who fled her home before her husband's body was scarcely cold, instead of remaining to greet the heir and see proper tribute paid to her late master. Not to mention, as any number of witnesses can testify, a mother who paid practically no attention to her son from his early years until his father's demise. Do you really think she has any chance to hang on to him? If you're such a *friend*, you should advise her to spare herself the embarrassment of having her conduct censured before the Court, and send the brat back now.'

So Diana was right; the miserable little muckworm did intend to exact his revenge on her son. His fighting instincts fully aroused, he said coldly, 'I certainly couldn't advise that.'

His eyes narrowing, the Duke examined Alastair's face. 'So that's the way it is, eh? I suspected as much. Though she has a pretty enough face, I suppose, and the same charms as any trollop, I still find it hard to understand how she entices men, but take some friendly advice. Have your fill of her and get out. She's about to face the consequences of her infamy, and it would grieve me to see a *gentleman* get dragged in it.'

'I think she has suffered quite enough already at the hands of the Dukes of Graveston.'

'Do you, now? Then let me assure you, the retribution she so justly deserves is only beginning. The investigation is in its early stages, but it's highly likely that she, ah, *assisted* my father's departure from this earth. It's common knowledge that she and the Duke did not get along, as every servant in this house would swear under oath. If this investigation bears fruit, I intend to have her brought up on charges of murder. So you'd be well advised to make your exit before she entangles you any further.'

Alastair first thought the Duke must be joking, but by the end of that incredible speech, realised Graveston was entirely serious. 'Bring her up on murder charges! That's preposterous! I advise *you* to consider your position before making such a ridiculous charge. It's more likely you, not the widow, who would appear reprehensible if Society learned that, not only had you no intention of honouring your obligations towards a woman who, despite your dislike of her, is still a dowager duchess, you are persecuting her with baseless and slanderous charges.'

'And I advise you again to consider your own reputation! How do you think Society will react to learning that, within days of the suspicious death of her husband, his widow hurried off to Bath to meet her former lover, with whom she is now conducting an illicit affair? Perhaps also the man who incited her to dispose of the husband he'd always hated for winning the woman he loved?'

Hot words hovered on his tongue to challenge the Duke then and there. But the man would probably welcome a confrontation—such behaviour would give credence to the absurd scenario of illicit passion and revenge the Duke was constructing.

Besides, Alastair was quite certain a man intent on exacting revenge against a defenceless woman was likely too much a coward ever to meet him; bullies preferred to attack weaker beings rather than confront a man equal to them in vigour and influence. Better for him to take his leave now, before Graveston could provoke him into losing his temper, then plan in the coldness of reason how to counter this threat.

Accordingly, he raised his eyes and fixed the Duke with a glare that had made many an errant subordinate quake. 'If it weren't beneath me to soil my blade with the blood of such a scoundrel,' he said softly, 'I'd call you out for such slander. I can promise you, I won't forget it, and there will be a reckoning.'

Keeping his temper in check with some difficulty, Alastair rose. 'Since it has become quite plain you are unwilling to recognise your responsibilities towards the widow, there is nothing to be gained from prolonging this interview.' He sketched the briefest of bows. 'I will no longer keep you, as you doubtless have many pressing duties,' he finished, with a last jab at the wait forced on him.

'Indeed I do, Mr Ransleigh.' The Duke nodded, looking very pleased with himself.

Alastair found it even more infuriating that the Duke appeared so supremely confident of his own power, so dismissive of the possibility that Alastair might devise some way to check him, that he gave no credence to Alastair's threat. His heart smouldering, he knew in that moment that even if Diana's welfare were not involved, he would have to bring the man down. He also knew he would do everything in his power to prevent the Duke from getting his hands on Diana's son.

The Duke accorded him a brief nod of dismissal. Fuming, Alastair stalked out of the salon.

Just outside in the hall, he encountered a tall, thin, hawk-nosed woman with housekeeper's keys hanging at her waist. She stared at him boldly as he paced by her, a thin smile on her face.

We'll see who laughs last, he vowed under his breath as the imperious butler shut the entry door behind him.

Several days' hard riding later, before returning to his sister's lodgings on Royal Crescent, Alastair rode instead to the townhouse at Green Park Buildings. He knew he owed his sister some attention after decamping with hardly a word, but he also knew Diana would be anxious, waiting to learn what he had discovered. He wished he had a better report, but the bad news wouldn't improve by putting off the telling.

He'd debated calling on her in Laura Place—if the Duke knew of their relationship, how many others were aware?—but on the chance that it had not yet been discovered by half of Bath, opted instead for discretion, sending her a note asking her to meet him at their usual rendezvous, as soon as she was able to get away that evening.

He would have to figure out how much to tell Jane, since, with his frequent absences in the evening and recent unexplained travels out of town, his needle-witted sister was certain to suspect something. But first, he needed to consult Diana.

Since he had no idea how early Diana might get away, he ordered a bath and an early dinner. As afternoon faded into evening, unable to distract himself with a book, he took to pacing.

At last, he heard her light step on the stairway, and leapt up to meet her as Marston ushered her in. She gave him her hands and lifted her face for his kiss, worry etched on every feature.

'I'm glad you returned safely. What did you discover?'

He swept her to a chair and poured her some wine. 'You're certainly entitled to something, probably a handsome something, whether from dower or as income from whatever jointure might have been established in your late husband's will. That is the good news. The bad news, although, is that if it involves dower, the local sheriff's court must oversee the administration. It's very possible a local man could be too intimidated to vigorously pursue his duty, if the Duke or his representatives resist the process at every turn.'

'As he certainly would. But I'm not so much concerned about jointures or dower. What about James?'

'The legality in that case is less clear.' Alastair paused, recalling the gloating expression on the Duke's face. 'I now fully understand and support your intention not to let the current Duke of Graveston gain control over your son.'

Diana gave a grimace of distaste. 'Has he already made himself so infamous that even your solicitor knows of him?'

She must have seen something in his face, for without giving him time to respond, she cried, 'Oh, Alastair— you didn't seek him out, did you? Tell me you did not!'

There seemed no point hiding it. 'I called on him at Graveston Court,' he admitted. 'I have to confess, I thought you were exaggerating the vengefulness of his character, but after talking with him myself, I'm forced to concede you were not.'

She sprang up and took an agitated turn about the room before halting abruptly before him. 'I should never have confided in you! Don't you see? Not just James is at risk now—you've placed yourself in harm's way as well!'

All too aware that he had been threatened, he said, 'I doubt there is much Graveston can do to me. But I fear I have complicated matters.'

She shook her head. 'You'd better tell me the whole.'

She seated herself again and remained silent through his recitation: the aggravating discourtesy of being made to wait, the Duke's sly baiting, his disparaging words about Diana, his demand that James be returned to Graveston Court, his certainty that Chancery would uphold his request for guardianship. Finally, reluctantly, he revealed the Duke's infamous design to have her brought up on murder charges.

Though her eyes widened at the mention of murder, she said nothing until he revealed the Duke had threatened to involve him, too, as a motive for the crime, unless he ceased to support her.

'Infamous!' she exclaimed. 'And how very like him!'

'Infamous indeed, but I must say, after repeating it to you here in prosaic candlelight, I find it difficult to credit. Making ungrounded accusations is a serious matter that could severely damage his own reputation. More probably, it was the ranting of the boy who never outgrew his rancour towards you for displacing his mother. He's a grown man now. When, in the coolness of reason, he considers the repercussions of making such accusations, I cannot see any rational man moving forward with such a project, nor any solicitor or adviser agreeing to assist—'

'You are wrong,' Diana interrupted, clutching his hand. 'Blankford is quite capable of moving forward in defiance of all reason, equally capable of doing whatever is necessary to discredit and destroy anyone who gets in the way. Only remember whose son he is!'

Tossing down his hand, she took another agitated turn about the room. 'How gleeful he must be at how cleverly we've played into his hands!' she said bitterly, turning back to face him. 'Had I withdrawn and lived quietly at the Dower House after Graveston's death, it would have been more difficult to hurl such accusations, though I suspect in his hatred, he would have done so anyway. But now—a widow fleeing her home to take up with an old lover with her late husband's body hardly settled in its grave—the bare facts of which we cannot deny? Only think how London's penny broadsides will love it!'

'It does look bad,' he had to admit. 'But I've no intention of abandoning you, so you needn't fear that.'

'On the contrary, that's exactly what you must do.'

Her reply was so unexpected, for a moment he thought he couldn't have heard her correctly. 'You think I *should* abandon you?'

She nodded. 'I learned long ago to take the Duke's threats seriously. My husband would have destroyed you then; the son will destroy you now, if you don't walk away. Even if he can't manufacture enough witnesses to convince the assizes to bind me over for trial, only think of the scandal! "Former lover helps unfaithful wife murder her husband!" Imagine the scurrilous cartoons in the print shops! The embarrassment to your sister, to your mother, the stain on your family name. No, it's unthinkable. You must sever all relations with me at once.'

Nodding to herself in final conviction, she backed away, as if preparing to leave.

'Wait a minute!' he exclaimed, jumping up to catch her hand again. 'Have I no say in this? Have you so little confidence in my abilities—this time, too?'

'You don't understand what you're facing. He will stop at nothing to obtain what he wants, just like his father!'

'No, I don't know what I'm facing,' he snapped back, anger over that long-ago episode resurfacing. 'You never told me, just made the decision for both of us. I understand the threat to your father was serious enough to prompt you to action, but I don't understand why you didn't trust me to help. I was no paragon, but I'd done nothing that could have given Graveston cause to ruin me. I can't imagine how he convinced you otherwise.'

'Can you not?' When he gave a derisive shake of the head, she sighed. 'Very well. Even now, it's difficult for me to utter the words, but I suppose you have a right to know what Graveston had designed for you.'

Seating herself beside him, she said quietly, 'At that time, you were not yet known as a valiant soldier, the hero of many battles, but had instead built quite a reputation as poet. You're surely aware it's often whispered that poets are…unmanly. Graveston warned if I told you anything of what he planned, he'd produce witnesses to testify that you'd forced them into…unnatural congress. Can you only imagine how such an accusation would have humiliated your family and destroyed your reputation, even if he couldn't produce enough witnesses to make the charges stick? And if he could—sodomy is a capital crime! You would have been forced to flee England. I couldn't risk it.'

Astounded, Alastair could think of nothing to say. He'd considered a few minor debts, some petty pranks played at university that might have been held against him. But nothing of that magnitude. 'That's…unbelievable.'

'Believe it. And believe the son just as capable of carrying out his threats as his father. Please, Alastair! What good is the sacrifice I made all those years ago, if I bring down destruction upon you now? Blankford would do it. And enjoy doing it.'

Recovering his wits, he countered, 'So, having persuaded you into an affair and gifted your persecutor with more ammunition to blast your character before a Court of Chancery, you expect me to slink away and leave you to suffer the consequences alone? What a fine fellow you must think me!'

'You *are* a fine fellow. I want your reputation to remain unblemished in the eyes of the world. I'm not prepared to let a venal man destroy your good name because of his vendetta against me.'

'It seems we are at an impasse, then, because I'm not prepared to let the threats of a venal man chase me away, so he may harass with impunity a woman already once victimised by his family. Besides, have you anyone else who could help you keep your son from his clutches?'

At once, the fire faded from her eyes. 'No,' she said in a small voice. 'Papa was an only son, as you know. All his near relations are dead, and the earldom to which his family is connected passed some years ago to a distant cousin I've never met. But if it comes to disaster, I do have a plan.'

'Running away again?' he guessed. 'Living the rest of your life looking over your shoulder? No, Diana. It's past time for confronting a bully and calling his dare.'

She shook her head wonderingly, tears pooling in her eyes. 'My brave, honourable, foolish Alastair. What can you do against the power of a duke?'

It pierced his heart to see her in such anguish—and hardened his resolve that this time, whatever was required, this Duke of Graveston would not have his way. This time, Diana would be freed of his menace, able to live her own life—whether she chose to keep him in it or not.

He pulled her into his arms, and to his immense satisfaction, she clung to him. 'Never underestimate the ingenuity of a rogue,' he whispered in her ear. 'I must go make peace with my sister, but I'll return later tonight, to plan what we should do next. Will you wait here for me?'

For a moment, she looked hesitant. As his mind scurried about, hunting up more arguments to persuade her, she nodded.

'Very well, I'll wait. If only so I can convince you tonight we must part for good.'

'You'll never convince me of that,' he said, giving her a kiss. 'I'll be back as soon as I can.'

And with that, he paced from the room, leaving her staring pensively after him.

Chapter Thirteen

Alastair hoped to catch his sister at home, preparing for dinner and whatever entertainment she'd chosen to attend that night. To his relief, Simms informed him as he took Alastair's hat and cane that his mistress was still at her toilette.

Alastair went immediately to his sister's room and rapped at the door. 'Jane, it's Alastair. May I come in and have a word before you head off to dinner?'

A moment later, his sister's maid opened the door. 'Please do come in, Alastair,' Jane called from her seat at her dressing table, where she was latching a necklace of pearls and diamonds about her neck. 'That will be all, Waters. I'll ring for you when I return; I shan't be late tonight.'

After the maid curtsied and went out, Alastair walked to his sister. 'I owe you an apology, Jane. I've neglected you dreadfully.'

She turned towards him as he approached, but when he bent to kiss her cheek, she gave him a roundhouse jab to the ribs. 'Oh, Alastair, how could you?' she exclaimed, and burst into tears.

'Damn and blast!' he muttered, certain he knew the

cause of her distress. For all his attempts at discretion, he might just have well have had the town crier stroll the streets, proclaiming the affair.

Still cursing silently, he held her at arm's length as, weeping, she tried to pummel him with her fists. 'Merciful heavens, Jane, get hold of yourself!'

Prevented from striking any further blows, she soon subsided. Pushing him away, she looked up at him accusingly, her lashes glistening with tears.

'I couldn't believe it when Hetty Greenlow whispered that you'd leased a house in Green Park Buildings. There could be only one reason for that. Oh, Alastair, how could you let yourself be drawn back into that evil woman's web?'

'Am I permitted to speak before you've condemned me utterly?'

'Say what you will. There's nothing that could reconcile me to the disaster of a renewed association with That Woman.'

'The circumstances surrounding Diana's marriage were more complicated than any of us could have imagined. I'd ask you to withhold any further judgement until I've acquainted you with the facts.'

And so he related the story Diana had told him of the Duke's machinations, her submission to them, something of the hardship of her life as the wife of a violent, controlling man, and her difficulties now with the new Duke, who wanted to deny her dower and take away her son. Jane sat stone-faced throughout.

'I don't blame you for being sceptical,' he coaxed. 'I didn't believe the story myself, at first. But as I've learned more, I've come to realise that she truly was coerced into the marriage to protect her father.' With his sister's expression still so sceptical, he left out the fantastical threat the former Duke had made against him, as well as the current Duke's threat, if he were to support Diana against him.

'She may have convinced you to believe that fairy tale, but I don't,' Jane said with a sniff. 'The only pressure upon her was her desire to be a duchess, and when she'd landed her prize, she broke your heart without a qualm. She deserves whatever she gets! And if, in her scheming, she wasn't clever enough to secure her financial future after her husband's death, that's her own fault. Hasn't she injured you enough? I cannot believe you would let her draw you into a tawdry fight over guardianship and dower! Her well-being and that of any offspring ceased to be of any importance to you the day she severed your engagement in front of half of London.'

'Jane, you can't believe I could, with honour, stand by and let any woman be bullied, threatened, and dis-possessed.'

'I could readily agree to it, if the woman involved is Diana.'

The mantel clock chimed. 'Drat,' she muttered, look-ing over at the timepiece. 'I must leave at once, or I shall be late for dinner at the Weatherfords'.'

As she rose from the bench and went to the wardrobe for her wrap, Alastair said quietly, 'Would you like me to leave?'

She halted and looked back over her shoulder. 'No! No, I want you to stay here. Away from her. Far away from her.' Her eyes glazing with tears again, her lip trembling, she said softly, 'I can't bear the thought of you being hurt again. And I'm terrified that the Dowager Duchess of Graveston still has the power to hurt you.'

He went over and drew her into a hug, which this time, she did not resist. 'I don't want to be hurt again either. I admit, there is still…something between us. However, whatever it is, whatever it might become, will have to wait until I've seen her protected from a family that has already treated her cruelly.'

'Just…be careful, Alastair,' Jane said, disengaging from his embrace. 'Promise me you'll be very cautious and very careful.'

'I can certainly promise that,' he said, before, smoothing her hair and catching up her shawl, Jane hurried from the room.

Alastair watched her go. Though sorry to have distressed his devoted sister, he was not about to be deterred from the course of action he'd already determined to be essential. Despite the danger that his involvement might draw him ever closer to Diana, a woman whose emotions he might never be able to touch, inviting a heartbreak that could decimate him.

Well, he'd not worry about that now. A small boy's safety was far more important than the risk to his heart. Telling himself he'd try again later to persuade Jane, after she'd had time to take in all he'd told her, he walked out of the bedchamber.

In the hall, he encountered a delighted Robbie. Anxious as he was to return to Diana, there was nothing for it but to return to the nursery with his nephew for a quick session with his soldiers until the nursemaid bore the boy off to bed.

By the time Alastair was able to quit the townhouse on Royal Crescent, it was already late. Would Diana still be waiting for him? Or, thinking it too late, would she have given up on him and returned to Laura Place. Even worse, might she think she'd convinced him that abandoning her was the best course?

Driven by his anxiety to see Diana again, Alastair was too impatient to wait for a sedan chair, deciding instead to cover the distance on foot.

He was still disappointed that Diana had had the same reaction as Graveston, discounting his ability to successfully counter the power and influence of a duke. Much as he appreciated her desire to protect him, her fatalistic acceptance that the only way to do that was for him to abandon her made him worry she might take her son and flee before he had the chance to convince her otherwise.

When he skidded over the threshold to be told by Marston that the lady still awaited him in the parlour, the sense of relief left him light-headed.

After ordering refreshments, he went at once.

Diana looked up as he entered, then ran to him. From the fierceness of her hug and the bleakness in her eyes as he leaned down to kiss her, he suspected she'd only waited in order to bid him a final goodbye.

He'd just have to persuade her that wasn't going to happen.

Marsden brought in wine and food. Not until after he'd coaxed her to sit and take some nourishment, did he finally return to the matter at hand.

'Thank you for waiting for me. I'm still not convinced Graveston is foolish enough to proceed with his ridiculous vendetta, but it would be best for us to make plans in case he does.'

She gave him a sad smile. 'I've already told you what we need to do. I would have returned to my lodgings when you went out, so I might begin my preparations—but I left you once without a word. This time, I wanted to give you at least the courtesy of a goodbye.'

'I thought as much. Thank you for giving me the opportunity to speak before proceeding alone. First, although it may not mean as much to you as it does to me, I consider that my honour is at stake in this matter. It was, after all, *my* suggestion that we began this liaison. Of course, I had no idea that an affair which should have remained a private matter would end up furnishing the Duke with ammunition to use against you. But so it has proven. I couldn't possibly abandon you to face the consequences alone and still call myself a gentleman—or a man.'

'You should not consider this in any way touching on your honour,' she countered.

'Shouldn't I? Were the circumstances reversed, and you had initiated something that caused me harm, would you walk away and do nothing to rectify the situation?'

She opened her lips—but remained silent, as he knew she would, for he had her there. 'I hardly think so,' he concluded. 'Else you would never have made such an enormous sacrifice eight years ago. I appreciate your continuing desire to protect my name and reputation. But I'm no longer a callow youth just out of university. I own a lucrative estate, my uncle is an earl and I, too, have powerful friends. After surviving dozens of battles, I've also learned a little about confronting a treacherous enemy.'

He could see the conflict in her face, the longing to believe him and accept his help warring with the long-ingrained habit of independence and her own sense of honour that drove her to spare him involvement, whatever the cost to herself.

Before she could speak, he pressed on. 'Besides, it is not just your safety at stake—I'm doing this to protect your son. With the stakes so high, don't you want to at least hear how I propose to counter Graveston's threat?'

At the reminder of her son's danger, she sighed. 'Very well, I'll hear you out.'

'Good,' he replied, relieved to have passed the first hurdle. Diana was shrewd, determined, and brave. Alastair knew if he could just get her to listen, he could convince her to fight instead of flee. Unless…she feared what he'd demand from her if she let him help her.

Better reassure her on that score immediately.

'I would hope you know this, but let me say it anyway. I assure you that when we win this battle, I will not press on you any…association you do not want. You'll be free to walk away. Your safety and that of your son is all the recompense I want.'

She smiled, relieving his mind and warming his heart. 'I do know that.'

'Very well, then. Let's begin with a rule of battle: the best response to attack is a well-designed counter-attack.'

'Counter-attack,' she repeated, light sparking in eyes that had looked tired and discouraged. 'I like the sound of that.'

Encouraged, he continued. 'First, we need to assess how strong a case Graveston could devise against you. Who might testify?'

She frowned, her gaze losing focus, as if she were running through a mental list in her mind. 'It could be anyone. As I told you, the staff at Graveston Court was loyal to the master—or more accurately, to Graveston's first wife, who had the running of the household for fifteen years before I was installed there. The former housekeeper in particular despised me. Since the staff didn't dare display hostility towards the Duke for his treatment of his first wife, they transferred that enmity to me.'

'Is the housekeeper a tall, thin, hawk-nosed woman?'

'No, Mrs Forbes is a rather rotund—' Her eyes widened. 'The current housekeeper is not, but the former one, the one who disliked me so, Mrs Heathson, is exactly that. You saw a woman of that description with the household keys?'

'I did. Blankford had obviously been informed of who I was and my connection to you before he came in to meet me. I had the impression that this housekeeper knew as well, and understood that anyone intervening on your behalf would be threatened with retribution. As I passed her in the hallway, she looked as pleased about the prospect as the Duke was.'

'I'm not surprised, if it was Heathson. She was fanatically devoted to her former mistress, doted on her son, and certainly would have been ranged on his side when he broke with his father. She'd been...retired; Blankford must have brought her back. With so many of the staff loyal to his mother, he could easily have recruited some of them to be his spies in the household after he left. He probably also instructed some to follow me to Bath after Graveston's interment.'

'So I concluded,' Alastair said, nodding. 'But what of his accusation? Are there any possible grounds for considering your husband's death suspicious?'

Diana stared into distance, frowning, before shaking her head with a sigh. 'I'm afraid I can't be of much help, since I avoided Graveston as much as possible. Thinking back, he did look somewhat pale. His hand trembled when he reached for the wine glass at dinner. I didn't think much of it; he went to work in his study every day as usual—a Duke of Graveston does not neglect business because of some trifling ailment, nor summon a physician to quack him. I suppose the estate agent did call at the manor more frequently than usual those last few months, rather than Graveston riding out with him.' She shrugged. 'I don't know—one might be able to make a case for some sort of slow poisoning.'

'Were you surprised when he died?'

She was silent for a long time. 'I never considered whether it was sudden or timely,' she said at last. 'After living for so long pressed down by a weight so heavy I could hardly breathe, once it was removed, all I felt was… relief. My sole thought, when his valet informed me of his death, was to get away before anyone could stop me. As soon as the coroner, after consulting Graveston's physician, declared that he had died of natural causes and authorised the burial—which by custom I would not have attended in any event—I left Graveston Court.'

'That's a point in your favour,' Alastair said, relieved. 'If the coroner did not suspect foul play, it seems unlikely Blankford will be able to turn up anything.'

'Perhaps. Perhaps not. The threat of prosecution might simply be a ploy to try to distress and intimidate me. But I don't think so. Blankford hates me enough to make accusations, even if he cannot unearth enough evidence to force a trial.'

Her description of determining to flee upon Graveston's death recalled to him the one detail of her account that still pricked at him.

'You lost your father less than two years after you wed the Duke. You were still childless, and I was with Wellington in the Peninsula, beyond his reach. Why did you not leave him then?'

'Oh, but I did leave him.'

He frowned. 'I don't understand.'

She rose and began to pace, a habit Alastair had noticed she often resorted to when distressed. 'Papa had been gone nearly a month when Graveston finally informed me of his death—and even then, he did so indirectly, by summoning me to his study to turn over some family jewellery. I recognised the pieces immediately as belonging to Papa's mother, and knew the only way he would have got them was if Papa had died.'

Alastair was struck by how unfeeling the Duke had been. 'I'm so sorry. You were always so attached to your father. It must have been terribly difficult.'

She shook her head. 'After the wedding, I distanced myself from Papa. Partly for his protection, but mostly because it would have been impossible to hide from him for long that I had not, as I assured him when he questioned me, thrown you over so I might become a duchess. Had he worked out the truth, it would have tortured him, and I didn't want that. But you asked about my leaving Graveston.'

She halted before the mantel and gazed into the flames, while he waited for her to begin, a sick feeling in his gut about what she was about to reveal.

'I left the same night I learned of Papa's death,' she said at last. 'Slipped out through the kitchen wing after all the servants were abed, taking only a portmanteau with a few old gowns and my family's jewellery. I made it through the village and almost to the posting inn on the mail-coach route before his men caught me. They dragged me, screaming and fighting, into a carriage and drove me back to Graveston Court.'

Shocked, he simply stared at her as she continued. 'It was, of course, unthinkable for the Duchess of Graveston to abandon her husband. He had me locked in my rooms, but he must have known I would try again, claw the wood out of the window frames if necessary, for he had me drugged. Downing the nourishment brought to me to keep up my strength to escape, I didn't notice until it was too late.'

'For how long?' Alastair asked, appalled.

'I don't know exactly. A long time. Once I had figured out what was happening, I tried keeping back some of the drugged wine, intending to drink it all together and escape that way.' She shook her head. 'Apparently Mrs Heathson—still the housekeeper then—figured out what I planned, and was quite willing to let me secrete away enough laudanum to carry me off. But for some reason, despite how often I'd displeased him, my husband wasn't. When I recovered from the overdose, Mrs Heathson had been "retired". And I discovered I was pregnant.'

She turned from the hearth to look at him. 'I didn't care what happened to me, but much as I hated bearing the son of such a man, I couldn't cause the death of an innocent child. Then, after his treatment of James, I couldn't flee and leave him at the mercy of a father like Graveston.'

Unable to restrain himself, Alastair went to Diana and pulled her into an embrace. She clung to him, her head pressed to his chest, shaking with tears she would not shed.

At length, she straightened and pushed against him. Knowing how cruelly she'd been imprisoned, he at once loosened his grip.

'I'm so sorry,' he said, running a fingertip down her cheek as he let her go. 'But you're free now, you and the boy. I won't let Graveston hurt you ever again. I promise, on my sacred honour.'

'My noble Alastair,' she whispered, squeezing his fingers. 'But even if you risk your reputation by getting involved, I don't know how you could prevent that.'

'Have a little faith, sweeting! First, I'll need to consult the solicitor again. I'm not an expert on the courts; I have no idea what evidence would be needed to persuade a coroner to open an inquiry into the death of a man already buried, with no suspicion of foul play. More than vague testimony from witnesses produced by a man well known to harbour a hatred of the woman he's accusing, I would think.'

'Even if that man is a duke, owner of nearly all the land in four parishes, employer of hundreds on the estate and in the adjoining villages, patron or supporter of most of the businesses, trade associations, and churches in the county?'

Alastair grimaced. 'True, with that much influence, Blankford could probably manage to get an inquest begun on his insistence alone. But an inquest is a far cry from convincing the assizes to convene a trial, and even further from a conviction. I'm confident it won't come to that.'

'You can't be sure. He'll pay for testimony, if necessary. There are always poor wretches ready to swear to anything, if the reward is rich enough.'

Payment for testimony was all too common, and frequently distorted the findings of a court. 'Perhaps,' Alastair allowed, 'but this isn't the matter of a thief-taker pointing the finger at some poor clerk in order to collect the reward offered for solving a burglary. Nor would the case be settled by a local magistrate, where a high-ranking lord could influence the outcome. For the possible murder of a duke and accusations against a duchess, a trial, if it came to that, would be held in the House of Lords. A chamber my uncle has run for years. Which is why I still believe, once he's recovered from his fit of petulance and thought it over carefully, Blankford will not push for a trial.'

She gave him a sad smile. 'To win, he doesn't have to. Accusations made against me in the county would be enough to poison the local officials against me and make it difficult to obtain any assets from the estate on which to raise my son. Enough to convince the Court of Chancery to take him away, even though he is still a minor child. Enough to create a scandal that would savage your reputation. I still see only one way to prevent all this.'

'Taking James and trying to disappear,' he summarised. 'Don't you see, Diana, doing that would give Graveston the ultimate victory? He'll have made you a fugitive and forced you to raise your son in obscurity, denying him the education, the comfort, the status to which his birth entitles him. Moreover, I'd be astonished if your husband hadn't made some provision for James in his will; disappearing so that legacy goes unclaimed—what a fitting revenge for the neglect Blankford feels you made him suffer! And as a final coup, a Duke of Graveston will once again have been able to drive us apart.'

She raised her face to him, frustration and fury in her gaze, and he knew he'd finally reached her. 'How do we prevent all that?'

We, she'd said, he noted, a thrill blazing through his heart. Stifling it before the gladness could distract him, he continued. 'We gather our own evidence, enough to convince Graveston it would be better not to make any public accusations—and I know just the rascal to do it. In the meantime, we need to move you and James some place safer, where a well-placed bribe won't risk tempting a low-moralled rogue to breach the security of your house and carry off the boy. There's only one place I can guarantee to be that safe—Barton Abbey.'

She looked at him incredulously. 'You propose to carry us to Barton Abbey? You can't be serious!'

'I'm completely serious. I doubt even the delusional Graveston would attempt to touch you there. Were he foolish enough to try, you'd have a small army of staff and retainers loyal to *me* to protect you. Who would turn away representatives from Chancery, if it came to that.'

'But would not my being at your house immediately bring down upon you just the scandal I wish to avoid?'

'There's nothing scandalous about my mother inviting a widow who was once a close family friend to spend part of her mourning period in the seclusion of Barton Abbey. Indeed, having you and James at my family home, under my mother's care, would further diminish the credibility of there being some clandestine plot between us. I assure you, no one in Society would believe Mrs Grace Ransleigh would be a party to something as dishonourable as that!'

'Quite true. Which is why your mother would most likely forbid me to enter the premises.'

'Leave Mother to me. Can you think of any place in England that would be safer? Your first duty, after all, is to protect your son.'

She looked up at him, her expression anguished. 'You know how much I want to keep you out of this. But… but you are right; my first duty is to James, and I cannot think of any place where I could be sure of protecting him, alone.'

'You would both be secure at Barton Abbey.'

Pensive, she turned once again towards the flames in the hearth, as if ultimate wisdom might be found in their dancing light—before abruptly whirling to face him. 'If I did agree to accompany you to Barton Abbey, and your mother did not turn us away, I—I could no longer come to you. Not in your mother's own house!' she finished, her cheeks flushing.

She looked so scandalised, Alastair had to laugh. 'My reputation is bad, I admit, but even I wouldn't embarrass my mother by conducting an affair under her roof. Once past the gatehouse, the agreement between us would be in abeyance, until Graveston is no longer a threat.'

'If all the trouble I envisage comes to pass, you will be thoroughly tired of me by then,' she said, reminding him of the terms he'd specified for ending their agreement.

'I will never tire of you…but you will still be free to do as you wish.'

She looked away and paced several more circuits around the room. Alastair waited, sure he was right, not wanting to coerce her, but hoping that after she'd considered all the possibilities, her own good sense would convince her his plan was the best course of action.

Hoping, though he knew it wasn't prudent, that accepting him as an ally would bring her even closer to him.

At last, she halted and turned to him. 'When do you propose to leave for Barton Abbey?'

'As soon as you can be ready,' he said, relief—and steely resolve—filling him.

This time, he would protect her and her son.

This time, the Duke's will would not prevail.

This time, they would defeat Graveston—together. And then, at last, find out whether or not they had a future.

She nodded. 'Tomorrow it is. Then we had best make the most of tonight.'

He held his breath, but she added nothing further— no admissions of affection, no confession that she had enjoyed their time together so much, she didn't wish it to end.

As closely guarded as she kept her emotions, he couldn't reasonably expect such a declaration—but he was still disappointed.

'We can both agree on that,' he said at last. Taking her hand, he led her up the stairs.

Much later, as they lay together in the aftermath of loving, still bone of bone and flesh of flesh, he whispered,

'Promise me you won't take the boy and run. Promise me this time, you'll trust me.'

She opened heavy-lidded eyes. 'I promise,' she said, and kissed him.

Chapter Fourteen

As arranged when they had parted late the previous night, shortly after daybreak, Alastair downed a quick breakfast and prepared to leave his sister's house at the Royal Crescent. His few belongings packed, he settled for penning Jane a note; he regretted parting from her on such unhappy terms without even a goodbye, but as she'd already been abed when he returned, and since leaving Bath early was imperative, it was the best he could do.

After hiring a post-chaise, he set off for Laura Place. A grim smile creased his lips as, for the first time, he knocked at her front door. At least now, there would be no more need for subterfuge.

Admitted within, he found Diana ready. The nursemaid had her sleepy son bundled up, and the small staff was busy closing up the house. A short time later, he ushered them to the coach.

'I still can't believe you talked me into going to Barton Abbey,' Diana murmured to Alastair, steadying the maid as Minnie carried her sleeping son up the step.

'You trust me to keep you safe, don't you?' he asked as he handed her in.

'If I didn't trust you to keep my son safe, I wouldn't have agreed to go.'

Tacitly accepting, for the moment, her slight change of emphasis, he followed her into the vehicle.

Soon, the coachman negotiated his way through Bath's busy streets and on to the road south towards Devon. Despite the jolting of the carriage, after a late night and an early rising, both the maid and Diana drifted off to sleep. Alastair sat watching them, savouring the feel of Diana's head nestled on his shoulder.

Finally, an end to shadow-boxing the family that had so drastically altered his life eight years ago. He couldn't wait to confront the Duke in open combat, drive home a victory, and free the two of them to explore their future.

Would Diana, compelled by extreme circumstance to rely upon him, continue to reveal herself after this episode was successfully concluded? Or would she close back in upon herself, refusing to admit him any further? So manipulated and constrained had she been, he knew he couldn't force or even cajole her to warm towards him.

Ah, but how he ached to help her further along the road to recapturing the joy, optimism and confidence she'd once possessed in such abundance.

Even if it meant, in the end, she took her revitalised spirit into a new life without him.

Initially too shy to speak, James soon overcame his reserve and proved an amazingly resilient traveller, eagerly watching the countryside and peppering Alastair and his mother with questions about the towns and vehicles they passed, the fields and workers observed out the windows. He'd also been delighted with the novelty of dining at public houses and spending the night at a busy coaching inn.

Forced to concede the necessity for it, Alastair had ordered two rooms, one for himself and a second for Diana, Minnie and James—and lain awake for hours each night, acutely conscious that Diana slept close by. Knowing that a period of enforced abstinence lay before them at Barton Abbey, its duration impossible to predict, he was sorely tempted to urge Diana to slip into his room after the others fell asleep.

But it wouldn't be wise. James's maid Minnie, Diana told him, had been informed they were travelling to visit an old family friend, who had sent her son to escort them. Alastair didn't know whether Diana's staff knew where— or with whom—she had spent her evening 'entertainments'. If the boy's nurse was aware that he was a more intimate acquaintance, she'd given no indication of it, and Alastair wished it to stay that way.

Who knew whether Graveston might summon the maid to testify against her mistress? Alastair meant to ensure the girl would have as little to say as possible.

After several long days on the road, even the curious six-year-old was tired of being cooped up in a coach, begging Alastair, who hired a horse to ride each day, to take him up in the saddle. Denied that treat, he and the rest of the party were increasingly impatient to reach their destination.

Finally, the longed-for moment arrived. Eschewing a mount for this last phase of the journey, familiar with every hill and turning from the last posting inn to his front door, Alastair joined the company in the coach. Eagerness, anticipation—and a touch of unease over the reaction of his mother to the guests he was about to foist on her—kept him on the edge of his seat.

'The entry gate's just ahead,' Alastair told James, who immediately thrust his small shoulders out of the window, impatient to get a look.

'It's not so big as the gatehouse at Graveston Court,' he pronounced as the carriage bowled through.

'Probably just as old, though, and full of nooks for boys to explore, as my cousins and I did when we were your age.'

The boy's eyes brightened. 'Could you take me exploring, too?'

Alastair smiled at the boy's artless assumption that he would still consider that a treat. 'When we have a chance.'

Diana, however, did not lean towards the window to get a glimpse of the estate of which she'd once expected to become mistress. Displaying none of James's excitement, she remained quietly in her seat, her impassive expression impossible to read.

Once, he'd anticipated bringing her here as his bride, envisaging her delight at seeing her new home for the first time. A sharp pain pierced his chest at the contrast between that old dream and the prosaic present.

They could never go back, he reminded himself. For now, it was enough that he'd persuaded her to come here, where he could keep her and her son safe. He'd content himself with that—and despite finally sheltering her under his roof, resist the deceptive illusion that the dreams he'd once cherished might still come true.

Despite that sober reminder, he couldn't seem to make himself stop watching her. Though her serene exterior gave no hint that she harboured any anxiety about what awaited them, he could read the small signs—the hands tightly gripping the seat, the rigid set of her shoulders—that said she was not as calm as she appeared.

He'd carefully refrained from any gesture of affection during their enforced closeness in the coach, with her son and his nursemaid always watching, but now, he leaned over to squeeze her hand. 'It will be all right. Trust me,' he murmured.

A short time later, the driver pulled the team up before the front entrance. As always, Alastair felt a surge of gladness at returning to the manor that had been his home since birth. Not even the uncertainty of his mother's reaction could dim that delight.

Then a footman was trotting over to let down the stairs. 'Mr Ransleigh!' he exclaimed, stopping short in the act of handing Diana from the coach. 'Welcome home, sir! But we weren't expecting you.'

'Nor any company,' he agreed with a smile. 'My mother shall certainly take me to task for that. Would you see that the baggage is carried upstairs?'

'Certainly, sir.'

Firmly taking Diana's elbow, he escorted the party up the stairs and into the hall, where the butler was hurrying to meet them. 'Wendell, you're looking well.'

Like the footman, the butler stopped short for a moment before giving him a bow. 'Master Alastair! What a pleasure to have you home, and your guests.'

'Would you have refreshment sent to the blue parlour, and let my mother know we're here?'

'Certainly.'

Once within the cosy blue chamber, Diana was invited to have a seat, while Minnie took James to the window to inspect the vista of the distant hills.

'Better not have the footman carry our bags too far,' Diana murmured when the maid was out of earshot.

'Nonsense. Mother would never be so discourteous as to ask someone I invited to my home to leave.'

Diana raised an eyebrow and made no reply. But her fingers twisted together even tighter, Alastair noted.

He truly did not worry that his mother would turn her away. To be sure, she would cloak her initial reaction to Diana's presence in politeness, and probably give him a furious earful once the guests were sent off to settle into their rooms. But he was convinced, once apprised of the truth of Diana's past actions and present circumstances, she would never turn away a woman and child in need.

If he were wrong, and she remained as opposed to his championship of Diana as Jane, she would simply have to take herself off to visit his sister. Barton Abbey belonged to him, and he would house there whomever he chose.

He hoped it wouldn't come to that. He would soon find out.

A few moments later, he heard his mother's quick step outside, and went to intercept her at the door.

In a graceful sway of skirts and a hint of rose perfume, she walked in, a delighted smile on her face. 'My darling Alastair! How wonderful to have you home again—even if unannounced, you naughty boy! And you've brought guests. How lovely!'

After hugging him, as she turned to greet those guests, her eyes widened and the smile fled from her face. 'Miss Northcot?'

'The Dowager Duchess of Graveston now, just recently widowed,' Alastair interposed smoothly. 'This is her son, Lord James Mannington, and his nurse, Minnie.'

The ladies curtsied. 'An unexpected honour, Duchess,' his mother said, an edge of irony in her voice. 'You and your son must be fatigued after your journey. I'll have Wendell show you to your rooms at once, so you may rest yourselves before dinner.'

At that moment, the butler returned, bearing a tray.

'Wendell, our guests are worn out from their travels. We should allow them to retire to their rooms at once. Escort them upstairs, please, and have John carry some refreshments to their chambers. I'm sure they will enjoy it much more after they are able to wash off the dust of the road.'

'As you wish, ma'am,' Wendell said, bowing. 'Ladies and young gent, if you would follow me?'

His mother waited only until the door had shut behind the visitors before rounding on him, incredulous fury on her face. 'Alastair, have you taken leave of your senses? How *could* you expect me to play hostess to the woman who put you and everyone who loved you through such agony? Jane wrote me that you were seeing her again! I've been praying ever since that if you didn't have the good sense to avoid her, you'd at least get your fill of her quickly and be done with it. How *dare* you bring her here?'

Not at all deterred by her reaction, he said, 'I dare, Mama, because it was the right thing to do. Please, calm yourself and hear me out! Once I've acquainted you with the facts, I believe you will agree with my decision.'

'That's highly doubtful,' his mother said with a sniff.

'But you are fair-minded enough to listen before making a judgement.'

'Wretch!' His mother gave him an exasperated look. 'When you put it that way, what can I do but listen?'

He waved her to a chair and pointed to the tray Wendell had left. 'Shall we have tea?'

'Probably wise. I've a feeling I'm going to need something to steady my nerves.'

She poured them each a cup and seated herself beside him on the sofa. 'So, tell me the whole.'

He took his time, and his mother did not interrupt,

sipping her tea thoughtfully while he related the circumstances leading to Diana's marriage, gave an account of her life after, and concluded with the present difficulties with the heir and the need to protect her son. After he finished, she remained silent for some time, while he held his breath.

'You believe the boy to be in danger?' she said at last.

'Diana certainly does. After my conversation with the Duke, I do believe he would mistreat him, exacting revenge upon the poor boy for an alienation of his father's affection that he blames upon Diana. He wants the boy to "suffer as he did", I believe he put it.'

'He actually said that?' His mother gasped. When he nodded, she grimaced. 'Peer or no, he seems thoroughly reprehensible.'

'So you understand why I felt it necessary to intervene, even though the child in question is Diana's.'

'I do, much as I wish the mother were anyone but Diana! Now, what else are you not telling me?'

A little startled, Alastair hedged. 'What makes you think there is more?'

'My dear son, you may be a man grown, and harder to read than you were as a child, but I have known you since the cradle. There's something else going on, isn't there?'

Alastair gave a rueful smile. 'I never could hide anything from you, could I?'

She smiled. 'As you got older, you didn't always confide in me, but I could still tell when there was something wrong. What is it this time?'

'I intended to tell you the whole, once I had your agreement to shelter the boy. Bringing him here may mitigate the accusations somewhat, but I'm afraid it's quite possible that by helping Diana, I shall be dragged into a rather ugly scandal. If, once I've related the circumstances, you'd prefer to take refuge with Jane until the storm blows over, I'll understand.'

With a sigh, she rose and poured them each another cup. 'I'm not likely to abandon either a helpless child or my son, but perhaps you'd best lay it all out.'

'Jane was correct when she told you that I'd…become involved with Diana again. I thought if I…could claim her for a time,' he said, his ears reddening at the thought of confessing this to his mother, 'I might finally rid myself of the lingering attachment that, try to deny it as I might, I never truly succeeded in stamping out.'

'But once she poured out to you the reasons for breaking your engagement, described how shabbily she was treated during her marriage, and threw herself upon your compassion, you felt you must become her champion?'

He gave a negative shake of the head. 'She made no such appeal. Oh, she told me why she had jilted me, of course, but that was all. The rest—what her life was like after her marriage, the threats against her son—I discovered only gradually, after inadvertent comments prompted me to make more pointed enquiries. She never could tell a lie, you know.'

'Nor even a convincing evasion,' his mother agreed, looking troubled. 'I do remember.'

'I know the story must seem fantastical to you. At first, I didn't believe her account either. But as I spent time with her, dredging out the facts bit by bit, I gradually came to accept it was true. Oh, Mama, can you imagine—Diana without paints, without books, without music? It makes my heart ache to envisage it. And so isolated. Alone, with no one to call upon for sympathy or protection.'

'So how does this lead to that great scandal you mentioned?'

'I told you that, wanting to get a sense of whether there was in fact a danger to the boy or not, I decided to call upon the Duke. At the conclusion of a rather unpleasant conversation, during which he refused to acknowledge that Diana, as his father's widow, was entitled to support from the estate and expressed his desire to punish her son, he boasted that he intends to accuse Diana of hastening his father's death. If I persist in championing her, he threatened to allege that I encouraged Diana to do away with her husband, in revenge for his father stealing her away from me years ago.'

'What?' His mother gasped again. 'But that's outrageous!'

'True. But since she did come to Bath immediately after his death, and we did…establish a relationship, the bare facts make such an accusation plausible.'

'But it's absurd! No one who knows you would believe such a calumny. I may hold Diana responsible for many sins, but murder? Surely Graveston isn't seriously going to try to implicate her in his father's death!'

'Diana seems to think he will at least make the attempt. Pointing the finger of suspicion upon her, as she well understands, would do enough damage to her reputation that she will have more difficulty accessing the funds due her from the estate, and would almost certainly induce the Court of Chancery to take away her son.'

'Being implicated as a widow's lover who persuaded her to murder won't do much for your reputation either,' his mother noted tartly.

'Which is why you might want to decamp to Jane's.'

'Surely you don't intend to let the wretch get away with this!' she said indignantly.

Alastair's face hardened. 'When it comes to Diana, I think the Dukes of Graveston have got away with quite enough already. The enmity between her and her late husband might have been well known, but so was the break between the former Duke and his heir. Fortunately, Will is back from Paris. I'm going to ask him to slink around Graveston Court and see what he can dig up. I'm betting he can gather enough counter-testimony that I can persuade Blankford to refrain from making any accusations, honour the estate's responsibilities to Diana and leave the boy where he is.'

His mother chuckled. 'If anyone can do so, Will can, the rascal. And love it, I'll wager. Last time he and Elodie visited, he admitted that all that respectability, as a trader and Crown representative, was getting a bit dull.'

'So he told me as well,' Alastair agreed, smiling. 'In the meantime, I want Diana and James here, where the Duke cannot bully or intimidate them. Frankly, it would be helpful to our cause if you would remain, so we can put it about that you invited Diana, an old family friend, to spend some time at Barton Abbey during her mourning period. Society would never believe *you* would countenance a murder plot, nor that I would dare to install a mistress under your roof.'

His mother raised an eyebrow. 'Are you trying to install a mistress under my roof?'

Alastair felt his face flush again. 'Whatever our relations might have been elsewhere, I would never insult you by attempting such a thing here.'

'Good,' his mother said, then surprised him by adding, 'Whatever my opinion of Diana, she deserves better.'

'Still, I have to warn you that though I am hopeful of resolving this without scandal, it might come to that. If you'd rather distance yourself, I'll understand. As long as you understand that, regardless of what happens, I will not desert Diana.'

'What, let my son oppose a child-threatening autocrat alone? I'm not such a pudding-heart!'

Love and gratitude warmed Alastair like the blaze of a welcoming fire after a long winter journey. He leaned over to give his mother a fierce hug, rattling her teacup in the process.

'Thank you, Mama. I knew I could count on you.'

'I should hope so. Heavens, if you can't trust in your mother's support, who can you trust? Just promise me, Alastair, you'll be…careful. I cannot bear to think of you suffering again as you suffered before.'

'Almost Jane's words,' he said ruefully. 'I've no desire to suffer either, so I'll do my best.'

His mother had paused, watching him. When he remained silent, she said, 'Very well. I'll put it about to my friends that I've…reconciled with Diana and offered her my support. I shall even do my best to be civil to her. As for the child, it's not been all that long since you and your cousins ran wild here. I think I can remember how to entertain a little boy.'

'Bless you, Mama. What would I do without you?'

She smiled and tapped him on the nose. 'You'd be desolate. Now, off with you. I must confer with Cook and the housekeeper and make sure we have something to tempt a child's sweet tooth.'

Giving her another hug, Alastair rose and walked out. He knew she'd hoped to have him confess what his intentions were towards Diana after the battle with Graveston was over. Fortunately, she didn't press him, because he wasn't sure himself.

The more time he spent with Diana, the less he could envisage letting her go. Perhaps, once she was safe, he'd feel differently. Perhaps, with her able to pursue a normal life again, like Napoleon on St Helena setting the world at peace, the momentous chapter of his life labelled 'Diana' would close, letting him finally move forward.

And perhaps Diana would go her own way.

The mere thought of her leaving made his heart squeeze in protest. Stilling it, he set his jaw. Winning her again—or not winning her—would have to wait. First, he had to protect her.

Chapter Fifteen

That night, as soon as the household retired to bed, Diana slipped along the darkened hallway to her hostess's room.

Mrs Ransleigh had been surprisingly cordial at dinner. Still, Diana knew it must chafe her extremely to be forced to house the woman who had so wronged her son.

Hopefully, that distress would be relieved after this interview.

Arriving at her destination, she tapped on the door. 'Mrs Ransleigh!' she called out softly. 'It's Diana... Northcot. May I talk with you for a moment?'

Her enquiry was met by a silence that lasted so long, she was debating how to proceed if her hostess refused her admittance, when suddenly the door opened. In gown and robe, with a frilly cap tied over her curls, Mrs Ransleigh stood on the threshold.

She looked Diana up and down, her expression wary, like someone approaching an unfamiliar dog, not sure if it would wag or bite. 'I suppose I shall have to hear you out sometime, so you might as well come in now.'

'Thank you.' Diana followed her hostess through the bedchamber into the blue-and-rose sitting room beyond.

'Take the wing chair by the hearth,' Mrs Ransleigh

directed as she reposed herself on the sofa. 'The fire's been banked, but there's still some warmth.'

As Diana hoped there would be, from this woman she'd once thought to embrace as her mother-in-law, for the child that might have been her grandson. Surely, regardless of her feelings for Diana, she would have pity on James!

'I wanted to thank you first for admitting us to your home. I'm sure Alastair pressed you, but, quite frankly, I wasn't at all sure you wouldn't refuse to take us in.'

As her hostess made no reply, merely nodding, Diana continued. 'I imagine you feel nothing but loathing for me and scorn for the dilemma in which I find myself. Let me assure you, I do not intend to impose upon your forbearance for very long.'

'Indeed?' Mrs Ransleigh responded, raising her eyebrows. 'Has my son exaggerated the menace Graveston poses to your son?'

'No! Not exaggerated. Or rather, as long as he sees my son as a means to make me suffer, James is in danger. But it's me upon whom he truly wants revenge. I believe that if he can obtain that, and James is protected by friends powerful enough to make proceeding against him difficult, he will content himself with me and leave James alone.'

Mrs Ransleigh frowned. 'What do you intend?'

'I once caused Alastair, and indeed your entire family, great suffering and embarrassment—quite enough for one lifetime, I think! I shall do whatever I can now to ensure that none of you is harmed by Graveston's anger towards me. I wouldn't have agreed to come here at all, except I knew Alastair would never bring James without me. But I plan to leave tonight, return to Graveston Court, and confront Blankford.'

'Return to Graveston Court!' her hostess echoed, obviously surprised. 'Are you sure you should do that? Would you not be placing yourself at Blankford's mercy?'

Diana shook her head. 'That doesn't matter. If Blankford wishes to order up an inquiry, or have me bound over to the assizes, let him do so. So long as James is safe, and Alastair's reputation protected. Before I go, though, may I beg of you one final, but most important favour?'

Mrs Ransleigh paused, opening her lips as if to speak, then closing them. 'What is that?' she said at last.

'I know it's a great deal to ask, but would you watch over my son? I've…not been much of a mother to him, but despite all he has been deprived of, he is a warm-hearted little boy, so anxious for and deserving of love. I couldn't imagine anyone more capable than you of guiding him to becoming a strong, intelligent, honourable man. A man like Alastair. Can you pity James, an innocent in all this, and forgive me enough to care for him?'

As Mrs Ransleigh stared at her, probably astounded by her audacity in demanding such an enormous boon, Diana held her gaze and prayed that compassion would triumph over dislike. Alastair would do whatever was necessary to protect James—but to become the man she'd want him to be he would need the kindness, wisdom and guidance of a mother. If she could assure that for him, she could return to face Blankford with an easy heart.

To her relief and joy, Mrs Ransleigh's eyes welled up with tears. 'Yes, I will watch over him.'

Overwhelmed, Diana went over to kneel at her hostess's feet. 'Thank you,' she whispered, humbled. 'I don't deserve such a favour, but he does.'

Now to put the rest of her plan in action. Rising once more, she curtsied to her hostess. 'I shall be gone by morning, so I'll bid you farewell. Would you convey my… goodbyes and my thanks to Alastair?'

'Shouldn't you do that yourself?'

Diana stifled the pang of longing before it could escape. 'No, it's best if I don't see him. Excuse me again for disturbing your rest, and may the Lord bless you for your mercy.'

This might even be a better solution, she thought, her anxiety lessening as she walked from the room. She might never become the mother James needed—but now she was turning him over to a woman who already was. With James safe, what difference did it make what happened to her?

As for the tantalising possibility of a future with Alastair—that was an illusion so cruel she should have crushed it the moment it whispered in her brain. Her emotions crippled and her heart stunted by years of living under Graveston's tyranny, she was as unsuitable a partner for a man like Alastair as she was unfit to be James's mother.

She hurried into her pelisse. The small portmanteau was already packed; a nearly full moon would illuminate the track to the village, several hours' walk away. Next morning, she could find a ride with some market-bound farmer to the posting inn on the main road and by midday, obtain a seat on a mail coach that would take her towards Graveston Court.

She couldn't bear to see Alastair—who would, in any event, try to dissuade her from a course of action of which he was certain to disapprove—but before she left, she would visit her son one last time.

Silently, she ascended the stairs and entered the nursery, setting the portmanteau by the door. Though unused for some years, she'd noted when she'd escorted James there earlier this evening that it was a cheerful place, its large windows overlooking the garden and bathing the room in light for lessons or play. Ranks of toy soldiers, tops, balls and a few precious books were arranged on shelves and a well-used rocking horse stood in the corner. Warm and inviting, it was as different as one could imagine from the formal, artefact-filled room her son had occupied at Graveston Court.

She hoped before long, Mrs Ransleigh would develop a fondness for James. He was a handsome boy with charming manners, who had already reanimated her deadened heart enough that she felt a real sorrow at having to leave him, just as she was finally beginning to know and appreciate him.

Tiptoeing past the sleeping Minnie, she eased herself on to the edge of his bed, careful not to disturb him. For a long moment, she gazed down on his face, cherubic in the moonlight.

'Be safe, my son,' she whispered. 'I know you will wonder why I left you, but some day, when you are old enough to compare Alastair's character to the Duke's, you will understand.'

She rose to leave before, driven by a compulsion beyond reason, she hesitated. Cautiously, as though attempting the forbidden, she leaned down to kiss James's forehead. From deep within, love long repressed and denied seeped up, bringing tears to her eyes.

He murmured and stirred, and she drew back. 'Goodbye, my dear son,' she mouthed silently, then picked up the portmanteau, and slipped out of the room.

Down in the darkened kitchen, Alastair paced, hoping his mother's warning had not brought him here too late. He'd checked Diana's bedchamber immediately and found it empty; he'd wait here by the hearth a few more minutes, but if Diana did not appear, he would set out after her. On foot, in the dark, she couldn't proceed with much speed, but though the home woods should not pose too many dangers for someone who kept to the road, he couldn't be easy about her being out there alone, undefended, in the middle of the night.

He exhaled an impatient breath, aggravated at her headstrong decision to confront Graveston without him. Not that he'd been truly shocked when his mother rushed to tell him what Diana intended. After years of being forced to rely on no one but herself, he had suspected that once her son was safe, she might set off independently.

Determined to confront her enemy alone, to spare him and his family.

Damn Graveston! He spat out a few well-chosen oaths. And foolish girl! When would he convince her that she no longer had to fight her battles unaided?

A few minutes later, he heard the soft shuffle of slippers on the stairway. Drawing back into the shadows, he watched as, carrying a small trunk, Diana appeared in the moonlit room.

'Just where do you think you are going?' he demanded, unable to keep a note of exasperation from his voice.

'Alastair!' she gasped, whirling to face him.

'Not the headless horseman. Though you deserve to confront a bogeyman, sneaking out like an ill-chosen guest absconding with the hostess's jewels.' His tone softening, he said, 'How could you think I would let you go off to face Graveston alone?'

In the stillness, he heard a little sigh that twisted his heart. 'I thought after I was gone, when you thought carefully about it, you would realise that was the best course. But how did you know I was leaving?'

'Mama told me. Quite in a rush she was, urging me to hurry so I could intercept you before you escaped.'

'Your mother?' she echoed, clearly astounded.

'Yes, though her warning didn't take me completely by surprise. I remember an account of a girl, freed of her obligations, sneaking out through the kitchens in the dead of night. I just hadn't anticipated it happening this soon.'

'I can't imagine why she would warn you,' Diana murmured.

'Here, give me that,' he said, taking the portmanteau from her slackened grip. 'Come up to the library and we'll discuss it.'

Realising how peremptory he sounded, and remembering how often she'd been coerced, he added in a softer tone, 'Please, Diana? I promise I will not force you to take any action with which you disagree. But let's discuss this again before you throw yourself headlong into danger.'

'Very well,' she said in a little voice, sounding tired and discouraged.

Heartened, he took her elbow and guided her from the room. Not that his assistance was really needed, but after envisaging Graveston dragging her before a magistrate, Graveston hurling accusations against her at the assizes…Graveston striking her, he needed the reassuring feel of her warm flesh under his fingers.

Once in the library, he rummaged up some wine and waved her into a chair.

'I still don't understand why your mother didn't just let me go. I would have thought she'd be relieved to be shed of me.'

'She hasn't quite forgiven you yet for what happened; the tale is a bit much to swallow all at once. But she believed enough of it to warn me—which is enough for now.'

He handed her a glass, noting how her fingers trembled as she sipped from it. He stemmed an overwhelming urge to gather her in his arms, to let his warmth and proximity reinforce the message she seemed so reluctant to believe—that he would stand by her, no matter the outcome. But she still radiated a brittle fragility, seeming half-glad he'd intervened, half-angry that he'd circumvented her will. He wouldn't risk pushing her too hard.

'I thought we'd agreed to face Graveston together,' he said instead. 'I thought you were going to trust me.'

'And I thought you understood I would rather die than destroy your happiness and reputation a second time.'

'Ah, Diana, do you truly think I could be happy, knowing you were going to sacrifice yourself for me? Perhaps if I tell you in more detail what I plan, I can convince you that proceeding together is the better way. You remember my cousin Will?'

A wisp of a smile touched her lips. 'Wagering Will? He went into the army too, didn't he? I suppose he tricked his way to general?'

'Not quite,' he said, momentarily diverted by the image of his reprobate cousin in a staff officer's uniform. 'Though I've no doubt he could have contrived it, had he wanted to. The army did use his skills in several clandestine ways on the Peninsula—who better to creep around and turn things up than Will? He also managed to find himself a wife while setting to rights the debacle with Max.'

Her eyes widened. 'Debacle with Max?'

'You didn't hear? It was quite the scandal.'

'I was exiled in the country the last few years,' she reminded him drily.

'While accompanying Wellington to the Congress of Vienna, he befriended a widow, hostess to a member of the French delegation who later plotted an assassination attempt against Wellington. Max's innocent association with the widow dragged him into it, ruining his political prospects. You remember how Will credits Max with saving him from the streets. He was so incensed by the affair—during which our uncle, the Earl of Swynford, made no attempt to assist his son—he set off to Vienna to find the woman and bring her back to clear Max's name. Succeeded so well, he ended up marrying her—and getting himself a post as a trader in Paris, while also representing the Crown on economic matters.'

'How can an economic envoy in Paris help us?'

'Will's back in England—and still possessed of those, uh, particular skills for gaming and subterfuge Max never succeeded in beating out of him. I intend to send him, in whatever guise he thinks most useful, to the village near Graveston Court and let him investigate the circumstances of your husband's death. We'll see whether he can turn up some counter-testimony to persuade the Duke it would be better not to make public his accusations. Given the enmity between father and son, I'm nearly certain we could find witnesses to support some counter-accusations.'

She sat silent for a moment, obviously considering the possibilities. 'Like his father, Blankford is supremely confident of forcing whatever outcome he wills. Anything Will "turned up" would have to be pretty convincing.'

'Will's a skilful rogue. Trust him. As I hope you'll trust me.'

He came over to take her hand and gazed into her eyes, willing her to believe him. 'I'm no longer an impetuous boy, ready to give up without a fight and slink off to nurse my wounded sensibilities. If I'd listened to the instincts that said you'd never willingly abandon me, pushed past the servant who said you wouldn't receive me and insisted on speaking with you eight years ago, how much misery and anguish would I have saved us both? You gave up your life to save mine then. Now I intend to fight to save yours.'

'But if you cannot convince Graveston to cry off, only think of the scandal! It is not just you who would suffer, Alastair. What of your mama, your sisters? How embarrassing it could be for them!'

He shrugged. 'I have thought about it. No one would believe ill of Mama, who made her choice to support us when she alerted me to stop you. Jane and Lissa are both married into important families with husbands who can protect them. Try as he might, Blankford would never find enough evidence to convict you in a court of law, so creating a scandal is all he could ultimately achieve. We can face it down together. Besides, neither of us cares a fig about whether we're received in Society or not.'

'You might become "Infamous Alastair" in truth,' she said with a flicker of a smile.

'And never look back. But I really don't think it will come to that. Won't you try this my way?'

He hesitated, wanting to say so much more. That neither honour nor affection would permit him to let her sacrifice herself a second time. That logic and reason demanded she choose his alternative. That he intended to keep her here and implement his plan whether she agreed or not.

But after all she had suffered, any attempt to coerce would probably trigger an instinctive resistance that would make her deaf to logic or reason. Holding her by force would only result in her trying to slip through his grasp again at the first opportunity.

So he waited, every nerve tensed for her answer.

At last, she gave a heavy sigh. 'Perhaps you are right.

Maybe Will can find something.' She gave him a rueful smile. 'I can always give myself up in the end.'

She turned to look up into his face. 'Maybe I should have trusted you more, eight years ago. Maybe Graveston would not have carried out his threats. All he needed, however, was for me to *believe* he would. A man of his rank, one who had imposed his will on others practically from birth…' She shook her head. 'What match was a girl of eighteen, with no experience of the world, against a man like that?'

'So this time, you'll trust me to keep James safe, to keep you safe. Trust *us*, working together?'

She squeezed his hand and nodded. 'I'll trust us.'

Overwhelming relief swept through him like a storm wind over the moors. Seizing both her hands, he kissed them.

'Thank you. I appreciate how hard it is for you to share control over your safety and James's with anyone,' he told her, both pleased and humbled by her trust. 'So, no more running away into the night! We'll stand and face Graveston, stare him in the eye, if necessary, in the full light of day. Fight, not flee.'

Taking a shaky breath, she nodded. 'Fight, not flee.'

He released her hands and motioned to her glass. 'Finish your wine, then, and get some rest. I'm off tomorrow to find Will—I could send a message and ask him to Barton Abbey, but it would be faster to seek him out. I'd like him to head to Graveston Court as soon as possible.'

Obediently, she sipped the last and rose to leave. As he escorted her out, she paused at the doorway to look up at him. 'Thank you, too. For protecting us.'

She lifted her face. He pulled her to him, and she clung to him through a lingering kiss that set every part of him throbbing with the need for fulfilment.

Oh, that he could make her his—truly his! But that couldn't happen here and now, so he'd better disentangle himself.

Heeding Jane and his mother's warnings, he'd better maintain a little more emotional distance, too.

Reluctant despite those cautioning thoughts, he released her. 'I only wish there had been some other, equally safe place to bring you. I'm already missing Green Park Buildings.'

She sighed as well. 'So am I.'

Chapter Sixteen

The next morning, Diana woke with a start. Her heart pounded through a moment of panic before she recalled where she was, in a pretty guest bedchamber at Barton Abbey, with James safe in the nursery on the floor above.

Safe.

It had been so long since she'd experienced the condition, she found it still difficult to believe. Like an injured soldier testing a wound, she prodded the edges of her anxiety, feeling for tender places where such concern was justified.

She and James were safe for the moment, but the confrontation had hardly begun. Still, Alastair had an ally who could probe into the circumstances of her husband's death and produce testimony to validate her innocence. Something she could never have managed on her own.

She leaned back against the pillows. Alastair was right: he was far more than the charming, impetuous young man she'd once loved. If he could face down a charge of French cuirassiers, facing down the Duke or a court of inquiry would hardly faze him. A battle-tested soldier of ingenuity, strength and courage, he would protect her and his family.

Her struggle with Graveston…might even end well. And if their plan were successful…what then?

She couldn't summon up a single image of a future beyond that. Despite her confidence in Alastair's abilities, the confrontation still to come loomed so large, her mind could not yet envisage anything beyond the yawning abyss of Graveston's threats.

However, until Alastair returned—and his cousin, if Will were amenable to assisting them, completed his work—there was nothing to be accomplished by worrying over the matter any further.

She should instead go down to breakfast and express her thanks to a hostess who, amazingly, had prevented her from departing in the middle of the night and taking her tawdry problems with her.

Hopping out of bed, she crossed to the bell pull. She was inspecting her meagre selection of gowns when a knock at the door heralded the arrival of an apple-cheeked maid.

'I'm Meg, Your Grace,' the girl said, bobbing a curtsy. 'Mrs Ransleigh says I am to attend you while you're here. I pressed and hung up the gowns; I hope I done it how you like them.'

'Thank you, Meg, they look quite fine. Is your mistress at breakfast now?'

'She should be, or if not, she'll be with the housekeeper. Shall I find her for you?'

'No, I'm sure I shall see her there, or later.'

Diana let the maid help her into a modest yellow day gown, then direct her to the breakfast room. She'd seek out her hostess, express her thanks, and go see James.

Having agreed to Alastair's plan, while he pursued the matter of testimony to dissuade the Duke from persecuting her, she'd have more time to get to know her son, she thought, her heart warming with gratitude. And perhaps while they sheltered at Barton Abbey, she might take some lessons from Mrs Ransleigh in how to become a proper mama.

A few moments later, after only a single wrong turn, she arrived at the breakfast room, to find Mrs Ransleigh still sitting over her cup of coffee. As Diana entered, her hostess rose and gave her a curtsy. 'Good morning, Duchess.'

Returning the curtsy, Diana grimaced. 'Please, Mrs Ransleigh, I should so much prefer that you not use the title. Could you not call me "Diana", as you once did?'

Mrs Ransleigh inclined her head. 'It's certainly not proper. But if you truly prefer it...'

'I would consider it a great favour.' She managed a slim smile. 'Anything that helps me put the last eight years behind me is preferable.'

'Very well...Diana. I hope you slept well—once you slept,' she added with a lift of an eyebrow.

Diana felt her face warm. 'I did sleep well, thank you. Though I cannot imagine why you didn't let me leave.'

'Can you not? I admit, I did not believe the circumstances of your marriage when Alastair first apprised me of them, but as I considered them again after you spoke with me, I changed my mind. Your testimony reminded me that when I knew you before, you never could lie—truth always rang in your voice and illumined every expression of your face.'

A lump rose in her throat. Convincing Alastair had been a gift—she'd never expected to regain the respect of his mother.

'Please, fill your plate!' her hostess urged her. 'Then we can chat.'

Marvelling that, if she'd followed her own plans, she'd now be riding in some farmer's cart towards her reckoning with Graveston, rather than sharing breakfast with the mother of the man she'd wronged, Diana served herself and took a seat.

Once the footman had poured her coffee and withdrawn, Mrs Ransleigh said, 'I liked you immediately when Alastair introduced us years ago, you know, and happily anticipated welcoming you to Barton Court as my daughter. Of course, I was appalled when you jilted Alastair. Incredulous, too,' she added with a smile. 'What girl of sense would give up my son for a mere title?'

Diana had to return it. 'What girl indeed!'

'I've been fortunate,' Mrs Ransleigh continued, 'I was allowed to marry a wonderful man for whom I cared deeply, to bear three children who returned a thousandfold in pride and pleasure for any trials experienced in raising them. But I know many women are not as lucky. Men have their land, or their skills or trade; they can choose how to earn their bread, settle in the community where they were born, or leave it to find new adventures—or to forget disappointments. Whereas most of *our* lives are dictated by others—fathers, husbands, brothers. But within the narrow range of our choices, I believe we women can display bravery and endurance equal to that of any soldier upon a battlefield. "Greater love hath no man than this, that he lay down his life for a friend." As you did. But one sacrifice was enough, Diana. This time, Alastair will fight to protect you, and I'll do all I can to assist.'

Diana's hard-won control seemed to be unravelling, for she felt tears prick her eyes. Once again, from deep within where she'd shut away all memories of that long-ago affair, a recollection slipped out: how much she,

who'd never known her own mother, had eagerly anticipated sharing Alastair's. The flush of warmth—and longing—that followed in its wake, she made no attempt to
suppress. 'Thank you for believing me,' she whispered.

'It's a travesty that you were distanced from loving
your son! To have been forced to miss his first six years!
Fortunately, you have several more before he's old enough
to prefer friends to his mama. You need to make the
most of them.'

'I know,' she replied, brought back to her first, most
pressing concern. 'But I'm not sure how.'

'Having already met the young lad, I think I can with
confidence advise you just to spend time with him and
let him be himself. He can't fail to delight you.'

Diana smiled faintly. 'Alastair gave me the same advice.'

Mrs Ransleigh laughed. 'That's how he was beguiled
by my rascal of a grandson! Robbie reminds me so much
of Alastair. Watching your son grow is a joy you must
experience. And now, you shall.'

Oh, how much she wanted to create for James the
sort of loving home that had produced an Alastair! 'Will
you...help me?'

His mother's face softened. 'I don't think you will
need much help, once you are truly convinced you may
love him openly without danger, but of course I will.
By the way, the two of you may stay here as long as you
wish. Treat Barton Abbey as the home we once hoped
it would be.'

She'd hardly dared expect forgiveness from Mrs Ransleigh—and never imagined she would be treated with
such generosity and compassion.

'There are no words to express how much I appreciate
your kindness, to me and to James. How can I repay you?'

'Be happy, for Alastair.'

Be happy. Could she ever discover how to do that—to thaw out the frozen lump of emotions still trapped within, let go of fear and restraint, finally allow herself to *feel* again freely?

'He still cares for you deeply. But you must not worry Alastair will try to push you into anything you do not want, once this is all over,' her hostess added quickly. 'Nor would I let him. You've been coerced quite enough.'

'He's already promised to respect my wishes, and I believe him.'

'Good,' Mrs Ransleigh said with a nod. 'What *do* you wish for, once this is all over? If I may ask—I don't wish to pry.'

'I really don't know,' Diana admitted. 'I lived a virtual prisoner for so many years, with no hope of escape, I ceased to imagine a life beyond the walls of the estate. I'm not even sure where to begin.'

'You might start by taking up activities you used to enjoy. We've a fine library; make use of it. There's a pianoforte at your disposal. Supplies for painting, sketching and needlework. You're welcome to borrow my mare, Firefly, if you'd like to ride. Join me for tea, for dinner, cards and conversation after if you like, or dine alone, if you prefer.'

Gently she took hand Diana's hand, and to her own surprise, Diana did not instinctively flinch away. 'You've been hurt and battered for too many years. Give yourself time to heal. And don't worry. Alastair will make sure no one harms you ever again.'

'I know he will try.'

'He will succeed,' his mother said firmly. 'Alone, my warrior son is a formidable force, but with Will by his side? Invincible! You will see.'

'I certainly hope so.'

'Never doubt it. You can relax and focus on your son—and regaining your life.'

Regaining her life… What would that life look like? Completely absorbed since her husband's death with protecting James—and dealing with Alastair—she hadn't begun to consider. Even now, it seemed somehow to be tempting fate to dare envisage anything beyond the end of Graveston's looming menace.

After taking a final sip, Mrs Ransleigh set down her cup. 'I enjoyed our chat, dear, but I must get to work.'

'Is there anything I can do to help?'

'It's a fine day, with the autumn flowers in the garden in brilliant hue. Perhaps you could gather some?'

Swift as a darting lark, a memory swooped back. Papa had delighted in having fresh greenery nearby as he worked, so she'd made a ritual of seeking the most unusual plants and flowers to arrange in every room.

A faint flicker of what she realised was anticipation stirred. 'I could arrange cuttings for the house, if you like.'

'I would like that.'

To Diana's surprise, her hostess leaned over to give her a hug. 'Life will be better. You'll see. Why not take that young scamp into the garden with you? Teach him about the plants his grandfather loved. I also seem to remember the coachman mentioning that one of the dogs had pupped. I wager James would love to have a dog of his own.'

A walk through a brilliant autumn garden, blooms to gather and arrange—and time with her son. From within a tender warmth welled up, like the small brilliance of the first yellow crocus emerging from the snow.

'Thank you, I'd like that.' After hesitating a moment,

she allowed herself to voice the other concern that had occupied her thoughts. 'Has Alastair gone yet, do you know?'

'Yes, he left at first light this morning.'

She felt a flash of disappointment, quickly squelched. Having settled everything last night, there was no reason he should have come to see her before he left.

As if privy to her thoughts, Mrs Ransleigh said, 'He asked me to pass along his good wishes. He would have delivered them in person, but he didn't want to disturb your sleep. More than anything, he wants you to rest—and heal.'

Diana nodded. 'He's been very good to me. As have you. Far better than I deserve, though I'm grateful for James's sake to have found such strong champions.' Foreboding about what that might cost Alastair swept through her.

'You mustn't worry about him,' Mrs Ransleigh said, seeming to sense Diana's concern. 'It's hard not to worry when you care for someone, as I know only too well. After Alastair's break with you, he was in such despair, I feared he might throw his life away in some great battle.'

Feeling the words as a reproach, Diana said quietly, 'I'm so sorry.'

'No point repining,' Mrs Ransleigh said. 'You had good reason for your actions, as I now know. In any event, I was so relieved when he returned from the war unharmed! But the man who came back brought me new worries. Harder, more distant, and cynical about everyone but his immediate family, he seemed to think females served only one purpose—and not one he would discuss with his mama! I could understand at first why he kept that distance, not wishing to risk a heart once so severely wounded. But as time went on, my worry deepened, for neither his many mistresses nor the proper young ladies to whom Jane tried to introduce him—whom he scrupulously avoided, I might add—seemed able to touch him. I have to admit, when Jane told me he was seeing you, I hoped the experience might break through the wall he'd erected around his heart. It has certainly done that. Whatever happens next, for that, and for the sacrifice you made for him earlier, I will always be grateful.'

Along with teasing out threads from the skein of memory Diana had kept so tightly wound within, Mrs Ransleigh seemed to be able to evoke long-repressed emotions. Once more near tears, Diana said, 'I never wished to harm him. I pray every night these new troubles will not.'

Mrs Ransleigh smiled. 'Prayer is always valuable. I'd best get along now, before Mrs Andrews sends a maid looking for me. We dine early, but if you wish something before then, nuncheon is available. Just ring. Shall I see you at dinner, or would you prefer a tray?'

Having not been given that choice for years, Diana hesitated. She could visit the library, choose a book, sit over her dinner reading.

But she didn't have to hurry off—she might choose a book at leisure, and read whenever she chose, for as long as she liked. The idea seemed strange—and wonderful.

But for the first time since she'd left her father and Alastair, Diana felt an inclination for company. To get to know better the remarkable woman who'd raised such a remarkable son—and forgiven her for hurting him. To learn all she could from her, to better raise her own son. 'I'd like to join you, if you don't mind.'

'I should be delighted. I'll look forward to those flower arrangements as well.' Giving Diana's hand another squeeze, she rose from the table. 'Try to enjoy the day, my dear. I'll see you at dinner.'

* * *

As her hostess walked out, Diana sipped her coffee. *Enjoy the day.* A whole day, for nothing but her pleasure.

The notion seemed almost impossible.

For all pleasures but one, she amended, remembering last night's single kiss. Her body aflame, she'd regretted as keenly as Alastair the need for the celibacy now imposed upon them. She hadn't expected to miss their intimacy quite so dreadfully.

Would Alastair wish to resume their relationship, once the confrontation with the Duke was over?

This last battle might be the end of the episode for him, the denouement that allowed him to finally close the chapter of his life labelled 'Diana'. Distress, a tangled mix of anxiety and sadness, arose at that possibility.

She would have to accept that, of course. The Alastair she'd known, the Alastair she was coming to know again, would support the cause he believed in and fight to the end. If that end was scandal and disgrace, he would see her comfortably established before moving on.

But what if he were not ready to move on? It required but a moment to conclude she'd welcome him back as a lover. More than that, she couldn't yet envisage. Would he be content for long with such a restricted offering? A man who should command not just the passion, but the unrestrained love of any woman lucky enough to be chosen by him?

She wouldn't think about that now.

Though slowly coming to believe she was truly freed of her prison, she hadn't yet untangled the twisted threads of her thoughts, desires and still-repressed emotions to figure out who she might become—whether it would ever be possible for her to love again with the passionate intensity she'd been capable of before Graveston. She hadn't the energy to contemplate her life beyond tomorrow. All she could manage at the moment was to begin working on dismantling the automatic ban she'd imposed over things which gave her pleasure, lest the Duke take them away.

The most important barrier to dismantle, before she could consider what might develop between herself and Alastair, was the one she'd been forced to erect between herself and the small boy whose emotional future depended upon her. With that thought, she set off for the nursery.

Chapter Seventeen

Diana found James rearranging the soldiers staged on shelves in the nursery. A delighted smile sprang to his face when she walked in. 'Mama, see what wonderful soldiers Minnie found for me! There's twice as many as my army!'

'So I see. Do you want to play with them, or go into the garden with me?'

James set down the soldiers at once. 'I should like to go outside, if you please.'

'Then outside we shall go. Minnie, if you'll get his jacket while I fetch my cloak?'

Diana hurried back to her bedchamber, gathering up a warm hooded cloak and her heaviest gloves. When she arrived back at the nursery, she noted approvingly that James was also warmly attired.

'You needn't go with us, if you'd prefer to remain inside,' she told the maid. 'I promise I won't get him too untidy.'

For a moment, the girl hesitated. 'Very well, ma'am, I'll stay here and catch up on my mending.'

Diana felt a little glow of satisfaction, as if she'd passed some sort of test. In the few short weeks since she'd begun making overtures to her son, this would be the first time she would spend time with the boy without Minnie hovering nearby.

'Are we going to a park?' her son's piping voice interrupted.

'To a garden,' she answered as she ushered him out and down the hallway. 'We're going to hunt plants.'

'Plant hunting? Is that like the fox hunting Papa used to do?'

Her jaw automatically tightened at the mention of his father. *He can't touch you any longer*, she told herself, pushing aside the reaction. 'No, it's the sort of hunting your grandfather, my papa, used to do.'

'The papa who taught you to paint?'

'The very one. We're going to find some flowers for Mrs Ransleigh's tables—giving flowers to your hostess is a very good idea, even if the flowers come from her own garden—and we'll look for some of the little plants my papa used to paint, too. I'll show you how later, or perhaps you'd like to make a portrait of some of your new soldiers.'

'Can I do both? I like painting.'

'And you are quite good at it, too.'

The child glowed at the compliment, and Diana felt a stab of regret. Her father had been lavish with his praise, whether complimenting her skill at reading and letters, or offering encouragement and advice as she began to experiment with paint and brush. James needed appreciation, too, and from more than just his doting nursemaid.

After asking direction of a footman, they set out for the cutting garden behind the kitchen garden. As Mrs Ransleigh had promised, the autumn flowers were reaching full bloom: chrysanthemums in rust and orange, asters in lavenders and whites, and Bourbon roses in the final flush of beauty.

After obtaining scissors and a trug from one of the gardeners, Diana let James carry the basket and helped him cut an assortment of the vivid blooms. They then returned to the kitchen garden, where she wandered among the rows to add sprays of mint, tansy, and rue to add a variety of green hues and a piquant aroma to the bouquet.

In between cutting the flowers, she allowed James to hopscotch down the flagstones of the back terrace, toss some pebbles from the gravel walk surrounding the herb beds into puddles left from the previous night's rain, and make friends with one of the kitchen cats sunning itself on a bench.

When at last the trug was full, she said, 'We'll arrange the flowers and greenery into vases when we go back to the house.'

His smiling face sobered. 'Must we go in already?'

She smiled at his disappointment. 'It's a lovely day, isn't it? No, I don't suppose we must return to the house yet. Would you like to walk some more?'

'Oh, yes! I can see woods from the schoolroom window. Could we walk there?'

'It might be too far away, but we can walk in that direction.'

So they set off, James full of curiosity, commenting on every wall, bench and tree, noting its similarities or differences from those in the gardens at Graveston Court.

'Why aren't there any stone people, Mama?' he asked suddenly.

She suppressed a smile at her son's description of the valuable antiques her husband had placed along the series of descending terraces that led away from the house at Graveston Court, where visitors could see them and be suitably impressed. 'Not everyone likes a very formal garden with statues,' she replied.

He nodded. 'Some of them were scary. I like this garden better.'

Smiling as she recalled some of the classical themes—the Rape of the Sabine Women, for one, which could in no way be considered appropriate viewing for an impressionable young boy—she said, 'I prefer just plants, too.'

Around a turn bordered by a wall of boxwood, they reached the end of the gravel walk. Beyond a wide expanse of grass stood a field of wheat, the long tassels nodding in the breeze, and at a good distance beyond that, the woods James had seen from his windows.

'Mama, it's so pretty—the tall grass that's all gold!'

'Part of that pretty grass is ground into flour to make your bread,' she told him.

'Really? Can I go see it?'

She tensed, wondering whether the watchers would allow them to cross the lawn to the edge of the estate's working fields. A second later she remembered: there were no watchers, ready to herd her back to the house—or drag her there, if need be—if she strayed too far.

A heady sense of freedom filled her, made her feel as light as if she were floating above the earth in one of those new Montgolfier balloons. 'Yes, let's go see the wheat.'

James set off at a trot, and she kept pace beside him. After a moment, tentatively, she reached for his hand. Eagerly, he grasped her fingers and together, they skipped over the uneven surface towards the golden sheaves beckoning in the distance.

Arriving, James realised the stalks blocking their path to the far-away tree line were nearly as tall as he was.

'Look, Mama, it's like the maze in the park we went to in the city.'

The Sydney Gardens maze had fascinated James and his friend Robbie, who had been taken there by kindly Uncle Alastair.

'Can we walk through it?'

'It's not cut in a pattern like the one in the city,' she explained. 'But I suppose we could walk down some of the rows, as long as we're careful not to harm the plants. This part…' she pulled a stalk closer and showed the kernels to James '…is ground into flour for bread.'

'Come, Mama, you walk down that row and I'll walk down this one.'

Amused by his imagination in turning a common farm planting into a playground, Diana agreed. For a few moments they walked parallel, before with a giggle, James darted several rows away. 'Come find me, Mama!' he shouted.

Warmed by the afternoon sun and her son's innocent enthusiasm, Diana walked along, peering through the sheaves and calling his name, pretending she couldn't find him, then bounding across the few rows separating them to seize him. His shrieks of laughter as she caught and released him made her laugh, too.

'Again, Mama!' he pleaded.

For a surprisingly enjoyable interval, Diana searched and pounced as James ran about, hiding among the wheat. When at last she told him they must return to the house, so they might arrange the flowers they'd picked into vases before they wilted, he'd protested.

She'd given him no more than a warning look before he instantly capitulated. 'Don't get angry, Mama. I'll go back. Minnie says I mustn't tease you, and I don't mean to.'

Another pang of sorrow for time and circumstance lost went through her. She couldn't ever remember worrying about 'teasing' her father with her questions or her presence—he had always had time for her. How many years had the nursemaid been protecting her son from the seemingly harsh scrutiny of his parents?

But time and circumstance were different now, and she meant for James to benefit from it.

'I know you weren't trying to tease me. There's a treat for you before we go back to the house, too. Shall we go see what it is?'

He brightened instantly. 'A treat! Is it ices?'

'No, but something I think you'll like even better.'

'I don't know,' he said solemnly. 'There's practically nothing as good as ices.'

As she had suspected, once they arrived at the stables, ices were forgotten in his delight with the mother dog and her pups.

'Mrs Ransleigh said you may choose one of the puppies to be your dog for our visit,' she told him.

'Can I? A dog for my very own?'

She nodded. 'You won't be able to bring it to the nursery; he or she is too young yet and must stay with the mama. Which one would you like?'

James took his time, his little face serious as, with a grinning groom's assistance, he held and examined each spaniel—until a brown-and-white-spotted puppy with fly-away ears stretched up to lick him on the nose. Drawing away at first in alarm, he then leaned forward to get another lick. 'I think this one is choosing me!'

'I believe you are right. What shall you name him?'

'How about Pebbles? He has little brown spots just like the pebbles I threw in the puddles.'

'Very well. You must say goodbye to Pebbles now, but we can visit him again tomorrow.'

Before setting the dog down, James lowered his face for another enthusiastic round of puppy kisses. 'He likes me, Mama!' James exclaimed with a giggle. 'I like living here. Can we stay for ever?'

Diana opened her lips, then closed them, the worry over their future that always hovered just out of mind surfacing at that remark. She didn't want to spoil her son's enjoyment by correcting his innocent assumption that Barton Abbey was now their home.

'Mrs Ransleigh is a very kind lady, isn't she?' she evaded.

'Oh, yes! She came to the nursery after Minnie found the soldiers and showed us where to get more. And she brought some teacakes Cook had just made. They were almost as good as ices.'

'I hope you thanked her politely.'

'Oh, I did! I told her she could bring me cakes any time.'

Diana grinned at his artless self-confidence. Oh, that she might share it about their future!

She wasn't sure where their eventual home would be, though it almost certainly wouldn't be Barton Abbey. As long as it was somewhere they could be together, beyond the Duke's reach, she would be content. She trusted Alastair to strike as good a bargain as he could for them; he'd also promised she would no longer have to be afraid—and she was trying to believe him.

But for now, until that eventual fate revealed itself, she vowed to be more like James, pushing aside worry about what the future held—with or without Alastair—and enjoying the respite he and his mother had given her. To breathe free and run through the fields, to get to know her son better, to read books, make conversation, paint and reacquaint herself with the pianoforte.

Her son was not the only one who was finding Barton Abbey a wonderful refuge, she thought as she followed him into the house.

A week later, after a futile stop in London, Alastair finally tracked his cousin down at Salmford House, the small estate Will had purchased in Sussex. Arriving in mid-afternoon, he was shown to the library, where the butler told him the master was going over the estate books.

'Alastair!' Will exclaimed with delight as the butler announced him. 'What an unexpected pleasure! Tate, would you bring some wine and see if Cook can scare up some meat and cheese? If I know my cousin, after the ride in, he'll be famished.'

Turning back to Alastair as the butler bowed himself out, he said, 'I didn't think we'd see you until we returned to London. Much as she loves Paris, Elodie needed some time here in her gardens before heading back to the city.'

'I did look for you there first, but no matter. A trip to Salmford is always a pleasure. Everything is well, I trust?'

Will nodded. 'It's always better when Elodie can bring Philippe to England with her. She's had her son back such a short time, she's never truly easy when he's out of her sight. Luckily, she was able to persuade the *comtesse* to let him accompany us on this trip. What brings you here?'

'Have you heard nothing?'

'About you? No. What have you got yourself into this time? Max didn't mention a word when we stopped to see him in Kent.' He shook his head. 'It seems I need to add to my network of informants. What is it?'

Well aware of Will's dislike of the woman who'd broken their engagement, he warned, 'Before I tell you, you must promise to reserve judgement until you've heard the whole.'

Will's grin faded. 'Must be serious indeed, if you're issuing such a warning to me, the most affable of men. Forget the wine, this calls for brandy.' Motioning Alastair to a chair, he walked to the decanter on the desk and poured them each a glass.

Seating himself again, he faced his cousin. 'Very well, begin.'

Alastair did. Though some thundercloud expressions darkened Will's face during the recitation, he honoured his promise and made no comment as Alastair related once again the reasons behind Diana's rejection of his suit, her ongoing battle of her marriage, and the new fight with her husband's heir.

Will's silence continued for some time after Alastair finished his account. Knowing he would not win approval by pressing Will, Alastair stifled his impatience and sipped his brandy, waiting while his cousin reflected on all he'd been told—and mentally trying to construct an alternate plan for thwarting the Duke, if Will refused to help him.

At long last, Will sighed. 'The tale is spectacularly unbelievable—which, I suppose, is the strongest recommendation for its truth. In any event, since I ended up marrying the woman I swore to drag back to England, to the gallows, if that proved necessary to vindicate Max, I suppose I don't have room to object to your championing the lady who injured you.'

'The story is hard to accept, I admit. Swallow that whole for a moment, and while it digests, let's move on to what we need to do now. Something I think you'll find much more palatable.'

'Something has to be done?' Will said with a grin. 'That does sound promising.'

'I called on Graveston to try to impress on him his responsibilities to his father's widow. Far from being convinced, he announced his intent to broadcast his suspicion that his father did not die of natural causes; he intends to accuse Diana of his murder.'

Will's eyebrows flew up. 'Has he any grounds?'

'Beyond his wish to punish her, not really. It's a ridiculous accusation that, were he anyone else, would probably be laughed at by local authorities. But because of his rank, he would probably be able to force an investigation. He seems certain he can find witnesses to support his version of events.'

'Or buy some?' Will interjected drily.

'I see you have as much confidence in the reliability of our legal system's evidence-gathering methods as I do,' Alastair replied acerbically. 'Now that I've had time to think about it, having his father buried already probably works in his favour. The coroner may well conclude there would be no purpose in exhuming the body, as it would be too late to find any evidence.'

'Either to prove—or more importantly, to disprove the charges,' Will said, shaking his head. 'I saw evidence enough during my years on the streets of how the law supports the mighty,' he added, his tone turning bitter. 'Boys transported because a shop owner claimed they stole bread, innocent men imprisoned over evidence from thief-takers intent upon winning a reward. So, what do we do to defend your lady?'

'Since I am too well known to be of much use, what *you* can do is more important. I'd like you to go to Wickham's End, the village nearest Graveston Court, and hang about. See what you can nose out from the locals about the old Duke's death, his relationship with his heir—anything of interest you can find. Anything we could use to persuade the heir not to drag Diana into a sordid public battle.'

'If it comes to that, we could buy witnesses of our own,' Will pointed out.

Alastair laughed. 'Yes, that's the rogue I need! I knew I could count on your expertise. But I'd prefer it not come to a trial.'

Will nodded. 'So you want me to poke about, see what I can find that might persuade His High-and-Mightiness not to move forward with charges? Excellent! I have to admit, though the give and take of bargaining on wine lots is exciting, much of the negotiation over trading rights between the Crown and our new French allies is damnably dull. I shall relish a bit of an adventure.'

'There's probably one more thing I should tell you.'

Will raised an eyebrow. 'Why is there always one more thing?'

'The Duke also threatened me. He had Diana watched, and so discovered that, very soon after she fled Graveston Court for Bath, we…began a relationship. He advised me to keep my distance, warning that if I intervened to help her, he would drag me into this, claiming that I'd encouraged her to do away with her husband so she might take up with the man who'd once been her lover.'

'The cad!' Will exploded. 'There'd be immense satisfaction in thwarting him just because he's a duke—but now, it's personal. No one can get away with threatening one of the Rogues. But devil's teeth, Alastair,' he added in exasperated tones, 'you certainly led straight into the Duke's trump suit with that play!'

'Well, I wouldn't have, had either of us any idea there was a game on. Or maybe not,' he admitted. 'Once I saw her again, once she approached me, the…need to be with her, to try to finish what had been between us, would have been too strong to resist, whatever the danger.'

Will studied him for a moment. 'Am I allowed to ask whether this *will* end once and for all what was between you?'

'You can ask,' Alastair said with a sigh. 'I just don't have an answer yet—and not because I'm trying to fob you off. It's impossible, of course, to recapture the innocence of the passion we shared eight years ago. Too much has happened, to both of us. This business with the Duke interfered before I'd been with her long enough to decide whether this was the bittersweet epilogue to something ended long ago, or the start of…something new. Either way…she's still in my blood. But all I mean to concentrate on right now is seeing her safe from his bullying—she and her son, whom, by the way, the Duke is also trying to take away from her so he may make the boy suffer. I'll worry about what happens next afterward.'

'He'd vent his pique on a child?' Will said in disgust. 'He truly is a piece of work! You do realise if the Duke continues to be unreasonable about this, there is no way, short of kidnapping and transportation—which I might be induced to attempt on a man vile enough to prey upon a defenceless woman and an innocent child—to prevent him from making the accusations public, however groundless they may be. You know how London loves a scandal. The demise of a duke, accusations against the widow, an illicit affair with a former lover when the earth has scarcely settled over her late husband's grave—the penny press would make a fortune! Not that anyone who knows you would credit your being involved in such a scheme, but the hullabaloo might seriously damage your reputation. You are sure you want to do this?'

Alastair looked at his cousin incredulously. 'You don't truly think I'd turn tail and abandon a woman— any woman—to face slander and intimidation alone, after walking her into it?'

'If you did, we'd have to ceremonially break your sword and drum you out of the Rogues,' Will agreed. 'I just wondered if, in your zeal to right this wrong, you fully understood the risk.'

Alastair shrugged. 'If we fail, and scandal is the result, so be it. After years of snubbing virtuous young maidens in favour of actresses, widows and matrons of dubious character, my reputation isn't that shiny-bright anyway. Whether the Duke's vendetta succeeds or fails, if he convinces the Court of Chancery to give him custody of the boy, I'll take them abroad. But I have a high regard for your powers of discernment and invention. If anyone can figure a way to pressure Graveston into reconsidering his attack, it's you.'

Will made a bow. 'Many thanks for the vote of confidence. Have you thought of speaking to our uncle? In case the Duke does manage to intimidate the local authorities into pressing forward to a trial?'

'I don't imagine the Earl would receive me with much enthusiasm. Last time we spoke, I left him in a cold fury for not defending Max—though I wasn't bold enough to take him to task for not supporting his son during the scandal.'

'Then you'll be happy to know Max and his father have reconciled,' Will informed him. 'Max told me when we stopped at Denby Lodge on our way from Paris. Not that the Earl admitted he'd been wrong not to embrace Max's cause, but he did apologise.'

'He apologised?' Alastair echoed incredulously. 'Wish

I could have heard that! Maybe he's mellowing, now that Max has produced a grandson.'

Alastair fell silent, thinking furiously. He'd not meant to approach his uncle unless absolutely necessary—but if the Earl had belatedly developed some family feeling, perhaps he should rethink that decision. Someone of the Earl's wide-ranging influence could be tremendously helpful in squelching whatever scandal the Duke could dredge up.

'Maybe I will consult him. I'd like his support, but even if he won't offer that, if yet another Ransleigh cousin is about to stir up a hornet's nest of trouble that might come buzzing into the Lords, I should give him a warning before he gets stung.'

'A good precaution. About your lady... I don't think any man can offer truly useful advice on a matter so individual but...let me just say this. Regardless of the scandal that might ensue, if you can't envisage life without her, don't give her up. The Earl's displeasure, the censure of those who know your name but not the man, the vast titillation you'd provide for Society's tattle-mongers—none of that matters a pin. To build a life with Elodie, I was willing to risk a break with everyone—even the Rogues, and you know how much all of you mean to me. If what you feel for Diana is that strong, the Rogues will stand by you—regardless of our initial doubts about the lady. And if she must flee England to keep her son, bring her to us in Paris.

'But enough of melodrama,' Will pronounced before Alastair could get past the lump in his throat to thank him. 'Let me pour you another glass while I put my reprobate brain to formulating a plan for evidence-gathering. I shall also have to think of an excuse to put off Elodie, lest she try to come along and keep a watchful eye over me.'

'You think she might be induced to visit Barton Abbey instead?' Alastair asked, taking another sip of his brandy. 'Mama would enjoy seeing her, and Diana's son is of an age with Philippe. James, I'm sure, would love to have another boy to explore with.' He gave a short laugh. 'Though Mama's come round to supporting Diana, I don't think my sister Jane has yet forgiven me enough for taking back up with her to lend me Robbie.'

'If I can convince Elodie I don't need her to guard my back, you could probably persuade her to visit. Our being safe and together, like her recovering Philippe, is still so new, we're hesitant to be apart. Though she was a full participant during our adventures on the road from Vienna to Paris, I think she views disguise and subterfuge as unfortunate necessities, rather than tricks that add spice to the game.'

'Still the same Wagering Will,' Alastair observed with a grin. 'Your journey being a continuation of the sleight-of-hand spectacles you organised at Eton to earn pennies? No, don't tell me—I'm probably better off not knowing. I always thought, though, you enjoyed the thrill of besting the other boys—and the risk of punishment if you were discovered—more than the meat pasties you bought with your earnings.'

'Spoken like a true privileged son, who's never known what it is to be hungry!' Will shot back, though Alastair noted he did not disagree. 'Elodie is looking for activities to amuse Philippe, so he will be as eager to accompany us on our trips back to England as she is to have him with us. I'm sure she'd be delighted for Philippe to make an acquaintance he can look forward to renewing each time we return.'

'Beginning a new generation of Ransleigh Rogue cousins?'

'Something like,' Will agreed. 'You can ask her your-self at dinner. You will stay a few days, won't you?'

'Just the night. Diana will be anxious,' he explained to Will's murmur of disapproval. 'I want to reassure her you will soon be in place, with our plan under way, and I think I'll take your advice and consult our uncle in London before I return to Barton Abbey.'

Will whistled. 'Your case must be serious indeed, if you'd rather face our censorious uncle than go rousting about with me.'

'If I thought I could be useful slinking about Wickham's End with you, I'd go without hesitation. But as someone once pointedly informed me that I look and act too much like a "privileged son of wealth" to pass unnoticed, I'd better leave subterfuge to the master.'

'Probably wise. I do understand the need to do everything you can for someone you've pledged to protect, so I'll not tease you any further. You'll want to change out of the dust of the road before dinner; Susan will show you to a bedchamber. Did you bring your valet?'

'No, I hired horses and brought only a portmanteau. Despite the awful paces of some of the job nags, it was the fastest way.'

'I'll send Maurice up; he'll fit you out in something of mine—we're enough of a size.' Will shook his head, a rueful smile on his face. 'Oh, the necessities of presenting a proper appearance in official circles! Cor, if any of me mates from Seven Dials could see me now—a regular toff, with a French valet!'

Chuckling, Alastair downed the rest of his brandy. 'I'll see you at dinner, then.'

'At dinner. And then, as quickly as I can run to ground the situation at Graveston Court, I'll report to you back at Barton Abbey.'

* * *

Following the maid towards the guest bedchamber, Alastair took a deep breath. Had Will not agreed to help him, he would have come up with some other way to pressure the Duke into dropping his plans for revenge. But he couldn't deny the vast uplift to his spirits, knowing that his ingenious—and if necessary, ruthless—cousin would be working for them.

He was nearly certain, given the long estrangement between Blankford and his sire, there was some animosity that could be turned to their advantage. With Will to sniff it out, he was more confident than ever their plan would prevail.

Then, with Diana safe, he could return to figuring out what the future might hold for them.

Chapter Eighteen

Four days later, on a late autumn afternoon whose crisp wind gave a foretaste of the winter to come, Diana stood at her easel in one of the north-facing parlours, a bowl of blooms set out on the table before her. For years, she'd only observed the colours of nature, barred by her defiance of Graveston from access to the supplies that would let her reproduce them on canvas. Now that she'd got a brush back in her hands, she found herself increasingly fascinated by the play of light over the vivid petals—rust and amber and coral, fading to ochre and chocolate in the shadows. At least twice daily, while morning and afternoon light lit the room to its brightest, she left James to his soldiers in the nursery and returned to her canvas.

'Beautiful hues—I like it.'

Her pulses leapt at the sound of Alastair's voice. Setting down the brush, she whirled around to find him standing in the doorway, smiling at her. Without further thought, she ran to him, leaning into his embrace as he took her in his arms.

'I've missed you,' he murmured into her hair.

'I've missed you, too,' she acknowledged, knowing as she said the words what an understatement they represented. Oh, how she'd missed him! His physical presence, his companionship—even the support she didn't wish to depend on but, from prudence and necessity, had accepted in order to prevail in the second-greatest challenge of her life.

With seeming reluctance, he set her at arm's length. 'I don't want to interrupt your work, but I did want you to know I was back. I expect you are anxious to know what transpired with Will.'

'I am. Can you tell me now?'

'I've estate business to tend, but it can wait until later. I'll have Wendell bring us some tea.'

He dispatched a hovering footman, then returned to take a seat beside her on the sofa. An almost tangible fire sparking between them, Diana found herself intensely aware of him.

A rapid series of images flashed through her mind—his mouth on her; his hands on her body; riding him, borne away on a tidal wave of pleasure. Heat flushed her face, spiralled through her body.

She looked up to see him watching her, an answering passion glittering in his eyes. With a little murmur, she angled her face up, her eyes drifting closed.

His kiss began gently, but rapidly turned hungry. Just as famished, she opened her mouth to him, her tongue urgent against his, then cupped his face and dragged him closer. Not until she almost succumbed to the impulse to work loose the buttons of his trouser flap so she might straddle him, right here in the parlour, did her brain manage to loosen the hold of her senses. Trembling, she broke the kiss.

She would have been embarrassed by her lack of control, if Alastair's breathing had not been as erratic as her own. 'How I miss Bath!' he said on a groan.

'Despite the necessity for it, I'm discovering that chastity is a good deal harder than I thought it would be,' she admitted. Shackled to a husband who neither aroused nor attempted to incite her desire, she hadn't realised, when she'd tumbled into an affair, how compelling and addictive passion could be.

'When we began this, I expected it would be of short duration, affecting only the two of us,' Alastair said, setting her gently back against the cushions. 'How wrong I was! But there's nothing for it now; I'll not abuse my mother's hospitality by forgetting myself again.'

'A wise resolution,' she said. 'Despite my reaction to the contrary, I entirely agree. Besides, I'm very concerned to hear what you've discovered.'

'Despite my reaction to the very great distraction you pose,' he said, running a fingertip along her lips, 'I'm very keen to give it.'

She'd closed her eyes on a sigh, savouring his touch, when Wendell arrived back with the tea tray. The ritual of pots, cups and cream gave them further opportunity for passion to cool while they sipped hot tea.

After Wendell bowed himself out, Alastair began. 'I'm happy to report Will has agreed to investigate at Wickham's End and Graveston Court. He'll pose as a pedlar; such a man, he told me, is welcome everywhere and can tease out the most interesting details while mesmerising the unwary with his shiny wares. He should be there by now, poking about to see what he can turn up.' Alastair laughed. 'If he finds no one else suitable, Will promised to hire us some witnesses, if circumstances require it.'

She grimaced. 'I hope it won't come to that—though I'm certain Graveston wouldn't hesitate to hire witnesses if *he* thinks it necessary.'

'There was one other favourable development. On

Will's recommendation, I stopped to see our uncle in London. I'd steeled myself to forewarn the Earl of the scandal that might turn up on his doorstep in the Lords, expecting to receive a proper jobation for getting myself into it. To my astonishment, he welcomed me with an apology for the harsh words we exchanged the last time we met, when I was defending Max's conduct in Vienna.'

'An apology?' Diana raised her eyebrows. 'As I recall, the Earl never apologised.'

Alastair laughed. 'Indeed! I couldn't have been more surprised if the stone dogs on the fireplace had leapt up and bit me. The Earl proceeded to explain that, after holding on by a single vote to the majority he'd ruled over in the Lords for thirty years, he'd realised that his decades of work could be wiped away in a few sessions—and that only what he accomplished with the family he'd ignored for so many years would live on. He said he regretted not having spent more time with us boys while we were growing up, and that he intends to change that now. Then, when I told him of your dilemma, he seemed positively enthusiastic. It appears he did not much like your late husband, and if the matter should make it to the Lords, found the idea of being able to put a spoke in the wheel of Graveston's son very attractive. He also pledged to tap his network of friends, acquaintances, and colleagues, if we have need of them.'

Diana felt a stir of excitement as a new thought occurred. 'Might he know any of the judges from the Court of Chancery?'

'Very possibly. With the Earl volunteering, not just to assist in the Lords, but to do whatever he can to prevent it coming to that, I'm more hopeful than ever that we can convince Graveston to give up his intention to harass or publicly accuse you. By the way, the Earl's last admonition was for me to bring you by to see him after all this is over.'

'Heavens! He has changed! I don't believe he even bothered to have me introduced when we were engaged!'

Alastair's smile faded. 'He was present at that political dinner the night you appeared in front of all of Graveston's guests wearing only your bruises for jewellery.'

She gasped as the memory of that evening's shame and desperation slashed through her like a sabre cut. 'He told you about the dinner?'

'No. Your former friend, Mary Ellington, now Lady Randolph, asked me to call on her in Bath. Not knowing we'd already met, and hoping to blunt any anger I might express if I encountered you, she told me about it. The Earl thought your bravery that night magnificent, as do I. But Heaven forfend, Diana, how could you have risked further angering a man who'd already brutalised you?'

'It wasn't bravery—not at all. Papa was gone, you were lost to me, and I hadn't yet borne James. I no longer cared what happened to me—and I wanted the world to know what kind of man Graveston was. I even taunted him when he came up later, furious.' She smiled grimly at the memory. 'The high-born Duke, who lost control and beat me like some gin-soaked labourer with a two-penny harlot. I'd thought it might incense him enough to finish me for good. Instead, it seemed to smite his pride; he never struck me again after that. Or perhaps it was the knowledge that beating me wouldn't make any difference.'

'Praise the Lord for that mercy, anyway,' Alastair spat out, a look of revulsion on his face. 'It sickens me that you were forced to live under his hand for years afterward. Well, soon you'll no longer need to fear the malice of a Duke of Graveston. With Will's help, and the Earl's if necessary, you will be free of their menace for ever.'

Reluctant as she'd been to reveal her tawdry circumstances, cautious as she knew she must remain about depending on help from anyone else, she couldn't help feeling a wave of relief and gratitude.

'Thank you for all you've done. Even now, it's difficult for me to place reliance on others, though I know you have only my best interests at heart. How can I resist, though, when you are risking your own reputation to protect mine?' she said, marvelling at the depth of his sense of honour and the strength of his resolve.

He gave her a wry smile. 'In a way, I should feel grateful for Blankford's nefarious scheme. If you hadn't needed to marshal every possible resource to protect your son, you'd probably never had confided in me—would you?'

'No,' she admitted, knowing it was true. Only desperation had pushed her to reveal the humiliating truth about her marriage that she would otherwise have carefully hidden.

'You would have pleasured me, held your innermost self aloof, and slipped away.' He shook his head. 'It scares me to think how close I came to losing you again without ever knowing you.'

'If Blankford ends up arm-wrestling you in the mud of a public scandal, you may be less sanguine about my asking for your help,' she retorted.

'Never,' he exclaimed, kissing her hands. 'I'm glad to assist you. Glad that you are allowing me to act for you. I can well imagine, after being forced and coerced and bullied for so long, it's hard to trust anyone but yourself.'

He gazed at her, an oddly expectant look on his face. Was he hoping she would deny it, assert that she was completely comfortable relying on him?

Much as she appreciated his efforts, she could not in honesty tell him that. Uncertain what to reply, she said, 'So now, we wait?'

The hopeful look faded from his eyes—and she feared she'd disappointed him. Tacitly accepting her evasion, however, he confirmed, 'Now, we wait. Will promised to come report as soon as possible. We may also have a visit from his wife, Elodie. The Frenchwoman who, you may remember, embroiled Max in the scandal that ruined his diplomatic career. Somewhere along the way from Vienna back to England, Will fell in love with her.'

'She must be quite a lady to hold Will's interest,' Diana said, grateful that he'd moved the conversation to less personal matters. 'As I recall, women always found him fascinating, and though he returned the favour, he was as fickle as the wind.'

'Yes, it's quite a love story, which I'll let her tell you when she visits. She also has a son a bit younger than James. I thought he'd enjoy having a playmate.'

'I know he would! It's so kind of you to think of him.'

'It's high time someone was kind to you both.'

Diana shook her head ruefully. 'Your mother seems to think so, too. Sometimes I feel I'm living in a dream! Paints and brushes at hand, an excellent pianoforte to play whenever I like, a library full of books to explore. Your mother shall be tossing me out of the house before long because I'm running through so many candles, staying up late to read. I keep thinking that one morning, I'll wake up and all this will vanish.'

'Be assured it will not.' He lifted her chin so she had to meet his gaze. 'The future is yours to determine, Diana. You'll never be constrained again.'

Though she still found it difficult to express her feelings, she made herself say, 'No matter how this turns out, I'll never forget it was you who thought to bring me the first paints I'd touched in seven years. You who lured me back to the piano bench. You who escorted me to the library at Barton Abbey and invited me to sample it.'

He shook his head. 'I still can't believe you existed for years without books, paints, music. How dull it must have been, with nothing to do all day but manage that vast house.'

She laughed shortly as another flood of bitter memories engulfed her. 'I didn't even do that.'

He raised his eyebrows and, flushing, she waved a dismissive hand, not wanting to admit the painful truth.

'Won't you explain, Diana? I want to understand. And I think, to move beyond the past, you must face it. I want to help. Won't you let me?'

Eight years of instinct pressed her to retreat, fall silent. But after a brief internal struggle, the sympathy in his gaze—and the memory of the sweet peace she'd found after confessing her dilemma about James—overcame her reserve.

Slowly she began. 'The Duke's first wife retained the sympathy of the staff, the housekeeper in particular. I admit, I made no attempt to take over the reins, but it probably would have been very difficult to pry them away, even had I wanted to.'

'Having spoken to Blankford, I can well imagine the hostility of anyone loyal to his mother. How did you occupy your time, then?'

'I was permitted needlework, since I expressed no fondness for it, and making garments for the poor was an approved occupation for the Duchess. I walked around the rooms, the Long Gallery, the garden. I *looked*—at the garden, the woods, the buildings, the tapestries, evaluating their textures and colours, imagining what paints

I would blend to reproduce their images, were I ever to paint again. I examined such grounds as I was permitted to stroll, noting plants I'd found with my father, ones he'd illustrated for his books and lectures.'

Once begun, she couldn't seem to halt the flood of words. 'I could sit or stand for hours, no doubt to the puzzlement of whichever menial had been assigned to trail me, listening in my head to Papa's analysis. Or in the house, I'd stare at some object, evaluating its shape in geometric terms, figuring how I would position it for sketching, where to place the lines of shading. Observed it as the light playing over it changed with the advancing hour, watching how it changed those patterns. Sometimes, if I passed by a book I'd enjoyed, I'd try to recall as much of its prose or verse as I could. And I spent a great deal of time training myself not to *feel*, or to at least be able to mask my emotions enough that *he* could not read my countenance and use my reactions against me. Quite an interesting and useful life,' she concluded bitterly.

In the next instant, anxiety seized her. Whatever had induced her to blather on so? Alastair must think her shallow, cowardly, despicable for allowing herself to exist in such a mocking echo of a life.

Wary, she looked up to see him studying her, but rather than disgust and condemnation, she read compassion in his gaze. 'I'm so sorry,' he said, lifting her hand to his lips for a kiss. 'Though I hesitate even to give such facile advice, you must try to leave all that behind you.'

For a moment, the relief that she had not alienated him held her speechless. 'I am trying,' she managed at length. 'After all those years at Graveston Court, Barton Abbey seems a wonderland. Like a starving man invited to a banquet, I hardly know what delight to taste first.'

He smiled. 'I'm so glad you are finding it so. But *are* you allowing yourself to *feel* delight?'

She nodded. 'I am, a little. It's still hard to believe that the things that bring me pleasure won't suddenly disappear again. But…I'm trying to believe it. Or I will, once all this is over.'

'Believe it, and believe also that it *will* soon be over. And then…'

Diana tensed. Would Alastair tell her what he envisaged for their future? Would he gently let her go—or ask her to remain his mistress? If he wanted that and more, could she possibly give him an answer now?

A knock sounded at the door, followed by the entrance of Mrs Ransleigh. 'I'm not disturbing you, I hope? Wendell just let me know you'd returned.'

'Not at all,' Diana told her, not sure whether she was relieved or disappointed by the interruption. She didn't want to think of a future without Alastair—but she wasn't sure, damaged as she still was, what she could offer him, beyond a temporary passion.

Would that be enough?

Alastair rose to give his mother a hug. 'Diana tells me you've been taking good care of her and James.'

'Indeed she is,' Diana confirmed.

'I'm so much enjoying her stay! James is delightful, and I've been grateful for her companionship. I even compelled her to play for me in the evening. I've missed hearing the pianoforte, with both your sisters now gone.' Mrs Ransleigh gave her a fond look. 'It's almost like having a daughter at home again. I must inform you, I've given her and James the run of house and invited them to stay as long as they like. And once this matter is resolved and it's safe for Diana to establish her own residence, I hope they will return to visit often.'

'Of course I approve.'

'Thank you, Mrs Ransleigh,' Diana said, touched by her kindness. 'It's been a long time since I lived with my father and felt like part of a family. It's something I very much wanted James to experience. I'll be forever grateful for your friendship.'

'As I esteem yours! But now, I must go check on dinner. I'm so glad you're safely home, Alastair. Will I see you both at table?

'Very good,' she said as they both nodded. 'I'll leave you to your chat. No naughtiness, now!' she added with a smile, waving a finger at them.

At the memory of the torrid kiss they'd shared, Diana blushed—and noted that Alastair's face reddened, too. 'I made you a promise, Mama, and I won't break it…no matter how tempting it might be.'

'You'd better figure out how you'll deal with it later,' came the enigmatic reply as with a wave of her fingers, Mrs Ransleigh glided out through the door.

Alastair looked back at her. 'I'd better go change out of my dirt. Mama isn't as much a stickler as my uncle, but she'd still not appreciate me leaving mud on her dining-room carpet.'

He bent to kiss her fingers, sending another sizzle of sensation through her. 'Mama's right. We will have to figure out what to do about this later, you know.'

Both delight and dread made her stomach churn. 'I know.'

'I won't tease you now, though. I'll see you at dinner.'

Diana watched him go. Their physical bond was, without question, as strong as ever. Would that be enough? And how long would it last?

She was trying hard not to depend on support which, once she was safe again, could well be withdrawn. She was trying not to hunger for the company of a man who, after having a husband who did everything possible to control, coerce, and deprive her, made it his task to indulge her, expand her horizons, and give her the freedom to choose her own destiny.

With complete freedom, what would that be?

She simply didn't know. She was, as she'd assured Alastair, just beginning to allow herself to experience happiness, while a love for her son, natural and unforced, seemed to increase with each interlude they spent together.

But she was still a long way from recovering from years of repressing all feeling, nor had she exorcised the demons left from her late husband's abuse. She'd shown she could be a mistress. She was not at all sure she could be more.

Well, she'd not tease herself either. For now, she must wait with what patience she could muster for resolution of the challenge from Graveston. Only then would she figure out what came next.

Chapter Nineteen

Two weeks later, the early morning sun a smouldering suggestion on the eastern horizon, Alastair was grabbing an early breakfast when Diana walked in.

Seeing him, she halted, her face lighting with a smile that made his heart swell in his chest.

'I thought you'd be gone by now. Your mother said last night you were meeting Hutchens today to visit some of the outlying farms.'

'Yes, and to arrange some assistance for one of the tenants. With crops about ready for harvest, the poor fellow fell off his barn roof and broke a leg. Hutchens has already talked with some of neighbours; today we'll arrange a schedule so they can work together to get all the fields harvested.'

'Will you be away the whole day?' she asked as she poured herself some coffee.

Alastair hoped he wasn't imagining the wistfulness in her tone. 'Much of it. What do you have planned?'

'The bouquets in the rooms need refreshing. I'll scour the cutting garden, then take James for a long tromp through the fields and see what plants we can find to augment them.'

Alastair smiled, remembering all the exploring through the woods and fields he'd done with his cousins. 'I'm sure he'll enjoy that. Barton Abbey is a wonderful place for an adventuresome boy.'

She nodded. 'Especially when he can bring his new puppy. I enjoy the walks, too. When we come across some interesting specimen, it recalls to me the particular plant-hunting expedition during which Papa first showed it to me. How he taught me to appreciate the lines and shapes of nature, as well as her colours. It's like getting a small part of myself back.'

'You'll bring your sketchbook?'

'Yes. James reminds me of Papa, too. It's not just a mother's prejudiced eye—he has a real knack for drawing. He seems to enjoy spending the time with me, sketching.' She sighed. 'He's missed out on so many simple things. Thanks to you, I'm beginning to make it up to him.'

'No, it's thanks to you, for thinking of them,' he corrected. 'You are a good mother, Diana.'

'I'm trying to be.' As her gaze traced his face, lingering on his lips, he felt heat rise within him.

She must have felt it, too, for she gave a little sigh. 'I am trying hard to be good—in many ways.'

His thoughts flew immediately to intimacy, and he had to suppress a groan. 'As are we both.' Then he grinned. 'I'd love to be "good" to you in a most different way, but that will be for later.'

'Oh, I hope so! Anticipation makes the heart grow fonder?'

'And other things,' he muttered. He rose and walked to her chair, fighting the urge to kiss her. She placed her hand on top of his, tracing the edge of his palm with her fingertip, setting his senses simmering, sparking his barely banked desire into flame.

'Witch,' he murmured when he could speak again.

'Wizard,' she replied, a little hitch in her voice. 'Sometimes doing the honourable thing is beastly difficult.'

'It won't be for much longer, sweeting. Once you are protected, settled with what is due you and James, we can move forward—to whatever you want.'

To his surprise, rather than looking relieved, her face clouded. 'I hope everything will transpire as you envisage it.'

'I'll never let you be hurt. You believe that, don't you, Diana?' He tilted her face up to gaze at him. 'I know with James in danger, you can't help worrying. But…try to be easy, won't you?'

She sighed. 'I will try. And I do trust you.'

He ought to go…but the desire to spend time with her while he could—and ease her apprehension—made him linger. 'I don't need to meet with Hutchens until later. How about I join you and James on your walk?'

'Do you have the time? I don't wish to pull you from your work.'

'I can spare an hour. And I know a few places an adventurous boy would enjoy visiting.'

To his delight, she chuckled, smoothing the worried creases from her brow. 'I'm sure you do! James would love to have you join us. He told me you've stopped by the nursery and played soldiers with him several times, which has quite won him over. I can't thank you enough for your kindness.'

'I enjoy spending time with him. He reminds me of Robbie.'

'Let me fetch him, then.'

'Finish your breakfast and we'll go up together.'

* * *

And so, after she'd nibbled her toast and sipped her coffee, they left the breakfast room and headed towards the nursery. As they climbed the stairs, Alastair felt an odd sense of déjà vu.

So it should have been, he and Diana going up together to fetch their son.

Too late for that, he thought, hauling back on the reins of his fantasy. *And too soon yet*, he reminded himself, *to picture anything for the future.*

As Diana had predicted, James was delighted to add him to their excursion. 'Are we going to explore the gatehouse, like you promised?' James asked after they'd descended the stairs and exited the house.

'We'll save that for a rainy day,' he replied, hoping they would be at Barton Abbey long enough for him to make good on his pledge. 'It's so lovely this morning, I thought we'd go to another special place.'

'Are we going to the woods?' James asked, skipping along beside him. 'Mama took me to the wheat field, but she wouldn't let me go all the way to the trees.'

'The woods are closer if you go this way, through the kitchen gardens,' he told them as he opened a gate into the walled enclosure.

'Mama and I walked here already,' James informed him. 'We picked the plants with smelly leaves.'

'The ones with fragrant leaves,' Diana corrected. 'Lavender, mint and rosemary, to add some scent to the bouquets,' she explained to Alastair.

Within a few moments, they'd traversed the neat arrangement of symmetrical beds filled with herbs and vegetables and reached the gate at the other side. Opening it, Alastair pointed to a path that set off into the woods beyond a border of shrubs. 'We're going that way.'

'What's there?' James asked. 'A treasure?'

'Of a sort,' Alastair replied. 'You'll see.'

'Let's hurry!' James cried, grabbing his hand and urging him forward.

'Steady on, wait for your mama,' Alastair said with a laugh. 'Ladies must walk at a more dignified pace. Their long skirts hinder them, you see.'

'Do they?' Diana said. 'Well, not this lady.' Raising her hem above her ankles, she took off at a trot while James, giggling, sped after her.

Chuckling himself, Alastair followed.

The trail twisted and turned among the trees before, several minutes later, it opened into a clearing. As they approached, the muted gurgle of water over stone announced the presence of a brook at the far side.

James rushed over. 'Mama, how pretty the water is! Can I go in?'

'Not yet,' Alastair said. 'First we need to find the treasure, and you'll frighten it away if you splash.'

Putting a finger to his lips to signal the child to silence, he took his hand and led him along the bank to where the stream broadened into a shallow pool. Along its edges, several frogs swam lazily.

'Have you ever caught a frog?' Alastair whispered.

The boy's eyes widened. 'No. Can you show me how?'

'You have to be quick. Watch.'

Stealthily Alastair approached, careful not to let his shadow fall over the pool. After choosing his target, he crouched down, and with a quick lightning thrust, snatched up the unsuspecting amphibian.

The frog squirmed and wiggled, trying to escape Alastair's grasp. 'Do you want to hold it?' he asked the boy.

'Oh, yes!' James breathed.

Alastair took the boy's hand and wrapped it around the struggling frog. 'Careful, he's slippery. You must hold him firmly, but not too tight.'

'Oooh, he's soft—and squishy!' James exclaimed. 'Mama, look! I have a frog!'

'So I see,' she said with a smile.

'Can I take it back to the nursery?'

'Unlike your puppy, who would love to join you in your bed, the frog prefers his pond,' Alastair said. 'We'll leave him here—so you can catch him again next time.'

'Do you want to catch one, Mama?' James asked, motioning towards the frog's fellows who, while hopping a safe distance away, still remained in the shallows.

'Ladies don't like to get their shoes muddy—or their hands squishy,' Alastair told him.

Diana raised her eyebrows. 'Well, this lady isn't so pudding-hearted. I'll have you know that, on plant-gathering expeditions with my father—your grandpapa,' she told James, 'the one who taught me to draw—I've caught any number of frogs.'

'Really, Mama? You know how?' James asked, awed.

'Really?' Alastair echoed, grinning at her.

She narrowed her eyes at him. 'I think I recognise a challenge when I hear one. Very well. *Attention*, Monsieur Grenouille!' Pushing up the sleeves of her pelisse, she walked to the edge of the pool.

'Don't fall in,' Alastair advised.

Ignoring him, she manoeuvred around a tree stump and crouched behind a big rock, eyeing her prey. Then, with a speed equal to Alastair's, she lunged forward, capturing a fat bullfrog before he could leap away.

'You did it, Mama!' James shrieked, almost dropping his own frog in his excitement.

'Bravo!' Alastair applauded. 'I'm impressed.'

'Would you like to hold it?' Diana asked Alastair in dulcet tones belied by the twinkle in her eye. When he demurred, she said, 'Shall we put them back, James, so they may swim for a while? Being held is very tiring for a frog.'

'Must I?'

'You can chase another one later. Why don't we sit here on the bank and watch them?'

With a sigh, James carefully lowered his frog to the water, where it leapt free and swam away. Diana pulled him to sit in front of her, smoothing his hair.

'Was this like the time you told me about,' he asked, leaning against her, 'when you went looking for plants with your papa and fell in the brook?'

'Yes, it was very like this.' To Alastair's look of enquiry, she explained, 'We'd gone hunting marsh irises. When I found one, I got so excited I slipped and fell in. Papa came to pull me out, scolding—but he slipped and fell in, too.' She smiled. 'We both started laughing, splashed water at each other, and then he wrapped me in his coat and carried me home for tea.'

'Well, if you fall in today, I promise to wrap you in *my* coat and carry you back,' Alastair said.

'Me, too?' James asked.

'Of course, you, too.'

'Good.' James snuggled back against his mother, who handed him a pebble to throw into the stream. 'You're Robbie's Uncle Alastair, aren't you?'

'Yes,' Alastair answered, puzzled by the question. Surely the boy hadn't forgotten him? 'We went for Sally Lunn cakes in Bath, you'll remember.'

'Oh, yes. They were very good. I just wondered, are you anyone's papa, too? 'Cause you'd be the bestest one.

You know about cakes and soldiers and frogs and everything.'

Alastair swallowed hard. *I might have been yours.* 'No, I'm not a papa...yet.'

'Mama says my papa's gone to Heaven and I won't see him any more.'

'I know. I'm sorry. I imagine you miss him.'

The boy shrugged. 'I never saw him much. Minnie said he was a great man and had much important business. He didn't have time for soldiers or cakes or frogs.'

'Then he missed something much more important,' Alastair said sharply, his bitterness towards the Duke expanding to include the outrage of a little boy ignored. 'Spending time with you.'

James gazed up at him. 'You think I'm important?'

'Very important.'

The boy's face broke into a smile. 'Good. 'Cause I think you're important, too. Isn't he, Mama?'

Diana looked over at him, her expression tender. 'He is indeed.'

For an instant, the stream, the child, the bird chatter and brook gurgle faded. All Alastair could see, could feel, was Diana, smiling at him, her face no longer tense and guarded, but open, almost innocent. As he remembered it from all those years ago.

'Mama, look!'

Startled out of his reverie, Alastair watched the boy scramble down the bank. 'Is this the plant you found with your papa?' he asked Diana, pointing to a wildflower covered in tiny white blossoms.

'No, marsh irises bloom in the spring. That's a wood aster.'

'It's so pretty! It looks like stars!'

The words seemed to spring from somewhere deep

within him. 'All the wonder of a starry sky/held in two small hands.'

'Lovely,' Diana said. 'Is that from a poem?'

He shrugged. 'Perhaps the beginning of one.'

'I hadn't thought to ask how your writing has gone. Interrupted by the army, I would imagine, but I should think you'd have completed several volumes of verse by now.'

'Actually, I haven't written since... Not for a long time.'

'Well, you should. You're a wonderful poet! If you considered it a travesty that I haven't painted for years, it's even more so for you not to be writing.'

'Can we pick some of the flowers? For the bouquets?' James was asking.

'That would be lovely. Maybe some of those ferns, too.'

As he watched them gather the plants, Diana looking as carefree as he remembered her from long ago, he thought the day could not be more perfect.

A long-forgotten warmth and tenderness expanded his chest until he felt he might burst with the fullness of it. Thick and sweet as honey, it suffused him, seeping into every cold and bitter crevice of his soul.

The intensity of it brought tears to his eyes.

With a sudden shock, he recognised the emotion: joy. Something he had not experienced in all the years since Diana had jilted him to marry Graveston.

In another sweeping flash of insight, with the words to follow the lines he'd quoted churning and bubbling beneath the surface, he realised that he'd not given up poetry because it was juvenile, or had no place in the army. That inclination, like joy, had died when he lost Diana.

Mesmerised, he watched mother and child, awed by

the wonder of it, swept away by the power of the emotion gripping him. The sun seemed warmer, the crystalline blue of the sky brighter, the breeze on his forehead softer. As if all his life, from then until now, had been lived under clouds, until Diana returned to dissipate them and bring him once again into full sunlight.

He'd known that Diana's years with Graveston had taught her to lock away her feelings. But he saw now that without her, he, too, had bottled up or suppressed his emotions. The restlessness, the unresolved anger, the fact that in no place and with no other woman had he found fulfilment, were mute testimony to a soul in bondage, waiting for the one catalyst that could set him free.

Diana. In some fashion beyond logic or reason, she… completed him. Made him whole again.

Savouring the joy, he knew in that moment that, whatever it took, however long it took, he had to win her back. He couldn't return to life in the shadows.

To win her, though, he'd have to help her find her own way back to the light. And once she was free of the ghosts of her past, he couldn't let her go.

In a daze, distracted by his new insights, he took the flowers and ferns the two had gathered, escorted them back to the kitchen garden and found them a trug to hold their bounty, then bid them goodbye and went off to find the estate agent.

He rode about the estate with Hutchens, setting up assistance for the injured farmer, consulting with other tenants about the harvest, but while he said and did what was necessary, his mind hovered around the imperative of saving Diana, loving her, and having her back in his life.

It had been two weeks now; if Will didn't show up soon, he'd break down and go hunting for him.

It would be satisfying to confront Blankford directly.

Alastair wished he might invent some pretext for challenging him, so he might get his fists on the man. Though, in his estimation of Blankford's character, the Duke probably didn't possess the physical courage to meet someone truly his match. He'd rather harass defenceless women, Alastair thought with scorn.

Well, Diana was one woman no Duke of Graveston would ever harass again. The sooner that business was done, the sooner he could begin his campaign to woo her back into his life.

Chapter Twenty

Fading daylight was turning the gold of the ripening fields to amber as Alastair rode back to the barns. After turning his mount over to a groom, he walked back to the house, his pace increasing, eager to wash, change, and seek out Diana.

Just thinking about seeing her made his heart leap with anticipation.

As he approached the side entrance, a carriage drove past him towards the stables. Excitement shocked through him. Might Will be back? Changing course, he sped towards the main entry.

To his delight, he did indeed find his cousin and his lovely, dark-haired wife in the hall, where his mother was embracing a little boy who looked a bit younger than James.

'Alastair, only see who Will has brought to visit us!' his mother cried as he ascended the steps. 'Elodie and Philippe! Well, young man,' she addressed the child, 'there's a boy here—and a puppy—who will be most happy to meet you!'

'C'est ma tante—et mon cousin?' the boy asked, pointing to Mrs Ransleigh and Alastair.

'*Oui*, Philippe, but you must practise your English now,' his mother said. 'Alastair, how good to see you again.'

'And you, Elodie. You're looking very well! Living in Paris must agree with you.'

'Paris is my heart, but it is my garden at Salmford that refreshes me, as my loving husband knows.'

'Let Wendell show you to your rooms, so you can get settled!' his mother said. 'Perhaps we can meet for wine and light refreshments before dinner, so our two young boys can become acquainted?'

'That would be lovely, Tante Grace,' Elodie replied. 'Philippe, *viens avec Maman.*'

'I'll be up in a moment,' Will said, squeezing his wife's hand before releasing her to ascend the stairs behind Wendell, while the boy trotted after her, gazing about this new dwelling with unselfconscious curiosity.

'I know you've been anxious, but I thought I'd stop long enough to bring Elodie and her son with me. Let the ladies and the boys get acquainted, while I let you know where things stand. Shall we talk now, or later?'

'Now—once I find Diana. I couldn't discuss what concerns her so nearly without her present.'

'She's like Elodie, then,' Will said. 'Not one to put up with men making decisions for her.'

'After what she endured at her husband's hands, one can hardly blame her. Even if she does trust us.'

'As I recall from years ago, she was always lively and spirited, discussing, with the expertise and directness of a man, topics far removed from the normal feminine concerns.' Will shook his head and laughed. 'A horse-breeder, a French exile, a maligned duchess? We Ransleighs do seem to find unusual women.'

'Truly! Let me go fetch this one. Shall I meet you in the library? If she's where I suspect, I'll be back directly.'

He did indeed find Diana at her easel in the north parlour she'd taken over as her studio. As she looked up upon his entry, he said abruptly, 'Will's back.'

Her eyes widened and she gasped. 'Did he tell you—?'

'Not yet. I thought you'd want to be there to hear his account, too.'

'I would, thank you. Shall I come now?'

He nodded. Hastily pulling off the apron that protected her gown, she tossed it beside the easel and walked to him. 'I'll worry about cleaning paint off my fingers later. Did he…give you any hint of what occurred?'

'No. But he tarried long enough to collect his wife and her son. If something were amiss, I think he would have come directly here.'

He held out his hand, and with a shuddering breath, she took it. 'I hope so.'

He gave her fingers a reassuring squeeze. 'Remember, whatever he has to report, I will make sure you and James are safe.' *Safe and with me*, he added silently.

She gave him a slight smile. 'I do trust you. I just don't want to put you at risk—again.'

'You won't. Not this time.'

They found Will in the library, lounging in one of the leather wing chairs, sipping his brandy. He scrambled to his feet as they entered.

And made Diana a deep bow. 'Duchess,' he said, his face unreadable.

A tiny frown came and went on her forehead. 'Never that. Once it was "Will" and "Diana". I'd prefer that, if you please.'

They stared at each other, Diana standing erect and unflinching under Will's hard, assessing gaze. Alastair held his breath, hoping what he'd told Will and what his cousin had learned at Graveston Court would triumph over any anger his cousin still harboured towards Diana for the anguish she'd caused him—and those who cared about him.

After a moment, apparently satisfied, Will nodded. 'Diana, then, if I'm to be Will again.'

'I would like that—if you can bear it.'

'From what I've discovered, it is you who had much to bear.'

'Please proceed, Will,' Alastair said. 'And leave out no detail.'

After motioning them to a seat, Will began. 'I arrived at Wickham's End in my guise as pedlar two days after Alastair left Salmford, bringing along two of my men, posing as horse-traders, in case I needed reinforcement. After taking a bed at the local public house, I proceeded to the taproom and announced, with some boasting about my wares, that I'd be making rounds of any interested households. Of course, they all were.'

'Played a few hands of cards, too, I'd guess,' Alastair interjected.

'Naturally. How else could a poor pedlar afford a room? While I won a little, lost a little, I got to hear all the local gossip. Since the death of a duke and the arrival of his heir were the most significant events to occur in that small village for a decade, talk soon turned to that.'

'What did you learn?' Diana asked.

'They'd heard nothing of the sort immediately after the old Duke's demise, but more recently, someone had been going about, stirring up rumours. Some said the new Duke's man was asking for witnesses, saying the

Dowager Duchess might be complicit in her husband's death. Opinion seemed divided over the possibility. Some said she was a cold woman, not properly submissive to her husband. Others denied that, telling of a friend or relation who'd received clothing or baskets of food from her, and argued it was she who'd done the most to share the Duke's wealth with the community. All knew Graveston as a hard, proud, unapproachable man.' Will laughed. 'One said "if his lady done him in, he probably deserved it".'

'And then what?' Alastair asked, impatient to get to the crux of the story.

'I made my rounds in town, then to some of the tenant farmers—where I had my first break. Gossiping while admiring a trinket she couldn't afford, the farm wife said her no-good brother-in-law was boasting of doing some work for new Duke, that was going to set him up right—serving as a witness against the old Duchess, who was for murdering her husband. It was the work of an afternoon to track down this Jamie Peters and invite him to share a pint. A few hands of cards and a great quantity of gin later, he confided he was to testify that he'd bought large amounts of laudanum for the Dowager Duchess, who told him she was going to slip a little more each day into the old Duke's food unnoticed.'

'The scoundrel!' Alastair exploded.

'You see?' Diana cried, grim-faced. 'I knew Blankford would do whatever it took to incriminate me.'

Will held up a hand. 'Calm down—I'm not finished yet. I asked Mr Peters if he was aware of the penalties for perjury. Painted a vivid picture of prison hulks, transportation and hanging. After giving him a moment to digest that, I suggested if he wanted cash, I would give him more than the Duke was offering if he would shut his mouth and resettle in another area of England. After some…encouragement, he was persuaded to take my money and leave.'

'Encouragement?' Alastair repeated, his eyebrows raised.

'Well, I might have suggested my sword could make short work of a man who'd shred a woman's reputation and risk her life for a handful of coins. I had one of my men escort him to Falmouth, so he might take ship and start a new life in the Americas. Farewell, incriminating witness.'

'Bravo!' Alastair cried.

'There's more. I also persuaded Peters to give me the names of the household staff who were supposedly assisting him and the Duke in their nefarious enterprise. During a trip to show off my wares at Graveston Court, I found all those he named owed their positions to the previous housekeeper, a Mrs Heathson, who just happened to be recently reinstated into her former position by the new Duke.'

'Tall, dark-haired, hatchet-faced?' Alastair asked. When Will raised his eyebrows, he explained, 'I encountered her when I called on Graveston.'

'I then paid a visit to Mrs Forbes, the displaced housekeeper, who, by the way, was turned off without a character and no settlement of wages by the new Duke. She'd gone to stay with the retired governess, eking out a living doing hand work. She told me the old Duke had hired her after the previous housekeeper, fanatically loyal to the Duke's first wife, nearly killed the second wife with overdoses of laudanum when the girl was being "sedated for a nervous condition".'

Will looked over at Diana. 'Nervous condition? I never thought you nervous in your life.'

'When you attempt to leave your husband, are dragged back from the posting inn by his minions and locked into your room, it can make you nervous,' she said bitterly.

Will's face hardened. 'I can well imagine. Mrs Forbes said all sorts of rumours flew around among the staff as the Duchess recovered, though none dared say or do anything for fear of losing their position. Some seemed sympathetic to the Duchess. Others, siding with Mrs Heathson, gave her trouble the whole time she remained at Graveston Court. During that time, Mrs Heathson continued to visit Cook and her other friends among the staff, who often spent their off-days with her. Apparently she never sought another position; Mrs Forbes suspected that the heir, Lord Blankford, was paying her. She was convinced Blankford was also paying some of the disaffected staff to spy on the Duchess and the household. In fact, when the Duke was discovered dead, Mrs Forbes had her suspicions that Cook might have been hired—or persuaded—to do to the Duke the laudanum trick Mrs Heathson had tried with his wife. But within hours of the old Duke's death, Mrs Heathson returned to Graveston Court with a letter under Blankford's seal, informing Mrs Forbes she had been discharged and must leave immediately, or the sheriff would eject her. With no other recourse, she had little choice but to depart.'

'Would she be willing to testify to all of that in court?' Alastair demanded.

'Yes, particularly as she no longer has to fear retribution for her honesty. It seems she very recently received a, um, handsome bequest to keep her comfortably for the next few months—and the offer of a new position at a fine establishment in Sussex.'

'Remind me to reimburse you the bequest and the resettlement money,' Alastair said.

Will gave an airy wave of the hand. 'No need. Happy to be of service to a fellow Rogue.'

'Are there any others who would testify for Diana?'

'Mrs Forbes named three or four, who fear for their positions now that Mrs Heathson has returned—or just don't approve of her actions against the Duchess. They could also assert that all those accusing the Duchess were hostile to her, if not actually in Blankford's employ even before his father's death.'

'So the primary witness against Diana is now missing, and Mrs Forbes can testify to Mrs Heathson's dealings in laudanum and previous attempt against Diana and her involvement with disaffected members of household,' Alastair summarised.

'That's about it,' Will concluded.

'Excellent job, Will! Even if Blankford has the local magistrate in his pocket and can induce him to write out a warrant, the evidence would never stand in a summary trial, much less in the Lords.'

'Our uncle would see to that.'

'As it happens, I had a very surprising interview with the Earl,' Alastair said. 'After confessing to him we might soon be providing a spectacle with more scandalous twists and turns than a penny opera, I braced myself for a tongue-lashing—that never came. He seemed positively...friendly. It was quite unnerving.'

Will laughed. 'Max can hardly believe the change in his father.'

'We have enough evidence now to convince Graveston it would not be wise to proceed,' Alastair concluded, exultant. 'If he's irrational enough to go forward in any event, so be it. Good work, Will.'

'Did you expect anything less?' Will asked with a grin.

'No—I had full confidence.'

'We aim to please. I'll leave the two of you to plot strategy. I'm famished, and I could use a wash. Diana, it's good to have you back from the wilderness.'

Her eyes widened in surprise before she said, 'Thank you, Will. It's not quite the same, but I think I feel some of what you must have felt, transported from the street into the bosom of the Rogues.'

'We're a shifty lot, but loyal. We'll never let you down.'

'So I should have believed years ago, and spared all of you—this.'

Will gave her hand a pat. 'Wouldn't have missed it. We Rogues like nothing so much as a good fight. I'll see you at dinner.'

As Will walked out, Diana, who'd said nothing during Will's recitation beyond her one outburst, looked over to Alastair. 'Do you think it's enough?'

'More than enough for any sane, rational man. Is Graveston sane and rational?' He shrugged. 'Only he knows that. I'll press him hard, and we'll see.'

At her troubled look, he gave her a quick hug. Holding her at arm's length, willing her to share the confidence he now felt, he said, 'One way or the other, we can move forward. Graveston can force a scandal if he chooses, but your final vindication is not in doubt. Regardless, we'll stand by you, me and all my family. James will stay with you, where he belongs, and we'll fight for what is due both of you. You believe that, don't you?'

'Yes. Just…I have no confidence that Graveston *will* prove reasonable. I wish it could be settled without a fight—without the danger of scandal for you.'

'You heard Will,' Alastair replied with a smile. 'We Ransleighs relish a scrap.'

She shuddered. 'I'll pray for Graveston to be reasonable. When…will we go?'

'*I'll* go,' he corrected. 'Tomorrow. I've been itching to confront the man again since our previous encounter.'

'I thought we were to confront him together this time.'

'Only if the matter went to court. I think we have enough to break him and keep it from going that far… but if he sees you, it might revive his anger and harden his resolve.'

'I suppose you're right,' she said with a sigh.

'You trust me, don't you?'

'You know I do.'

'Besides, do you really want to go back to Graveston Court?'

She shuddered. 'No. Never.'

'Then let me do this for you. Let me do it for us.'

He didn't think there'd been anything threatening in his tone, but Diana frowned. 'Promise me you won't beat him to death. Then we really would have to flee to Paris.'

'I'll try to restrain myself. Mama will take care of you while I'm gone.'

'She's been very kind. But I can take care of myself too, you know.'

Alastair's smile faded. 'You've had only you to care for you, for too many years. But that's over. You'll never be without friends and allies again.'

'Avenging Alastair.'

'For you, yes. It's time to finish this.' *And move on to so much more.*

Noting she still looked troubled, he added in a lighter tone, 'I'm hoping for a quick resolution—and then a swift end to chastity.'

As he'd hoped, the anxious lines in her face smoothed

and she laughed. 'Rogue. I hope to make that end worth your while.'

In a flash, his imagination raced off like a thoroughbred at the starting gun. Battling back images of her smooth naked skin under his hands, he groaned. 'Temptress! I'd better get myself ready for dinner, before I think too much about what I'd rather be getting ready for.'

She smiled that naughty smile that made his breath hitch and his body harden. 'Don't worry. I'll be ready, too.'

Chapter Twenty-One

Next morning, Diana bid Alastair goodbye in the break-fast room—all too formally, under the eye of his mother, when she would have preferred to send him off after a luxurious episode in bed.

Praying earnestly that Blankford would surprise her by being reasonable, and too agitated to concentrate on her painting, Diana set out for the garden. She'd restlessly circled the cutting garden, intent on walking towards the woods, when she encountered Will's wife, Elodie.

'Mrs Ransleigh has lovely gardens,' Elodie said after greeting her.

'I understand you are quite an enthusiastic gardener.'

She nodded. 'I've found such peace in a garden, during some of the most difficult times of my life.' She smiled. 'My Will, he bought Salmford for us because of the gar-dens. The fields were fallow, the tenants surly and in need of guidance. The seller was surely laughing behind his hand, thinking he'd made a bargain over a city man who didn't know a plough from a potato. But the gardens of the manor were magnificent and now, the fields too have responded to love and care.'

Responded to love and care. 'Like a neglected child,' she murmured, reminded at once of her own situation.

'And men. Will tells me Alastair is protecting your son.'

Diana felt a wave of gratitude. 'My son, and me—though he had no good reason to do so.'

'They act for honour, these Ransleighs. What is life, without your child? You are wise to defy even the greatest to keep him.'

'You give me too much credit. I hardly cherished him for most of his years, but I'm trying to do better.'

Elodie's eyebrows shot up. 'You were estranged from your son?'

'Factors…prevented me from becoming close to him.' At the incomprehension on Elodie's face, she said, 'The situation was…complicated.'

'I know what it is to battle against powerful men. One caused me to lose my son, too, when he was still very small. Every day I missed him, longed for him, cherished all the memories I had of him. And when I finally found him again, Philippe…didn't even recognise me.' Tears welled in her eyes.

How would she feel if James were indifferent to her, rather than eager for his mother's love? Something painful twisted in her chest. Maybe shutting herself off from her son was not the worst thing that could have happened.

'It must have been terrible.'

'Not so much, for him. He had a stepmother with a high position in Society, who lavished him with love. But he is *my* son, and I wanted to be part of his life. Will helped that happen.'

'Does he remember you now?'

'Sometimes, I think he does. But no matter. His stepmother is a good woman. She works with me.' Elodie laughed. 'She must, for if she did not, my rogue of a husband, knowing how much my son means to me, told her he would simply steal him away.'

'Will would protect you at all costs.'

'He would. You ache for all the lost years with your son, no? So did I. But it is coming back, the bond we once shared. It will for you, too.'

Diana sighed. 'If I don't end up on the gallows, or so disgraced that the Court of Chancery takes my son away.'

Elodie shook her head. 'Will would never allow that, nor Alastair. If he must turn up more rogues and reprobates to testify, he would do so. In the meantime, we rebuild, eh? Love is important, the most important thing. For children. For women. Hold on to your Alastair.'

Diana shook her head. 'He's not "my" Alastair.'

'He would be, if you want him. Good men, they are not so easy to find.'

'I'm well aware of that,' Diana said with a wry smile. 'But good men...deserve good women.'

'Then be one.'

'I'm not sure I can. I'm not sure I know how,' she admitted, voicing her deepest anxiety.

'When life has treated you roughly, it is hard to imagine it becoming better. Believe in it fiercely enough, though, and you can make it so. But I'll not tease you any more. Now, shall we return? There are two boys who, I think, will have the nursery destroyed if we do not hurry back.'

Nodding, Diana turned with her, and the talk moved to a discussion of the flowers they were passing. But as they walked back to the house, Diana wondered: could she put the shattered pieces of herself back together to make a woman good enough to deserve a man like Alastair?

And what would the future hold if she couldn't?

After a week closeted with his solicitor, doing some investigation of his own, Alastair presented himself once again at Graveston Court.

As he was being escorted by the butler to the same imposing salon, he encountered the housekeeper. The expressionless stare he returned to her mock of a curtsy chased the knowing smirk from her lips and sent her retreating in the opposite direction.

Forewarned by his previous visit, he came prepared for the Duke's reception, pulling a small volume of Shakespeare's sonnets from his pocket as soon as he took an armchair near the cold hearth. When the Duke's arrival was announced by the butler a goodly time later, Alastair did not lift his eyes from the page, continuing instead to read for some minutes before at last looking up to greet his host.

'I hope I'm not interrupting?' the Duke said, an edge of irritation in his voice.

'Not at all,' he replied amiably. 'While on campaign with Wellington, I found reading a wonderful diversion to occupy the tedium between battles.'

'Is it to be a battle, then? You will choose to sacrifice your reputation by supporting That Woman in a losing cause? I am grieved to hear it.'

Since neither the Duke's expression nor his tone carried a hint of sadness, Alastair grinned. 'So I see. I had hoped that, given the time to consider your course of action, you would reconsider.'

The Duke made a scornful sound. 'It sounds like you are still taken in by her. I never understood the spell she seems able to cast on men—even one as disciplined as my father!'

Holding on to his temper, Alastair said evenly, 'Since we'll never agree on the character of the Dowager Duchess, shall we dispense with discussing her? I'm hoping you will see reason in not proceeding with what could only become an ugly scandal, that would have the great name of Mannington gossiped about by every groom, footman, and busybody from here to London.'

'I'm not concerned about that,' Graveston said loftily. 'Only with justice.'

'Indeed? Of course, you may rush ahead like a fool if you choose, but before you embarrass yourself, perhaps even place yourself and your reputation in danger, there are some points you should consider.'

'Place *myself* in danger?' The Duke laughed. 'I hardly think so.'

Not bothering to contest that boast, Alastair continued. 'First, there's the matter of claiming guardianship of your half-brother. If it came to the Court of Chancery, I would feel compelled to repeat for them the threats you made against the boy.'

'Threats?' he exclaimed. 'What nonsense! I told you only that I wanted to have him raised as befits his birth!'

'True. But you also said you wanted the boy to "suffer as you suffered" and "learn to serve your son". Observations I imagine the gentlemen of the court would find most interesting.'

The Duke's eyes narrowed. 'Even if you made such accusations, it would be your word against mine.'

Alastair fixed on him a steely-eyed stare. In a quiet voice, he said, 'I'm sure you don't mean to imply you would question my veracity before the court. Think carefully before you answer, lest you have a need to choose weapons and find a second.'

Alastair almost hoped Graveston would be too irrational to step back. His fingers itched for a sword or pistol, to make this man with all the advantages of wealth, position and authority face someone more his equal than a widow whose only resource was the loyalty of her friends.

To his satisfaction, the Duke looked away first. 'Let's not be so hasty.'

'Then you'll agree you have no reason to appeal to Chancery for custody of the boy. Now, on the question of making accusations of foul play against Dowager Duchess, I've made some enquiries on my own, and discovered a number of witnesses who can attest to your hatred for the Dowager, even of threats to harm her when you inherited.'

Graveston stirred uneasily. 'I'm sure I made no such threats.'

'You did so to me. In any event, the Dowager did not stand to gain materially by her husband's death. You, however, did. I understand you've accumulated some debts.'

'How did you—?' the Duke sputtered. Recovering himself, he said, 'Nothing exorbitant.'

'Then there's the former housekeeper, who I understand was dismissed by your father for attempting to poison the Dowager. One would have thought, faced with the enmity of as powerful a man as a duke, she would have taken herself far, far away. Yet she stayed nearby, even coming and going to this house to visit members of the staff, all who were known to be loyal to you. If your father *was* poisoned, this woman, who had attempted it once before, who was discharged by your father and thus had a motive to wish him ill, had both access and expertise to do so. A woman who, I believe, you have reinstated in her former position as housekeeper. How much did you intend to pay her for her work, once all this was settled?'

'Pay her for—?' he echoed incredulously. 'You can't seriously contend that *I* had anything to do with my father's death!'

Continuing as if he'd not heard, Alastair said, 'The court might wish to have your father exhumed, though I understand coroners disagree on whether poison would leave any trace in someone this long buried. The court would certainly want to know more about your relationship with Mrs Heathson and why you reinstated a woman accused of attempting to murder your stepmother. And then there's the matter of your mistress. Very expensive, I'm told, with a rapacious appetite for jewels. So expensive, you approached your bank in the City to borrow more funds.'

While Graveston gaped at him, Alastair shook his head. 'I have to say, I don't think it would look good. An heir in need of cash hiring a disgruntled former employee to do away with his father, then threatening the poor widow's reputation to try to cheat her of her portion so he can drape diamonds around his mistress's neck. The penny press would be salivating at the courtroom door.'

Leaving Graveston no time to reply, Alastair continued, 'For the sake of argument, let's say the assizes believed your version of events. There's still the matter of a trial—in the House of Lords, which my uncle has run for years. I regret to say, he's no admirer of your late father, either.'

The Duke was looking less certain by the minute. 'Are you so sure the Earl would wish to become involved? After all, he didn't lift a finger for his son Max. I expect he'd be even less inclined to be saddled with cleaning up your scandal.'

'What's one more scandal to a Rogue?' Alastair asked with a shrug. 'Besides, "cleaning up" is what my uncle does best. He thrives on it, or so he assured me when I warned him about possible proceedings.'

'You've talked with him about this?'

'Of course. I'd never have pressed forward in so critical a matter without his approval.'

After giving that a moment to sink in, Alastair changed tactics. 'A distasteful business,' he said with a dismissive wave of the hand. 'It's not seemly that the noble name of Graveston, the family of the Manningtons, who've served their country since the Conquest, should be associated with such a sordid tale. Nor is there any need that it should be. If necessary, however, I'm quite willing to match my witnesses against yours. It's up to you.'

At that, he sat back and gazed out the window, calm, confident and at ease.

For a long time, the only sound in the room was the tick of the mantel clock. Finally, the Duke said, 'What does the bitch want?'

'If you take that tone,' Alastair snapped, 'I shall be forced to proceed regardless. I'm quite willing to let Society weigh my reputation against yours, in the court of public opinion or in the Lords. A hero of Badajoz, frequent leader of the "forlorn hope", valiant defender of Waterloo against a provincial aristocrat who has done—what have you done? Ah, married a wealthy girl and attempted to coerce a helpless widow. Now, would you like to rephrase your question?'

His expression simmering resentment, Graveston stared at Alastair with sullen eyes. 'What does the Dowager want?' he said at last, enunciating each word separately, as if they were being pulled out of him.

'*She* wants nothing. What I want, though, is merely what is due to her. She will waive dower, while you facilitate transfer of the reasonable amount already stipulated in your father's will—yes, I've seen a copy of it, already filed for probate—plus what was bequeathed to Lord James. Who is, as you've pointed out, the son of a duke and should be reared as such. I want you to cease your harassment and abandon any attempts to prosecute her, a process that would in any event never get further than the local court you could control. Win a judgement against her in the Lords? That horse won't jump, Graveston. You have the title and a lucrative estate. Why not show yourself worthy of both?'

The Duke sprang up and took a turn about the room. 'Just—let her go, with no retribution? You cannot know what it was like to have your mother, who lived for your father's approval and wanted only to please him, ignored, scorned, once he was besotted by *her*. I might have understood it if she seemed to care for him, for anything. But all she ever showed was an icy disdain. Still, my father was consumed by her! He had no time for me; I was packed off to school, and when I was older and protested his excessive absorption in her, he even raised his hand to me!'

Despite his disgust for the Duke's campaign for revenge, Alastair could hear in the man's voice the lingering pain of an abandoned boy who'd seen his beloved mother humiliated and discarded. He knew only too well how abandonment and humiliation could fester within, a canker in the gut.

'It must have been difficult,' Alastair said quietly, a reluctant sympathy tempering his disdain. 'But that neglect was the fault of your father, not the Dowager, who had no more choice over your father's actions than you did.'

'Choice?' he scoffed. 'What was there to choose? He made her, the daughter of a nobody, into a duchess!'

'Impossible as you—and he—seem to find it, she had no desire to be a duchess, as her behaviour made quite evident. But I understand the need to exact retribution for the unfairness of it all. I suggest a remedy with a more suitable opponent.' Alastair lifted his hands and flexed them into fists. 'Me.'

The Duke's scowl turned to astonishment. 'Meet you? For fisticuffs?'

'We can resolve this here and now, man to man, out of the vulgar public gaze—more fitting behaviour for the heir to a great and noble title. Or we can have fisticuffs by lawyer, in full view of gawking spectators in the gallery of the Lords and in front of print-shop windows. That way, I promise you, you will surely lose, dragging your title and name into the mud when you do.'

Graveston frowned, looking furious—but uncertain. 'You can't seriously think a few well-placed blows could right all the wrongs done to me and my mother.'

'Nothing can undo that—not fisticuffs, nor a public vendetta against the Dowager that would shame you more than it would her. All one can hope for is to assuage the sting of past injustice, and let it go,' he advised, the truth of those words in his own situation resonating within him.

He held up his fists again. 'That is, if you're man enough. Or would you rather vent your spleen on a woman?'

'I'm no coward, despite what you insinuate,' Graveston snarled.

'Then meet me. Expend that anger and resentment, and call it done.'

While Graveston appeared to weigh the matter, Alastair added, 'It's difficult to give up a grievance, especially one well founded. But it's better for the soul.'

'A ridiculous solution,' Graveston muttered.

'Perhaps. Before I leave you to stew in bitterness, might I ask the courtesy of knowing your intentions? If you won't tell me, I shall feel compelled to proceed with the evidence I've gathered.'

Anger and frustration played across the face of a man too engulfed by tumultuous emotion to mask them. 'Very well,' he said at last. 'Fisticuffs it is. Not here, though.'

'Certainly not. I wouldn't wish to damage any of your father's carefully collected knick-knacks,' Alastair said, running his finger over a vase on the table beside him.

'Heathen!' Graveston said with a reluctant smile. 'That Greek hydria from the third century BC is probably worth more than your entire stable.'

'Ah, a stable! That would be just the place.'

And so it was that the Duke of Graveston and Mr Alastair Ransleigh of Barton Abbey retreated to the stable, banished the gawking grooms and coachmen, claimed an unoccupied stall and proceeded to try to pummel out each other's frustration.

Having obtained what he sought, Alastair intended to go easy on the peer, but found to his surprise that the young Duke held his own pretty well. He even managed to land two or three well-disguised feints that were going to leave Alastair with a bruised jaw for the foreseeable future.

Sometime later, after they were both panting and bloodied, Alastair held up a hand. 'Shall we call a draw?'

Holding his sides, the Duke nodded. When he could catch his breath, he said, 'You were right. It doesn't change the past, but it did…help.'

'I'm glad,' Alastair said in perfect truth. A man who would persecute a woman was despicable. But a man who could finally realise he was in the wrong, alter his course—and could throw quite a respectable right hook in the bargain—deserved a second chance. 'Then we are agreed.'

Graveston sighed. 'I've spent the last five years dreaming of revenge for my mother…and myself. It's hard to let that go. There's the temptation to keep fighting, even at the cost of tarnishing my reputation.'

'Shooting your best hunting dog to take down a pigeon? Not wise.'

'No—though oh-so-satisfying. But…yes, we're agreed. I'll inform my solicitor not to delay any longer the execution of Father's will. Your Dowager will get her properties. I'd prefer that she and the brat not use the Dower House, though. I'd prefer they remain out of my sight permanently.'

'I see no difficulty there. She has no more desire to set foot at Graveston Court than you do to see her here, and since the boy will inherit other properties, there's no need for him to reside here either. In return, I'll pledge that as long as you keep our bargain, I'll not present my evidence to the Lords.'

Pleased to have achieved the results he wanted, Alastair felt he could be magnanimous and forgive the insults Graveston had flung at him. Smiling, he offered his hand.

Reluctantly, the Duke shook it.

'One last bit of advice. When you take your seat in the Lords, I'd still be wary of my uncle.'

'Thank you; I'll remember that.' Graveston shook his head. 'I'll never understand the fascination she elicits in men. She certainly won a strong champion in you.'

'So she did. If you're tempted to forget our agreement, remember that.'

Chapter Twenty-Two

Euphoria in his heart, Alastair set off for Barton Abbey, riding as fast as he could change horses. He knew Diana was anxious, despite her trust in him. He couldn't wait to set her worries at rest.

Finally, they could move on to resolve the situation between them, resume the progress of their relationship that had been arrested when the threat against her demanded her removal to safety under his mother's roof.

How would she choose to resolve it? Anticipation and anxiety warred within as he contemplated her possible reaction.

She'd more or less said she wished to resume their physical relationship. Would she allow more than that? Could he be satisfied with less than a full commitment from her?

Ah, how he wished to cosset and care for her! Shower her with so much attention and love that the grim years with Graveston receded into distant memory, blurred by time until they seemed like events in the life of a stranger.

Would she let him?

The only thing he knew for certain was he didn't want her to walk away.

* * *

Three days of hard riding later, he had arrived at Barton Abbey in the late afternoon. Leaving his lathered horse at the stables, he had jogged to the house, impatient to bathe, change, and seek her out as quickly as possible.

A bare half-hour later, his still-dripping hair slicked down and his damp shirt sticking to his back, he found her at her easel in her north-salon studio.

He'd approached quietly, easing the door open, anxious to drink in the sight of her for a moment before she was aware of his presence.

How lovely she was, he marvelled, his heart contracting with joy and longing at the sight of her. Even better, her expression looked intent but serene as she studied her canvas, with no dark shadows of worry beneath her eyes and the once-wary set of her shoulders relaxed.

After a moment, some sixth sense must have alerted her she was under scrutiny, for she stilled, then looked over at him. 'Alastair,' she cried, the happiness in her voice the sweetest music to his needy ears.

Unable to resist, he paced towards her, picked her up and swung her around in his arms when she ran to meet him, then sat her down and kissed her thoroughly.

'Ah, how much I've missed that!' he murmured, cradling her to the rapid beating of his heart.

She looked up at him anxiously. 'It must have gone well. You wouldn't look so happy, if it had not.'

How much he wanted to sweep her into his arms, carry her up to his chamber, and make love to her for a week! 'I could be happier. But alas, that will have to wait a bit longer. Come, sit, and I'll tell you all about it.'

Contenting himself, for the moment, with one more quick kiss, he escorted her to the sofa and gave her a full accounting of his interview with the Duke of Graveston.

'He will truly let it go?' she asked, her tone disbelieving. 'Are you sure?'

'I think so. But if he should change his mind, he's been warned.'

She gave a little sigh. 'So there's still the possibility he might try to destroy your reputation.'

'Though we can't totally eliminate the risk, I think it unlikely. If it should happen, we'll deal with it. Your ultimate vindication is sure, even if he were so unwise as to proceed.'

'As is scandal and disrespect to your name, if he should proceed.'

How he wished he could set her mind completely at rest! 'Sweeting, we can't live in fear of shadows.'

'Live in fear of shadows,' she repeated with a sad smile. 'Ah, Alastair, I've done that for so long, I don't know how to live in sunlight.'

'You'll learn. I'll help you.'

'After all those years in the shadows, I know I'm... damaged. I don't know how to forget them, how to heal. If I can heal.' She traced his cheek, her touch tender. 'You deserve so much more. Someone whole, whose love has no shadows.'

It wasn't the full-fledged avowal he longed for, but... Once, sensing how close she was to telling him everything he wanted to hear, he might have pushed her for more. But she'd been pushed and manipulated enough. More than that, if they were to have a future together, it would have to be her choice, free and clear.

He gave her a wry smile. 'Diana, there is no one for me but you. For too many years, I tried to deny it, but after finding you again, I no longer fight that truth. I love you and I want you in my life, in whatever way you are comfortable. I'd prefer you as my wife, but I'll take whatever you can give me. Mistress. Friend. Adviser. Just let me stay close and help you heal. If you needed friends and allies against a duke, you'll need them even more battling the demons of the past. But that's what I desire. What do you want?'

She rubbed his hand, her expression anxious. 'I'm still not sure. A place of my own, to start over.'

'You can stay at Barton Abbey until the provisions of your husband's will are carried out. Which, by the way, buttress your position. Despite the animosity between you, Graveston left a substantial sum to you and an even more handsome one to your son. Not quite the act of a man at war with his wife.'

'It was war, though, most of the time. The Duke had won his trophy, but he could not make me compliant. Having given up all I wanted and everything I loved, defiance was all I had left. It…confounded him. He'd never met resistance that couldn't be broken. After all, he'd been raised since birth to believe the world should rearrange itself to suit him; he had only to express a desire and it was gratified. I think he found it incomprehensible that a woman, especially one who'd not been born into the highest aristocracy, would not abandon her childish opposition and go from reluctance to delight that he'd deigned to make her a duchess.'

'He should have believed it,' Alastair said. 'You told him forcefully enough.'

'It took him a long time to finally realise it. Years of tracking down and then removing everything that meant anything to me, until he had nothing left with which to try to control me.'

Alastair hadn't wanted to ask—the prospect made him sick to contemplate—but somehow the words forced themselves out. 'Not even beating you?'

'Ah. Beating. That was perhaps most frustrating of all to him. Eventually he realised—unlike, I suspect, his poor first wife—that I had no fear of physical punishment. What was physical pain, compared to the agony of all I had lost, what I would never have?'

Rising, she paced away from him, making a circuit of the room. Though he wanted to go after her, pull her into his arms, offer comfort, he knew he had to leave her be.

Finally, she looked back at him. 'I've had time these last few weeks, finally free of his menace, to think about all that happened. I found myself wondering if I did indeed overestimate his power. Perhaps he would only have threatened, but never actually used Papa's debts to put him in prison or find perjured witnesses to ruin you. All I knew was that I loved you so much, I would rather die than destroy you. He understood that and was shrewd enough to use it.'

'That doesn't make him less despicable in my eyes. I do wish, though, that you'd doubted his influence enough to come to me then.'

'So do I. But wishing won't change the past. By the end, I think in his own way, he was…fond of me. Not that he would have let me leave him, but I think he respected my courage in resisting him, even as it infuriated and perplexed him. Of course, a Duke of Graveston could not admit he'd been wrong; he never returned the books or paints or musical instruments he'd had taken away. But when he came back from London, things would appear. An exquisite antique Greek vase in my sitting room. New gowns and costly furs in my wardrobe. His way, I suppose, of reaching out, asking for peace between us. If I had deferred to him then, even a little, he might have considered his victory finally won, given me back all he'd taken and treated me as less of a prisoner. But after years of suppressing all emotion save defiance, I didn't know any other way to be. I *couldn't* yield to him—if I had dismantled any of the barriers that had kept me upright through years of siege, I risked the whole edifice tumbling down.'

She sighed. 'It may be bad of me, but I'm glad he's dead, and I'm free at last.'

'Perhaps one day, you'll be able to forgive him. But I can't deny that I, too, am glad he's dead and that you are free to do whatever you want.'

'What I want,' she repeated, shaking her head. 'Once I knew exactly what I wanted—you. Us. Our future together. When I had to give that up, I merely survived, holding on to the few pieces of myself by resisting. Now that I don't have to fight any more, I'm not sure what to do, where to go. I spent nearly nine years of my life virtually alone, pushing back against the forces of the world, first Graveston, then his son. Like a game of tug of war one plays as a child, pulling and pulling and pulling, until suddenly, when your opponent gives way, you fall backward into nothingness.'

'Is that how you feel—that you've fallen into a void?'

She shivered and rubbed her arms, as if chilled. 'Yes,' she admitted in a whisper. 'I loved you. I always loved you. I never stopped. But I pushed the emotion deep within, until it was frozen far below the surface of my thoughts. When I was a child, tromping a winter field with Papa, intent on finding a particular plant, I'd go on until my toes and fingers were numb. Once home by the fire, I'd slowly unthaw, feet and hands burning and tingling in pain. I don't know how long it will take me to unthaw my heart from all the years with Graveston, or how much pain there will be. It's…frightening, to not know who you are any more.'

He couldn't help it then; he had to take her in his arms. To his relief, she clung to him willingly. The shivering increased, until he realised, for the first time, she was weeping.

Her sobs grew in intensity until her whole body shuddered in his arms. His heart aching for her anguish, he tightened his grip.

'I'll be here for you always, however long it takes. Whatever happens. You'll never be alone, never again afraid,' he whispered into her hair. 'I love you, Diana. I always have; I never stopped. I will always love you.'

For a long time, he simply held her, until at last the sobbing lessened, then ceased and she leaned against him, limp in his arms.

He closed his eyes, savouring the feel of her cradled to his chest. Even as his body clamoured for more, he rebuked it.

Yes, he wanted more; he wanted everything. But he was wiser now, no longer an impetuous boy, insisting on having it all *now*. Breaking a nervous, green filly, one couldn't force her; she must come to him on her own terms.

He could wait as long as it took.

After several grim years lost in an emotional wilderness, he'd once again found the centre of his universe. And he would never, ever give her up again.

Pulling away from Alastair, Diana sat up, feeling dizzy and disorientated. She'd wept—in Alastair's arms. Actually shed tears, something she hadn't done since the terrible night she'd realised she must marry the Duke and Alastair was lost to her for ever.

Embarrassment replaced surprise as she looked at

the soggy cravat, now hanging limply at his throat. 'I'm afraid I've ruined your neckcloth. I'm so sorry.'

He made a gesture of dismissal. 'Don't be. I've got others. Besides, the first part of healing is letting go.' He smiled, the tenderness of his expression making her chest ache. 'I should know.'

'I'm not sure I can let go. There's so much.' She pressed her hands to her chest, feeling as if a lead weight were imprisoned there. 'So much pain and ugliness, I don't dare open up, lest it all rush out, and I...I drown in it.'

'I'll be here. I won't let you drown.'

'Attentive Alastair. So you intend to protect me?'

'In every way I can. Whatever grief and pain bedevils you, we can meet it, conquer it, together.'

After the bout of tears she felt—strange, fidgety. The idea that Blankford could no longer threaten her still seemed impossible to believe. Uncertain, her whole world shifting around her, all she knew for sure was she could not bear to be pressured.

Even by Alastair.

When he reached for her again, she held up a hand to fend him off.

'I know you care for me and want to help. But...I need time to myself—to find out how to breathe freely again. I do love you, Alastair, but I don't know if I *can* become a woman who could share her life with you. I don't even know if I can succeed in mothering my own son!'

Compelled by a distress she didn't seem able to control, she jumped up again and began pacing.

What was wrong with her? Alastair had just affirmed what she would have given her life to hear eight years ago—that he'd forgiven her betrayal and loved her still. That he wanted to help her heal. That he wanted her as his lover—his wife.

Why could she not accept that offer with joy, and move on to a future with him?

It made no sense. But with her whole body trembling in anxiety, her thoughts in turmoil, all she knew was that she couldn't.

She looked back to see him watching her, his expression unreadable, his hands rigidly at his sides, as if he had to fight with himself to keep them there.

Foolish tears stung her eyes again. 'I'm sorry, Alastair. I don't mean to hurt you, and I'm grateful—'

'Sweet Diana, don't apologise,' he interrupted. 'You've lived through eight years of torment, had your child and your very life threatened, and have only just learned you can in safety move forward. How could you not need time to let the upheaval settle before you can decide what you want to do with your life?'

Another tear escaped. 'Thank you…for understanding.'

'Shall I tell you what I suggest? Just a suggestion, of course. You shall do whatever *you* feel is right.'

That sounded less threatening. The pressure in her chest easing a bit, she said, 'Very well. What do you suggest?'

'The late Duke's will stipulates you are to receive as a widow's portion the incomes and rents from four of Graveston's most prosperous properties, the land itself to be owned in trust for your son until he reaches his majority. The estates are located on good land and should earn you a comfortable income. There happens to be a small property in this county, not too far from Barton Abbey, that the absentee owner is interested in selling. The property, Winston Hollow, is close enough for Mother to call on you. She's grown quite fond of that son of yours, and would hate to give him up. I suggest that you settle at

Winston Hollow, plant a garden, paint, enjoy running a household again, as you did for your father. Take time to find yourself.'

A place of her own, staffed with servants of her own choosing. A place to rediscover who she was, to purge the mistrust, the grief, the regret of the past and build the courage to believe in a future.

She'd battled against a strong-willed master for as long as she could remember, existed under the scrutiny of his watchful, disapproving staff. Never in her life had she lived both alone and free. The prospect was both liberating...and alarming.

'Will you...call, too?'

'If you want me to. I spend most of my time at Barton Abbey; Mama is a good manager and Hutchens knows his job and the land, but an estate this size requires a lot of work, and I don't like to burden her. Call on me whenever you want advice or company.'

Alastair—close, but not pressing her to do anything or be anyone. The tension within her dissipated a bit further. 'I think I would like that.'

'Then I'll notify my solicitor to start drawing up the necessary documents for you immediately.'

If she had her own house, they could begin again as lovers. Heat fired within her at the realisation.

But she could hardly take him as a lover while protesting she needed to keep him at arm's length. Could she? After such a forceful rejection, he wasn't likely to proposition her any time soon.

Her body protested the idea of further chastity, but her skittish mind rebuked it. Everything had changed since their sojourn in Green Park Buildings, when she'd thought he disliked her and would soon tire of the liaison. While she hungered for him, she knew right now she couldn't bear the weight of any expectations he might cherish for a future.

So it seemed, for the time being, she would burn.

'Thank you. I'm sorry I…can't offer more.'

He smiled. 'You are a brave, resourceful, strong woman. You will heal, Diana. And as adviser, friend—or lover—I will always be available. But now, I must go find Mother. She doesn't yet know I've returned.'

He came towards her and she tensed, but he simply lifted her fingers for a kiss. She searched his face—was he angry, impatient, disappointed? She couldn't tell.

'I'll see you at dinner.'

She stared after him as he walked out, then turned to sink down on to the sofa.

She'd greeted him as a long-lost lover and sent him off like a nervous virgin. Almost literally pushed him away, and then been illogically disappointed that he hadn't tried to kiss her before he left.

How could she expect him to comprehend her behaviour, when she didn't understand it herself?

But she'd been uncertain all along, she reminded herself, retreating in confusion every time she'd tried to contemplate a future, putting off making any decisions until the threat of Graveston was settled.

Well, now it was, and she'd just met the first challenge by, at the least disappointing, if not actually insulting, the man who'd won her back her life.

She put her head in her hands. Alastair seemed confident she would heal in time. She could only hope he was right—and that by her intransigence, she wouldn't risk losing for ever a man she might soon decide she didn't want to live without.

Chapter Twenty-Three

The following morning, Alastair hesitated outside the door to the north parlour Diana used as her painting studio. He'd speculated many different endings to the meeting at which he conveyed the glad tidings of her deliverance from Blankford's revenge, but he'd never anticipated her withdrawing from him so completely—and right after he'd comforted her in his arms.

He'd had a hard time concealing a dismay and disappointment that cut even deeper that night when, after visions of having her fall rapturously into his arms upon hearing the news, he took himself off instead to a bed that promised to remain cold and empty for a good long time. He could only be glad he'd listened to the instincts that told him not to press her, or he might have frightened her away completely.

But the rejection stung nonetheless.

Well, enough repining. One skirmish lost did not determine the course of a war, and he was far from ready to retire from the field. He might not be able to cosset and care for her as he'd like—or make love to her for a week—but he'd pledged to aid her recovery in whatever way he could, and he intended to do so.

Besides, there was no need to despair—she *had* confessed that she still loved him, had always loved him. She might not believe it yet, but he had full confidence that the courageous, determined, resilient woman who'd resisted the intimidation of a duke would eventually fight her way out of the prison of her past, back to a free and vibrant life.

Back to him.

He just had to stay patient and lure her slowly, gently, gradually out of her self-imposed isolation.

He'd take the first step this morning. After a deep breath, he rapped on the door.

He walked in when she bid him enter, but rather than cross the room to claim a kiss, as he might have only a day ago, he remained near the door.

The alarmed expression that swiftly crossed her face before she schooled her features made him glad of his caution, even as it struck a blow to his heart. How could they have become so awkward with each other in only a day?

Ah, Diana, do you not yet realise I would never do anything to hurt you?

Pushing back the sadness, he summoned a smile. 'Mama thought you'd be at your easel. I noticed yesterday that you'd almost finished your painting of the asters. I thought you might like to start one for these.'

From behind his back, he produced a bouquet of late-blooming damask roses.

To his relief, the gesture seemed to put her at ease. 'How lovely!' she exclaimed, coming over to him.

'The cool autumn nights give the petals an interesting mix of shades—pink, salmon, cream, pale pink, with a touch of saffron. When I saw them this morning, I immediately thought you'd enjoy trying to capture the different hues.' He handed over the bouquet. 'And as James would say, they are wonderfully smelly.'

'They are indeed,' she said, bending down to inhale a deep breath of the sweet, spicy aroma.

'James dotes on you, you know. I watched him while you were gathering asters and ferns by the brook that day. He mimics what you do and hangs on every word you utter. By offering affection and responding to his needs and interests, you've made a great start at reviving your relationship. It will only grow deeper over time.'

'You truly think so?'

'I do. But you needn't trust the word of an old bachelor—ask my mother.'

She smiled shyly. 'She said much the same.'

'Well, there you have it. Enjoy the flowers.'

Curbing the ever-present longing to touch her, he made himself turn towards the door.

'Alastair!' she called as he reached the threshold. When he looked back over his shoulder, she said, 'I do appreciate you thinking of me, even if I'm...still not very good at expressing gratitude.'

'You have to start trusting that good things will happen to you. How would you react to a gift if you had no reservations, felt no fear, no sense of threat?'

She paused, considering. 'I suppose I would be... delighted.'

'Then let yourself be. For eight years, you merely endured. This is what you endured *for*—so you might feel delight, and happiness, and enthusiasm again. I'll hope to see the painting when you've finished it.' With a bow, he exited the room.

Thank heaven the estate required a great deal of work and long hours in the saddle, he thought as he headed for the stables. Else, thrown together with Diana day after day in the house, stymied love and frustrated desire would drive him mad.

He'd be glad when Reynolds finished obtaining her new property, so she might establish her own household. Once secure and independent, in a home of her own making, she could begin to heal—and he'd be that much closer to winning her back.

Six weeks later, Diana sat at her desk in the morning room at Winston Hollow, making notes on the menus left by Mrs Jenkins, her new housekeeper. After living in the manor for a month, served by staff she'd chosen herself, a sense of anticipation had begun to replace the foreboding with which she'd awakened for as long as she could remember.

Trust that good things will happen to you, Alastair had advised. It had been difficult at first, but as she became immersed in the rhythm of her own household, taking up the duties she'd enjoyed performing in her father's house, the dread that had haunted her for so long had gradually begun to dissipate.

Putting down her pen, she gazed out the window that overlooked the gravel drive, empty of visitors, and sighed. She'd begged Alastair for time to herself, and he'd certainly given it to her—rather more than she would have liked.

Indeed, almost as soon as she'd set him at a distance— and he complied with her wishes—she'd begun to regret pushing him away. After all his care and consideration, how could she have feared he would pressure her, force on her anything for which she was not ready?

Until she'd left Barton Abbey, she'd continued to see him—in company at dinner, in passing as he rode out on estate business. Several times, he'd joined them as she walked with James, to her son's delight, showing him how to skip pebbles in the brook, tossing him a ball, and one rainy day, taking him to explore the old gatehouse that had so fascinated him the afternoon they arrived.

Often, he dropped off little gifts—a book of poetry from his library he thought she'd enjoy, a colourful plant he'd found while riding through the meadows, some fresh berry tarts from the kitchen to share with James. He was unfailingly kind, gentle, patient—and he never touched her.

Oh, how she missed his touch! The mere thought of the passionate nights they'd shared in Bath made her body throb with need and her soul ache with longing.

But as much as she yearned for him, she knew that coming here alone had been the right choice. Living under threat for so long, she'd existed in a constant state of alarm, her nerves taut, her body rigid. In the sheltering cocoon of Winston Hollow, where every activity was directed by her, where no one but herself made any demands on her, where she did not have to prepare herself each night for the next day's battles, the tenseness in her body had seeped away along with the sense of dread, leaving her feeling lighter and more relaxed than she'd been in years.

She was, in short, ready to embrace a new life. But no such life would be complete without Alastair.

While he had agreed to give her time and space, he'd also said he would call. She'd expected, once she was established in her new home, he would find some pretext to stop by. Every time there was a clatter of gravel on the drive, or the sound of voices in the entryway, her spirits leapt, expecting him.

But though Mrs Ransleigh had come twice for tea, Alastair had not appeared. Not that she could fault him—

she'd been the one to bring their relationship to a halt. Necessary as that had been initially, she was finding that each day, she missed him more.

His counsel. His ready smile. The delight of discussing poetry or painting or the events reported in the London newspapers with a man of wisdom and discernment. And always, his touch.

Not wishing to press her, was he waiting for an invitation to visit?

Perhaps it was finally time to send one.

Almost upon the thought, Clarkson, her new butler, appeared in the doorway. 'Madame, you have a visitor. I put him in the morning room.'

Excitement blew through her like a fresh breeze. Since she had no other male acquaintances in the county, it must be Alastair.

'Mr Ransleigh?' she asked hopefully.

'Yes, ma'am. He's just back from London, he said.'

Perhaps that was why he'd not called earlier. Gladness filling her, she smoothed her skirts, tucked in a curl that had escaped her careless coiffure, and hurried into the morning room.

He stood as she entered, looking so handsome and irresistible her breath caught in her throat. 'Alastair, what a pleasant surprise!' she said when she could speak again. 'Can you stay for tea?'

'If you are sure I'm not interrupting. I found something for you in London; I debated just sending it over, but since I was riding by anyway, I thought I'd chance delivering it myself. I hope you don't mind.'

'No, I'm delighted! Please, do sit!' Motioning him back to the sofa, she gave instructions to Clarkson, then came to take a seat beside him.

He studied her, a smile slowly lighting his face. 'I

think you *are* delighted. I'm so pleased. Running Winston Hollow was what you needed, then.'

She nodded. 'I can't thank you enough for suggesting it! I'm finding I love being mistress of my own household, with all the small routines of daily life—consulting with the cook and the housekeeper, painting in the morning, lessons with James in the afternoon, taking him and the puppy your mama insisted he bring with him for walks around the property. He's such a delightful companion, eager to explore, excited by every new discovery. I love him better each day—as you assured me I would. I can never thank you enough for making it possible for me to keep him.'

'Your pleasure—and his—is reward enough. You do look lovely—and you sound happy. Have you found at last the peace you sought?'

'I think so. Just recently, I've dared to unlock the memories I suppressed of those happy times before my marriage—wonderful memories of that spring we fell in love. I've even been able to let go some of the misery of the years after, without the flood of anguish I feared. Instead, there's been this slow…trickling away of the fear and bitterness and anger that held me as much a prisoner as the walls of Graveston Court once did. I go for days now without thinking about it.'

She laughed. 'Now, this will surprise you! I believe in time, I may even be able to forgive Graveston.'

'Then your healing will be complete.' He leaned towards her and she sucked in a breath, supremely conscious of his nearness, every nerve anticipating his touch.

Running a fingertip gently down her cheek, leaving sparks of sensation in its wake, he declaimed. *"'Her merest smile to me is a delight. Her brow uplifted, finally free of pain. Her joy like the uprush of a lark to flight. My joy to win her back to life again.'*

Without question, he'd written that for her—about her. Humbled, she said, 'So you've taken up your pen again?'

'Yes, I have. It seems my muse is back. Though she is still often maddeningly elusive. But here, let me show you what I've brought.' Producing a wrapped package, he handed it to her.

She peeled off the paper to reveal a small leather volume. *'Pride and Prejudice,'* she read the title on the spine.

'My sister Lissa recommended it. The author has a unique voice and a sense of humour I think you'll enjoy.'

Flipping open the book to the first page, she read aloud, *'"It is a truth universally acknowledged, that a single man in possession of a good fortune must be in want of a wife."'* Chuckling, she said, 'Yes, I think I shall like it. Thank you so much.'

'So you can enjoy a gift now—with no fear, no sense of threat?'

'Less every day. As you promised.'

'It's gratifying to be proven right,' he acknowledged with a grin. 'You're beginning to trust that the future *will* be full of possibilities? That you *can* learn to love again?'

Did he mean her son—or him?

She knew which love she needed to affirm.

'There may be nothing as sweet as one's first falling in love,' she said softly, her heart accelerating as he fixed his gaze on her, 'except, perhaps, recapturing a love once lost.'

She watched as the intensity of his regard turned to something else. Something impossible to resist.

She angled her head up, inviting his lips. He gave her just a gentle brush with his mouth, but at the first contact, her body seemed to catch fire.

He must have felt it, too, for his kiss deepened. Any possibility of breaking it off shredding to ash and disintegrating, she opened her mouth, and with an inarticulate sound, he sought her tongue with his own.

Only her brain's insistent warning that at any moment, the butler might return with the tea tray, gave her the strength to break away.

Breathing hard, obviously as reluctant as she was to end the kiss, Alastair let her go.

'I've missed you,' she explained, blushing a little.

'"Missed" doesn't begin to convey the enormity of it,' he muttered, moving away from her.

She caught his sleeve, pulling him back again, suddenly desperate for more. 'Another kiss?'

'You're sure?' he asked, studying her. 'You'll let yourself enjoy, with no fear, no sense of threat?'

'With you, yes.'

Tenderness softened the passion in his gaze. Pulling her into his arms, he kissed her forehead. 'No fear, no threat,' he whispered as he kissed her ear, the slope of her throat, her chin while her senses swam and tiny explosions of delight and pleasure ignited whenever his mouth touched her.

'No fear, no threat,' he whispered again before claiming her mouth.

This kiss was long, gentle, and so achingly sweet she could almost weep with the joy of it. Her long-denied body trembled and burned, eager for completion.

With surprising ease, she let go her last reserve, like a ship slipping its moorings to set off fearlessly on uncharted seas, while her unfettered heart rejoiced with love for him.

She must have been demented to have denied them

this—denied *him*, for so long. 'Please, stay,' she whispered when at last he broke the kiss.

'Now?' He raised his eyebrows. 'In full daylight? With the butler about to bring tea and your son in the nursery?'

'Bother the butler and Minnie has charge of James. Oh, how I've missed *you*—and this!' She traced his mouth with a trembling finger, until he groaned. 'You will stay, won't you?'

'You know I can deny you nothing.'

'I'm so glad!' Feeling impossibly wicked, she took his hand and led him from the morning room. Tiptoeing down the hallway to the stairs, scanning around them like a pair of naughty children, they went swiftly hand in hand up to her bedchamber.

It was mad, delicious—and she couldn't wait to taste him again. And at last, to offer him all of her.

A long, leisurely time later, Alastair woke from a deep sleep to find himself in a shadowed bedchamber—with a delectably naked Diana beside him. For a moment, he thought muzzily that he must be dreaming.

Then consciousness returned, and with it, the memory of calling on her and being finally—praise Heaven!— invited back into her arms.

Diana stirred against him. He kissed the top of her head, relishing the feel of her body against his, the silk of her hair under his lips. *Diana*, free and unafraid beside him, where she belonged.

A few minutes later, she roused and gave him a sleepy smile. 'Alastair?'

He placed a kiss on the tip of her nose. 'Yes, my beloved.'

'Am I your beloved?'

'You know you are.'

'Then…is your offer still open?'

An electric flash of anticipation instantly dispelled any residual sleepiness. 'Which offer?' he asked cautiously, trying to restrain a rising hope and excitement.

She blushed a little. 'Your offer to make an honest woman of me.'

'You mean…marriage?'

She nodded, looking suddenly shy.

He could have teased her, but he was far too eager for delay. Detaching her from his arms, he slid out of bed, pulled her to sitting position, and went down on one knee.

'My dearest, darling Diana, will you marry me, and make me the happiest man in England?'

'Amorous Alastair.' She chuckled. 'Accepting Alastair. My Alastair-for-Always. Yes, yes, a thousand times yes.'

He didn't want to ask, to give her a chance to entertain any doubts, but he'd waited too long not to know for certain. 'Are you sure?'

'The innocent, joyful girl I'd once been is gone for ever, but as I've resumed the habits of my old life, the most consistent, most important joy I remembered and have found again…is you. I've no need for wariness any longer. *He* took away and pressured and intimidated; *you* give and support and encourage, asking for nothing in return but for me to rebuild my life and be happy.'

'I did ask to be part of it,' he pointed out.

'Now I have a new life I owe to you—and I can't envisage living it without you.'

Elated, he gave her a passionate kiss, then jumped up and hurried about, gathering up his scattered clothing.

'I tell you I can't live without you, and you respond by leaving?' Diana asked, looking disgruntled.

'Absolutely! I must ride to London today and arrange for a special licence. Talk with Mama; shall we be married in the parlour at Barton Abbey or here?' He stopped suddenly. 'Unless you want a grand wedding in London? The Dowager Duchess, re-emerging triumphant in Society?'

She shook her head. 'I never wanted to be part of Society. The only thing I wanted, almost from the moment I met you, was to be your wife.'

'So you shall be, then. For ever and always, my beloved,' he declared, and gathered Diana to him for another kiss.

* * * * *

THE RAKE TO
REVEAL HER

To my husband and hero:

Never give in.

Never give up.

Chapter One

Suffolk—spring 1816

His ears still ringing from the impact of the fall, Dominic Fitzallen Ransleigh levered himself to a sitting position in the muddy Suffolk lane. Air hissed in and out of his gritted teeth as he waited for the red wave of pain obscuring his vision to subside. Which it did, just in time for him to see that black devil, Diablo, trot around the corner and out of sight.

Headed back to the barn, probably, Dom thought. If horses could laugh, surely the bad-tempered varlet was laughing at him.

It was his own fault, always choosing the most difficult and high-spirited colts to train as hunters. Horses with the speed and heart to gallop across country, jumping with ease any obstacle in their paths, but needing two strong hands on the reins to control their headstrong, temperamental natures.

He looked down at his one remaining hand, still trembling from the strain of that wild ride. Flexing the wrist, he judged it sore but not broken. After years of tending himself from various injuries suffered during his service with the Sixteenth Dragoons, a gingerly bending of the arm informed him no bones were broken there, either.

His left shoulder still throbbed, but at least he hadn't fallen on the stump of his right arm. Had he done that, he'd probably still be unconscious from the agony.

Resigning himself to sit in the mud until his muzzy head cleared, Dom gazed down the lane after the fleeing horse. Though the doctors had warned him, he'd resisted accepting what he'd just proved: he'd not be able to control Diablo, or any of the other horses in his stable full of hunters, with a single good hand.

Sighing, Dom struggled to his feet. He might as well face the inevitable. As he'd never be able to ride Diablo or the others again, there was no sense hanging on to them. The bitter taste of defeat in his mouth, he told himself he would look into selling them off at Tattersall's while the horses were still in prime form and able to fetch a good price. Sell the four-horse carriages, too, since with one hand, he couldn't handle more than a pair.

Thereby severing one more link between the man he'd been before Waterloo, and now.

Jilting a fiancée, leaving the army, and now this. Nothing like changing his world completely in the space of a week.

Could he give it all up? he wondered as he set off down the lane. Following in his hunting-mad father's footsteps had been his goal since he'd joined his first chase, schooling hunters a talent he worked to perfect. Before the army and between Oxford terms, he'd spent all his time studying horses, looking for that perfect combination of bone, stamina and spirit that made a good hunter. Buying them, training them, then hunting and steeplechasing with the like-minded friends who called themselves 'Dom's Daredevils'.

Stripped of that occupation, the future stretched before him as a frightening void.

Though he'd never previously had a taste for solitude, within days of his return, he'd felt compelled to leave London. The prospect of visiting his clubs, attending a ball, mixing with the old crowd at Tatt's, inspecting the horses before a sale—all the activities in which he'd once delighted—now repelled him. Sending away even his cousin Will, who'd rescued him from the battlefield and tended him for months, he'd retreated to Bildenstone—the family estate he'd not seen in years, and hadn't even been sure was still habitable.

He'd sent Elizabeth away, too. A wave of grief and remorse swept through him as her lovely face surfaced in his mind. How could he have asked her to wait for him to recover, when the man he was now no longer fit into the world of hunts and balls they'd meant to share?

Ruthlessly he extinguished her image, everything about her and the hopes they once cherished too painful to contemplate. Best to concentrate on taking the next small step down the road ahead, small steps being all he could manage towards a future cloaked in a shifting mist of uncertainty.

Fighting the despair threatening to suck him down, he reminded himself again why he'd left friends, fiancée, and all that was familiar.

To find himself…whatever was left to find.

Wearily he picked up his pace, his rattled brain still righting itself. He traversed the sharp corner around which his horse had disappeared to find himself almost face to face with a young woman leading a mare.

They both started, the horsing rearing a little.

'Down, Starfire,' a feminine voice commanded. Looking up at him expectantly, the girl smiled and said, 'Sir, will you give me a hand? I was almost run down by a black beast of a stallion, which startled my mare. I'm afraid I wasn't paying enough attention, and lost my seat. I'll require help to remount.'

His mind still befuddled, Dom stared at her. Though tall enough that he didn't have to look down very far, his first impression was of a little brown wren—lovely pale complexion, big brown eyes, hair of indeterminate hue tucked under a tired-looking bonnet, and a worn brown habit years out of date.

The unknown miss didn't flinch at his eye patch, he had to give her that. Nor did her eyes stray to the pinned-up sleeve of his missing arm—the sleeve now liberally spattered with mud and decorated with leaf-bits, as was the rest of his clothing. Heavens, he must look like a vagrant who'd slept in the woods. It was a wonder she didn't run screaming in the opposite direction.

His lips curved into a whimsical smile at the thought as her pleasant expression faded. 'Sir, could you give me a hand, help me remount?' she all but shouted.

Dom flinched at the loud tones. *She must think me simple as well as dishevelled.* As his mind finally cleared and her request registered, his amusement vanished.

The images flashed into his head—all the girls he'd lifted in a dance, tossed into saddles…carried into bed. With two strong arms.

Anger coursed through him. 'That would be a bit of problem.' He gestured to his empty sleeve. 'Afraid I can't help you. Good day, miss.'

Her eyes widened as he began to walk past her. 'Can't help me?' she echoed. 'Can't—or won't?'

Fury mounting, he wheeled back to face her. 'Don't you see, idiot girl?' he spat out. 'I'm…impaired.'

Crippled would be a better description, but he couldn't get his mouth around the word. He turned to walk away again.

She hurried forward, the horse trailing on the reins

behind her, and blocked his path. 'What I see,' she said, her dark eyes flashing, 'is that you have one good arm, whether or not you choose to use it. Which is more than many of the soldiers who didn't survive Waterloo, including my father. *He* wouldn't have hesitated to give me a leg up, even with only one hand!'

Before he could respond, she shortened the lead on the horse's reins and snapped, 'Very well. I shall search for a more obliging log or tree stump. Good day, sir.'

Bemused, he watched the sway of her neat little bottom as she marched angrily away. With well-tended forest on either side of the lane—deadfall quickly removed to provide firewood for someone's hearth—he didn't think she was likely to find what she sought.

Turning back towards Bildenstone, he set off walking, wondering who the devil she was. Not that, having spent the last ten years either with the army, at his hunting box in Leicestershire or in London, he expected to recognise any of the locals. That girl would have been only a child the last time he'd been here, seven years ago.

He'd probably just insulted the daughter of some local worthy—though, given the shabby condition of her riding habit, not a man of great means. He meant to limit as much as possible any interaction with his neighbours, but in the restricted society of the country, he'd likely encounter her again. Perhaps by then, he'd be able to tender a sincere apology.

Stomping down the lane without encountering any objects suitable for use as a mounting block, Theodora Branwell felt her anger grow. After a fruitless ten-minute search, she conceded that she might have to walk all the way back to Thornfield Place before she could find a way to remount her horse.

Which meant she might as well abandon her purpose and try again tomorrow.

Not the least of her ire and frustration she directed at herself. If she'd not been so lost in rehearsing her arguments, she would have heard the approaching hoofbeats and had her mount well in hand before the stallion burst around the corner and flew past them. After all the obstacles they'd ridden over in India and on the Peninsula, how Papa would laugh to know she'd been unseated by so simple a device!

No sense bemoaning; she might as well accept that her lapse had ruined the timing for making a call on her prospective landlord today.

She had Charles to check on, she thought, her heart warming as she pictured the little boy she'd brought up. Then there were the rest of the children to settle, especially the two new little ones the Colonel had just sent her from Brussels. Though the manor's small nursery and adjoining bedchamber were becoming rather crowded, making settling the matter of the school and dormitory ever more urgent, Constancia and Jemmie would find them places. But she knew the thin boy and the pale, silent girl would feel better after a few sweetmeats, a reassuring hug, and a story to make them welcome.

How frightening and strange the English countryside must seem to a child, torn from the familiar if unstable life of travelling with an army across the dusty fields and valleys of Portugal and Spain. Especially after losing one's last parent.

It was a daunting enough prospect for her, and she was an adult.

The extra day would allow her to go over her arguments one more time. She liked Thornfield Place very much; she only had to convince Mr Ransleigh, her mostly absentee landlord who had now unaccountably taken up residence, that turning the neglected outbuilding on his property into a home and school for soldiers' orphans would cause no problem and was a noble thing to do.

A guilty pang struck her. She'd really been too hard on the one-armed, one-eyed man in the lane. Though he might have been injured in an accident, he had the unmistakable bearing of a soldier. Had he suffered his wounds at Waterloo? Recovering from such severe losses would be slow; frustration over his limitations might at times make him wonder if it would not have been better, had he never made it off the battlefield.

She knew it was. She'd have given anything, had Papa been found alive, whatever his condition. Or Marshall, dead these five years now.

The bitter anguish of her fiancé's loss scoured her again. How much different would her life be now, had he not fallen on that Spanish plain? They'd be long married, doubtless with children, her love returned and her place in society secure as his wife.

But it hadn't been fair to take out her desolation on that poor soldier. Wholly preoccupied with her own purpose, she only now recalled how thin his frame was, how dishevelled his rough clothing. When had he last eaten a good meal? Finding employment must be difficult for an ex-soldier with only one arm.

He'd not carried a pack, she remembered, so he must be a local resident. Country society comprised a small circle, she'd been told, much like the army. Which meant she'd probably encounter the man again. If she did, she would have to apologise. Perhaps in the interim, she might also think of some job she could hire him to perform at Thornfield Place.

Satisfied that she'd be able to atone for her rudeness, she dismissed him from her mind and trudged down the lane back towards Thornfield.

* * *

Nearly an hour later, Theo finally reached the stables and turned over her well-walked horse. Dismissing her irritation over an afternoon wasted, she entered through a back door, to have Franklin, her newly hired butler, inform her that a visitor awaited her.

Since she had no acquaintance in the county beyond the village solicitor she'd written to help her find staff, she couldn't imagine who might be calling. Curiosity speeding her step, she'd reached the parlour threshold before it struck her that, according to the dimly remembered rules of proper behaviour her long-dead mama had tried to instil in her, she ought to have gone upstairs to change into a presentable gown before receiving visitors.

But the identity of the lady awaiting her drove all such thoughts from her head. 'Aunt Amelia!' she cried in surprise and delight.

'My darling Theo! I'm so glad to have you home at last!' the lady declared, encircling her in a pair of plump, scented arms.

Theo's throat tightened as she returned the hug of her last remaining close relation. 'I'm so glad, too, Aunt Amelia. But what are you doing here? And how did you know I was at Thornfield Place?'

'I'd hoped you'd come to see me in London after you left Brussels. When you wrote you'd already consulted Richard's lawyer, found a suitable country manor, and wished to get settled there before you visited, I just couldn't wait.'

'I'm so glad you've come, although I fear you'll not find the establishment nearly up to your standards. I'm still hiring staff, and everything is at sixes and sevens.'

Pushing away, she surveyed the lady she'd not seen in over five years. 'How handsome you look in that cherry gown! In the first crack of fashion, I'd wager—not that I would know.'

'You're looking very well, too, my dear—though I can't in good conscience return the compliment about the habit.' After a grimace at the offending garment, she continued. 'Now that you're finally back in England, we must attend to that! One can understand the unfashionable dress, living in all the God-forsaken places my brother dragged you, but how have you managed to keep your complexion so fresh? I thought to find you thin and brown as a nut.'

'I've always been disgusting healthy, or so the English memsahibs used to tell Papa.'

'Unlike your poor mama, God rest her soul.' Sadness flitting across her face, she said, 'I still can't believe we've lost Richard, too.'

Steeling herself against the ever-present ache of loss, Theo said, 'I'm glad you've given up your blacks; the colour doesn't suit you.'

'You don't think it too soon? It's only nine months since…' Her voice trailed off.

'Since Papa fell at Waterloo,' Theo replied, making herself say the words matter of factly.

'It just doesn't seem fair,' Lady Amelia said, frowning. 'My brother surviving all those horrid battles, first in India, then on the Peninsula, only to be killed in the very last action of the war! But enough of that,' she said after a glance at Theo—who perhaps wasn't concealing her distress as well as she thought. 'Shall we have tea?'

'Of course. I'm devilish thirsty myself,' she said drily. 'I'll ring for Franklin.'

After instructing the butler to bring tea and refreshments, Theo joined her aunt on the sofa.

'How long can you stay? I'll have Reeves prepare you a room. It's a bit hectic with the children not settled yet, but I think we can make you comfortable.'

'Children?' her aunt repeated. 'So you still have them— Jemmie, the boy your father took in when his sergeant fa-

ther died? And the little girl you wrote me about. Besides
Charles, of course. How is the poor little orphan?'

'Doing well,' Theo said, her heart warming as she
thought of him. 'A sturdy four-year-old now.'

'Goodness, that old already! His father's family never...'

'No. Lord Everly's commander, Colonel Vaughn, wrote
to his father again when I returned with Charles after the
birth, to inform him of the poor mother's death in childbed, but the marquess did not deign to reply.' She neglected
mentioning how she'd rejoiced at learning she'd be able
to keep the child. 'So, he's still with me. Indeed, I can't
imagine being parted from him.'

'You're quite young enough to marry and have sons who
truly *are* your own,' her aunt replied tartly. 'I suppose you
had to do your Christian duty and accompany that unfortunate girl, *enceinte* and grieving, back to England after
Everly was killed. I do wish you'd made it to London for
the birth, though. How unfortunate to have his mama fall
ill, stranding you at some isolated convent in the wilds of
Portugal! Naturally, after her death, you felt obliged to
take charge of the infant until he could be returned to his
family. But with that family unwilling to accept the boy
and Richard gone—are you sure you should continue caring for him? As for the others, would it not be better to
put them into the custody of the parish? Under a colonel's
guardianship, such an odd household might have been tolerated in the army overseas, but even with your papa present, such a ménage here in England would be considered
very strange.' She sighed. 'You were ever wont to pick up
the stray and injured, even as a child.'

'I'm sure you would have done the same, had you been
there to see them, poor little creatures left on their own
to beg or starve.'

'None the less, without Richard... It's just not fitting for
a gently reared girl to have charge of...children like that.'

Theo laughed. 'After growing up in India and all those years following the drum, I don't believe I qualify as "gently reared".'

Her aunt gave her a fulminating look. 'You're still gently *born*, regardless of the unconventionality of your upbringing, and are as well, I understand, a considerable heiress. Despite your…unusual circumstances, I wouldn't despair of having you make a good match. Won't you come to me in London for the Season, let me find you a good man to take your father's place in your life?'

With a firm negative shake of her head, Theo said, 'I can't imagine a prospective suitor would look kindly on the idea of taking in a child not his own. Since I won't give up Charles, I doubt my fortune is large enough to tempt any man into marrying me. That is, any man I'd consider marrying.'

'You do yourself a disservice,' Lady Amelia protested. Giving Theo a quick inspection, she said, 'Your figure is fine, your complexion lovely, and those brown eyes quite luminous. I'm certain my maid could do wonders with that curly dark hair. You're a bit taller than is fashionable, but with the proper gowns, I think quite a number of eligible gentleman might come up to snuff. You are the grand-daughter of an earl, after all.'

Waving Theo to silence before she could protest again, Lady Amelia continued. 'If you love Charles as you say you do, you must know the best thing for him would be for you to marry! Give him a father to pattern himself after, someone who could teach him all those manly pursuits so important to gentleman, and introduce him to the clubs and societies he must frequent to be accepted by his peers. As for the other children… I don't wish to set your back up, but it really would be better for them to be placed in an institution where they can learn a vocation. You do them no favours, to raise them above their stations.'

Ignoring her aunt's words about Charles, which had the uncomfortable ring of truth about them, Theo said, 'I don't intend to raise the others above their stations. In fact, arranging for their proper care is the main reason I decided to come here. I have to admit, I'm looking forward to having a settled home again myself, something I've not had since we left India.'

She left unspoken her fear that making a life alone in England, the ancestral home in which she'd never lived, whose ways often seemed as strange to her as India's would to her aunt, might prove a daunting task.

No matter, she would master it. She must, for the children and for herself.

'I did wonder why you chose a manor in Suffolk. As I understand the provisions of the will, Richard left you numerous properties, along with your mama's considerable fortune. Why did you not settle on one of them?'

'The solicitor informed me that all the properties are let to long-term lessees, whom I wouldn't wish to displace. So I asked Mr Mitchell to find me a suitable country manor to rent, something with a sturdy outbuilding nearby of sufficient size to be turned into a dormitory and school. A place where the children can learn their letters and be taught a trade.'

Her aunt laughed. 'Goodness, that sounds like a great deal of trouble! Wouldn't it be simpler to send them off to the parish? It's only two children, after all.' At the look on Theo's face, she said, 'It is just the two?'

'Well, you see,' Theo explained, well aware of her aunt's probable reaction to the news, 'Colonel Vaughn told me before we left Brussels how much he appreciated what Papa and I had done for the orphans. After Waterloo, I… found two others, and in a reply I've just posted to his letter enquiring about the possibility, I assured him I would be happy to take in more.'

'Theo, no!' her aunt cried. 'You can't mean to bury yourself in the country and turn into some glorified—*orphanage matron*, looking after the children of who knows who!'

'Who else will look after them, if I don't? Should I just stand by and see the offspring of our valiant soldiers end up in a workhouse? Besides, I need something useful to do with my life, now that…now that I won't be running Papa's household any longer,' she finished, proud to have made it through that sentence without a tremble in her voice.

'My dear Theo, you're far too young to behave as if your life is over! I know you believe you buried your heart when Marshall fell at Fuentes de Oñoro. But I promise you, one can find love again—if you will only let yourself. I'm certain Lieutenant Hazlett wouldn't want you to dwindle away into an old maid, alone and grieving.'

'At seven-and-twenty, I imagine society already considers me at my last prayers,' she evaded. Though it had been more than five years now, she still couldn't speak of the horror of losing Marshall. Loving so intensely had led to intolerable pain, all she could endure. She had no intention of subjecting herself to that ever again.

Besides, she could never marry someone without telling him the truth—and she didn't dare risk that.

'I'll not argue the point—for now!' her aunt said. 'But I would like to persuade you to come to London. Though I perfectly understand why you felt it your duty to remain with Charles's mother during her Hour of Need, I was so disappointed when you didn't come stay with me as we'd planned. I've hoped since then we'd have another chance for me to spoil you a bit, after all the time you've spent in the wilds, billeted who knows where, never knowing where your next meal might come from, and with the worry of impending battle always weighing on you!'

'One never completely escaped the worry,' Theo admit-

ted, 'but battle was the exception. Most of the time was
spent training, moving between encampments, or billeted
in winter quarters. Provisions were generally good, with
game to supplement the soup pot. As for accommoda-
tions…' she chuckled, remembering '…Papa and I shared
everything from a campaign tent to cots in a stable to the
bedchamber of a *marquesa's* palace! It was a grand adventure shared with marvellous companions, and I wouldn't
have missed it for the world.'

It had also brought her Charles, and, she thought as a
stab of grief gashed her, a fiery passion she didn't expect
ever to experience again.

Which also reminded her that not all the companions
had been marvellous. After the devastation of her fiancé's
death, one officer who was no gentleman had sniffed at her
skirts, certain she must eventually succumb to the blan-
dishments of a man of his high birth and social position.

The only benefit of leaving the regiment was she'd never
have to deal with Audley Tremaine again.

'Game in the soup pot and a cot in a stable!' her aunt
cried, recalling her attention. 'Call me pudding-hearted,
but I prefer a bed with my own linens under a sturdy roof,
awakened by nothing more threatening than the shouts of
milk-sellers.'

'Campaigning would not have been for you,' Theo
agreed. 'But I must leave you now to check on the children. Constancia—you remember Constancia, the nursemaid I brought with me from the convent after Charles
was born?—will show you to your room. I hope you'll
make a long visit!'

'I am due back in London shortly, and you'll have much
to do, getting your establishment put together. Unless I
can dissuade you from this enterprise? Coax you to leave
the children with those used to dealing with orphans, and
concentrate on your own future?'

'Abandon them to a workhouse?' Theo's heart twisted as she thought of those innocents turned over to strange and uncaring hands. 'No, you cannot dissuade me.'

Lady Amelia sighed. 'I didn't think so. You're as head-strong as Richard when you get the bit between your teeth. The whole family tried to talk him out of going to India, but no one could prevail upon him to remain at home, tending his acres like a proper English gentleman, once he'd taken the idea in his head.'

'I do appreciate your wishing to secure a more suitable future for me,' Theo assured her. 'But having never lived in England and being so little acquainted with the society's rules, I fear I'd be an even greater disappointment than Papa, were you to try to foist me on the Marriage Mart.'

'A lovely, capable, intelligent girl like you? I don't believe it! Though I admire your desire to aid those poor unfortunates, I refuse to entirely cede my position. I still think marriage would be best for you *and* them, and I shall be searching for a way to make it happen!'

Theo laughed. 'Scheme, then, if it makes you happy.'

'It's your happiness I worry about, my dear. You're still so young! I want you to find joy again.'

Joy. She'd experienced its rapture—and paid its bitter price. She'd since decided she could make do with contentment, as long as Charles was safe and happy.

'I expect to be happy in my life, helping those "poor unfortunates",' she told her aunt firmly as she kissed her cheek.

So she must be, she thought as she walked out of the room. It was the only life left to her, a choice she'd sealed years ago when she left that Portuguese convent with a swaddled newborn in her arms.

Chapter Two

By the time Dom, beyond exhausted by the long walk home, arrived back at Bildenstone Hall, all he wanted was a glass of laudanum-laced brandy and something soft on to which he could become horizontal. Instead, he was met at the door by the elderly butler, Wilton, who informed him the Squire, Lady Wentworth and Miss Wentworth awaited him in the parlour—and had been waiting more than an hour.

'Send them away,' Dom ordered, limping past the man, desperate for that drink to ease the headache that was compounding the misery of his throbbing wrist and shoulder.

'But, Mr Ransleigh,' Wilton protested as he trailed after Dom, 'the Squire said the matter was urgent, and he would wait as long as necessary to see you today!'

The words trembled on Dom's lips to consign the lot of them—the Squire, Lady Whomever, the girl in the lane, Diablo and the butler—to hell and back. With difficulty, he swallowed them.

While Dom hoped to socialise as little as possible, he'd known that, once the Squire learned the owner of the most extensive property in the county had taken up residence, courtesy demanded he pay a call at Bildenstone Hall. Though his head pounded like an anvil upon which a blacksmith was hammering out horseshoes, he knew that it would be the height of incivility to send away sight un-seen so distinguished a neighbour.

Unless he wished Wilton to tell that worthy and his party that, having fallen off a horse and been forced to walk home, Mr Ransleigh was in no fit state to receive them.

He might not have resided at Bildenstone Hall for years, but beyond doubt, every member of the gentry for miles around knew of 'Dandy Dom' and his exploits on the hunt-ing field and in the army. Call it foolish pride, but even more than being branded as churlish, he dreaded being considered a weakling—a conclusion his injuries might make strangers all too quick to draw.

Dredging up from deep within the will that had kept him in the saddle through the fatigue and strain of many long campaigns, Dom said, 'Very well. Tell them I'm just back from…riding the fields and will need a few moments to make myself presentable.'

'Very good, Mr Ransleigh,' the butler said, obviously relieved not to have to deliver a message of dismissal to a man of the Squire's stature.

Hauling himself up the stairs, he rang for Henries. He had his mud-spattered garments removed by the time the batman arrived to help him into clean ones. Battle-ready within minutes, he squared his tired shoulders and headed for the stairs.

Though he ached for a soothing draught and a deep sleep, he figured he could stay upright for the length of a courtesy call. He was too tired to wonder why Lady Somebody and her daughter had accompanied the Squire.

A few moments later, he forced a smile to his lips and entered the drawing room.

'Squire Marlowe, how kind of you to call! And whom

do I have the honour of addressing?' He gestured to the ladies.

'So good to see you, too, Mr Ransleigh, after so many years!' the Squire replied. 'Lady Wentworth and Miss Wentworth, may I introduce to you our illustrious neighbour, Mr Dominic Ransleigh. A captain in the Sixteenth Light Dragoons who charged into the teeth of Napoleon's finest, one of the heroes of Waterloo!'

'Ladies, a pleasure,' Dom said as the callers curtsied to his bow.

'We've heard of your gallant deeds, of course, Mr Ransleigh,' Lady Wentworth said. 'Everyone in the county is so proud of you.'

'We were all of us delighted to learn you intended to take up residence at Bildenstone Hall again,' the Squire said. 'Your father and mother, God rest their souls, were sorely missed when they abandoned Suffolk to settle at Upton Park.'

Had the neighbourhood felt slighted by his father's removal to Quorn country? Dom wondered, trying to read the man's tone.

'When she learned I meant to call today,' the Squire continued, 'Lady Wentworth, head of the Improvement Society for Whitfield Parish, begged leave to accompany me. With her lovely daughter, Miss Wentworth, the ornament of our local society who, sadly, is soon to join her godmother for the Season in London.'

So that was why Lady Somebody had come, Dom thought, his mind clearing as he caught this last bit. As closely as news about his family was followed, he suspected that word of his broken engagement had already made it to Suffolk. The nephew of an earl with a tidy fortune and important family connections would be considered an attractive prospect by country gentry like Lady Wentworth, regardless of his physical shortcomings.

Equally obvious, the enthusiasm engendered in her mother by his matrimonial assets was not entirely shared by the daughter. Dom noted her gaze travelling from the pinned-up sleeve to his eye patch and back, her expression a mingling of awe and distaste.

First the girl in the lane scolding him for making excuse of his limitations, and now Miss Wentworth's fascinated disdain. As if he were the prime attraction in a raree-show.

He had the ignoble urge to sidle up to her and see if she would flinch away. When his continued attention finally alerted her that he'd caught her staring at him, she coloured and gave him what he supposed most men would consider an enticing smile.

With her pretty face and glossy blond locks, she was as lovely as the Squire had pronounced her—and he felt no attraction at all.

Perhaps he ought to relieve her anxiety by assuring her he was in no danger of falling for the charms of an *ingénue* who'd probably never set foot outside her home parish. Then, rebuking himself for his uncharitable thoughts, he turned his attention back to the mother, who was nattering on about her reasons for accompanying the squire.

'...take the liberty of accompanying Squire Marlowe, when in the strictest sense, I should not have called until my husband, Sir John, called first. However, there is a matter of urgency at hand. My society oversees the parish poorhouse, where honest folk in need are offered assistance. As I'm sure you'll agree, it's imperative that such unfortunates, their morals already weakened by low birth and squalid surroundings, not be made more vulnerable by exposure to additional corruption. As they certainly would be, were children of that sort allowed to reside here!'

'Children of that sort?' Dom echoed. 'Forgive me, Lady Wentworth, but I have no idea what you're talking about.'

'Have you not yet been informed of the matter?' the lady cried, indignation in her tones. 'Infamous!'

Resigning himself to the fact that, though Lady Wentworth's main purpose might be to show off her attractive daughter, her secondary one was not likely to be quickly accomplished, Dom said, 'Shall we be seated? I see Wilton already brought tea; can he refresh your cups?'

Resisting the devilish urge to seat himself close to Miss Wentworth, and see whether the inducements of his wealth and lineage won out over her distaste for his damaged person, he took a chair opposite the sofa.

After Wilton had served the guests, he turned to the Squire, hoping his explanation would prove briefer. 'Won't you acquaint me with the matter?'

'Certainly,' the Squire said. 'Two days ago, Mr Scarsdale, the solicitor in Hadwell, mentioned to me that Thornfield Place, which abuts your southern boundaries, had been let by a Theo Branwell. He then informed me that this man, already in residence, intends to approach you about renting the old stone barn your father once planned to turn into a cloth manufactory. For the purpose of setting up a *home for soldiers' orphans.*'

'A terrible prospect!' Lady Wentworth cried, seizing hold of the conversation. 'Having been with the army, Mr Ransleigh, you know better than we how rough a life it is! Lord Wellington himself referred to the common soldiery as "the dregs of the earth". Only consider the offspring of such persons, growing up around vulgarity, drunkenness, and the company of...' With a glance at her daughter, she leaned closer to whisper, *'Camp-following women!'*

Settling herself back, she continued in normal tones. 'They could not help but have been corrupted since birth. I'm sure you understand our horror at the prospect that such children might be lodged nearby. Unthinkable enough that gently raised folk be subjected to their presence! Only consider how much more injurious association with them would be for the orphaned poor, with their innate bent to depravity. As head of a society devoted to their well-being, I felt it my Duty to speak with you at once about this nefarious scheme. Doubtless, this Mr Branwell means to play upon your sympathies as a former soldier. But as a gentleman of wit and discernment, I'm sure you could not wish to lend yourself to such an enterprise.'

In truth, Dom didn't wish to lend himself to anything, particularly not to the lady whose strident voice was intensifying the pounding in his head. Knowing that responding would encourage her to embellish, likely at enough length that he got a good eyeful of her beauteous daughter's neatly turned ankles, he meant to give her no excuse to prolong the interview.

'I understand your concern, Lady Wentworth, and yours, Squire Marlowe. I assure you, when and if I'm approached by Mr Branwell, I will give the matter my most careful consideration. After such a long wait, I'm sure you must be pressed to return to other engagements. I myself am overdue to consult with my steward,' he lied smoothly. 'So you must excuse me, but do finish your tea before you depart.'

He rose as he spoke, continuing quickly. 'Squire, a pleasure to see you again. Miss Wentworth, I wish you well on your Season, and best of luck with your society, Lady Wentworth.'

Deaf to their expressions of gratitude and protestations that they were in no hurry, Dom bowed and left the parlour.

Retreating to his chamber with as much speed as he could muster, he barely made it to the bed before his legs crumpled under him. Bracing himself with his good arm, he sank face-down on to the blessedly soft, flat surface and fell instantly to sleep.

With dim memories of having awakened in the dark to glug down a glass of the laudanum-laced brandy at his bedside, Dom pulled himself from sleep late the next morning, groggy and aching. He took another quick swallow of the brandy, thinking as he sank back against the pillows that he'd not indulged in strong spirits before breakfast since his salad days at Oxford.

After a few moments, the liquor soothing the sharp edges off his ever-present pain, Dom felt human enough to ring for his batman. Hot coffee and a hot bath would dispel the grogginess, after which he could dress and ready himself…for what?

Once, he would have headed for the barns to check on his horses. How he'd prided himself on his reputation for finding the most spirited yearlings with jumping promise and bending the difficult horses to his will, schooling them to jump obstacles they'd rather avoid. Gloried in the excitement of sitting astride a ton of barely controlled wildness while galloping through woods, fields and meadows, jumping streams, brush and fences.

There'd be no more of that, as yesterday had demonstrated with painful clarity.

He should go to his study, check the London papers and the current prices for prime hunters at Tatt's. Or write to some hunting enthusiasts, asking if they were interested in purchasing any of his horses.

His spirits, already at a low ebb, sank even more at the prospect.

No, he couldn't face that today. He'd go poke about in the library, which was as respectably large and well filled a room as he remembered. The pleasure of reading, a pastime often indulged while in winter quarters on the Peninsula, had been restricted by the dearth of books available. The single bright spot in his decision to retreat to Bildenstone was having access to the wealth of volumes his grandfather had accumulated.

Finding something intriguing would distract him from his misfortunes and raise his spirits, he told himself. Maybe he'd wander outside to read, see if the gazebo in his mother's garden was still a pleasant place to sit.

He needed to start figuring out his future…but not yet. Once the additional aches of yesterday's disastrous episode faded, he'd be in a better frame of mind to move forward.

An hour later, fed, dressed and feeling marginally better, Dom walked towards the library. Encountering the butler on the way reminded him of the previous day's meeting, and he paused.

'Wilton, I don't wish to receive any more visitors. I mean *no one*, not even if God Himself turns up on my doorstep!'

Looking pained at that sacrilege, Wilton nodded. 'As you wish, Mr Ransleigh.'

'That's what I wish,' he muttered, and continued to the library.

After browsing through Caesar's *Commentaries*, lamenting his inattention during Latin studies, Dom settled on a volume of Herodotus. The day having turned cloudy, he abandoned thoughts of the garden and settled in a wing chair before a snug fire.

As he'd hoped, the discussion of the struggle between Xerxes and the Spartans soon absorbed his attention.

When Wilton bowed himself into the room later, he realised enough time had passed that he was hungry.

Unwilling to leave the comfortable chair, he said,

'Would you ask Cook to prepare some of the ham and cheese from last night, and bring it here to the library?'

'Of course, Mr Ransleigh. But first…' the butler hesitated, an anxious expression on his face '…I'm afraid I must tell you that…that a young lady has called. I explained that you weren't receiving anyone, under any circumstances, but she said the matter was urgent and she would not leave until she saw you.'

Yet *another* lady on an urgent errand that would not keep? Who might it be now?

Though he'd happily tilled his way through fields of accommodating beauties before getting himself engaged, he'd always been careful; he had no fears that some dimly remembered female stood on his doorstep with a *petit paquet* in arms.

Curiosity was soon submerged by a lingering irritation over yesterday's unwelcome visitors. 'You didn't admit her, did you?'

'No, sir. Following your instructions, I closed the door—in her face, as she refused to move, a thing I've never done in my life, sir!'

'Sounds like problem solved,' Dom said. 'Eventually, she'll tire of waiting and go home. Will you have that tray brought up, and some more coffee, please?'

The butler lingered, looking even more distressed. 'You see, sir, as the young lady arrived at just past eight this morning, while you were still abed, I felt no hesitation in refusing her. But it's now nearly two of the clock and… and she's still waiting.'

Annoyed as he was to have yet another person try to intrude upon his solitude, Dom felt a revival of curiosity which, as he reluctantly reviewed the situation, intensified.

He hadn't mingled with society here for years, and only a few knew he'd returned to Suffolk. He had no idea who the woman might be, or what matter could be compelling enough to prompt her to come alone and wait for hours to consult him.

Arguing with himself that he would do better to ignore the caller, and losing, he finally said, 'Who is it? Not the girl from yesterday, surely.'

'Oh, no, sir,' Wilton said, sounding scandalised. 'Miss Wentworth's mama would never allow her to call alone on a single gentleman. The Young Person didn't give me her name, saying it wouldn't be known to you anyway.'

It *would* be scandalous for an unmarried girl to call on him, Dom belatedly realised. He'd been out of England so long, he'd initially forgotten the strict rules governing the behaviour of gently born maidens.

Maybe she wasn't so gently born.

There might be possibilities here, he thought, his body now taking an interest. Not that he was sure he was yet healed enough that such pleasant exercise wouldn't cause him more agony than ecstasy. 'You called her a "young lady", though. Why, after such brazen behaviour?'

'Well, she is young, and in speech and dress, she appears to be a lady, however improper it might be for her to come here.'

'Alone, you said.'

'Yes, sir.'

'What has she been doing all this time?'

'When I last glanced out, she'd seated herself on the brick wall at the end of the courtyard. She appeared to be reading, sir.'

'She hasn't knocked again?'

'No, sir. I suppose, sitting where she is, she knows the household must be aware of her presence.'

So his unwelcome caller had been waiting for hours. Without trying a second time to force herself upon them.

Reading a book.

Persistence he understood, but he knew few men, and no females, that patient.

After an irresolute moment, that bedevilling curiosity overcame his body's urging that he remain seated. Dom rose from his chair and paced to the mullioned windows.

Glancing out, he could see, below to his left, the three-foot wall that set off the courtyard spanning the space between the two Tudor wings projecting from the main block of Bildenstone Hall. Sitting there, wrapped in a cloak, was a female, her figure so foreshortened by height and distance that he couldn't accurately estimate her shape or stature.

The day, already gloomy when he'd made his way to the library, had darkened further. As he gazed at her, a gust of wind rattled the window.

'It's going to rain shortly,' he said, after a soldier's inspection of the clouds. 'That should send her on her way. I'll have that tray now.'

'Yes, sir,' Wilton said, looking brighter. Apparently feeling that, having discharged his duty to the fairer sex by informing his master of the girl's presence, he could now absolve himself of responsibility for her welfare, he trotted off for the tray.

A responsibility he obviously felt he'd transferred to Dom. Though his will tried to tell his conscience he wouldn't accept the charge, within a few minutes of seating himself again, he felt compelled to return to the window.

The rain he'd predicted was pelting down from clouds that didn't look likely to dissipate for some time. The girl was still there, though she'd tucked the book away and huddled in upon herself, as if to provide the smallest possible target to the besieging rain.

Her choice, he told himself, returning to his chair.

But after a few more minutes of reading the same paragraph over and over without comprehending a syllable, he tossed down the book and returned to the window.

She sat as before, huddled on the wall.

Uttering a string of oaths, Dom stomped to the bell pull and yanked hard.

A few moments later, Wilton reappeared, panting. 'I came as fast as I could, sir!'

Dom walked back to window and stared down at the female, still sitting immobile as a gargoyle rainspout on a cathedral roof.

Probably didn't shed moisture as efficiently, though.

'Damn and blast!' he muttered before turning to Wilton. 'I suppose we'll have to admit her before she contracts a consumption of the lungs.'

'At once, sir!' Wilton said, sounding relieved. 'I'll show her to the small receiving room.'

'Better put some towelling down to protect the carpet. She must be drenched.'

Wondering when he was going to find the solitude he sought, angry—but more intrigued than he wanted to admit by the mysterious female—Dom exited the library and headed for the receiving room.

After entering, he took up a commanding position before the cold hearth—the lady might have won the first skirmish, but Dom had no intention of looking defeated— and awaited his uninvited visitor. Underscoring the caller's lack of pedigree, she was being conducted to a small back parlour, rather than the formal front room into which the Squire and his ladies had been shown yesterday.

Dom wondered if she'd recognise the subtle set-down.

He heard the murmur of approaching voices and his body tensed. To his surprise, he found himself looking forward to the encounter.

But then, this female had already shown herself a skilled campaigner. Using neither force nor threat nor any of the tears and tantrums upon which ladies, in his experience, normally relied to soften male resolve—relying instead on his own sense of honour and courtesy—she'd induced him to yield.

The female entered. He had only a quick impression of a tall girl in an attractive, if outdated, green gown before she bent her head and sank into a curtsy.

'Thank you for receiving me,' she said, her throaty voice holding no hint of the reproach he would have anticipated from someone subjected to so long and discourteous a wait.

His unwilling admiration deepened. Yet another good tactic—unsettle an opponent by not responding in the expected manner.

Noting she was not, in fact, dripping on the carpet, as she rose to face him, he said, 'I suppose I should apologise, but you seem no worse for a drenching, Miss…'

'No need to apologise. My sturdy cloak has protected me through many a…'

Her voice trailed off and her eyes widened as Dom's brain added together luminous brown eyes, pale skin, and slender form.

'You!' she cried at the same moment Dom realised he recognised his persistent visitor.

The girl from the lane.

Chapter Three

For a long moment, they simply stared at each other.

Recovering first, the girl sighed. 'Oh, dear, this is…unfortunate! I suppose I should start by apologising for being so judgemental and inconsiderate yesterday. I do beg your pardon, Mr Ransleigh.'

If she could be magnanimous, he supposed he should be, too. 'Only if you'll accept my apology in return. There was no excuse for my rudeness…even if I'd just had my limitations rather forcibly demonstrated.'

Her eyes narrowed. 'The stallion!' she said. '*You* were riding that black beast that nearly trampled me.'

No point in denying what, with impressive quickness, she'd already figured out. 'Until he dumped me off,' he admitted.

'I don't wonder he unseated you. I expect you'd need the hands of a prize fighter to keep that one under control.'

'True. But, oh, can he fly like the wind! And jump anything in his path,' Dom said wistfully, remembering.

'Waterloo?' she asked, pointing to his arm.

'Yes.'

'I'm sorry.'

He nodded an acknowledgement before the memory

surfaced. 'I seem to recall you saying your father fell there? My condolences on your loss.'

Anguish showed briefly on her face before she masked it. 'Thank you,' she said softly.

Watching, Dom felt her pain echo within him. It had been difficult, losing comrades with whom he'd ridden and fought, but he'd never lost anyone who was truly family. How much more agonising would it have been had some battle claimed one of his cousins—Will or Max or Alastair?

Recovering her composure, the girl said, 'Had I known you were recuperating, I should have asked first for your lady mother. That is, I imagine she is here, caring for you during your recovery?'

'I'm afraid I lost my mother years ago.'

'Ah. So who is here, assisting you? Surely your family didn't leave you to cope alone.'

She must have sensed his withdrawal, for before he could utter some blighting set-down, she said, 'Now I must beg your pardon again! I didn't mean to pry. I should confess at the outset that, never having resided in England, I have trouble remembering the rules governing polite society. I've spent my life in the compounds of India or in the army, where everyone knows everyone else's business. I'm afraid I'm deplorably plain speaking and have no sensibility at all, so if I say something you find intrusive or inappropriate, just slap me back into place, like Papa's sergeant-major always did when I was too inquisitive.'

Having just been given permission to ignore her question, he felt unaccountably more inclined to answer. Unlike his former hunting buddies and the society maidens who had spent the war safely in England, she'd evidently lived through it with the army. She understand hardship, danger—and loss.

'My cousin Will found me on the field after the battle,

had me removed to a private house and cared for, then stayed with me until I was able to be transported back to London, about a week ago. He urged me to accompany him to our cousin Alastair's home, so our aunt could tend me. But she would have cosseted me within an inch of my life, and I…I didn't think I could bear that.'

She nodded. 'Sometimes one must face the bleakest prospects in life alone.'

The truth of her words, uttered with the poignancy of experience, resonated within him. The death of her father and returning to an England she didn't know were certainly bleak enough.

'But here I am, taking up your time while you're probably wishing me at Jericho! Let me state my business and leave you in peace. I'm Theodora Branwell, by the way,' she said, holding out her hand. 'My father was Colonel Richard Branwell, of the Thirty-Third Foot.'

She offered the hand vertically, for shaking, rather than palm down, for a kiss. Amused, he grasped her fingers for a brisk shake—and felt an unexpected tingle dance up his arm.

Startled for an instant, he dismissed the odd effect. 'Dominic Ransleigh,' he replied. 'Though I suppose you already knew that.'

'Yes. I recently leased Thornfield Place, specifically because it abuts your property. Or rather, one particular part of your property.'

Suddenly the connection registered. 'Theodora—Theo!' he said with a laugh. 'I'd been told to expect a call. Except the folk hereabouts seem to think you're a man.'

A mischievous look sparkled in her eyes. 'Though I didn't deliberately try to create that impression, I might not have used my full name when I contacted the local solicitor. So, you've been told that I'd like to lease the stone building in your south pasture and convert it into a home and school for orphans?'

'I have. I must warn you, though, the neighbourhood isn't happy about the idea. To quote the head of the Improvement Society of Whitfield Parish, whom I had the misfortune of receiving yesterday, such children, growing up around "vulgarity, drunkenness, and the company of loose women" must have been "corrupted at birth" and could only be an affront to decent people and a deleterious influence upon the county's poor.'

Miss Branwell's eyes widened at that recitation. 'No wonder you didn't wish to receive anyone today.'

While Dom swallowed the laugh surprised out of him by that remark, she turned an earnest look on him. 'Surely you don't share that ridiculous opinion! You're a soldier, Mr Ransleigh! True, the conditions in the army were… rougher than those the children might have encountered in England. I would argue, though, that the hardships they've survived make them stronger and more resilient, rather than less suited for society.'

Like she was? he wondered. Stronger, perhaps. Suited for *polite* society—that might be another matter.

'Besides, what they become will be determined, not by the circumstances of their birth, but by how they are treated now,' she went on. 'The best way to avoid having them fall into vice is to make them literate and give them training in a proper trade. Do you not agree that is the least we can do for the orphans of the men whose valour and sacrifice freed Europe from Napoleon's menace?'

Though her words were stirring, Dom found himself more arrested by the lady delivering them. How could he have thought her a little brown wren?

Her cheeks flushed, her eyes sparkling, her enticing bosom rising and falling with every breath, her low, throaty voice vibrant with conviction…. As his skin prickled with awareness and his body tightened in arousal, he felt himself almost physically drawn to her.

Surely a woman so passionate in her defence of the orphans would bring that passion to every activity.

To her bed.

'What happened to Christian charity, to compassion for the innocent, to leaving judgements to God?' she was demanding.

Her reference to the Almighty a rebuke to his lust, he told himself to concentrate on the subject, rather than the allure of the lady. 'Abandoned for preconceived notions, probably,' he replied.

That brought her flight of oratory to a halt. Sighing, she said, 'You're probably right. But...*you* don't share such notions, surely?'

She gestured towards him as she spoke. He had to force himself to keep from taking her hand, now near his own. Tasting her lips, still parted in enquiry. So nearly tangible was the pull between them, surely she must feel it, too?

For a moment, she did nothing, simply standing with her hand outstretched. Just as he was concluding that his previously reliable instincts must have gone completely array, she raised her eyes to meet his gaze. Some *connection* pulsed between them, wordless, but eloquent as a sonnet.

Hastily, she retracted her hand and stepped back. 'I shouldn't harangue you—though I did warn you I'm deplorably outspoken! If allowing me to use your building would put you at odds with the neighbourhood, perhaps I should come up with another plan.'

Dom thought of yesterday's call by Lady Wentworth. How many other mothers of marriageable daughters lived within visiting distance of Bildenstone Hall? Finding himself at odds with his neighbours might not be a bad thing.

'What would you do if I refuse permission?' he asked, curious.

She shrugged. 'Break the lease on Thornfield and make enquiries about settling elsewhere.'

'Wouldn't that be a great deal of trouble? To say nothing of the disruption to the children.'

'Having known nothing but following the drum, they're used to disruption and trouble.'

Despite his automatic inclination to do the opposite of whatever the officious Lady Wentworth had urged, with his desire to be left in solitude, he had been leaning towards refusing, should the then-unknown Theo Branwell approach him about renting his property.

Now he wasn't so sure.

Apparently sensing his ambivalence, Miss Branwell's face brightened with new hope. '*Would* you consider it? I promise we shall not intrude on your peace! You needn't make a final decision now; let us stay on a provisional basis. If you find the school a disturbance, you can send us all packing!'

That sounded reasonable enough—and might have the added benefit of keeping the Lady Wentworths of the area at bay. 'Very well, I agree.'

'Splendid!'

The delight in her smile warmed him, and he couldn't help smiling back.

Though she'd claimed she would not cut up his peace, with that…*something* simmering between them, Dom wasn't so sure. With a little shock, he realised that for the first time since the urge for solitude had consumed him, the possibility of company didn't displease him.

'Do I have your permission to inspect the building at once, while the solicitors discuss terms?' she asked, pulling him from his thoughts.

'Certainly.'

'Thank you. I need to determine what materials and

supplies might be necessary to make it suitable. I shall cover all the costs of renovation, of course.'

'The building hasn't been inhabited for years,' Dom felt it necessary to warn her. 'My father constructed a second floor, intending to convert it into a weaving factory, but the rest of the work was never completed. Getting it into shape may be quite costly.'

'My father left me well provided for.'

Suddenly it occurred to him how odd it was for a girl of her age and situation to undertake such a project. 'It's one thing for a *Mr* Theo Branwell—doubtless an idealistic cleric of some sort—to open an orphanage. Why are *you* doing this?' he asked. 'If I have relations to cosset me, surely you have family in England to take you in—or find you a proper husband. Maybe a prospective fiancé waiting in the wings?'

He wasn't sure what imp had induced him to add that last, but at the stricken look on her face, he instantly regretted it.

'He fell at Fuentes de Oñoro,' she said quietly. 'For many months afterward, I wish I'd died, too. But the orphans needed someone. Now, with Papa gone, so do I. I've sufficient funds for the endeavour, and some of the children have already been with me for years. We're good for each other.'

So that explained why such a vibrant girl wasn't already riveted, mothering a quiverful of her own children. The odd notion struck him that though he *missed* Elizabeth, he'd never felt he would perish without her. Shaking off the thought, he returned to the topic at hand.

'I should probably go with you to inspect the building.'

'You needn't! I've just promised we wouldn't be any bother. Your estate agent can accompany me.'

Again, she'd offered him a graceful way to disengage—and again, he was curiously disinclined to take it.

'Not having seen the building in years, I've no idea what would be a suitable rent,' he countered.

'I have seen it—at least from the outside—and had a figure in mind,' she said, naming one that sounded quite generous to him.

'You are certainly…well organised,' he observed, substituting a more flattering adjective for the one that had initially come to mind.

'Managing, you mean,' she acknowledged with a smile. 'You're quite right. You see, I've overseen my father's household since I was the merest child. Then, on the Peninsula—well, you were there, you know how it is. Having to anticipate movements, preparing for every contingency! Water, or none. Provisions, or none. Shelter, or none. Having your gear and supplies ready to move at a moment's notice, should battle threaten or the army's plans change. Which,' she added with a chuckle, 'they always did. Which regiment were you in, by the way?'

Before he could answer, she waved her hand in a silencing gesture. 'There I go, prying again, after just assuring you I would not. Please excuse me.'

'It's not prying to ask about the experiences of a fellow campaigner,' he replied, surprised to discover he meant it. 'I was with the Sixteenth Light Dragoons.'

'Did you charge with the Union Brigade against D'Erlon's Corps at Waterloo? A magnificent effort, I was told.'

Dom shrugged, having never sorted out his feelings about the event that had so drastically altered his life. 'When the trumpet sounds, one goes.'

'Duty, in spite of fear or likelihood of success, Papa always said,' she murmured, grief veiling her face again.

'Duty,' he agreed, struggling himself with a familiar mixture of pride, sadness and bitter regret for what he had lost that day.

After a silent moment, both of them doubtless recalling what duty had cost them, Dom shook himself free of the memories. 'When do you want to inspect the property?'

'Now, if possible.'

'I appreciate that you don't mind the damp, but the weather is rather inclement. Are you sure you wouldn't prefer to wait until tomorrow?'

'Oh, no! I'm impatient to begin. Besides, the worst of the rain is over now. But truly, you needn't bother yourself to accompany me.'

'It won't be a bother. If I'm to reside here, I must know what's going on with the property. Did you come on horseback?'

'Yes, but as I recall, the building isn't too far from the manor. We could walk.'

Was she recalling his admission that he no longer possessed a horse he could ride? he wondered. 'If you'll wait until I get my coat, I'll escort you. By the way, in spite of what you saw me wearing yesterday, I do own a coat respectable enough that you needn't fear being seen with me.'

To his puzzlement, she gave a peal of laughter, quickly stifled.

'What?'

She shook with silent mirth, her eyes merry. 'It's nothing.'

'Come, you must tell me. Have pity on a man whose face now frightens children.'

That sobered her. 'You can't be serious! Don't you ever look in a glass? You must know you are quite handsome.'

It being obvious by now that Miss Branwell was incapable of toadying or flattery, he knew she spoke the truth as she saw it. His spirits, consigned to the lowest of dungeons after yesterday's ignominious ride, climbed several storeys at this verbal confirmation that the unusual girl who attracted him so strongly found him attractive, too.

As he gazed at her, their physical connection, simmering just below the level of consciousness, intensified again. Struggling to resist its pull, he said, 'Now, tell me what was so amusing.'

She remained silent for a long moment, her eyes locked on his. Then gasped and shook her head, as if breaking a spell.

That, he could understand. He felt a bit enchanted himself.

'What was amusing,' she repeated, as if trying to recover her place in the conversation. 'Well, you see, reflecting upon your appearance after parting from you yesterday, I concluded you must be a poor, unemployed ex-soldier. I'd decided to make up for my rudeness by hiring you to perform some tasks at Thornfield Place.' Another chuckle escaped. 'How ridiculous! Thinking I was doing a favour, offering odd jobs to a man who owns half the county!'

'Not so ridiculous, given how disreputable I looked,' he said, amused, but also touched by the compassion she'd felt for a chance-met stranger—and a surly one at that.

No wonder she had a heart for homeless orphans.

'You'll wait while I get my coat?'

'I really shouldn't task you with this…but if you are truly sure it wouldn't be an imposition, and I'm not keeping you from other matters?'

'It won't be, and you aren't.' He refrained from mentioning he had nothing on his calendar—now or any subsequent day. 'I consider it an opportunity to become better acquainted with my new neighbour.'

Which, though perfectly true, he thought as he left the room, was certainly singular, given his original intention not to mingle with any of them.

Chapter Four

Reviewing their conversation as he climbed the stairs, Dom marvelled at himself. Was the solitude he'd sought wearing on him already, that he felt such a lift at the prospect of inspecting some musty old building?

But thinking about London, or Leicestershire, or even Elizabeth, still brought an automatic shudder of distaste. Perhaps what he really sought was not so much solitude, but a world completely different from the society he'd once enjoyed and the company of those who'd known him there.

Miss Theodora Branwell was certainly different. Though his little brown wren had been more attractive today in a green gown that accentuated her graceful figure, made her skin glow and emphasised her lovely dark eyes, were the stunningly beautiful Lady Elizabeth to have entered the room, most men wouldn't have given Miss Branwell another glance.

Compared to Elizabeth, who'd been trained since her youth in the art of conversation designed to make her companion feel himself the most fascinating man in the room, Miss Branwell, with her frankness and total lack of subtlety, would be considered unpleasantly plain-spoken and offensively inquisitive.

And yet, though he'd always appreciated Elizabeth's

beauty and avidly anticipated the pleasures of the wedding bed, he didn't remember ever having the sort of immediate, visceral reaction he'd felt for Miss Branwell. Perhaps that response was intensified, coming as it did after Miss Wentworth's distaste and representing as it did the first time since his injuries that he'd felt a sense of his own masculine appeal. The first evidence as well that a woman who attracted him could find him desirable for who and what he was now, rather than as the damaged remains of the man he used to be.

But enough analysing. Like today's rain, Miss Branwell had blown a freshness into his life, lifting his spirits and imbuing him, for this moment, with a sense of lightness and anticipation he hadn't felt in months. He'd accept it as a gift from Heaven.

Recalling that the walk to the stone building was rather far, he took a swig of the laudanum-laced brandy at his bedside. He didn't want to end up so cross-eyed with pain by the time they arrived that he was incapable of accurately assessing the building. Or appreciating the company of the lady he was escorting.

Miss Branwell awaited him in the entry as he descended the stairs. 'I took the liberty of asking your butler if there was a pony trap we might use. He's having one sent up.'

'Afraid I might collapse on you?' he tossed back. And regretted the hasty words, as his mind jumped to other ways he might cover her that had his body immediately hardening in approval.

'...nursed enough soldiers to know,' she was saying by the time he got his thoughts back under control. 'You have the look of a soldier still recovering from his injuries. Did you suffer a lingering fever?'

'For months,' he confirmed, no longer surprised at how easy he found it to speak frankly to her. 'I wasn't well enough to leave Belgium until quite recently.'

She gave him a quick inspection that his body hoped was more than an assessment of his level of recovery. 'You're still rather thin. In my judgement, you should have more careful tending—but that's for you to decide, so I shall not mention it again. However—' She stopped herself with a sigh. 'No, excuse me, I shall say nothing.'

Dom shook his head with a chuckle as they walked out to the vehicle a groom had pulled up outside the entry. 'You shall have to tell me, you know.'

She looked back at him, smiling faintly as she shook her head. Remembering her rebuke of the previous day, he offered her a steadying hand as she climbed into the vehicle, savouring more than he should the touch of her gloved fingers.

She didn't turn to see if he had trouble climbing up himself. And though, army veteran that she was, she probably could drive the trap better than he, she made space for him on the bench seat and waited for him to take the reins with nary a solicitous look nor a concerned enquiry about whether he felt well enough to handle them. That, after just pronouncing her nurse's opinion that he was not fully recovered.

A tiny glow of satisfaction lit within the gloomy depths of his battered self-esteem. She assumed he was adjusting to his handicap, continuing with his life. Expected he would eventually master it.

As he would. Feeling better about his condition than he could remember since his wounding, Dom motioned for the stable lad to release the horse and jump up behind them.

After yesterday's fiasco with Diablo left him doubting his ability to do anything, his spirits rose further as he discovered he could handle the single horse and simple carriage with ease. The expertise honed through years of practice returned without thought, and as the trap rattled down the lane, he found himself relishing the business of driving.

As Miss Branwell had predicted, the rain had ceased, leaving the air cool and scrubbed clean. Dom exulted in the wind ruffling his hair, the scenery flashing by, the taut feel of the reins in his hand and the horse responding to his commands. With a rush of gratitude to the Almighty, he realised at least one of the pleasures of his former life wasn't totally lost to him.

Of course, this was only a pony trap, the nag pulling it far from a high-stepping carriage horse. But effortlessly controlling horse and vehicle felt…good. He told himself to stop equivocating and just enjoy it.

His mastery of the reins allowed him to enjoy watching Miss Branwell as well. After noting her chattiness at the house, he was encouraged to discover she could remain silent as well. Sitting relaxed, her hands resting on the rail to steady her over the bumps, she gazed from side to side, her eyes bright with interest. Trusting this one-armed soldier to drive her safely while she investigated her new surroundings, he thought, buoyed by her confidence.

The spring woods just coming into leaf were lovely, and so was his companion. Though, he noted in a reprise of the discriminating standards from his days as 'Dandy Dom', the battered-looking bonnet and well-used cloak would go, if he had the dressing of her.

Then again, he'd rather have the undressing of her.

Preoccupied by reining in that line of thought before it bolted into ever more inappropriate directions, he started when she cried out, 'Goodness, what is that, just ahead?'

Squinting in the direction of her pointing finger, he saw around the corner a stretch of lane bordered on both sides by an expanse of flowers. 'It's a bluebell wood,' he replied. Not having been at Bildenstone during the spring for years, he'd forgotten this part of the lane, less densely treed than the one they'd travelled yesterday, was home to thousands of the little bulbs.

'Can you slow down?'

'Of course,' he said, reining the horse to a stop.

She gazed around her in delight at the sea of blooms surrounding them. 'It's as if an ocean had been cast down under the trees! How beautiful!'

Looking at the expanse, he realised it *was* beautiful. And that, had she not been with him, he would have passed through it, preoccupied by his own problems, with scarcely a glance.

Turning back to him, she said, 'I can't get enough of gazing at the woodlands here, the tall trees with their leafy canopies. After the dry plains of India and the scrub of Portugal and Spain, I find them endlessly fascinating.'

He, too, would do well to appreciate every simple pleasure, instead of brooding on what he'd lost. To the attraction and interest she'd generated in him today, he added gratitude for bringing him to recognise that truth.

'We are fortunate in our forests,' Dom replied, clicking the horse back into motion, 'especially those lucky enough to possess a bluebell wood. Now, what was it you were going to tell me and decided not to?'

He laughed at the surprise on her face. 'Did you think I had forgotten? I must warn you, I have a mind like a poacher's trap. So…confess.'

'Very well, but as I had resolved to say nothing, you may not afterwards accuse me of interfering! It's just…I noticed that your butler is rather elderly. I expect, having been around him for years, you haven't marked the passing of time, but the truth is, he struggles to open that heavy door. Does he still bring in the tea tray? I imagine it's difficult for him. Of course, that's only my observation. It's really none of my business.'

Dom recalled Wilton carrying in the service to his

callers yesterday, lugging a tray full of victuals from the kitchen up to the library for him this afternoon.

'It's been more than seven years since I visited, and years before that since the family resided here,' he admitted. 'Beyond noting in a general way that Wilton had aged, I'm ashamed to say I never considered whether resuming duties he'd not had to perform for years would be hard on him.'

He'd come up from London in a laudanum haze that enabled him to bear the jolting of the journey, then shut himself in the master's chamber and, until yesterday, hadn't set foot out of the house. To his mortification, he hadn't given a thought to how his unexpected arrival must have upset the routine of the handful of servants who'd remained to oversee Bildenstone Hall during the family's long absence, or the strain on all of them required to extract the place from its holland covers and make it habitable.

'Even though I don't intend to entertain, I should probably hire more servants,' he admitted. 'While I'm at it, perhaps I will put Wilton out to pasture.'

'Oh, I don't think—' she began before closing her lips.

Dom laughed outright. 'You might as well tell me the whole. I promise not to accuse you of interfering.'

'Wilton has been long at Bildenstone Hall?'

'He's been butler since I was a lad.'

'Then I don't think I'd retire him—not immediately, after such a long absence, lest he feel you are dissatisfied with his service. Why not find someone to serve as underbutler, whom Wilton can train up as his eventual replacement? Then, after a suitable interval, you can offer him a cottage nearby and a generous settlement for his lifetime of loyalty. If the family hasn't resided here for some time, it probably would be wise to hire more staff, which will also earn you the good will of the neighbourhood—

paying jobs are always prized, especially now, with so many being let go from the army.'

'That sounds like excellent advice. If you have any other suggestions, pray offer them.'

She uttered a delightful gurgle of a laugh. 'As if you thought I could keep my opinions to myself! Goodness, though, your family must possess some magnificent properties, if they chose to leave the beauties of Bildenstone for another location.'

'It's worse than that—Papa actually had to purchase the other property. Having always loved hunting, both haring and fox, he happened to meet Hugh Meynell, now of Quorn Hall in Leicestershire.'

He paused, but as no hint of recognition dawned in her eyes, he continued. 'Meynell, another hunting enthusiast, believed there was no reason that hounds couldn't be bred for a good nose and for speed, which would allow fox hunting at any time of the day, not just early in the morning when the foxes, weary after a night of hunting, return to their dens too tired to outrun the slow hounds. My father thought it an intriguing idea, and along with Meynell and some others, experimented with producing fast-running hounds. So absorbed did he become in the project, he determined to obtain a property in Quorn country, where he could continue the breeding experiments and hunt with Meynell's pack.'

He paused, remembering. 'I'd just outgrown my first pony when we relocated to Upton Park. It took only one hunt to make me as keen about the chase as my father. So I can't say I regretted leaving Bildenstone, despite the beauties of its bluebell wood.'

'Appreciation for flowers isn't generally a trait possessed by young boys,' she replied. 'I don't wonder you found the excitement of Leicestershire much more to your liking. So you devoted yourself to the hunt?'

'Single-mindedly. Which reminds me,' he said, recalling her hours waiting on his wall. 'What would you have done if I'd not relented and admitted you today?'

Following the sudden change in topic without a blink, she said, 'Waited a bit longer, then tracked down your estate agent. When I first proposed to lease Thornfield, I was told your family hadn't occupied the property for years, so finding an owner in residence was an unwelcome surprise. If the agent thought you were indifferent to the use of the building, or were not planning to remain long at Bildenstone, I would have proceeded. Otherwise, I would have made plans to go elsewhere.'

He had to laugh. 'You really are resourceful!'

'Papa always said you can never count on the enemy to do what you expect; for a sound battle plan, one must devise alternates for every imaginable contingency.'

He smiled down at her. 'I hope you don't consider me the enemy.'

She gazed up into his eyes. 'No, I consider you...' Her words trailed off, her lips slightly parted as she stared at his face...his mouth.

Attraction crackled like heat lightning between them again, scorching his face, leaving his mouth tingling. Immobilised by its force, Dom wasn't able to tear his gaze from hers until the jolting of the vehicle over a particularly large bump forced him to return his attention to his driving.

Chapter Five

Patting her flaming cheeks with one hand, Theo took a deep breath, her heart thudding as she surreptitiously watched Mr Ransleigh manoeuvre the pony trap.

Goodness, what was wrong with her? First her runaway tongue, and now this firestorm of sensual awareness!

Granted, she'd never been shy about expressing her opinions, but what had possessed her to be so free with her advice—to a man she'd scarcely met, and one with whom she needed to establish good relations, if she hoped to settle her orphans at this location? If that almost instantaneous sense of rapport she'd felt with him was an illusion, she might have doomed her mission before it even began.

And yet, she was convinced Mr Ransleigh, too, felt the connection between them.

After an initial surprise and dismay upon discovering her potential landlord to be the one-armed man she'd been so rude to in the lane, she'd been immediately drawn to this ex-soldier, who matched her apology with a generous one of his own. Then, to confirm that his life had, like hers, been upended in the aftermath of Waterloo and to learn they shared the same army experiences...

Having made her awkward way these last few months through an unfamiliar civilian society in an unfamiliar land, to stumble upon someone who'd been part of the world she'd lost was like coming home. Within a few moments, she'd been more comfortable in his company than she'd felt since leaving the regiment in Belgium.

Yet at the same time, upon meeting the man again, properly garbed and in his own element, she'd been struck by the potent masculinity he radiated, in spite of his injuries. The fever-induced thinness of his frame only served to emphasise his impressive height and the broadness of his shoulders. Caught up in gazing at the strong chin, sensual lips and brilliant blue eye, she'd several times, like a moment ago, lost track of where she was in the conversation.

A fact as sobering and even more dismaying than learning the identity of her new landlord.

Just sitting beside him in the pony trap, close enough that the next bump in the road might bounce her into contact with his body, kept her heartbeat skipping at an accelerated pace. The air between them seemed to simmer with a palpable tension.

As an unmarried woman, society might expect her to be an innocent, but she was no stranger to passion. In the arms of the man who'd intended to make her his wife, she'd revelled in kissing and touching, eager to explore Marshall's body, wanting him to explore hers. Though she'd lived mostly in the company of men for the years since his death, not until today had she felt again that unbidden, instinctive, intensely physical connection.

She knew exactly how powerful it could be—and how dangerous.

Oh, this would not do at all!

She should have insisted on delaying this visit until Ransleigh's estate agent could accompany her.

Instead, disbelieving, intrigued—and tempted—she'd permitted his company, compelled to discover if that incompatible pairing of feelings—welcome ease, and dangerous attraction—would dissipate upon further acquaintance.

Well, it hadn't. Despite the distractions of the drive and the delight of the bluebell wood, the ease had only increased, and so too the attraction. As evidenced a moment ago by her losing track of every thought save the impulse to run her finger over his lips and watch that undamaged eye drift closed as she tangled her fingers in the shaggy mane of blond hair and pulled his mouth to hers.

Just recalling that desire sent another flush of heat through her.

But there was no time now for her to figure out what she was going to do about this unwelcome complication, with Mr Ransleigh pulling up the pony trap in front of the stone building. Forcing her thoughts away from that dilemma, she made herself calm.

The spark that singed her fingers as he helped her down momentarily distracted her. But Theo would never have survived the last four years had she not been able to summon the will to focus only on the problem at hand.

Putting a deliberate distance between them, Theo followed Mr Ransleigh as he led her on an inspection of the stone building.

The fact that the structure appeared nearly perfect for her purposes helped her concentrate. Originally designed as a barn, the building had a main floor of smooth paving stones; the stalls had been removed, leaving an open, rectangular space that would do well as a schoolroom. The hayloft above, its partially floored area finished out and with railed wooden stairs constructed to reach it, would serve splendidly as a dormitory.

'This will be excellent!' Theo declared as, having made use of the railing rather than her escort's arm to steady her, she returned from the upper floor to the main room. 'It will require very few alterations: partitions upstairs, to divide the boys' area from the girls', and cordoning off a small section on this floor to install a kitchen, where meals can be prepared and girls can be schooled in cooking and household management.'

'Are you sure?' Mr Ransleigh said dubiously. 'It looks like a cobweb-infested wreck to me.'

'Compared to some of the structures I had to make habitable on the Peninsula, it's a virtual palace! I dare say the roof will not leak, half-drowning some hapless orphan in the middle of the night, nor a wall give way, letting in cows to munch next morning's bread, nor do I see any ancient piles of rotted straw that might house a host of vermin.'

'Sounds like you were billeted in the same places I was,' Ransleigh said.

'Doubtless,' she agreed, dragging her mind back before it could jump to contemplating the idea of being billeted... or bedded down...with her compelling landlord. 'A good scrubbing and a competent carpenter, and I believe I can turn this into just the school I envisioned. If you're agreed, I'll consult the solicitor at once to find the necessary workmen, so they may begin as soon as the lease is signed.'

'You might consult Bildenstone's steward, Winniston. He seems to have kept the manor house in reasonable repair, despite the family not having resided there for years. And he would know where to find the craftsmen you'll need.'

'That would be most helpful, if it won't be too much bother.' Laughing ruefully, she shook her head. 'Here I've been assuring you I wouldn't intrude on your peace! I've already dragged you from your house and am now thinking of imposing upon your estate manager.'

Mr Ransleigh shrugged. 'He hasn't been imposed upon for years. Every soldier needs a little prodding to keep him marching in the right direction.'

'Very well, I shall ask. Now, I should allow you to get

back to Bildenstone and whatever business I interrupted when you felt obliged to accompany me here.'

Theo worked to keep the wistfulness from her voice. Unwise as it was, she was enjoying this outing more than she could remember enjoying anything in a long time. The easy camaraderie and sense of shared experience made her forget for a while that she was now alone in an unfamiliar world. And his tantalising presence revived dim memories of what an energising delight it was to bandy words with a handsome man, a titillating buzz of attraction humming between them.

Settling the details of the lease was a matter for solicitors; once they completed their tour today, there would be no need for her to consult again with the property's owner. She would go back to her children and their needs, and firmly shut behind her the door into this glimpse of what life spent with a congenial, beguiling man might have been like.

Since that life was lost to her for ever, the sooner she did so, the better.

Setting her shoulders, she walked back to the pony trap and hauled herself to the bench before her escort could offer a hand.

Which didn't mean she was any less cognizant of the simmering heat of him, once he climbed up beside her, she thought with a sigh.

'That was exceedingly dusty,' Mr Ransleigh said as he set the vehicle in motion. 'Can I offer you tea when we get back?'

Theo steeled herself against the temptation to accept. 'That's very kind, but I shouldn't.' A more disturbing thought occurred and she frowned. 'Indeed, now that I think of it, with you being a bachelor and having no lady mother in residence, I seem to recall that it would be considered improper of me to take tea at your house—or indeed, even to call upon you.'

She sighed with exasperation. 'English mores! Dashed inconvenient, with you being our landlord, but there it is. I only hope I haven't blotted my copybook already! It wouldn't help the children's reception—already dubious, according to what you've told me—if your servants carry tales hinting that I'm a lightskirt.'

Her companion choked back a laugh. 'You really are plain-spoken, aren't you?'

'I'm completely devoid of maidenly sensibilities,' Theo admitted. 'Perhaps I should try to acquire some, if it will make the idea of the school more acceptable to the neighbourhood.'

'Though you may be right, I'd hate to see it. I find your candour refreshing.'

'So is a dunk in the Channel, but most people would rather avoid it,' Theo said wryly. 'I'll have to learn to curb my tongue—and think more carefully about my actions.' She made a mental note to ask Aunt Amelia, before she returned to London, to review with her the most important rules of propriety.

'You're probably right about tea,' Ransleigh allowed. 'Talking over experiences on the Peninsula, it's too easy to fall back into army ways and forget the rigid notions of conduct that apply here. Since I've been back in England less than a month, after years away, my memory of those rules is probably as rusty as yours. But let me assure you, no tales of our lapses today will be heard beyond the walls of Bildenstone—or the offenders will answer to me.'

Surprised, she looked up at him. Though linked by their memories of campaign, he was still little more than a stranger. No connection between them required him to watch over her reputation, and she was impressed that he intended to do so.

He truly was an officer and a gentleman.

'I wouldn't expect you to go to such trouble, but I do appreciate it.'

'Don't want you to run afoul of the Lady Wentworths of the county before you've even got your building renovated,' he said, turning his attention back to his driving.

All too soon, they arrived back at Bildenstone Hall. Once again resisting the temptation to continue their conversation, Theo refused his offer to proceed to the drawing room while a groom fetched her horse.

'There's no need for you to tarry here, truly!' she said when he gallantly insisted on waiting outside with her. 'I shall be off as soon as Firefly is brought up. The children will be missing me, and there's still so much to do, getting the house up to snuff and filling in until I can secure a teacher.'

He raised an eyebrow. 'You don't intend to teach the children yourself?'

'No. While we were with the army, I helped Jemmie with his letters and sums, but we hadn't the materials, nor I the training or inclination, to give him a proper schooling. Not that the children should study languages and philosophy—just gain a thorough grounding in reading and arithmetic. While they learn, we shall ascertain what most interests them, then train to that trade, for which I'll need to hire instructors as well. I doubt I could sit still long enough to manage a classroom. I have to be out and about, moving around, accomplishing things.'

'I can appreciate that. After months of being cooped up, mostly bedridden, I can't tell you how much I've enjoyed this drive in the fresh air.'

'Then you must drive about often—as long as you don't tire yourself. You're not fully healed yet, remember.'

'Don't worry. My arm and shoulder will remind me, should I be tempted to forget.'

From the stable lane, a groom paced up, leading her mare. 'Here's Firefly,' she said, turning back to him, 'so I will take my leave.'

After giving the mare a quick inspection, Mr Ransleigh nodded his approval. 'Good, deep heart, nice level croup, and well muscled—she must be a fine goer.' Reaching out to stroke the horse's neck, he crooned, 'What a lovely lady you are! Such a graceful neck, pretty eyes and small, perfect ears!'

As the mare nickered and leaned into Ransleigh's massaging fingers, Theo chuckled. 'I believe she's preening for you. Which is quite a compliment! Firefly doesn't take to just anyone. You must have a way with horses.'

'I've always loved them. Spent most of the last fifteen years when not in the army breeding and training them. Hunters and steeplechasers who—' Abruptly he went silent, leaving the sentence unfinished.

Even if I just had my limitations forcefully demonstrated, his cryptic comment came back to her as she recalled the fractious stallion who'd almost trampled her. *But oh, he can fly like the wind and jump anything in his path.*

'You trained that black beast from yesterday,' she said, putting it all together.

'And many more like him,' Ransleigh said tightly. 'For all the good it does me now.'

All horses he could no longer ride. Theo felt an ache in her chest. One more loss, one more joy stolen from him. How terribly cruel life could be!

'It must have taken remarkable skill, just to get him to accept a rider,' she said, wanting to ease the tension in that clenched jaw. 'He looked like he would have enjoyed running us down.'

He rewarded her with a slight smile. 'He would have, the evil-tempered devil.'

The urge to linger and question him further teased at her. Clenching her teeth against it, she told herself she should bid him farewell before this intriguing man charmed her any further.

'Well, I must be off. You're welcome to call any time at Thornfield Place and meet the children. Or not, as you choose,' she added, unhappily aware he was unlikely to take her up on that offer.

Before the groom could assist her, Ransleigh offered his hand. 'You were right,' he said as he lifted her into the saddle. 'I can do it, if I want to.'

Our last contact, she thought with a little sigh as he released her boot. 'I am sure you will soon be able to do whatever you wish, Mr Ransleigh. Thank you again for giving my orphans a chance.'

With a wave of her riding crop and a foolish sense of regret, she turned Firefly and set off towards Thornfield.

She felt the warmth of his gaze on her back, all the way to the turn in the drive.

By the time she'd ridden most of the way home, Theo had convinced herself she'd not really responded as strongly to Mr Ransleigh as she'd first imagined. After all, it was only natural that she would feel comfortable around a man who'd spent nearly as many years with Wellington's army as she had, especially after more than a month of dealing with civilians.

Nor did she deny he attracted her. The scarred face and eye patch did nothing to detract from his commanding profile, nor the missing arm from the vitality that emanated from him, despite the fact that he was not fully recovered from his injuries. Indeed, in her eyes, the marks of the suffering he'd endured in defending his country enhanced his already arresting physical attributes.

But that attraction, like the welcome relief of finding herself once again in a soldier's company, had doubtless been heightened by not having experienced the feeling in so long.

She could only imagine how much more potent his appeal would be when he was fully healed. A heated flutter stirred in her stomach.

Fortunately, she was too old and wise now to be caught again in passion's snare. Or she certainly should be—she need only remember the agony she'd suffered over Marshall.

Still, she was a woman, and vain though it might be, she was glad she'd worn the most attractive of her gowns for the call. She'd couldn't help being pleased that, if her instincts were correct, that compelling man had found her attractive as well.

A flush of embarrassment heated her face as she suddenly recalled she'd actually told this wealthy, well-connected bachelor how handsome she thought him.

Drat candour! Hopefully, he would only think the comment shameless—and not suppose her to have marital designs upon him. The very idea that he might interpret her comment in that manner made her a little sick.

Nothing she could do now to correct that impression, if he had so interpreted her remark. With any luck, there'd be no further need to contact him, so any awkwardness on that score could be avoided.

Then perspective returned, and she had to laugh at herself. How foolish of her to think this commanding man, whose wealth and pedigree doubtless focused upon him the attention of every woman in the vicinity, would think twice about any supposed lures cast his way by a plain, outspoken spinster—with a crowd of orphans in tow!

The only lasting result of her visit today was her landlord's agreement to lease her the property. Once she was immersed in overseeing its renovation, adding that task to those of getting Thornfield running properly and finding the necessary teachers, today's interlude would fade to a pleasant but vague memory.

Ignoring the eddies in her stomach that warned otherwise, Theo fixed that conclusion firmly in mind and turned Firefly down the drive to Thornfield's stables.

Chapter Six

Dom awoke the next morning with a sense of anticipation, the first he could recall since his injuries. Questioning the source of that unexpected sensation, he remembered meeting his unusual new neighbour the previous day, and smiled.

The drive to the stone barn had been energising. As he recalled, there was a tilbury in the carriage house and a high-stepper with a bit more fire to pull it. After his successful driving of the pony cart, he was reasonably sure he wouldn't end up flat on his back in the mud again if he tried taking it out.

This morning, he decided as he rang for Henries, he would.

After consuming breakfast with a keener appetite than he'd possessed in some time, Dom walked down to the stables to collect horse, carriage and a stable boy to watch them, should he need to stop and inspect a field or cottage. It required but a moment's thought to decide where he meant to drive first.

Miss Branwell had invited him to call at Thornfield Place, and so he would.

Setting the carriage in motion, he wondered at himself. After all his firm intentions to avoid contact with the neighbours, here he was, the day after meeting Miss Branwell, ready to encounter her again. If he felt like visiting, he ought to first return the Squire's call.

He pictured his bluff neighbour and frowned. Stopping there didn't appeal in the least.

Seeing Miss Branwell again did.

Perhaps it was because she didn't expect anything of him but to be her landlord. Unlike every other resident in the county, she didn't know his reputation, had no connections to hunting or its enthusiasts—she didn't even recognise the name of the great Meynell! And, praise heaven, she wasn't evaluating his worth on the Marriage Mart.

Indeed, Miss Branwell, self-confessedly ignorant of English customs, might not even be aware that, with his wealth and connections, he was still a prime matrimonial prospect.

No, all she had seen was a dishevelled one-armed soldier walking down a lane—and decided to offer him employment. He laughed out loud.

Direct, plain-spoken and completely focused on her objectives, she worked and thought like a soldier. Only she was much better to look at.

Picturing her immediately revived the strong attraction she'd inspired yesterday. His mind explored the idea of dalliance and liked it, his body adding its enthusiastic approval. However, Miss Branwell was still a *miss*, a gently born virgin. As strongly as he was attracted to her character and her person, he'd never debauched an innocent, and he wasn't about to start.

With a disappointed sigh, he allowed himself to regret she wasn't the widowed *Mrs* Branwell. They couldn't, alas, be lovers. But perhaps they could be friends. A friend who knew him only as the man he was now.

There was freedom in that: no preconceived notions to

meet, no pressure to perform up to the standard of what he'd once been.

Besides, he had to admit he was curious to see this assortment of orphans she'd collected. He tried, and failed, to imagine the problems one must overcome in order to follow the army with a troop of children in tow, then to transport them to England.

He shook his head and laughed again. What a remarkable girl!

Without doubt, calling on her would be much more interesting and enjoyable than perusing the London papers to determine the current value of hunters.

An hour later, at Thornfield Place, Theo was sipping a second cup of coffee while her aunt finished breakfast when Franklin informed them that Mr Ransleigh had called.

Surprise—and a delight far greater than it should have been—sent a thrill through her. After instructing the butler to inform the visitor that the ladies would receive him directly, she turned to her aunt.

'Thank goodness I had Mrs Reeves straighten the parlour first thing this morning,' she said, trying to pass off her enthusiasm as approval of prudent housekeeping. 'It appears my new landlord is paying us a visit.'

Her aunt opened her lips to reply, then froze, her eyes opening wide. 'Did Franklin say a Mr *Ransleigh* had called?' she asked at last.

'Yes. Mr Dominic Ransleigh. The building I want to turn into the children's school sits on his land. I told you I planned to call on the landlord yesterday, remember?'

'Of course I remember. But why didn't you tell me your landlord was a Ransleigh?'

'The owner of that much land would doubtless be a

member of a prominent family. I didn't think it mattered which one.'

'Not matter? Good heavens, child, don't be ridiculous! One must always be aware of the social position of the individuals with whom one associates—as you army folk want to know the rank of a military acquaintance.'

'I suppose you're right,' Theo conceded. 'Enlighten me, then.'

'Do you know anything of his background?'

'Only that he was in the army for the duration of the war.'

'So he was—he and his three cousins. The 'Ransleigh Rogues,' the boys have been called since their Eton days. They grew up inseparable, and when Alastair Ransleigh ran off to the army after being jilted by his fiancée—quite a scandal that was!—the other three joined up to watch over him. The eldest, Max—younger son of the Earl of Swynford, who practically runs the House of Lords!—was involved in a scandal of his own, something about an affair with a Frenchwoman at the Congress of Vienna and an assassination attempt on Wellington. The youngest, Will, the illegitimate son of the Earl's brother, spent his first decade on the streets of St Giles before being recovered by the family.'

'My, that is an assortment!' Theo said with a laugh.

'Your landlord, Dominic, was known as "Dandy Dom", the handsomest man in the regiment, able to ride anything with four legs and drive anything with four wheels.' I don't know about the former, but I've seen him in Hyde Park, impeccably dressed, navigating a coach and four through the crowd as easily as if it were a pony cart on an empty country lane. He is—was—absolutely fearless on the hunting field, I'm told. His late father moved the family to Quorn country so long ago, I'd forgotten their primary estate was in Suffolk.'

The details about his family drifted into the background of her mind like dust settling on a window-sill. All that struck Theo was the image of a runaway horse and a one-armed man shuffling down the lane, his garments spattered with mud and leaves, his face strained and angry. *Able to ride anything with four legs...*

Her heart contracted with a sympathetic pain. How much more bitter it must be to bear his injuries, knowing he'd been renowned throughout the polite world for those skills!

'Does he seem...recovered?' her aunt asked, pulling her from her thoughts. At Theo's questioning look, she continued. 'I only wonder because he was engaged to a duke's daughter, and broke with her as soon as he returned from Belgium. It was quite the *on dit* before I left London, the young lady making it known that it was Mr Ransleigh who wished to cry off, not her.'

'I had no idea,' Theo said. She ran through her observations of his behaviour before continuing, 'He didn't seem to be brooding over a lost love, but then a man would hardly wear his heart on his sleeve, especially before a stranger. Certainly he's not yet fully recovered physically.'

'Retired to the country to finish healing,' her aunt said, nodding. 'Here, rather than in Leicestershire, where the memories of his hunting days would be sure to torment him.' Lady Amelia shook her head wonderingly. 'Dominic Ransleigh, living practically at your doorstep! Thank heaven you wore something at least moderately attractive when you called on him yesterday!'

Then she realised what she'd just said, and gasped. 'Oh, Theo, you called on *him*? You took Constancia with you, I hope?'

'I'm afraid not. Really, Aunt, I had no idea my landlord was a bachelor. I was expecting a doddering old man with an ear trumpet, rather than a most attractive young man.'

'He is—still attractive? I'd heard he was grievously wounded.'

'He lost an arm and an eye, and his face is scarred. But he's still a very handsome man.' A heated awareness shivered through her as she remembered just how arresting he was. 'Perhaps even more compelling now, given the grace with which he bears his injuries.'

Her aunt's expression brightened. 'And he's once again unattached!'

'Don't look at me with that light in your eye!' Theo warned. 'For one, if Mr Ransleigh has just broken an engagement, he's unlikely to start angling after some other female. Nor, having rejected a duke's daughter, is he apt to consider anyone less lofty. I expect he came to the country to find space and time…especially if his circumstances have changed so drastically. So promise me, no hints from you about how superior my lineage and prospects are, despite my current situation.'

The very idea that Ransleigh might suspect she was trying to attach him made Theo feel ill. Patting her hand, Lady Amelia said, 'Don't upset yourself, my dear! I would never do anything to embarrass you.'

Theo relaxed a little—until her aunt gave her a smile Theo didn't entirely trust before saying, 'In any event, we've kept him waiting long enough. Shall we go in?'

A few moments later, Theo and Aunt Amelia entered the parlour. The warmth of Ransleigh's smile as he rose to acknowledge them sent an immediate surge of response through her. Trying to curb it—and her dismay at how strong and involuntary a reaction it was—Theo made the necessary introductions.

'Delighted to meet you, Lady Coghlane,' Ransleigh said.

'As I am to meet you, Mr Ransleigh. And may I add my thanks for your gallant service with the Dragoons? I can't tell you how much better we all sleep, knowing that Napoleon is vanquished for good!'

Ransleigh inclined his head. 'Doing my duty, as so many others did. My condolences on the loss of your brother, by the way. Too many good men fell at Waterloo.'

Her aunt's eyes misted over. 'Richard's life was the army, but it's been…difficult. Enough of that, now. By the way, I knew your late mother well—we came out together. A lovely, sweet girl, who became an elegant and much-admired lady. The carriage accident which claimed your parents' lives was a sad day for all of us. Though it's been years, you have my deepest sympathy. It's not a loss from which one recovers easily.'

Ransleigh nodded. 'I was fortunate to have my cousins and their families to help me bear it. So my mother was said to be elegant?' He laughed and shook his head. 'I remember her in a worn riding habit, mud on her boots and her windblown hair escaping from her bonnet. She was as hunting-mad as my father, at a time when ladies weren't supposed to hunt.'

'I seldom leave London, so I didn't see her often after the family relocated to Upton Park. Which happened so long ago, as I told Theo, I'd forgotten Bildenstone was your primary estate. How are you finding it?'

'After being away with the army for so many years, I'm just reacquainting myself with it. My grandfather did accumulate a superb library, which I'm enjoying.'

'I understand my niece wishes to rent one of your buildings for her project. Though I applaud the tender feelings which inspire her, I have to admit, I have tried to talk her out of it. Such a weighty responsibility for someone so young, do you not agree?'

Theo threw her aunt an indignant look, to which that lady returned a bland smile. 'Really, Aunt Amelia, delighted as I am that you journeyed here to welcome me back to England, I'll not be so happy if you induce Mr Ransleigh to have second thoughts about allowing me to use his building!'

'I, too, think establishing the school a laudable aim—if a bit unusual an undertaking for a gently born lady,' Ransleigh said. 'However, from my brief acquaintance with your niece, Lady Coghlane, I don't think she's likely to be dissuaded.'

Her aunt sighed. 'She takes after her father in that—once she's fixed a project in her head, there's no dislodging it.'

'Will you be staying to help her begin the school?'

'Heavens, no! I have neither training nor inclination. As Theo said, I came only to welcome her to England. I'm too fond of London's comforts to tarry long in the country. I have been trying to persuade her to visit me, perhaps for the rest of the Season.' She gave Theo an arch look. 'There are, after all, other laudable goals for a young lady to accomplish.'

'If you're hinting at marriage, Aunt, I've no intention of accomplishing that goal, as you well know,' Theo said, irritated. 'I'm happy in the country, and I fully expect the children to occupy all my time. That is—' she looked over at Ransleigh as the dismaying thought suddenly occurred '—assuming you didn't come here to tell me you intend to withdraw your permission to rent your building.'

'No, I have not,' Ransleigh replied. 'Although I hope that won't put me in your black books, Lady Coghlane.'

'For the fondness I bore your mother, I shall try to forgive you,' she said with a twinkle.

'I am relieved! I should hate to offend my mother's good friend. As for why I appeared on your doorstep, it's such a fine morning for a drive, I decided to take your good advice, Miss Branwell, and get some fresh air. While pondering where I might drive, I recalled your invitation and thought perhaps I might meet the orphans whose school building I've agreed to lease to you.'

Surprised—and impressed, for how many young men would trouble to acquaint themselves with a group of children—and orphaned commoners at that?—Theo said, 'I'm sure they would be delighted to meet you. Especially Jemmie, the oldest, who will have to be restrained from monopolising you, once he discovers you're a soldier. I've already ordered a farm wagon brought up so I might drive them over to the building this morning. They've walked so often in the van of the supply wagons; the opportunity to *ride* in one is quite a treat. If you don't mind including in your drive a stop at the stone barn, may I wait to introduce them until after we arrive? They will be much more attentive once the ride takes the edge off their exuberance.'

'Of course. I brought my tilbury, Lady Coghlane. May I offer you a ride?'

'That's kind, Mr Ransleigh, but I will not be going. The prospect of a gaggle of children running about, shrieking at each other at the top of their lungs, does not appeal. As for the barn, Theo tells me it is presently unoccupied, needing a good deal of work before it will be fit for her purposes.' Lady Coghlane shuddered. 'Not a task I'd willingly undertake! I prefer my rooms already cleaned, polished, heated and well furnished before I enter them—preferably to find a comfortable couch upon which to sit, and a butler at the ready to bring refreshments.'

Theo laughed. 'It's good that Papa didn't ask his sister to follow the drum, then. Shall you feel neglected if I leave you for a time?'

'Certainly not, my dear. I have letters to write.'

'I'll bid you goodbye, then,' Ransleigh said, making her a bow. 'Once again, it was a pleasure to meet such a charming lady, and doubly so to meet a friend of my mother's.'

'Goodbye, Mr Ransleigh. Do call if you find yourself

in town. I would be pleased to receive you in that comfortable parlour and offer some excellent refreshments!'

Ransleigh laughed. 'I will certainly avail myself of your hospitality when I'm next in London.' Turning to Theo, he said, 'Shall I meet you and your charges at the barn, Miss Branwell?'

'Yes. I'll go collect them at once. Until later, Aunt Amelia. Let me escort you out, Mr Ransleigh.'

While they walked towards the entry door, Theo said, 'As she told you, my aunt has been trying to dissuade me from establishing the school. Failing that, I suppose she hopes I'll set it up and then turn it over to some good vicar to run, resuming my place as a proper English maiden.'

Her attraction to him, doubtless evident to a man of Ransleigh's experience, made it even more important to her that Ransleigh understand her views on marriage. So, despite the embarrassment of discussing such a topic with an eligible bachelor, she forced herself to say, 'Having no daughter of her own, Aunt Amelia always hoped Papa would ship me back to England so she might launch me into society and find me a husband. Neither Papa nor I were ever interested in accepting her kind offer, and with the school to establish, I certainly am not now.'

'Are you so uninterested in marriage?' Ransleigh asked, his tone curious.

'Papa left me very well settled. Unlike most of my sex, I don't have to marry for security or to have a place in the world.'

'What of…companionship?' he asked, his expression turning warmer.

Ah, *companionship*… With him standing at her shoulder, his gaze locked on her face, the physical pull between them intensified. Resisting the desire to step close enough to feel the heat of him up and down her sensitised body, she said, 'I was once engaged, I believe I told you. Having already found—and lost—the love of my life, I don't expect to find another. Nor would I even wish to. Losing Marshall w-was...' Her voice breaking, she swallowed hard, unable to find words to express the shock, horror and desolation of learning that he'd been killed in battle.

They'd reached the stairs, giving her an excuse to wrest her gaze away from his. She took a deep breath to slow the pounding of her heart. 'I'll leave you here, and see you at the barn in half an hour?'

Tacitly accepting her retreat, he nodded. 'Half an hour it is.'

Theo watched him walk away, then headed up the stairs to the nursery.

She hoped her avowals of uninterest in marriage had negated any little hints Aunt Amelia, drat her, had made about London and a maiden's duty. She also hoped Ransleigh didn't feel as strongly as she had the tingling connection that seemed to hum between them from the moment he'd entered the parlour. That had intensified as she walked beside him down the hallway, a tantalising hand's breadth apart.

Only recalling the agony of losing the man she loved had broken its bewitching hold over her.

Alas, the immediate attraction she'd felt at their first encounter at Bildenstone, that she'd tried while riding home to convince herself had been a trick of the moment—an amalgam forged of an unexpected meeting with a like-minded soldier who also happened to be a handsome man—had resurfaced in full force upon their second meeting. Every instinct, reinforced by the innuendo in his tone when he mentioned *companionship*, told her he found her alluring, too.

She wrestled with that fact, finding it at once deliciously appealing and alarming.

Focus on the 'alarming' part, her sensible nature urged. If only she could, without having to arm herself against him by calling up painful memories she would rather keep buried. And she absolutely must submerge again the dangerous passion he seemed to call forth so readily from where she'd banished it after Marshall's death.

Like putting the genie back in the bottle, the task was proving much harder than she'd anticipated.

She'd probably not see Ransleigh again after today. Surely she could restrain her inclinations for one more outing—with a bevy of children as chaperones!

Chapter Seven

As she'd expected, the children chorused their excited approval of a drive. Exuberant, Charles jumped up and down, clapping his hands in glee before delighting her with a kiss on her cheek. She gathered him close, drinking in the cherished feel of his small body nestled against her.

The ever-silent Maria merely nodded, but even the new children, Anna and Georgie, left off their guarded looks to smile at her.

She shepherded them downstairs to where a groom had pulled up the wagon. After helping Constancia settle the little ones in the back, Jemmie climbed up beside her, begging to handle the ribbons. Promising she would offer driving lessons on another occasion, when they did not have someone waiting on them, she took the reins and set the horses off.

A short while later, she pulled up the wagon in front of the stone building. Mr Ransleigh, already arrived in his tilbury, awaited them before the entrance. Just seeing him standing there sent an anticipatory shiver through her.

She tried to quell it while she helped the children down from the wagon—though, alas, she did not need to be looking at the man to be fully aware of his presence. Once they were safely disembarked, she said, 'Mr Ransleigh, may I present Jemmie, Charles, Maria, Anna and Georgie. And this is Constancia Bracamonte, their nurse and my assistant.'

'Pleased to meet you, children, Miss Bracamonte,' Ransleigh said, inclining his head.

'Mr Ransleigh owns this building, which as I told you, children, we plan to make into a home and school for you.'

Five young heads turned as one to look at it. 'Seems sturdy enough,' Jemmie said after a swift inspection.

'Very sturdy—made of good stone. Why don't you all go inside and have a peek?'

Charles, who'd been impatiently shifting from foot to foot after the introductions, needed no further invitation. 'C'mon, Georgie, I'll race you!' Shaking his head, Jemmie loped off after them.

Anna looked at Theo, who nodded. 'It's quite safe. Maria, would you take Anna's hand? Constancia will accompany you, too, so you will be all right.'

'Come, *meninas*, I will see you take no harm.' Beckoning the girls to follow, the maid walked them after the boys.

Theo turned back to Ransleigh. 'Your colour is better this morning! I believe driving agrees with you.'

'You may have the satisfaction of knowing you were right; I do feel better, getting out into the fresh air. Shall we walk towards the pasture while the young ones explore?' He offered his arm.

She hesitated. Given his effect on her, it would be wiser not to accept—but it would seem rude to refuse. At the questioning lift of his brow, she capitulated, laying her fingers on his arm. Despite the layers of broadcloth and kidskin, she felt a connection sizzle between them.

She suppressed a sigh, torn between annoyance and letting herself, for the few more moments she'd have to spend with him, simply enjoy the delicious disturbance he created whenever he was near her.

'So, tell me about your little group,' he was saying. 'Where did you find them?'

Glad that he'd invoked the children—the surest way to ground her—she said, 'Jemmie, the oldest, is the son of Father's sergeant-major, who was already with the regiment when we joined it in India. His mother died in childbirth—all too common an occurrence for English women in Calcutta, I'm afraid. The sergeant-major was killed by a sniper while directing the rear guard during the retreat to Corunna. Jemmie's about twelve, we think, and more than ready to begin training for an occupation.'

'Maria, the older girl with the sweet smile, is about seven. We found her at a convent after the Siege of Bajados, brought there with her dying mother, who'd been... abused by French soldiers. The sisters suspected Maria had witnessed the attack, for she's never spoken, and is very shy around men—quite a disadvantage for a female travelling with an army! She grew to be easy with my father, and accepts Jemmie and Charles, but she prefers to stay close to me or Constancia.'

'Anna and Georgie are the newest, just arrived from Belgium. I understand Anna's mother died in Brussels right before Waterloo, and her father was killed in the battle, leaving the five-year-old orphaned. Georgie we found at the docks in Calais, as he was about to be turned over to a gendarme for filching a meat pie from one of the army provisioners. He's about seven as well.'

Jemmie had approached them as Theo finished that last, and shook his head. 'Still not sure it was such a good idea, taking in a thief, Miss Theo! The Colonel always said them that thieves small will thieve big, sooner or later.'

'Which may be true for soldiers, but I don't know that the rule applies to a starving child, Jemmie,' Theo said.

Jemmie shrugged. 'S'pose we'll see. Right clever she was about nabbing him, though,' he said, turning to address Ransleigh. 'Fat pieman about had his thumbs around ol' Georgie, hollering as how he'd stolen a pie and he was goin' to turn him over to the provost. Miss Theo nips over, cool as you please, and spins him this faraddidle about how she'd sent Georgie to get pies for us, and how Georgie was naughty to make the man chase after him, rather than just buyin' the pies from his stand.' Jemmie chuckled. 'The man just stood there, gogglin' at her, cause he weren't born yestiddy and knew as how she was bammin' him, only when Miss Theo gets her "colonel's daughter" agoin', who's to gainsay her?'

He turned back to face Ransleigh. 'So you see, sir, Miss Theo kin look after herself, what with me to help out. And Miss Theo, though that building is sturdy enough to make a fine shelter if we wanted a billet, I don't see why we need a school. I'm too old for one, Maria never lets out a peep, and Master Charles will be getting a tutor anyway, won't he?'

'That's as may be, but remember, there will be more children coming to join us. All of you will need to learn your letters and a trade.'

The boy's frown deepened. 'Sure you got enough blunt to keep more army brats, after paying to rent that fancy manor house?'

'You watch my money closer than I do,' Theo said with a chuckle.

'Don't want you to run short,' the boy said seriously. 'Not afore I'm old enough to join the army, so's I can earn enough coin to support us. I promised the Colonel before he died that I'd take care of you, and I mean to.'

'I know you will,' Theo replied, an ache in her throat as she looked at his earnest young face. There would be time later to argue over his desire for an army career—

and its potential financial returns. 'But to earn enough to take care of a family, one has to have schooling. You'll like it, Jemmie.'

'Mebbe,' the boy conceded. 'I'd rather watch out for the horses, like I did for the Colonel. I will be able to tend horses here, won't I?'

'We'll see,' Theo replied diplomatically. 'You'll need to do lessons as well, though. Now, will you round up the others for me? It's time we went back.'

Jemmie nodded. 'Whatever you say, Miss Theo.' Turning to Ransleigh, he said, 'Nice to meet you, sir. I expect we can manage on our own now.'

After giving Ransleigh a bow, he trotted back towards the barn.

'I think I've just been warned off,' Ransleigh said, watching the boy walk away.

Theo shook her head ruefully. 'He's grown quite protective since Papa died. Though he's a boy still, he's at that awkward age, not yet a man, but thinking to take on a man's responsibilities.' She laughed. 'Which I guess explains why he tried so hard to demonstrate how clever I am and how well we are able to hold our own in the world, without anyone else's help.'

'You *are* clever. Nor do I think I'd want to cross swords with you when you've got your "colonel's daughter" goin'.'

'You already know I'm managing. I suppose it doesn't take much of a stretch to think of me as manipulating as well.'

He raised his eyebrows. 'I seem to remember a caller waiting on a wall in the rain until the reluctant host felt obliged to receive her.'

She laughed again. 'I object, sir! That was tactics, not manipulation.'

'And quite effective,' he admitted. 'You've told me about the others, but what about the one he called "Master Charles"? Who's not to attend the school, but to have a tutor?'

'Ah, Charles.' She gathered herself to give him the story she always told of how the boy had become like her own. 'He is an orphan, but not the offspring of a common soldier. His late father, Lord Everly, was the youngest son of the Marquess of Wareton. Before joining his regiment on the Peninsula, Everly persuaded the daughter of a curate to run away with him. They were both of age, and wed by an army chaplain after their arrival, but the marquess, who was furious at his son's union with a girl whose father was barely a gentleman, never recognised the marriage.'

'Everly,' Ransleigh said, frowning. 'I knew him slightly. He was at Cambridge when I entered Oxford. Didn't last long, as I recall; sent down before the first term ended. Wild to a fault. Poor girl.'

'Poor girl, indeed. He got her with child almost immediately, and a very difficult time she was having of it. I persuaded her to accompany me back to London to my aunt's house for the birth, but before we reached Lisbon, we received word that Lord Everly had been killed. Distraught and hysterical, she was unable to travel further. We ended up staying at a convent until the child was born, and sadly, she did not long survive his birth. I brought Charles back with me, only to learn upon my return that Lord Everly's father had no intention of acknowledging the woman or a brat from a marriage he refused to recognise. So Papa and I kept Charles. Indeed, I look upon him as my own son now, and shall do my upmost to see that he receives an upbringing and education suitable to his birth—whether or not he is ever received by his grandfather.'

'Raise a child on your own? Once again, a commendable aim, but isn't that an even weightier responsibility for a young lady?'

'With Papa gone now, too weighty, my aunt would say.

But why should an innocent child suffer for the folly of his parents, the hard-heartedness of a grandfather and the death of a male sponsor? Especially as dear and clever a boy as Charles. Which is, of course, another reason a Season in London would only disappoint my aunt. I don't imagine many gentlemen would be eager to court a lady who comes with a child attached, one whose blood family refuses to receive him. And I will never give him up.'

Before Ransleigh could attempt a reply—fortunately, for Theo wasn't sure what a gentleman could safely respond to such a startling revelation—Constancia trotted up with the children in tow.

The full truth of her circumstances should effectively snuff out whatever attraction he might have felt for her, she thought, both relieved that the temptation he represented would soon be removed—and a little sad to lose it. Like the last vestiges of her youth, disappearing for good.

Immured in the country, he might find flirting with a safe but willing female mildly attractive. Even flirting with one who had a troop of orphans to supervise might not be too daunting. But trying to flirt with a woman surrounded by a gaggle of orphans who also had a child clinging to her skirts would doubtless not seem worth the effort.

'The children are all here, Senhorita Theo, except for Jemmie,' Constancia said.

Pulling herself back to the present, Theo said, 'I thought he was doing the gathering. Where could he have got to?'

She was about to call him when her attention was drawn to a flicker of movement glimpsed from the corner of her eye. Turning, she saw in the adjoining pasture the boy approach a tall, prancing stallion.

Jemmie—drawing near the black beast who had nearly trampled her.

At Theo's gasp, Ransleigh saw them, too. 'Great Lucifer, is the boy mad?'

'Too late to warn him! What should we do?'

'Stay here, and don't call out to Jemmie!' he said, restraining her when she would have run towards the fence. 'Any loud noise or sudden movement could set the horse off and he'll kick out, or run the boy down. Don't come any closer, and for heaven's sake, keep the rest of the children away!'

But as he set off at a measured pace for the pasture, Maria gave a guttural cry and leapt forward. Before she could take a second step, Ransleigh grabbed her, murmuring soothingly to the child as he turned slowly, calmly towards Theo, who stepped forward to take the girl in her arms.

'Keep her safe,' he said softly, and set out again towards the pasture.

Much as it chafed Theo to stand still and do nothing more useful than murmur reassurances to the trembling Maria, she knew Ransleigh, from his long association with the horse, would be more likely to safely rescue Jemmie.

As she watched anxiously, Ransleigh approached the fence. Meanwhile, rather than retreating from the agitated stallion, Jemmie—whose neck she was going to wring once Ransleigh extracted him from the pasture—had moved slowly closer. As she held her breath, he leaned towards the huge beast, his lips moving, doubtless talking in the soothing tones he used with the army horses.

The stallion stopped pawing the ground and watched the boy. Cautiously he extended his head, his nostrils quivering. A moment later, his body and muzzle relaxing, he let Jemmie stroke his neck.

Slowly and silently Ransleigh scaled the fence, his gaze never leaving the boy and horse. As the stallion's aggressive posture changed to curiosity and then acceptance, he walked slowly over to the pair and put a hand on Jemmie's shoulder.

'That's enough of a visit for now,' he said, giving Jemmie's shoulder a tug.

'Is he yours?' the boy asked, awe in his tones. 'What a prime goer he must be!'

'He is, but with a disposition to match his name—Diablo,' Ransleigh said, a touch of acid in his tone. 'Let's leave while he's still feeling amiable.' Keeping his body between the horse and the boy, he walked Jemmie back and over the fence.

Theo rushed over to greet them. 'Jemmie, what were you thinking? You shouldn't just go right up to a horse you don't know!'

Jemmie looked at her, puzzled. 'But I done that all the time, Miss Theo. The cavalry boys always wanted me to tend their horses.'

'Yes, but we're not with the army now, and Diablo isn't a cavalry mount, he's much less steady! Besides, one shouldn't approach a horse in a private pasture without getting the owner's permission first.'

'Which would not have been granted, not for that horse!' Ransleigh said. 'You might have been bitten, at the least, kicked in the head at worst. I've seen Diablo scatter a stall full of grooms on a whim.'

'He'd never hurt me, sir,' Jemmie said. 'I could see he were a bit riled up at first, but once I started talkin' to him, he calmed down right quick. They generally do, once they know you understand them and don't mean them no harm.'

Ransleigh shook his head and looked at Theo.

'He does have a way with horses,' she explained.

'That may be. But, young man, you are not to approach Diablo again. He was moved to be amenable today, but he can change in an instant. Promise me you won't go near him.'

'You don't need to worry he'd be harmin' me,' Jemmie

repeated confidently. 'But it's your horse, so I guess I have to promise. Will you let me visit him again?'

'We'll see about that later,' Theo said. 'Now, please help Constancia load the children back into the wagon.'

'Yes, Miss Theo. Thank you again, sir, for lettin' me talk to your horse.'

'As if I'd given him permission,' Ransleigh muttered to Theo as Jemmie ushered the children away. 'He does have the touch, though. I've seen grooms with years of experience afraid to go near that horse.'

'Perhaps Diablo allowed it because he sensed that Jemmie was not afraid. I, however, was terrified! Thank you so much for seeing him safely out!'

Ransleigh made a gesture of dismissal. 'It seems he would have been fine on his own. But I couldn't risk that.'

Theo felt a swell of gratitude, which only redoubled her admiration for him. 'I do think Jemmie would make a fine trainer—which would be a better use of his skills than sending him to the army.'

Ransleigh nodded agreement. 'A skilled trainer can forge a fine career working for a large stable, like the Duke of Rutland's racing stud. If he can quiet Diablo, Jemmie should be able to work wonders with more even-tempered beasts.'

'From what you've told me of your work with horses, you should know.' A sudden thought occurred, and Theo's eyes lit. 'Might you work with Jemmie? If you were able to train Diablo, there must be so much you could teach him!'

As soon as the words left her lips, she caught herself. 'No, don't answer that,' she said before he could speak. 'Forgive me again! I get so caught up envisioning their futures, I blunder on as if everyone takes a similar interest. But I would ask one other, more acceptable favour.'

He shook his head at her. 'Poor Lady Coghlane. I sincerely doubt she's going to be able to tempt you away to London. Now, what would that favour be?'

'In your years of working with horses, you must have met any number of trainers. I do think it would be a perfect occupation for Jemmie. If you can think of a good one who might consider working at the school, I would very much appreciate the recommendation. I'd like to see Jemmie—all of them—become useful members of the society their fathers gave so much to protect.'

'You may have trouble convincing the Lady Wentworths of the neighbourhood, but I wholeheartedly agree.' He shook his head. 'Despite the fright Jemmie gave me over Diablo, I'll even see if I can think of a trainer you might use.'

Nothing could incite her gratitude more than his engaging himself to help her orphans. 'Thank you for understanding,' she said fervently. 'And for your compassion.'

Impulsively she grasped his hand, intending to shake it. But the moment she touched him, a palpable current flashed between them, so strong she nearly gasped at its force.

He must have felt it, too, for his pulse leapt under her fingers. But rather than pulling his hand away, he tightened his grip.

Her breathing stopped, her vision narrowed until only he filled it—the handsome face with the slash of the scar running down from the eye patch, his vivid blue gaze watching her so intently. Her hand throbbed beneath his touch, the vibrations radiating from her fingers up her arm to the whole of her body.

He murmured something, her name maybe, and bent his head. Her eyes fluttered shut, her lips tingling in anticipation of his touch.

A sharp tug at her gown snapped her eyes back open.

Dazed, she looked down to find Charles beside her. Her face flaming, she yanked her fingers from Ransleigh's.

'Can we go back now, Miss Theo! I'm awfully hungry.'

Shaken by what had passed between her and Ransleigh, she seized the boy and lifted him into her arms, hugging him against her, a reassuring reminder of where she belonged.

Heavens, Theo, pull yourself together!

'I'm ready to get in the wagon now,' Charles said, squirming in her grasp.

She set the boy down and gave Ransleigh a curtsy, her breathing still unsteady. 'Thank you again for lending us your barn, Mr Ransleigh,' she said, relieved that the words emerged in a natural tone, rather than a gasp. 'Perhaps you will honour us with another visit after the school has begun, if your engagements permit.'

'I expect they might. Good day to you, Miss Branwell,' he said with a bow.

She felt his gaze on her as she walked away, her body still humming and fizzing like a Congreve rocket about to erupt. Which she might have done, had Charles not interrupted them. Or would Ransleigh have come to his senses first?

She'd need to regather her wits in order to drive the children home without running them into a tree, she thought as she hoisted Charles into the wagon and took her seat. And leave until later, when her brain was functioning again, the problem of figuring out how to halt the madness that seemed to overcome her every time she came near Dominic Ransleigh.

Chapter Eight

After watching Miss Branwell drive off with her orphans, Dom reclaimed his vehicle and set the tilbury in motion. What was it about the lady that affected him so strongly? Though she looked no more like a siren than a sparrow resembles a peacock, something about her seemed to light him off faster than a fuse touched to powder.

She felt it too, he was certain, just as unbidden and just as strongly. And seemed to have no more idea where it came from or how to counter it than he had.

It certainly wasn't her beauty, nor a sophisticated wit that played seduction's game. To be sure, she had a natural grace and a keen, if often biting, intellect. But far from trying to entice him, she proclaimed she had no interest in men or marriage. He had to believe her; the surprise and confusion with which she reacted, each time attraction flared between, was too convincing to be a sham. Besides, if she were trying to lure him on while playing the innocent, she'd surely allow a touch or a kiss, just to inflame him further.

Even if she weren't too straightforward to make those claims to try to cozen an eligible bachelor, the fact that she had taken in a child she intended to raise underlined the truth of her uninterest.

A child she meant to keep even without her father to help smooth his way, she'd said, raising her little chin as if she meant to defy everyone and the world who might try to take him from her.

Which should provide protection enough from seduction and wedlock. As she'd noted, few men would want to begin married life with someone else's cuckoo in their nest, a boy his own blood family refused to recognise.

Nor could he blame his reaction to her on the fact that he'd been too long without a woman—though it had been too long. Just two days ago, he'd kissed the hand of delectable blonde, blue-eyed Miss Wentworth, whom any sane man would consider far more beautiful than Theodora Branwell. And felt…nothing.

Was it the passion so evident in her eloquent defence of her orphans and her brisk, restless movements that called to him? A strain of barely controlled wildness he sensed thrumming beneath her skin, which drove him on some instinctive level to try to free it?

Whatever fomented it, the urge was strong. If that urchin hadn't distracted her, he would have kissed her in full view of the whole group of orphans and their nurse. For no more reason than something primal in her called urgently to something in him.

Just thinking about taking her mouth, pulling that lithe, slim body against him, made his pulses race and his body harden further. He sighed and blew out a breath.

Pay attention, Dominic Ransleigh, he told himself sternly. Had that long fever addled his brain? Nothing about Miss Branwell's circumstances had changed since the last time he'd speculated about his attraction to her. She was still a gently born virgin, therefore not a female available for seduction.

Unless he was thinking of marriage.

Ah, there was a brake to halt this runaway carriage!

Attracted he might be, but having just extricated himself from one attachment for the express purpose of discovering what he meant to do with his life before committing himself to anyone, he had no business letting his senses lead him into another entanglement. Miss Branwell was not some experienced widow or bored society matron, whom he could dally and then part with amicably, both satisfied with the arrangement and no one the wiser. Keep less than a stranglehold over his passions, and he might compromise her, forcing him to do the honourable thing and compelling into wedlock a girl who'd expressed even less desire to marry than he had.

To save himself frustration—and temptation—he probably ought to avoid her.

Except…he'd just more or less promised her he'd look into the matter of a trainer.

Though he might know nothing about children, he did remember being a boy mad about horses, an enthusiasm he saw mirrored in Jemmie. He shuddered as he recalled the boy in the pasture with Diablo. A lad who could get near that beast without injury already possessed instincts that could not be taught, that needed only refining to turn him into a superb trainer.

Maybe he should help, sharing his love of and skill with horses. Guiding the sergeant-major's orphan into a secure future would be a worthy task.

Then he had to laugh. Was that his destiny—becoming an orphanage instructor? He could just imagine the shock, disbelief, and derision among the toffs of the *ton*, were they to learn Dandy Dom had turned his hand to bear-leading youths.

But then, who cared what the toffs of the *ton*—or Lady Elizabeth's ducal father, or the earl his uncle, the 'King of the Lords', thought of what he did? It was his life—his to remake.

He'd felt for so long like the old brown leaves scattered beside the lane he drove down, crumbling into nothingness as the new grass of spring grew through them. But maybe he was more like a skittering seed pod blown on the wind, just needing to reach fertile ground to take root.

Still, he'd be prudent not to make a premature offer he might later decide was unwise.

Besides, training the orphan would mean spending way too much time around Miss Theo.

Recalling her allure heated his simmering senses anew.

He could seduce her—he was sure of it. Contemplating the passion promised in that lush mouth, those vibrant eyes sent an anticipatory thrill through him.

Wise or not, he couldn't seem to bury that fact that he wanted her. More intensely than he'd wanted a woman in a very long while.

If he couldn't subdue the craving, maybe he should try to assuage it in a more acceptable way. He'd had mistresses before his engagement to Lady Elizabeth. If it would distract him from this frustrating desire for Miss Branwell, maybe he should consider setting up another.

He conjured up the image of a lush female in a diaphanous gown, her mouth in a seductive pout, her bosom covered with jewels and little else. Somehow, beside Theo Branwell's fresh, straightforward appeal, such a woman seemed...overblown.

He uttered a curse, startling the horse he'd just turned down the drive to Bildenstone.

He had too much free time on his hands—that was part of the problem.

Now that he could manage more than sleeping half the day and lifting his head to sip some gruel, he needed something more challenging to occupy him.

He'd been with the army so long, he had trouble recalling the rhythm of his days before he'd become a soldier.

Blocking out the hunting and steeplechasing activities still too bitter to contemplate, he tried to remember. In the country, he'd been up early, he mused, consulting with his grooms, training horses, or travelling to fairs or farms to evaluate others he might wish to purchase. Studying bloodlines in the evening if alone, or socialising with like-minded friends. In town, he'd stop by Tattersall's to check out the horses for sale, visit the tailor and bootmaker and haberdasher, pay calls by day and spend his evenings at dinners, balls or entertainments, charming the ladies.

Contemplating returning to most of these activities still evoked distaste. The only endeavour that called to him was working with horses.

Putting that thought away to consider later, he returned the tilbury to the stable and walked to the house.

Wilton met him at the entrance. 'Some refreshment in the library, sir?'

'Thank you, some ham and ale would be good,' he said, pleased to find, after months of no appetite, that a morning of driving and walking about had left him both hungry and not too fatigued to eat.

He'd found his place again in Herodotus by the time Wilton knocked at the library door. Miss Branwell's advice came back to him as he watched the man carry the tray to the table. To his chagrin, it did seem the elderly butler struggled to manage the heavy item, his thin frame bent back under its weight as he balanced it.

Deciding on the instant, he said, 'Wilton, a word, if you please.'

'Of course, Mr Ransleigh.'

'I've been intending to ask you to convey my appreciation to the staff for the excellent work they did, preparing Bildenstone Hall for my arrival. I know it took a great deal of effort, after the house had been closed up for so long.'

Expressions of surprise, then gratification, illumined the butler's face. 'I'm pleased you found everything satisfactory, Mr Ransleigh, and I'll certainly pass your approval on to the others.'

'With the increased workload of having a family member in residence, we should hire some additional employees. I'm thinking we will need an under-butler, an assistant for Cook, plus a couple of maids and perhaps another footman, as a start.'

The butler's eyes lit with enthusiasm. 'That would indeed be helpful, sir. We had nearly twice the staff when the late Mr and Mrs Ransleigh resided here. Though as a bachelor, of course, you won't do as much entertaining.'

'Consult with Mrs Greenlow and hire as many as you think necessary. '

The butler nodded. 'Very good, sir. I shall be honoured to assist you in reviving Bildenstone Hall.'

'Thank you, Wilton.'

The butler bowed himself out. Dom sat for a moment with a bemused smile. *Well, Miss Branwell, I've taken care of the house,* he thought, satisfaction warming him. Perhaps it was time to arrange a tour with his estate agent and check on the tenants. If the lord of the manor was going to reside here—and it appeared he was—he ought to become better acquainted with his land and the people who farmed it.

That should keep him occupied, away from the school—and the tantalising Miss Branwell.

Though even as he resolved it, he doubted he'd stay away long.

Chapter Nine

Two days later, the afternoon turning fair, Dom toted the volume of Herodotus to the bench in his mother's rose garden. An agreeable hour of reading later, a footman trotted up to inform him Miss Branwell had called.

Surprise, pleasure—and a bit of alarm—filled him. He thought at their last encounter they'd settled, regrettably, the fact that propriety forestalled her from calling on him again.

It might be wiser to send her away unseen, but it took him only an instant to conclude he'd not be able to force himself to do that. Curiosity alone demanded he discover what was so urgent that she felt moved to disregard the irksome rules of proper conduct and come to Bildenstone.

While he debated whether it would be better to receive her inside, in the parlour, where there would be fewer prying eyes to observe them, or out in the garden, in the open, where the many household staff could witness nothing improper was transpiring, the lady herself walked over.

'Good day, Mr Ransleigh,' she said with a smile.

It was certainly not prudent, but Dom couldn't help himself—he *had* to walk forward and take her hand, just to see if the tingling connection fired between them again.

He felt it immediately as he touched her—shock, then a force surging through him, flooding his senses. Without further thought, instead of shaking her hand as he had before, he turned the hand palm up and kissed it, fiercely resenting the buttons that prevented him from moving his lips to taste the bare skin at her wrist.

After a moment of savouring her warmth and an intoxicating violet scent that made his senses swim like strong brandy, he made himself release her. Straightening, he saw her gazing down at her still-extended hand, eyes wide, lips parted, her breathing quick and shallow.

Ah, she'd felt the connection just as strongly! he thought, triumphant. Desire ignited, sending awareness and need flaming through him. Had she leaned even infinitesimally closer, he could not have stopped himself from kissing her. Fortunately, more discreet than he, she took a wobbly step backward. He had a moment of furious regret before reason returned to make him glad she'd halted the encounter before it flared ever further out of control.

It took him a moment to reassemble his scorched wits.

'Good day to you, Miss Branwell,' he managed to say at last. 'I'm very happy to see you—though I am surprised you called, given the conclusion of our last conversation on the matter. Nothing alarming has happened, I trust?'

She gave a shaky laugh, further defusing the sensual tension. 'No, nothing alarming. Encouraging developments, actually. Not only am I emboldened to call on you, I believe you can offer me tea with impunity. Which, in fact, I should very much like. The day seems to have become suddenly over-warm.'

He could sympathise; his cravat—not to mention his breeches—now seemed over-tight. 'Let's walk back to the house, then. I'll order tea, and you can explain.'

He offered his good arm, and to his delight, she took it. Though as a result, he scarcely heard what she was saying, too distracted by her body so near his and that elusive violet scent, which seemed to emanate from her glossy brown hair—or perhaps from behind her ear. His mouth watered as he envisioned tasting her there, before his gaze drifted down to focus on the glimpse of tongue behind soft lips as she spoke. Wind-loosened wisps escaped from the braided tangle beneath her hat, and he itched to pull the hair fully free of its pins.

In short, he wanted her more than ever. It took all his will-power to force back that need and focus on her words.

'...probably not wise to visit too often,' she was saying as he guided her to the large receiving room, 'but I did need to call just this once, to warn you. I'm afraid you may be angry when I confess the rather presumptuous statements I made to Lady Wentworth, whom I called on this morning.'

'Presumptuous?' he echoed, amused. With so outspoken a girl, he couldn't imagine what outrageousness she'd uttered—and to Lady Wentworth! 'So you bearded the lioness in her den? I'm impressed by your courage,' he said as he waved her to a chair and sent a footman off for tea.

'Papa always said it's best to take initiative and confront your adversary on ground of your choice, rather than wait and wonder when and where you're going to be attacked. If Lady Wentworth intended to be an impediment to my establishing the school, I needed to know sooner rather than later.'

'Will she be an impediment?'

Her grin looked almost—smug. 'I think I've defused the problem, for the present, at least.'

'Have you, now?' he said, dubious. 'She seemed rather strongly opposed to it when she and the Squire called on me, and she didn't strike me as a person who is easily persuaded to change her opinions.'

'Quite true. But Papa also said one must learn everything one can about one's adversary before facing him, so I preceded my visit with a call on the local solicitor, Mr Scarsdale. I wanted to thank him anyway for his efforts in helping me staff Thornfield Place and discover from him which were the most influential members of the community, whose approval I must obtain if the school is to succeed. '

'Your father is right—that was good tactics,' he said approvingly. 'I'm sure Mr Scarsdale was gratified to be consulted.'

'I believe he was. Solicitors seem to me akin to sergeants in the army, performing many useful functions, knowing everything about everyone in their community, yet too often undervalued by those outranking them.'

Struck by the comparison, Dom nodded. 'I expect you are right. So, what did you discover?'

'After describing the most important families in the area—Squire Marlowe, Baron Southwick, and the Ransleighs—' She halted as Dom groaned.

'I hope he didn't recount too many adventures of my misspent youth.'

She shook her head, regarding him seriously. 'You must know how very highly you are regarded here, both your reputation before you entered the army, and for your valour in serving. He merely repeated what you yourself already told me—your ability with horses, your family's growing interest in breeding foxhounds and hunters, which led to their removal from Suffolk, to the great disappointment of all in the county. But he also provided the information I needed about Lady Wentworth.'

'Such as?'

'An only daughter doted upon by her father, she was the most beautiful and the most richly dowered maiden in the county in her début Season. Which makes it more understandable that she is accustomed to pronouncing judgements that permit no opposition, expressing desires that must be swiftly accommodated, and having others defer to her. I discovered the local charitable organisation of which she is now the head was established by her father, which she carries on in his honour. So naturally, in our conversation, I emphasised how the greatest wish of my late father, one of the heroes of Waterloo, was to establish a home and school for orphans of the soldiers he'd led into battle. That after his death, I felt it my solemn duty to carry out his wishes.'

Dom lifted an eyebrow. 'Was it his greatest wish?'

'Well, he never said it *wasn't*,' Miss Branwell said, with a twinkle in her eyes that made him laugh. 'To be fair, he had a war to win before he figured out what was to be done with the orphans we'd begun to accumulate. It's quite possible he would have decided to establish a home for them.'

'I begin to believe you incorrigible, Miss Branwell,' he said severely, his amused expression belaying the censorious comment.

'Determined, certainly,' she allowed, seeming not at all apologetic about manipulating her adversary.

After a break while Wilton brought in the tea tray, she continued. 'Mr Scarsdale said her father was a man of strict morals. So I emphasised that children brought up around an army are instilled with discipline from their earliest years, which makes them more amenable to following directions in moral training and improvement— moral improvement being something else her late father felt quite important.'

'I never noticed that strict discipline had any morally improving effect on soldiers.'

'As adults they have grown too set in their ways,' she countered. 'In any event, I ended by begging that she avail me of the experience she's garnered in running her own establishment. Which is quite true—I *would* appreciate her recommendations in staffing the school, and I certainly can't obtain the calibre of employee I want or find positions for the students later, if she sets the neighbourhood against me.'

'Very true. Well done, Miss Branwell!'

She nodded, her cheeks pinking at his praise. After draining her cup, she set it down and lifted her chin. Taking a deep breath and looking for the first time a bit uncomfortable, she said, 'I'm afraid I haven't yet confessed the truly incorrigible bit.'

Intrigued, and bracing himself for something outlandish, Dom said, 'Better do so straight away.'

'Well, if you're angry, there's nothing for it, but under the circumstances, I felt the…evasion justified. You see, before I left, Lady Wentworth took me to task about the nature of my relationship with you.'

Irritation washed through him. He'd never before resented quite so fiercely that birth and position would make everything about him of great interest to his neighbours for ever. 'Interfering creature,' he muttered. 'However, with the servants at Bildenstone all interrelated to families in the county, the fact that we've met several times was bound to get out.'

'Yes, and this is the…presumptuous part. I felt I'd mostly won her over, but with an unmarried daughter who might need to look closer to home for suitors if her Season isn't a success, and with her initial opposition to the orphans still making her approval uncertain, I knew she'd seize upon any reason to discredit me—and any stain upon my honour would give her exactly the excuse she needed! So I'm afraid I inferred that our acquaintance was of long standing, that you were a sort of protégé of my father's whom I looked upon as a sibling, and had been pleased to meet again as a fellow campaigner.'

Dom paused a moment to absorb the implications. 'You told that plumper without a blink? You *are* shameless!' he cried, torn between annoyance and admiration.

'Oh, no, I didn't lie!' she protested. 'I simply mentioned that Papa had mentored a number of young officers, of whom I grew quite fond and looked upon as brothers. As my comment followed her enquiry about our relationship, she *assumed* that you were one of the young men I was describing. Though I did not, I confess, contradict that erroneous assumption. In any event, I felt you should know about it, so you may decide how you wish to respond if anyone dares to question you about it.'

'So I can be prepared to insert a suitable evasion, which infers a relationship that never existed without precisely lying about it?'

She grinned. 'If your conscience will allow, I would much appreciate it.'

'Miss Branwell, I begin to have serious doubts about your character.'

She lifted an eyebrow and shrugged. 'Subterfuge and misdirection, when necessary, are legitimate tactics.'

'Perhaps you should abandon the idea of caring for orphans and take a post in strategy at Horse Guards.'

'With Boney on St Helena, they don't need me any more,' she said, then burst into laughter. 'Very well, I admit, I enjoyed leading her on. Someone so obviously full of herself, with a heart hard enough to consign innocent children she's never met to poverty without a blink, deserves to be hoodwinked from time to time.'

He shook his head, wondering at what a marvel she was. 'I only wish I'd been there to witness the performance. It must have been masterful!'

'Adequate, at any rate. With effects lasting long enough,

I hope, that I can launch the school and staff it before she has second thoughts about my respectability. Though it would still be wise not to invite those second thoughts by visiting here too often. So I'd best take advantage of this opportunity and ask you now if you've come up with any trainers whom you think I could approach about teaching at the school.'

'I did make a list. But I fear all those with the qualifications and experience you'd prefer are presently employed training horses for very wealthy men. It would probably be beyond your budget to hire any of them.'

She gave a negative shake of her head. 'If adequate salary is all that prevents them from accepting a position, that won't be a problem.'

'I should think, for one who's always managed on an army officer's pay, finances would be a pressing concern. Unless you have tucked away somewhere an India nabob or a rich brewer for a grandfather?'

'Actually, as you may have discerned with Lady Amelia being my aunt, my grandfather was an earl. My father, his youngest son, bedazzled my mother, a marquess's daughter with an enormous dowry that made her the prize of her début Season. I've inherited wealth from them both.'

Unconventional, outspoken, independent—and an heiress. Dom whistled. 'Miss Branwell, you amaze me!'

She looked down, her cheeks pinking again. 'I know, I hardly look the part,' she said, totally misunderstanding his compliment. 'Another reason I've resisted my aunt's urging that I come to London for the Season.'

Before he could come up with a tactful way to reassure her, the thought struck him of how Lady Wentworth would react to the news, and he had to laugh again. 'Wait until the officious Lady Wentworth discovers you outrank her—with a lineage that makes you far outshine the attractions of her daughter!'

'Not in that young lady's estimation,' Miss Branwell said, and chuckled. 'I met her during my call on her
mother. One look at me and my less-than-stylish raiment,
and Miss Wentworth accorded me half a curtsy and a murmured greeting before relegating me to the background,
as being of no more interest than the sofa.'

Having often observed the treatment acclaimed beauties meted out to those they considered of lesser stature,
Dom wasn't surprised by the girl's discourtesy. He *was*
surprised to find how strongly he resented the treatment
on Miss Branwell's behalf.

'Sad to discover her breeding doesn't equal her beauty.'

'No harm done; I found it amusing. In fact, her disdain turned out to be useful. Deciding it might be helpful in securing Lady Wentworth's approval, I let slip my
aunt's name. Upon realising her daughter had just been
rude to the niece of one of society's leaders, she couldn't
have turned more agreeable. So agreeable, she offered to
scotch any rumours that might be generated by my calling
on you—allowing my visit today. So I can only be thankful for the beauty's self-absorption. Though,' she added,
her smile faded, 'it would be less amusing, were I forced
to put up with such treatment through the whole of the
Season Aunt Amelia would drag me to.'

'Your aunt would guarantee you were too fashionably
gowned and too surrounded by persons of superior intellect and breeding to receive snubs from ill-mannered
country nobodies.'

'I'm not so sure. Nor could I imagine enduring the
rounds of visiting and shopping my aunt described as necessary for acquiring a suitable wardrobe. And the cost! I
may have inherited wealth, but I find it almost scandalous
that society ladies fill wardrobes with gowns intended to
be worn only once or twice.'

'What sacrilege!' he said, even more amused. 'Quite

true; with opinions like that, you'd not only *not* become fashionable, you'd be lucky if society's female population did not hire a sharpshooter to silence you before their menfolk could be exposed to so treacherous a notion.'

'No danger of my becoming fashionable, Aunt Amelia's protests notwithstanding. New gowns wouldn't change who I am—and what I am not. You can put a wagon mule into shiny harness, but that won't make him a cavalry horse.'

'That's a bit harsh,' Dom protested. Giving her shabby habit a glance, he said, 'You may not follow the latest fashion, but you have many admirable qualities.'

She raised an eyebrow. 'Such as?'

'Honesty, courage, ingenuity, perseverance, and a keen wit,' he shot back, naming off what had so quickly impressed him.

Obviously taken aback, her eyes widened. 'Thank you for that,' she said after a moment. 'But surely you can't claim those to be qualities highly prized by society gentlemen on the lookout for suitable wives!'

Before he could find a way around that irrefutable statement, she said, 'Not that it matters a particle. Only desperation would ever drive me to the Marriage Mart, and with Papa's inheritance and Mama's portion, I don't see that happening. As I mentioned before, unlike most of my sex, I'll never need to marry to avoid ending up with no roof over my head, or be reduced to begging a post as a companion or governess. Which is fortunate,' she added with a grin. 'Since I've never learned to keep my opinions to myself, I probably wouldn't last long as anyone's employee.'

Dom couldn't imagine her in that role, either. Though he did find it somehow sad that she seemed to think it her destiny to remain alone in the world. Such a unique, engaging personality deserved nurturing and appreciation—just as the sensual side to her called out for a lover's fulfilment.

His breath quickened and his body hardened at the thought; ah, how he'd like to guide her along that path, explore their explosive connection to the inevitable, exquisite conclusion!

While he once again struggled to rein in that fruitless desire, she rose and shook out her skirts. 'Thank you for the tea. With my news now delivered, I should get back to Thornfield Place.'

An immediate reluctance to let her go had him scrambling to his feet. Seizing on the first excuse that came to mind, he said, 'Before you leave, let me show you my grandfather's library. Anyone who could spend hours sitting on a wall, reading in the rain, must appreciate books, and Grandfather amassed quite a collection.'

Her face brightened. 'You mentioned to my aunt how extensive it is. I would love to see it! We could carry so few books with us on campaign. What I missed most about not having a settled home was the lack of a library.'

'So did I,' he said, struck by how she'd echoed his own feelings on the matter, and delighted to be able to share his grandfather's treasure with someone who would appreciate it as much as he did. Like braiding another thread into a strand of rope, that common interest further reinforced the bond that pulled them together.

Offering her his arm, Dom led her from the parlour to the library.

Three steps into the room, she came to a dead halt, her eyes wide with wonder as she looked up and down the shelves that covered every wall, from the floor up to the high vaulted ceiling.

'It's magnificent!' she breathed. 'May I?' She gestured towards the shelves.

'Of course,' Dom replied, her response all he had hoped. 'I must warn you, though, Grandfather's passion was collecting, not archiving, so I'm afraid the books are not shelved in any particular order.'

As Dom watched, she practically ran to the nearest bookcase. Something tightened in his chest as he watched her avidly scanning the shelves, sometimes running her fingers reverently over the spine of a particular volume, occasionally removing one to browse a page or two before carefully replacing it.

A lady who disdained new gowns, but went into raptures over a well-stocked library, was a unique creature indeed. The avid delight with which she examined the books, completely absorbed in discovering the treasures surrounding her, reinforced his instinctive sense of the deep passion that animated her, simmering beneath her matter-of-fact façade—and calling to him to fully reveal it.

After ten minutes, she shook her head and looked back at him.

'You warned me it was extensive, but this is overwhelming! How wonderful that your grandfather had a passion for collecting books, instead of rocks or jewellery or snuff boxes! I haven't enough time now to explore as I'd like. Might I come back later?'

'Whenever you wish. It's a pleasure to make it available to someone who truly appreciates it. Should I chance to be away when you call, Wilton can show you in.'

She turned towards the exit, then halted and looked back at the shelves, as if the volumes had an almost physical hold she was reluctant or unable to break. Then, with a sigh, she crossed the room to his side and looked up, her expression rapturous.

She stood so near, he burned to touch her, the delight still animating her face intensifying that desire. Struggling to restrain himself, Dom could barely breathe. When she placed her hand on his arm, his body tensed as he fought the need to pull her into his arms.

'I know life treated you cruelly, but you still have such blessings. A beautiful home, loyal servants, this magnificent library—and a bluebell wood!'

'And an enchanting new neighbour who appreciates books as much as I do,' he murmured.

'It is enchantment,' she whispered, and raised her chin.

Mesmerised, he cupped her face in his hands. As he lowered his mouth, her eyes drifted shut, one hand coming up to clasp the back of his head, the other trailing beside her, over a stack of books on a side table.

Which tumbled over the edge and hit the floor with a tremendous clatter.

At the sound, Miss Branwell gasped and jerked away from him. Bereft, shocked, Dom let her go.

For a long moment, they stared at each other, panting. Miss Branwell, her eyes wide and unfocused, brought a hand to her trembling lips, as if unable to sort out what had just happened.

A knock at the door, followed by Wilton bowing himself in, broke what remained of the spell holding them motionless. 'Should you like me to bring refreshments here, Mr Ransleigh?' the butler asked.

'N-no,' Miss Branwell answered for him. 'Thank you, Wilton, but I'm already overdue to return to Thornfield.'

'Very good,' the butler said, bowed himself back out.

Miss Branwell turned back to Dom, high colour still in her cheeks. 'I suppose I should be grateful for disorganised stacks of books. Otherwise, my actions might have been… embarrassing, to say nothing of scandalous.'

'I'm the one who should apologise, Miss Branwell,' Dom said, making the obligatory statement, though he was not sorry at all. Or, with his needy body still clamouring for the kiss denied it, only sorry they'd been interrupted.

'I should not have taken such advantage of you, a guest in my house.'

'You hardly "took advantage",' Miss Branwell admitted frankly. 'It goes without saying that the lapse mustn't be repeated, but in honesty, it was as much my fault as yours. And quite unsisterly! That's what I get for browsing through Ovid.'

Before his shocked mind could come up with a reply, she went on, 'I should like to browse through the library again, but next time I'll bring my maid as chaperone. And oh, how I would like to borrow some of the books for the school!'

As soon as the words left her lips, she shook her head. 'Forgive me! Presumptuous again! You would certainly not wish to risk loaning valuable books to children who would not appreciate how costly and delicate they are. But if you would permit it, might I myself borrow some books? I could copy out passages for the students.'

'Of course you may. Though you are correct; it would not be wise to put them into the hands of grubby school-children.'

'I shall ensure they are not.' Not meeting his eyes, she bent to gather up the scattered books and stacked them back on the table. 'I should leave before I wreak any more havoc. Thank you again, for your hospitality—and your understanding.' She turned to go, halted a moment to press his hand, then hurried out.

Fingers tingling, Dom watched her walk away, then took himself to the sofa. His unsatisfied body still raging, he tried to settle a mind in turmoil and make sense of what had just happened.

Only one thing was clear: Miss Theo Branwell, unlikely siren, just made him forget a host's duty to protect his female guests, a precept that had been drilled into him since childhood. He'd better stay away from her until he figured out what he was going to do about it.

Shaken, Theo gripped Firefly's reins with trembling hands as she directed the mare down the lane back towards Thornfield Place, alarm over the episode in the library extinguishing her satisfaction in having outmanoeuvred Lady Wentworth. Whatever had come over her?

Her ladyship's chagrin over her daughter's discourtesy might have initially put to rest the worry that Theo's association with Dominic Ransleigh might harm her orphans' cause. But had the butler entered the library a few moments earlier, with her practically embracing his employer, even Aunt Amelia's influence as a society hostess wouldn't have been enough to salvage her reputation. Loyal retainer Wilton might be, but such gossip would be too delicious to repress—and impossible for Ransleigh to halt or punish.

Hadn't she learned that lesson well enough, having to endure Audley Tremaine's sly innuendoes after Marshall's death? She'd paid dearly for her indiscretion in slipping away into the sunset-washed Portuguese hills to spend one halcyon evening alone with the man she loved. She should know better than to act so impulsively.

Besides, her imprudence now would injure not just her, but the innocent children she'd pledged to nurture and protect.

A part of her protested the clear conclusion that, having shown herself so susceptible to Ransleigh's appeal, she should avoid him entirely. True, in his company she was able to recapture the ease and comfort of her years in the army with Papa, and she'd been completely delighted by the treasures of his library. But Ransleigh's ability to slip through her guard and fire a passion she'd thought long extinguished was a danger against which she needed to remain much more vigilant.

Work was the answer, she told herself, shutting out the pleading voice that urged her not to end her association with her intriguing neighbour. Set up the school, care for the children, and fill her days loving the little boy who meant more to her than any transient passion.

No matter how much, at this moment, she might regret letting it go.

Chapter Ten

A week later, Herodotus finished, additional staff hired, and restless, Dom wandered around a rose garden freshly weeded by the new assistant gardener. Though he was pleased at returning Bildenstone to the elegance and comfort he remembered from his childhood, he hadn't yet managed to force himself to proceed to disposing of his now superfluous horses and carriages, nor had he ventured out to inspect the estate.

Having only recently been able to manage more than eating, sleeping, and reading, Dom told himself that taking on restoring the house was task enough for the moment. As he regained strength and immersed himself in the rhythm of country life, he'd feel more like he belonged here, begin figuring out what he was meant to do next—and find it easier to part with the relics of the past.

At least, he hoped so.

With a sigh, he halted his aimless ramble and turned back towards the house. He'd check on the progress the carpenter from the village had made on the repairs to the kitchen roof, then find another book to replace Herodotus.

Pacing into the kitchen, he found a neat pile of supplies, but no carpenter. The assistant cook looked up from peeling vegetables to bob a quick curtsy.

'Can I help you, sir?'

'Is Young Joe around?'

'He left after setting the new beams in the corner,' the cook replied. 'He said while he was waiting for the plaster to dry, he'd be down at the stone barn, building some partitions for Miss Branwell.'

'Did he say how much longer it would take him to finish the work here?'

'No, sir. Shall I send one of the boys down to the barn to ask him?'

Dom hesitated. He should tell her to dispatch someone, or wait until the carpenter returned on his own. But if work were being done on the school building, Miss Branwell was undoubtedly present.

After the incident in the library proved beyond doubt how strong his attraction to her was and how difficult to resist, he'd told himself to put her out of mind. Had Wilton or any of the other servants come in while he was practically devouring her, the vicar would even now be calling the banns. Since compromising her meant marriage, something neither of them wanted, the best remedy to buttress a suddenly deficient will-power was to avoid her.

But damn, he missed her. That keen wit, the winsome smile, the sparkling laugh, how she could shock and amuse him with her honest, unexpected and sometimes outrageous observations. She'd brought back to him the pleasures of driving and pointed him towards increasing the staff, which had led him to the admittedly limited activities that now occupied his days.

And that dangerous, irresistible, visceral attraction that sparked between them had made him feel more virile, more alive, and more happy to be alive, than he'd felt since before his wounding.

Why not go to the barn himself? In addition to consulting Joe about the progress on Bildenstone's kitchen, as the owner of the barn, he probably ought to inspect what alterations were being made.

Once admitting the possibility of seeing her again, the need to do so rose to swamp him.

And why shouldn't he? A man who'd faced down a company of Napoleon's fiercest cuirassiers needn't fear handling one tall, brown-haired girl. If he felt his willpower slipping, there would be workmen and children about, chaperones aplenty to restrain him from making any untoward moves. Besides, as eager as Miss Branwell was to avoid being compromised, she'd undoubtedly be on her guard as well.

He could indulge in the pleasure of her delightfully unconventional conversation for a few moments, with little risk. Before returning to his lonely existence at Bildenstone.

There was no need to be so blue-devilled. If he were beginning to regret burying himself alone in the country, there were any number of friends and at least two of his cousins he could invite to divert him.

But after running through a list of possibilities, he didn't hit upon a single one whose company tempted him to alter his solitary state.

No one but Miss Branwell.

The implication of that truth was so unsettling, Dom shied away from considering it.

Hell and damnation, enough introspection! He wanted some intelligent conversation, and he wanted it with Miss Branwell. Surrounded by workmen and urchins, he could indulge in half-an-hour's chat without requiring a priest and a wedding band at the end of it.

Suddenly aware the cook was still staring at him, awaiting an answer, Dom shook his head. 'No, you needn't send someone. I'll speak with Joe later.'

About thirty minutes later. Nodding as the woman

bobbed him another curtsy, Dom paced out the kitchen door and headed to the stables to order the tilbury.

Scarf around her hair to keep off the dust, an apron over her oldest gown, Theo was directing Jemmie and Maria to carry in water to wash down the grimy stone walls when she heard the rattle of a carriage and the clop of hoofbeats. Looking up, she saw a familiar tilbury approaching, and a shock of anticipation raced through her.

Her landlord, coming to inspect the alterations to his property, that was all, she rebuked herself, trying to settle her fluttering pulse. After her shameless behaviour in his library—her cheeks burned hot as she recalled how, but for some carelessly positioned books, she would have made a complete fool of herself—he'd not wish to be near *her* unless a number of chaperones provided protection.

She would concentrate on behaving like a proper lady and give neither of them any further occasion for embarrassment.

But she couldn't seem to stop the thrill that ran through her as he pulled up the vehicle and she watched his lithe, broad-shouldered form climb down. A technique, she noted, he'd now mastered, swinging down on his single arm with none of the awkwardness he'd displayed on their first drive ten days ago.

Nor could she slow her accelerating heartbeat when a shock of energy flashed between them as their gazes met.

Not daring to permit his touch, she tucked her hands behind her and made a quick curtsy. 'Good day, Mr Ransleigh.' *It is, now that I've seen you.* 'Have you come to check our progress, or to reclaim the carpenter I stole from you? Young Joe told me he's doing some work in Bildenstone's kitchen.'

'I need to talk with him, yes. But I also wanted to see the changes you're making.'

His tone seemed normal, friendly, with no edge of the disapproval she might have expected after he'd had time to consider her forwardness in the library—and no embarrassment, either.

Reassured, she said, 'Young Joe has most of the partitions constructed in the sleeping loft, and is now framing out the part of the downstairs that will become kitchen and dining areas. Should you like to see them?'

'I would, if I'll not be taking you from your work.'

'I'd enjoy a break from scrubbing and sweeping, and I'm sure the children will, too. Jemmie, Maria, there's a basket in the wagon with water, cheese, and some of the apple tarts Cook made for dinner last night. Have a bite while I show Mr Ransleigh around the building.'

To her surprise, Jemmie, who normally would have set off at a run to claim apple tarts, merely stood, eyeing Ransleigh. 'I can show him around, while you rest yourself with Maria.'

The bitterness of loss echoed within her. She appreciated Jemmie's protectiveness—the need he apparently felt to take over from Papa. Then a less sanguine thought occurred: did Jemmie, a young male of the species, sense something between her and Ransleigh?

Devoutly hoping he could not, Theo said, 'No, go enjoy your treat. The inspection tour will not take long.'

'I don't think Jemmie trusts me,' Ransleigh murmured. 'Perhaps you'd better assure him I won't ravish you in the sleeping loft.'

'I might rather assure him *I* won't ravish *you*,' Theo muttered, feeling herself flush. 'Once again, I do apologise—'

'Please, don't!' he interrupted, his teasing tone turned serious. 'First, I assure you that, if circumstances permitted, I would welcome being ravished by you, and second, the…mistake in the library was mutual. An episode that, much as I regret the fact, cannot safely be repeated, so I suppose we shall both have to be on our best behaviour. See, I have not even attempted to take your hand.'

Grateful there was nothing further she was required to say, she murmured, 'Thank you. That forbearance will lend me the courage to escort you up to the sleeping area. Though as a mercy, there aren't yet any beds.'

His quick chuckle made her smile, too, and relax— at least, as much as she could, with every hair on her arms and neck quivering at his nearness. Forcing herself to concentrate on the building, she showed him the girls' and boys' sleeping areas, the sections partitioned off for washing up and for storage. Descending the stairs again, over the racket of Young Joe's saws and hammers, she described the planned addition of two fireplaces, finishing up with the news that the stove and kitchen equipment, desks for the schoolroom, tables for the dining room, and beds for the dormitory were expected from various providers within a fortnight.

'So, what do you think?' she asked, dropping her voice back to normal tones after leading him back outside. 'You approve of the alterations, I hope.'

'I think you've done a wonderful job, though I would hate to estimate the cost.'

'That's of little consequence, as long as it turns the building into a home and school the children find welcoming. By the way,' she recalled, thinking it might amuse him, 'I've just received the first fruits—or perhaps the second, if I count my permission to call on you—of my interview with Lady Wentworth. We now have a teacher!'

'Indeed? Who did Lady Wentworth deign to recommend?'

'One of the charges from her institution, Helen Andrews, the orphaned niece of a retired governess who passed away, leaving the girl with no resources. Her aunt had completed her education, but being so young and without references, she'd been unable to secure a post. Lady Wentworth sent her to Thornfield; she's quite eager to take the job. Jemmie approves, and he's very cautious about accepting strangers.'

'So I noticed.'

Flashing him a look, she continued. 'Maria liked her, too. Not that she actually spoke with her, of course, but she consented to sit beside her when Helen came up to meet the children. I think she'll do very well.'

'When will classes start?'

'Probably next week.' After which time, she should be busy enough that squelching her stubborn attraction to a certain dashing neighbour should become easier. 'As soon as the schoolroom is finished and the desks arrive. The dormitory and kitchen will not be fully functional for several weeks yet, so we'll be bringing the children back and forth from Thornfield, but I'm anxious to have Helen begin the lessons. Travelling in the van of an army makes for a haphazard education, and I'm eager for the children to catch up.'

Since she could think of nothing further to discuss about the school, she ought to say goodbye and send Mr Ransleigh on his way. Still, protected by the presence of so many chaperones and knowing, once classes began, there would probably be few occasions to indulge in the delicious thrill of his nearness, she found herself hunting for conversational excuses to make him linger.

'Young Joe tells me you are doing a good deal of work at Bildenstone,' she ventured.

'Yes, I took your advice and hired more staff—doing my bit to contribute to employment in the county. Then, since I needed to give them something to do, it seemed a good idea to begin restoring the old place to its former glory.'

'It must be satisfying to watch it become the showpiece you remember.'

'It's a long way from that yet. With dusting and polish, the rooms are looking better—and the kitchen roof no longer leaks! But my favourite place is still the library. For several reasons.'

Those words drew her eyes to his face as steel to a magnet, to find him regarding her with an intensity that brought back all the mesmerising passion of that interlude. Her body heating, she gave him a little nod, silently acknowledging she remembered the episode as vividly as he did.

His molten gaze and her subtle response suddenly recalled the looks she'd exchanged with Marshall after their engagement, when they were in camp, surrounded by soldiers…smouldering, secret glances that reminded her of intimacies exchanged, promised intimacies to come.

Flustered, she shook her head. How ridiculous a comparison! In this case, there would be no intimacies to come. The fact that she could even erroneously connect the experiences, however, did warn her to be mindful of the strength of her attraction to Ransleigh, a passionate connection the like of which she'd not experienced since she had fallen in love with her fiancé.

This time, she'd not be able to indulge her passion.

She should only need to recall the spectacular heartbreak in which that passion ended to be thankful there would be no repetition.

Annoyed at herself for the turmoil Ransleigh seemed to provoke in her, she steered him towards his tilbury, which the stable boy was walking on the verge by a fence that divided the roadway from a field of newly sprouted wheat, the tiny plants swaying in the light spring breeze.

The younger children not being of practical use in cleaning the building, she'd had Constancia take them for a

walk. The maid, Charles, Georgie and Anna approached
from down the lane as she and Ransleigh reached his vehicle.

Anna ran up and held out a bouquet of wildflowers.
'They are pretty, just like you, Miss Theo!'

'How sweet of you, Anna,' Theo said, accepting the gift.

Warmth filling her as it always did when she saw
Charles again after an absence, no matter how brief, she
drew the boy to her for a hug—which he tolerated for a
moment before wriggling free.

Growing up already, she thought, releasing him with
regret.

Meanwhile, Georgie had wandered to the fence. Leaning over it, he took a deep breath. 'The dirt smells good.
Not like in the cities.'

'It's rich, fresh earth, newly turned over so the crop
could be planted,' Ransleigh said. Gesturing towards the
young plants, he added, 'That's wheat growing in the field.
When it gets tall, it makes kernels that are ground into
flour. The kind that is made into bread, not the sort Anna
just picked.'

Georgie looked up at him. 'Those little plants turn into
bread?'

'It's a bit more complicated than that, but, yes.'

As Georgie surveyed the field, rows of plants rolling
into the distance, his eyes widened. 'There's so much of
it! We never had enough bread on the march. That there's
probly enough so's we'd none of us ever be hungry again.
Wish I had a field I could grow bread in,' he said, his
voice wistful.

'Would you like to learn how to plough the land and
grow wheat?' Theo asked.

Georgie wrested his gaze from the field to look up at
her. 'Could I really, Miss Theo?'

Theo turned to Dom, who held up a restraining hand. 'I

know, I know. Let me check with the estate manager and see if any of the tenants would take on a young farmhand.'

Georgie looked from Theo to Ransleigh and back. 'Do that mean I'll get to grow the bread plants?'

'Wheat,' she corrected. 'We'll see. You'll still need to go to school, though. Now, you must all be thirsty from your walk! There's water and apple tarts in the wagon; Jemmie will help you get some.'

'Apple tarts!' Charles said, clapping his hands. 'C'mon, Georgie, let's go fast before Jemmie eats them all!' The two boys pelted off, Anna and the maid following.

'Do you really think you could arrange for one of your tenants to take Georgie under his wing?' Theo asked. 'I would so appreciate it.'

'When you look at me with that appeal in your eyes, how can I refuse?' he murmured. 'As long as you don't expect me to find positions for all your urchins.'

'Of course not. But I cannot tell you how much I appreciate your kindness in looking out for them—Jemmie, and now Georgie.' Holding up Anna's bouquet, she laughed. 'I suppose I should thank *you* for the flowers, too, since they were filched from your lane. They are beautiful.'

'Spring is such a lovely time of year here—I've been away so long, I'd almost forgotten. With your school about to start, I expect you'll soon be too busy to notice, and it would be a shame not to enjoy it. If you can spare a few hours, why don't I drive you around the estate tomorrow? So you can say you didn't miss the beauties of your first Suffolk springtime.'

Shirk her responsibilities for a morning, and explore the verdant paths, mossy woods and brilliant fields of wildflowers of this homeland she was just discovering? Guided through the lanes and fields by a man whose similar interests and experiences made her feel as much at ease as she'd been since losing Papa?

Theo wanted very much to accept the offer, but…being seated beside him as he drove her down deserted lanes and paused to explore bluebell woods and newly planted fields would be dangerous. As much as she felt secure with him, she'd also proven on several occasions how very strong the attraction between them was—far stronger than the rules of propriety, strong enough to lead them into disaster, if her vigilance in resisting him lapsed for even a short time.

If the treasures of an exceptional library hadn't been enough to restrain desire, she doubted the English countryside, no matter how delightful, would succeed in distracting her from its insidious call.

She'd reluctantly decided prudence demanded she refuse the offer when an alternate solution occurred—and she pounced on it.

'I should love to have a tour—but I'd much rather ride. Firefly could use the exercise, and surely you have something in your stable less temperamental than Diablo.'

He started to speak, then halted, looking troubled.

'You've not attempted to ride any other mount, have you?' she guessed. When, with a wry grimace, he nodded, she said, 'Your balance is still excellent. There's no reason you shouldn't be able to ride—as long as you don't choose a bully who'd rather bite, buck and unseat you than follow your commands.'

'I've always rather enjoyed mastering those bullies who'd rather bite, buck and try to unseat me.'

'Why not try a more amenable mount, and see if you can enjoy that, as well?' If she could only persuade him, she'd win herself an extended ride through the countryside—a pleasure she'd not realised how much she'd missed until Ransleigh proposed this expedition. It would enable her to spend a few more precious hours in his company, stashed in a saddle a safe distance from him, the need to pay attention to her mount distracting her from the constant temptation of his nearness.

She was reasonably sure she could manage it—as long as she stayed in the saddle.

Finally, he shrugged. 'I suppose I must try riding some time, though the prospect of mounting a slowtop doesn't appeal.'

'There are alternatives between a beast and a slug,' she pointed out.

His unexpected smile was like the sudden appearance of a winter sun on snow, dazzling in its brilliance. *Gracious, but he was appealing,* she thought dazedly, curling her fingers into fists to keep herself from reaching out to touch him.

'You're right, and I should stop being churlish. Very well, I'll give it a try. I warn you though, if I can't abide it, I reserve the right to return to Bildenstone and fetch the tilbury.'

'Agreed,' she said, delighted she would have her treat. 'But I'll wager you won't need to.'

'Shall I call for you at Thornfield—about nine?'

'Nine would be quite convenient.'

'Until tomorrow, then, Miss Branwell.'

'I shall look forward to it.' *More than you can imagine,* she added silently.

Prudently he refrained from taking her hand, and prudently she didn't offer it. But she felt the lack of his touch almost like a physical ache as he turned to climb up into the tilbury. She waved as he flicked the whip and the equipage set off down the lane.

After it disappeared from sight, she turned back to her buckets and brooms, savouring the knowledge that before the responsibilities of managing the school and caring for the orphans relegated her permanently into matronhood, she could look forward one last time to spending a few hours in the company of that attractive, witty and intriguing man.

And it had better be the last time, she warned herself. Before her growing yearning for her dazzling neighbour destroyed any chance that she could satisfy herself with a lifetime of mere contentment.

Chapter Eleven

Just before nine the next morning, Dominic Ransleigh trotted a seasoned gelding down the lane towards Thornfield Place. He'd trained this horse, too, rejecting him as a mount since the animal lacked the fiery temperament he always sought in a hunter. He would have sold him off, but the animal had a soothing effect on Diablo and the speed and endurance, if not the spirit, to match the stallion. Still, though responsive to command, he wasn't so docile Dom felt he was riding a hobbyhorse.

A little more spirit wouldn't have been amiss, though. Any challenge that forced him to direct his attention away from the beguiling lady he was about to meet would be helpful.

He really did want to introduce Miss Branwell to the beauty of an English spring, but she had been wise to suggest they do so on horseback, not seated in the far too intimate confines of a carriage. Somewhere along the way to recovering his strength and vitality, he seemed to have misplaced most of his good judgement and all of his powers of resistance.

At least when it came to the appeal of the unconventional Miss Branwell.

Still, he was glad she'd overcome caution and agreed

to accompany him. Were she any other maiden, she'd be bringing along a maid or a groom, but Dom bet the notion of a chaperone would never occur to her. Riding alone wouldn't be as proper, but if she met him unescorted, he certainly wasn't going to suggest adding one to the party.

For this excursion, he wanted her all to himself. He had a strong feeling she meant to severely limit their interactions in future—and an even stronger feeling he was going to miss them acutely.

A rising excitement gripped him as he approached Thornfield Place. To his relief, Miss Branwell, sans groom, stood near the entrance, her mare on a lead. As he rode up, she climbed on to a mounting block and tossed herself into the saddle.

She wore the same old riding dress—Dom thought again how he'd enjoy introducing her to more fashionable styles and colours that would bring out the chestnut in her hair and the velvety brown of her eyes. He recalled the disdain she'd expressed for shopping and laughed. How 'Dandy Dom' would love teasing and bedevilling her through a succession of modistes and dressmakers!

How much more he'd love easing her out of the old habit, using lips and hands to show his appreciation for her unclothed form, before fitting the new garments over her naked skin...

To his frustration and regret, there'd be no chance of that, so he'd best enjoy the innocent delights of conversation and companionship. They made excellent friends, after all. In fact, she was the cleverest, most entertaining and engaging individual he knew, excepting his Ransleigh Rogue cousins.

She rode up to meet him. 'Good morning, and what a glorious one it is! As if England herself ordered up a perfect day to show me her wonders.'

'What, you're not going to credit me with arranging it?' he teased.

She chuckled. 'Very well, Mr Ransleigh. I'm sure there is nothing you could not arrange! So, which way first—to the bluebell wood?'

'No, it's been a fortnight, and their display will have faded. Along the lane leading north, there's a stand of jonquils that should be coming into bloom, as well as meadow buttercup and red clover. The land rises as we go; from the highest point, we'll get a good view over the estate.'

'Lead on!'

They set off at a trot. Dom didn't attempt conversation, content to watch Theo ride. As he'd expect for one who'd followed the army, she sat the horse effortlessly, moving as one with her mount, fluid, graceful, and lovely to observe.

They exited the Home Woods into an area where fields bordered both sides of the road. And just as he remembered, up ahead was a glorious stand of jonquils.

With an exclamation of delight, she spurred her mount. He followed, smiling at her excitement as she gazed at the tall yellow flowers nodding in the wind.

'Papa told me about England's daffodil meadows—but this is more beautiful than I imagined. And the scent! Sweet as vanilla.'

'Heavenly, isn't it?' he agreed. 'Shall we ride on? I seem to recall a patch of wood violets along the banks of the brook just ahead.'

For the next hour, they rode slowly from wildflower display to wildflower display, past a handful of farms. But as the ride continued, Dom's initial enthusiasm began to dim.

The first farm they'd passed had seemed somewhat run-down, the roof thatch of the farmhouse old and dark, some of the surrounding field still fallow, with an old wooden-bladed plough left in the soil, as if the farmer had been unable to force it to finish its task. He'd noted it with some concern, wondering whether the tenant was old and in need of assistance.

But by the time they'd passed four such farms, each seeming more dilapidated than the last, he knew it couldn't be a question of aged tenants.

Angry and troubled, he pulled up near a patch of red clover.

Looking at him soberly, Miss Branwell said, "I'm no agriculturalist, but it seems something is wrong. I thought your estate was profitable?"

'It has been. It is. I'm no agriculturalist either, but the places we've just passed remind me more of the abandoned farms we saw in Spain after the French had plundered them, than a prosperous estate in the heart of England. I cannot imagine how they have deteriorated to this point, but I certainly intend to find out.'

She nodded. 'Of course you must. These are your people, dependent on your leadership as surely as the men who served under you in the army. They need you to watch out and care for them.'

She hadn't meant the words as a reproof, but they stung anyway. 'These *are* my lands and my people, and their welfare *should* be my concern. I'd thought about riding the fields ever since I arrived—but there's no excuse for my not having done so sooner. I find it strange, though, if the farms are in such dire straits, that I've not heard a word of complaint or dissension from anyone on the household staff.'

'You said you'd been absent for seven years, and your family hadn't resided here for much longer. It's probably been like this for some time.'

Dom nodded grimly. 'It might well have been. My father had little interest in agriculture. He prized Bildenstone only for the income it provided him to spend on his hounds and horses. Winniston, the agent, has been here for years, and his father before him. Trusting them to manage things, Papa came only to collect the rents. If the amounts were sufficient, he probably didn't even check the account book.'

'He must not have ridden the estate, either.'

'Probably not. I know he was never gone long from Upton Park.'

'Well, someone needs to fix this.' She waved her hand towards another pasture half-grown up in weeds, with a dilapidated farmhouse in the distance. 'Do you think you could take up the tasks of an agriculturalist? I shouldn't think it would be so different than evaluating and cultivating horses—though less exciting than a gallop across the countryside.'

Memory returned in a vivid flash: mounting a horse so fresh he fought the bit, coaxing him to accept Dom's weight, moving him forward. And then the sheer soul-filling wonder of leaning low over the beast's head while the countryside flashed by him, the exhilaration as the horse gathered himself and threw heart and body over fence or pond or fallen log, the possibility of a rough landing or a fall ever present, adding a spice of danger.

Wonder, exhilaration, and excitement he'd never experience again.

'I don't know,' he answered frankly. 'By the time I went up to Oxford, I knew I wanted to spend my life breeding and training horses that were the strongest, fastest, most fearless jumpers in England, both to follow the hounds and to race cross-country.'

'Like Diablo.'

'Like Diablo,' he said. 'Horses which, as you know, I can no longer ride. With the endeavour that was the focus of my life since I outgrew short coats no longer feasible, I've come back full circle, to Bildenstone, looking for something to replace it. Thus far, singularly bereft of inspiration, I've been drifting along, unable to force myself to sever those ties with the past, unable to see a future I want to pursue.'

She nodded, offering him no empty platitudes, for which he was grateful. But as she sat regarding him thoughtfully, Dom wondered what had possessed him to confess his failings to her. Just because they'd shared the same experiences and challenges in the army—just because a potent sensuality pulled them together—didn't mean she was interested in his inability to redefine his life. A difficulty, incidentally, about which he'd said nothing to Max or Alastair, and admitted only to Will, who'd tended him with a mother's care after his injuries.

'So many never made it off the killing fields of Waterloo,' she said softly, startling him out of his reverie. 'For you to be so severely wounded and survive, yet be ill equipped to continue your previous pursuits, it seems to me that you must have been spared for a purpose. To become a new man, meant to pursue something that lies in an altogether different direction. Your challenge is to resist looking back, regretting what you've lost, and discover instead what is meant for you now.'

'As you have?' he asked, well aware that his wasn't the only life whose course had been shattered by the case shot of Waterloo.

She gave him a brave smile. 'Easy for me to offer advice. I already know what I'm to do.'

'Taking care of soldier's orphans. Are you so sure that's your destiny?' he asked, wishing he could find such a clear sense of his own.

'Despite Aunt Amelia trying to dissuade me, I believe it is.'

A new man with a new purpose. Maybe that's why it seemed so easy to confide in her, he thought. Because, rightly or wrongly, he felt Max and Alastair and even

Will would always be comparing him to what he'd been, whereas she knew only who he was now.

She saw him and his future as a blank slate, and she expected him to pick up the chalk.

Right before him loomed at least one worthwhile endeavour. And she was right; it was past time for him to start moving forward.

'Is that why you broke your engagement—because you felt your future would be completely different from your past, and you didn't think the lady would want to go there with you?'

The question startled him, but by now he should expect Theo Branwell to boldly ask what no one else would dare enquire about. 'Yes. I didn't feel it was fair to hold her to her promise when I was no longer the sportsman whose suit she'd accepted. When I no longer could, nor wanted, to move in the same circles, doing the things I'd done before.'

'So she didn't pass the test.'

He frowned, not sure what she meant. 'Test?'

She nodded. 'If she'd really loved you, she wouldn't have let you walk away.'

'That's a little unfair!' he protested. 'I didn't give her a choice.'

'That may be, but if Marshall had been wounded and sent me away, I wouldn't have gone. I've have stayed and tended him, and if he wouldn't permit that, I'd have sat at his doorstep until he relented.'

'Like you sat on my wall?' he said, bemused.

'Yes. And if he had me evicted, I would have written him every day, telling him how much I loved him and wanted to be with him. I would never have given up.'

Dom sat silently, pondering. Had he, on some level, meant his insistence on breaking the engagement as a test—for them both?

If so, he had to admit, he had failed it, too. Since coming to Bildenstone, he'd hardly thought of Elizabeth.

'Well, in any event, look at me! I'm not the gallant cavalier who had the gall to persuade a duke's daughter to marry him.'

She stared at him, her eyes narrowed. 'Maybe that was part of it—the audacity of carrying off the prize on your part, the thrill of flouting convention on hers. Of course, it's not my place to speculate.'

He chuckled. 'But you did anyway.'

'What *I* see when I look at you is a man as audacious as he ever was. Brave, powerful, immensely attractive, and full of potential. He may be a bit nicked up on the exterior—' she motioned to his eye patch and missing arm '—but the outside isn't important. It's the essence of the man within that matters.'

'I'm not sure what my essence is,' he admitted. 'I suppose, before this, I could always rely on what was outside, so I never had to look. I'm looking now, and I'm not sure I like what I'm seeing.'

'What did you do before?'

'Oh, followed the seasons as a sportsman. Buying, training and hunting horses in the autumn and winter; balls, entertainments, cards at my club, visits to the tailor in London during the Season, house parties and more horse training in the summer...'

His voice trailed off at the look of incredulity on her face. 'Pretty useless stuff, actually,' he allowed, 'when compared to fighting Boney—or caring for orphans.'

'Maybe what happened, happened, so you'd have to confront your life and choose to do something different. Something more...important.'

'Had this not happened, I probably never would have examined it,' he said, realising that fact for the first time.

'Nor am I sure what that "something more important" should be.'

'While you ponder it, do something for the tenants here.'

'Like hiring an estate manager who knows what he's doing,' he said acerbically.

'Yes. And hopefully,' she added with a grin, 'one willing to take on some junior apprentices.'

'Ever watching out for your orphans! Maybe I *should* become an estate manager. Fattening up little boys like Georgie would be an aim worth striving for. My cousin Alastair is master of his own profitable estate—I'll write and seek his advice. I also remember him nattering on about the spring shearing at Holkham Hall in Norfolk; where a group of agriculturalists gather to discuss new techniques. Maybe that will ensure I no longer let my tenants down,' he added, his ire resurfacing.

'You didn't know they'd been let down. What matters now is what you do to correct the deficiencies.'

They set off again, Dom still angry and unsettled. How he wished he had Alastair's expertise, so he would know immediately how to rectify all the problems he'd seen!

As they reached the next farm, Dom noted a man in the field, ploughing behind a heavy-set draught horse. Pulling up his mount, he said, 'If you don't mind, Miss Branwell, I'd like to speak with that farmer. I can at least assure him that I intend to begin at once to correct some of the problems he will doubtless want to point out.'

'Please, go speak with him as long as you like. I even promise not to gift you with my opinions on his suggestions.'

He smiled slightly, appreciative of her efforts to make him feel better. Though nothing but a transformation of the cottages and fields he'd just seen would do that.

'I won't be long.' At that, he slid from the saddle and set off, leaving his mount to graze at the roadside.

Seeing him approach, the man pulled up his horse, watching him warily.

'I'm Ransleigh,' Dom said as he approached. 'And you are…?'

A flash of emotion—resentment, probably—briefly coloured the man's expression before he nodded a greeting. 'Willie Jeffers. Heard you'd come back to Bildenstone, Mr Ransleigh.'

'Pleased to meet you, Mr Jeffers. That's a fine horse and plough you have. Unfortunately, I haven't seen others like it on my inspection today.'

'I reckon not,' Jeffers said with a short laugh.

'Your fields look to be in prime shape as well. As you know, I've not been to Bildenstone for years, and am shocked by the condition of the farms. Can you tell me what has happened here? Please, speak frankly. Anything you say will be held in confidence. I give you my word.'

After studying Dom for a moment, the farmer said, 'Folks say you were a brave soldier and a man that keeps his word. So, you want the truth about the farms?'

'I do,' Dom replied, meeting the man's steady gaze.

'The truth is that Winniston's always been more concerned with collecting rents than using any of the blunt to improve things—even make necessary repairs. Don't think he holds back extra for himself. Just doesn't seem to understand he'll get more profit from the land if he ploughs some back into it, instead of wringing out of it every farthing he can get.'

'You seem to have held on to enough to improve yours.'

'Aye,' Jeffers acknowledged. 'My family has farmed these acres for generations, and I'm always looking for ways to do it better. I've a brother up near Holkham Hall, and he passes along to me the things they've tried up there.'

'To very good effect, judging by what I've seen. First, let me assure you that Winniston will not be supervising

Bildenstone's farms much longer. I *am* interested in improving things, and want to do so as soon as possible. But as you noted, my experience is with the army, not the land. I'd appreciate any suggestions on techniques you've found useful in your fields.'

The wariness in the farmer's expression turned to the enthusiasm of a master describing his craft. 'Iron-tipped ploughs help, especially when the ground's mostly clay. And having the right draught horse. At the last county fair, I talked with a farmer from around Needham Market way. He'd heard of breeding a Suffolk sorrel with a Norfolk trotter, to give the offspring more flesh and stamina. Gentle, tractable, strong, and love to work, those sorrels! If we could breed more stamina in them—now that would be a combination! I already have a trotter—can't ride around all these acres on some weak-kneed thing that would give out under my weight in an hour. One of the farmers the other side of Hadwell has a sorrel out of Crisp's stallion. But when it came right down to it, neither he nor I knew enough about breeding to give it a try.'

The idea immediately piqued Dom's interest. 'I might. Not by borrowing your stallion—you need him to ride your fields. But I must return to Newmarket soon to complete the sale of some stock, and will see about purchasing a good trotter stallion and several sorrel mares.'

'A lot of your tenants would like a horse that could hold the plough longer over heavy ground,' Jeffers said. 'Especially further east, where the land's low and marshy.'

'Thank you very much, Mr Jeffers. I shall certainly look into it.'

'Right happy to have you back in residence, sir,' Jeffers said, before turning back to his plough.

I hope you will be, Dom thought, energised by the conversation. He'd never considered breeding anything other than steeplechase animals, but creating a crossbreed that could allow farmers to plough their fields faster and perhaps grow crops in land previously thought too heavy to cultivate would be an admirable goal.

Was this to be the worthy endeavour he was meant to pursue? A rising sense of anticipation dispelled the last vestiges of his anger and frustration.

'Looks like it was a profitable conversation,' Miss Branwell observed as he walked back to her.

'It was. I may have found something useful to do after all.'

'Excellent! That calls for a celebration. How about a good gallop? Let's find an unploughed field just begging to be ridden.'

The disaster with Diablo had so shaken his confidence, Dom wasn't sure he could manage more than a canter. *Well, why not?* he thought, buoyed by a newfound enthusiasm. If he could discover a new vocation, maybe he could find a way to keep his seat at a gallop.

'I'll see if my mount and I can oblige.'

As if sensing his hesitation, Miss Branwell said, 'You need only pretend you're mounted on your cavalry horse, sabre in hand, leading the charge.'

If he were going to land on his rump, better to find out now. He couldn't envision another person whose witnessing of that failure would bother him less than the compassionate Miss Branwell.

Not only would she neither laugh nor carry tales, she'd probably make judicious notes about the cause of the fall and advise him how to correct his position.

Smiling at that notion, he rode with her past the rest of Jeffers's acreage, down a hill and around a bend, where they found an invitingly fallow meadow.

'Ready?' she asked.

'Ready.' *As I'll ever be,* he added silently. Dom set his mount off slowly, signalling the gelding through his paces.

He found him responsive to his touch, not fighting him for control, as Diablo always had. He'd about convinced himself he was ready to try a full-out gallop when Miss Branwell, in the lead, looked back over her shoulder and shouted, 'Race you to the stone wall!'

No Ransleigh had ever refused a challenge. As her mare took off in a burst of speed, Dom spurred his gelding to follow.

As the horse moved faster and faster, he found his body adjusting instinctively into the rise and fall of the horse's stride. His hips and legs easy, the shift of his weight automatic, within minutes, he was able to transfer energy from worrying about balance to urging on his mount.

The gelding accelerated, stretched himself out to a ground-eating pace. Wind whipped at his hat, air rushed through his lungs, his heartbeat accelerated…and joy began to bubble up from deep within, the pure joy he always felt when he became one with his mount in a full-out gallop.

Miss Branwell looked back once, a brilliant grin on her face as she saw him closing behind her. Taking that as a tossed gauntlet, Dom pushed the horse harder. Just before they reached the stone fence at the far end of the pasture, he edged her mare out by a nose.

Miss Branwell pulled her horse up and sprang down from the saddle. Energised, exuberant, he slid down beside her.

'Not very chivalrous to beat you at the end, I'm afraid.'

'Oh, but what a run! How I've missed the good gallops I used to have with Papa, out on the plains of Spain and Portugal. And you—you were magnificent! Not many could beat Firefly when she's got a lead, but you managed it. I knew you could do it!'

With a joyous laugh, she threw her arms around him and tilted her head up.

Despite a whisper of conscience that warned it was dishonourable to take advantage of her impulsive act, a company of French cuirassiers at the gallop couldn't have kept him from claiming the lips so temptingly close.

The kiss began slow and sweet, a soft brush of his mouth against hers. But then she made a small sound deep in her throat and parted her lips.

A surge of heat and desire swamping him, he swept his tongue to claim hers. To his elation, she met his and fenced with it, laving him with slow, lush strokes that fired passion to a searing heat.

With his one good arm, he pulled her against him and deepened the kiss while she wrapped her arms around his neck. He slid his hand down to cup her bottom, bringing her closer still, and she rubbed herself against his aching groin.

White-hot lust obliterated everything but his need for her. One tiny, still functioning part of his brain applied itself to considering whether there was any usable surface where he could lay her down, raise her skirts and lose himself in her.

The sound of a horse's whinny finally penetrated the fog of lust. Shocked that he'd almost tried to ravish her at the edge of a field, where some farmer might at any moment have come by and discovered them, he released her and staggered a step away.

Her eyes dreamy and unfocused, she stared up at him, her moist, kiss-rosy lips so appealing it was all he could do not to step closer and kiss her again.

'If you apologise for that, I'm going to punch you,' she murmured.

Trust his Theo to say the unexpected, he thought, her unconventionality a joy. 'If I did,' he replied, smiling, 'it would only be for form's sake. I've wanted to kiss you practically from the moment I met you.'

'As I've wanted to kiss you. Shocking, I know, and un-maidenly, but there you have it. So I am very, very glad I got to kiss you—and it was everything I'd dreamed it would be. But it must stop here. I wish…' she sighed be-fore continuing '…but wishing changes nothing. Episodes like this, if discovered, would ruin my reputation, and I cannot risk that, when any disgrace of mine would harm the future of my orphans. And you—well, you need to find that new direction for your life before you involve yourself with anyone.'

Dom knew what she intended. Everything within him wanted to resist the conclusion, but she was right—which didn't mean he had to like it. 'Time to part?' he said.

'Time to part,' she agreed. 'Thank you, Dominic Rans-leigh, for making my return to England easier and more joyful than I could ever have hoped, so soon after losing Papa. Thank you for all you've done, and continue to do, for my orphans. I wish you the best as you work towards your future—and you *will* find what you're meant to do, I'm sure of it. I would ask only one more thing.'

'Only one?' he asked, amusement at that unlikely pos-sibility breaking through his dismay over the note of fi-nality in her speech.

'Well, I can't promise never to ask anything in future for the children, but I do promise never to ask anything else for me. Nothing but this. May I kiss you goodbye?'

After a moment of shock at the unexpected request, he answered by pulling her into his embrace. She slid her fin-gers into his hair, sending shivers down his body as she tilted her head up and opened her mouth to him.

Twining her tongue with his and moulding herself against his body, she kissed him with everything in her—lips, tongue, fingers stroking his head, legs and torso rub-bing against him, even her booted foot wrapped around his ankle. She kissed him as if the world were about to end, as if there would never be anything of fire and passion and intimacy again.

He took everything she offered, and returned it.

When at last she released her hold on him, he was breathless and so dizzy he nearly fell over. For a few moments, there was nothing but their panting breaths and the almost tangible connection sparking in the air between them.

'I would really rather consider that hello,' he muttered when he'd assembled wits enough for speech.

She gave him a little smile, so sad he felt an immediate need to assuage whatever hurt had caused it. His confusion and concern mounted as tears sheened her eyes.

While he stood frozen, unsure what to do, she opened her lips as if to speak, closed them and shook her head, as if the situation were hopeless. 'Goodbye...my very dear Mr Ransleigh,' she whispered and turned away.

Before his muzzy brain decoded her intent, she'd led her grazing mount to the rock ledge, scrambled up and launched herself into the saddle. Without another word, she kicked the mare to a gallop.

Dom stood watching her ride away, his body still afire with unsatisfied desire, his thoughts in turmoil, while within the raging cauldron of chaotic emotion something shouted that letting her go was *wrong*.

After a few more dazed moments, he shook himself free and went to claim his own horse. Leading it to the ledge, he remounted and nudged the gelding towards Bildenstone Hall.

Hello, not goodbye, kept echoing in his brain.

Chapter Twelve

Two weeks later, Dom was looking through records in the estate office, trying to make sense of harvest quantities, when Wilton came in, out of breath. 'Sorry to disturb you, Mr Ransleigh. We've just had a soldier stop by, asking for directions to the stone barn. He said he meant to call on Miss Branwell.'

An immediate stab of jealousy struck him, so surprising he didn't quite hear Wilton's next words.

'…so you might ride over and check on her,' the butler was saying.

'Ride over and check on her?' he repeated.

'She may be there by herself, with just that young female teacher and the little ones, and no man to protect her.'

'Did this soldier look like someone she might need protecting from?'

'I can't rightly say, sir. But he was young, and…vigorous.'

While that observation didn't make Dom's struggle to suppress the unaccountable jealousy any easier, he did wonder about Wilton's unusual level of concern for a girl he'd met only a handful of times. Had Miss Branwell confided to the butler that increasing the staff at Bildenstone—and thus easing his burdens—had been her idea? Somehow, that didn't sound like her.

'You seem rather worried.'

'All the neighbourhood thinks highly of her, sir. Giving a place to Miss Andrews, when other families in the area that could have didn't lift a finger. Employed many others, too, and Young Joe told me that she paid all the workers she hired twice the going rate, since she wanted the building completed as soon as possible. And made sure there was ham, cheese and ale available for all, so they didn't have to bring their own. Mrs Greenlow was just telling Cook what a shame it was she lost her man in the war and fair broke her heart, her being so young to be alone, no matter but it's noble for her to dedicate herself to those poor unfortunates. Anyways, no one would want to see any harm come to her.'

Good thing she's not hunting a new butler, Dom thought, awed at that paean of praise from the normally laconic Wilton. Still, he felt a swell of pride in her; some Christian folk gave lip service to the need to do good in the community, but the concern Theo Branwell showed for her orphans, the care she urged him to show for his employees, she showed to everyone.

A pang of longing echoed through him. While he was dampening down that equally unsought-for emotion, Wilton said, 'You will ride over and make sure everything is all right, won't you, sir?'

A rush of excitement stirred his senses. Though he felt somewhat guilty at taking advantage of this situation to break their self-imposed separation, he wouldn't be staying long, and there would be a school full of witnesses to make sure he didn't indulge any carnal longings. And though he was reasonably certain the redoubtable Miss Branwell, who'd followed the army from India to Portugal to Brussels, would have no trouble taking care of herself if some soldier turned importunate, she might still be alone and unprotected out there.

Maybe it would be wise to check on her, he thought, a niggle of unease stirring.

'Better send to the stables for my gelding.'

'Thank you, Mr Ransleigh,' Wilton said, obviously relieved.

'I shall do my best,' Dom assured the butler before trotting up the stairs to change into his riding gear.

Ten minutes later, spurring his mount down the lane, Dom let his thoughts stray to the object he'd been trying so hard *not* to think of since the incident by the wildflower meadow.

That kiss—heaven and stars, what a kiss! It's a wonder he hadn't turned molten on the spot. If she kissed like that, he couldn't imagine what ecstasy a full loving could promise.

But what pulled him to Theo Branwell was more than just a promise of sensual heaven. The fact that she'd shared and understood the demands, the sacrifices and the unequalled camaraderie of the army had drawn him to her from the first. He'd been gratified and delighted to find they shared a love of books and horses. She stimulated his mind as much as she stirred his body, challenging easy assumptions, jolting him to think in different directions, startling him with her unusual perspectives and her clear, bright honesty. She made him think more, dared him to do more, to *be* more.

How much brighter his days had become since he stumbled into her in that lane! She'd pushed him into trying to drive and ride again, restoring those pleasures to him much sooner than he probably would have discovered them on his own.

He admitted to himself that he'd been jealous when she'd talked about her lost fiancé. From what he'd seen of Theo Branwell, the man she loved would have been wrapped in a devotion so complete, so intense, nothing would ever have been able to penetrate it. Her fierce declaration of unlimited loyalty only underscored how easily he'd been able to part from Elizabeth, and how easily she'd let him go.

In fact, thinking back on that kiss—a pleasure he'd sternly denied himself—he was convinced that, though Miss Branwell might be still unmarried, she was not completely inexperienced. She *had* been engaged to a man she loved completely; it wasn't beyond possibility that they'd anticipated their vows.

His body rejoiced at the idea of Theo Branwell coming to his bed, prompting his mind to consider possibilities for making that happen.

Only a moment's contemplation reminded him there were none. Experienced or not, he concluded with a sigh, she was still technically a maid. And she was quite right that an affair discovered would tarnish her reputation and make the lives of her orphans that much more difficult.

Unless…unless he decided to court her with honourable intent?

Shockingly, the voice of self-interest and prudence didn't immediately reject the notion. Though, as they'd discussed, he didn't yet have a clear idea of his future, and thus had no business asking anyone to share it, he could at this juncture not imagine finding a lady more delightful, challenging, and sensual than Theo Branwell.

Fortunately, there was no need to make an immediate decision. He could let the tantalising notion rattle around in his brain and see where it ended up. Miss Branwell and her orphans were only just getting established in their new homes, and neither he nor she were going anywhere else any time soon.

Pleased and intrigued by the possibility of being able to

pursue an association with Theo Branwell after all, Dom kicked his mount to a canter and guided him down the lane to the stone barn.

Meanwhile, Theo stood in the kitchen area at the school, supervising the installation of the new cooking stove. In the open space beyond, students at their desks recited a lesson, after which Miss Andrews had asked Theo to read them a story copied out of Bildenstone library's volume of *Arabian Nights*.

She needed to make one more trip to Thornfield, to fetch the rest of the linens for the beds and the kitchen. Within a few days, her vision would be fully realised as the students began using the building as both home and school.

She'd not seen Dominic Ransleigh when she ventured back to Bildenstone's library, a bored Constancia at her side. She hadn't really expected to, but she'd been shaken anew by the strength of her disappointment and regret at missing him.

The hard truth was she'd already grown too attached to him, and not just by the physical magnetism that drew her to him whenever he was near. She had come to crave his company and look forward to discussing all manner of topics with a mind as active and even more far-ranging than Papa's. She loved listening to him talk about horses, discuss farm management and reminisce about his army days. She would love to scour the shelves in the Bildenstone library while they compared their favourite books.

She recalled their wildflower ride, the disarming humility with which Ransleigh confessed he was still floundering to find his place, the deepening intimacy of friendship that had surrounded them as they talked so frankly, a bond as close and powerful as the more physical connection they'd shared after.

Even now, she felt the urge to throw herself and all
her energies into helping him identify the life's work that
would replace the calling he'd lost, sure whatever endeavour he settled upon, he would pursue it with vigour and
competence.

It would take but very little more involvement to find
herself falling in love with him. Which would be a disaster on so many counts.

First and foremost, she had only to remember the catastrophe of losing Marshall. She'd fallen for her fiancé
quickly and completely, investing every particle of her
mind and heart. Imbued with the confidence of youth, she'd
expected him to go through all the campaigns unscathed,
as Papa always had. The loss of Lord Everly and his be-
reaved wife's pain had scarcely shaken her confidence in
the future she and Marshall would share.

When, on the road to Lisbon, she'd received the terrible news of Marshall's death in battle, she'd been at first
incredulous and denying. Once the messenger her father
dispatched was able to convince her of its truth, she'd fallen
to her knees, struck down by a physical pain as great as if
her chest had been cleft in two.

She'd told everyone their long sojourn at the convent
was because of Alicia's ill heath, but in truth, her companion could probably have made it to Lisbon. It was Theo
who, after reaching the nunnery where they'd arranged
to spend the night, had collapsed, inconsolable. Paralysed
by grief and despair, she lay for days unmoving, pushing
away the meals the nuns brought her, scarcely able to dress
or groom herself.

If it hadn't been for the need to care for the infant
Charles, she wasn't sure she would ever have emerged
from that spiral of misery.

Now, when she looked up at Ransleigh's face, caught
in that mesmerising blue gaze, wrapping herself up in his

brilliant smile, her mind captivated by his wit and beguiled by his charm, she thought how easy it would be to fall again just as completely for Dominic Ransleigh.

Her illusions of safety destroyed by the deaths of Marshall and her father, she wasn't sure she could survive losing anyone else.

And if she couldn't risk falling in love with him, no more could she risk *making* love to him. She no longer had any doubt about the strength of the physical pull between them; if she kept seeing him, sooner or later the siren song of passion would drown out the voice of prudence and caution—she'd been reckless enough already, kissing him with total abandon in that farmer's field. The results of discovery, for herself and her orphans, would have been too dire to contemplate.

But even if she did become so lost to reason and prudence as to take those risks, an involvement between them wouldn't be fair to Ransleigh. He'd shown disarming candour in confessing that he was still at his life's crossroads. It would be wrong to try to attach him now. Sooner or later, he would find the occupation he sought, and land on his feet again. Once launched upon the new endeavour—and some interaction with society would inevitably be part of it—he deserved far better than an old maid past her last prayers with a troop of children in tow, a woman whose position in society would do him not a particle of good in advancing along whatever path he chose to pursue.

The keenness with which she missed him, and strength of temptation to seek him out, only reinforced her conviction that parting from him was necessary.

It was also miserable. Well, she'd endured 'miserable' before; she must simply grit her teeth, keep moving forward, and wait until the need for him faded.

As it must, eventually. Mustn't it?

A touch at her arm shocked her out of her melancholy

reverie. Beside her stood one of the footmen who'd accompanied her from Thornfield to transport the heavy items. 'Miss Branwell, there's a soldier outside asking to see you.'

Curiosity replaced introspection. She didn't recall that any of Papa's troopers hailed from Suffolk. 'Did he give you his name?'

'Lieutenant Audley Tremaine. He said he'd worked with your father.'

Distaste soured her stomach and she frowned. What could Audley Tremaine want with her? She wished she'd been able to repeat to her father some of the crude insinuations he'd made after her return from the convent; Papa would have used him for target practice, and she'd not have to deal with him now.

Though she had no wish to see him, neither would she give him the satisfaction of thinking he intimidated her. Still, not wanting to have the children witness the unpleasantness that would probably arise at their exchange, she decided to meet him outside.

'I don't want the students disturbed. Tell the lieutenant I'll join him by the pasture fence.'

After giving the footman time to deliver her message, she took a deep breath and girded herself for what was probably to come. *You will be cool, distant—and will not let him make you lose your temper,* she instructed as she exited the building.

She saw him immediately, lounging by the fence, his black gelding tied to a nearby tree. Before she'd met Marshall, she'd found the attentions of the tall, handsome, arrogantly charming Lieutenant Tremaine flattering and exciting. Until acquaintance with a man far his superior made his attractions look as insignificant as a copper farthing beside a gold sovereign.

He straightened when she reached him and made a

mocking bow. 'Well, well, Theo Branwell, imagine finding you in the wilds of Suffolk!'

'Indeed,' she said, not offering her hand. 'Whatever brings you to the wilds of Suffolk?'

'The desire to renew your charming acquaintance?'

'Since we didn't part on friendly terms, I doubt that.'

'We could have been friendly. We could still be very... friendly.'

Trying not to grit her teeth, she said, 'Weren't you selling out? So you could resume attending house parties where there are bored matrons to seduce?'

The smile on his handsome face faded. 'Not kind to remind me that my ancient name came unaccompanied by the funds to maintain it. Yes, I've sold out, but ladies find a man in uniform so appealing! I'm sure you noticed the effect.'

'I'd say it depended on the man.'

Ignoring that jibe, he continued. 'My business elsewhere didn't preclude my stopping by to see you. Quite a fuss you've created in the neighbourhood, I understand! Over a pint at the King's Arms in Hadwell, I heard all about your pious zeal for the poor orphans. How are the little tykes?'

'Please don't pretend now you have any interest in them. I remember too well your disdain for father's sergeant-major's son.'

'Hanging on to them after the old man's death to remember him by? How pious and proper. Ha!' He laughed. 'If the townspeople here only knew.'

'Now that you've offered the usual insults, isn't it time to leave?'

'I might have offered you marriage instead, once upon a time. Though after Marshall arrived with his handsome face, large fortune, and future title, I knew I didn't have a chance. Now that he's met his sad end, however, there might be…other opportunities. Not marriage any longer, of course.'

'Not now that I'm "damaged goods", you mean?'

Tremaine laughed. 'I always admired your spirit. I knew a lass with your energy and enthusiasm would have to be passionate—and we both know how right I was, eh? I figure by now, you've had time to finish grieving and become…lonely.'

'I will never be *that* lonely. But don't despair; at this house party or the next, you may find an heiress with less-than-vigilant relations you may cozen into marrying you before she realises what you are. Not everyone can be as fortunate as I was.'

He merely smiled. 'You always had a sharp tongue on you. I've always hungered to taste it…and more.'

At that moment, Charles ran over to tug at her sleeve. 'Miss Theo! Teacher says she needs you to come tell our story now.'

'Very well,' she said, patting the boy on the shoulder. 'Tell Miss Andrews I'll be with you in a moment.'

Turning back to her tormenter, who stood regarding her with a smirk she longed to slap off his face, she said, 'I'm afraid I can't stay and trade insults any longer.'

'Cute little urchin, and too well spoken to be an enlisted man's leavings,' Tremaine said, watching Charles skip back towards the building. 'Was that Everly's brat? Funny, with him and his doxy so dark, to have the boy turn out so fair. He's almost as blond as…'

Tremaine's words trailed off and amazed recognition lit his eyes. Consternation filled Theo as the lieutenant turned back to scrutinise the child until he was lost to sight inside the building.

'Well, now, what an interesting development,' he murmured, looking back at Theo. 'Ah, the stories I could tell! Maybe you'd like to reconsider my offer?'

Desperately Theo schooled her face to indifference, hoping Tremaine hadn't seen the flash of fear in her eyes.

'Why ever would I wish to do that?' she asked in a bored tone. While her mind raced, trying to decide whether it would be more effective to add another dismissive disclaimer, or say nothing further, she suddenly noted the sound of approaching hoofbeats. Relief filled her when she turned to see that Dominic was nearly upon them.

'You'll have to excuse me. Here's my landlord, coming to consult about the property.'

Tremaine looked over her shoulder. 'Dominic Ransleigh! Might not have recognised him, but for the missing arm. I'd forgotten his family had an estate in Suffolk. "Consulting about property", eh? Darling, if you're still giving it away for free, why waste your charms on a cripple? A real man could make it so much better for you.'

At that insult to Ransleigh, her control, already pushed to the edge by Tremaine's insinuations and her own panic, finally snapped. Stepping forward, Theo slapped his face with all the force she could muster.

Chapter Thirteen

Trembling with rage and dismay, Theo jumped when Ransleigh suddenly materialised right behind her.

'Is something amiss?'

Theo forced her voice to calm. 'Nothing I can't handle. Lieutenant Tremaine was just leaving.'

'Am I? With all the stories I have to tell?' Tremaine said, a challenge on his face as he rubbed at the scarlet mark of her palm on his cheek.

With a great show of indifference, she shrugged. 'Tell whatever tales you like. No one of discernment gives any credence to what you say anyway. Now, you really should be leaving.'

'Perhaps you need further encouragement?' Ransleigh said, his voice a snarl and his one hand curling into a fist.

Tremaine looked from Theo to Ransleigh and back. 'Not this time. Wouldn't want to distress the urchins. But you may be hearing from me again, Theo.'

Motioning Ransleigh, who looked ready to have a go anyway, to stay where he was, Theo said, 'I devoutly hope not. Have a pleasant life, Lieutenant Tremaine.'

He stared at her, but she faced him down, unsmiling, until finally he broke eye contact. 'Sure you won't reconsider?'

At her curt negative shake of the head, he said, 'Your choice. Don't blame me if you—and your little urchins—have cause later to regret it.'

At that, with a negligent nod to Ransleigh, Tremaine strode to his mount, threw himself in the saddle, and rode off.

As Theo took a shuddering breath, trying to slow the racing of her heart, Ransleigh said, 'Why did you stop me? If that varlet said something meriting a slap, I would have enjoyed planting my fist in his face. Although, accustomed as I am to your plain speaking, telling him no one believes anything he says was a bit harsh.'

'It wasn't kind, perhaps, but I hope to prevent him carrying tales. My reputation is…already sullied, but I would like to prevent him tarnishing yours.'

'Sullied?' Ransleigh said, an odd note in his voice. 'Forgive me, I overhead some of your conversation as I approached. Surely he didn't say you were "giving it away for free"? How could you keep me from punishing him for uttering something so scurrilous?'

Theo sighed. 'Will you walk with me? I don't want the children to overhear, and after what you saw—and heard—you'll want an explanation.'

'I wouldn't wish to pry into the private details of your life.'

She laughed without humour. 'Unlike me, who had no hesitation about prying in yours. But there has always been honesty between us, and you ought to know the truth about your tenant—unless you'd rather not hear it.'

After a short pause, he said, 'If it concerns you, I'd like to hear it.'

'Very well. Let me tell Miss Andrews I'll be another few minutes.'

After informing the teacher she'd be delayed, Theo rejoined Mr Ransleigh. She hoped he'd have enough compassion for the children not to reveal to anyone what she was about to confess. Even though, she knew with a sick certainty that made her stomach churn, she would surely forfeit his respect once she'd told him.

No point delaying the unpleasantness any further.

Waving him to follow, she set off walking. Once they were out of sight and hearing of the school, she said, 'Let me come straight to the point. While Tremaine's wording was crude, it's still…true. I suppose, after that kiss in the wildflower meadow, you suspected that I'm not an innocent. I've told you how much I loved Marshall. We were to be married as soon as I returned from escorting Lord Everly's wife back to England.'

She fell silent a moment, lost in the memories. Probably shocked speechless to find that a woman he'd thought virtuous, wasn't, he didn't prompt her to continue.

'How many times I've regretted not insisting we find the nearest chaplain to marry us before I left!' she said at last. 'But Marshall wanted me to have a proper wedding when the army went into winter quarters in Lisbon, with a reception for all our friends and Papa giving me away in a smart new gown. So we waited—for the wedding. But I didn't want to wait to belong to him completely…and he didn't deny me that.'

'Unfortunately, the night we slipped away, Tremaine followed us. And watched, apparently. When I returned from the convent with Charles, he started shadowing me, making suggestive overtures whenever he caught me alone. He seemed to think that if I'd allowed Marshall to touch me, I was fair game for any man.'

'And you never told your father of this?' Ransleigh interrupted. 'I can't imagine he would have tolerated it!'

'No, Papa would probably have shot him, or at least run him out of camp. But Tremaine was very careful not to make his insinuations where others could overhear him.

It would have been difficult to accuse him to Papa without having to confess the whole and I...I dreaded forfeiting Papa's good opinion. As, I fear, I've now lost yours.'

He frowned. 'Do you know me so little as to think I would disdain you for giving yourself to the man you meant to marry, when men take women lightly all the time without reproof? If I did not know you must be upset by Tremaine's visit, I'd be insulted.'

Her throat felt tight, and tears threatened. 'Most men have different standards for themselves and for women. When a maid gives herself to a man, and does not end up marrying him, she is scorned.'

'Miss Branwell, I have never known a woman more principled and honourable than you! And before you insult me again by asking, I have no intention of betraying your confidence to anyone.'

Knowing what she'd *not* told him, his unqualified support was almost worse than disdain. She considered confessing the whole...but gentleman though he was, the risk was still too great.

Swallowing hard, digging her nails into her palms to keep the tears at bay, she whispered, 'You are too kind.'

'Not at all,' he retorted, 'though I was too courteous. For his insults and for upsetting you, I should have pummelled Tremaine anyway, despite the possibility of the children overhearing us.'

'I'm glad you did not. I have a singular dislike of a man being punished for telling the truth. Besides, he was the best pugilist in the regiment.'

'All the better to prove what I can still do with one hand. But can he make trouble for you?'

'If he were to cast aspersions on my character, Lady Wentworth—and others—would likely withdraw their support. But with the school already staffed, and with agreements in place for the local masters to apprentice willing students, the effect wouldn't be as devastating as it would have been earlier. I'd have to press Aunt Amelia to find places for the girls.'

'I couldn't do much for the girls, but I'd certainly be willing to help find positions for the boys.'

'I don't think it will come to that—but now you've made the offer, I will hold you to it!' she warned. 'Tremaine probably only discovered I was here by chance, when he broke his journey at the public house in Hadwell. A younger son with expensive tastes and no means, before the war he cultivated those who could entertain him in the style he prefers, drifting from country estate to hunting box to the London town houses of wealthier friends. Technically now out of the army despite the uniform, he's taken up that pastime again.'

'I am glad that his call provided me opportunity to see you.'

She looked up at him, surprised. 'You knew about it?'

'Tremaine stopped at Bildenstone for directions to the school. Wilton—and the rest of the staff, apparently—were concerned about the safety of you and the children out here, alone and unprotected.'

Embarrassment—and gratitude—warmed her face. 'That was kind of them.'

'You shouldn't find it surprising. The Lady Wentworths of the county may look down their noses at your efforts, but your concern for the welfare of the lowliest in the parish has won you the admiration of everyone else.'

'Take care of your soldiers and your sergeants, and the men will take care of you, Papa always said,' she murmured, feeling again that ache at his loss.

'True, and some commanders do so out of self-interest. But the men recognise those who treat them well out of respect and concern, and they don't forget it.'

'Much as I appreciate your reinforcements, I hope you

didn't feel compelled to interrupt your work to come rescue me. As you saw, I was able to handle it myself.'

'I was glad to come. I know we agreed—or rather, you dictated—that we should avoid one another, but I owe you thanks for your advice. After the horrors you observed when we rode about the estate, I thought you might like to know how things are progressing.'

Despite knowing how important it was to start distancing herself from him, she couldn't help feeling a flush of pleasure. 'I would indeed.'

'The first project was riding the rest of Bildenstone's acreage, followed by an inspection of the estate ledgers. Unsurprisingly, I concluded that Winniston was at best incompetent and worst, skimming more off the top than he was entitled to. After Father's death, he had no oversight; all the estate income was kept by him or deposited in the accounts, with nothing reinvested in the land or the tenants.'

She nodded, thinking of the old equipment and rundown dwellings they'd passed. 'That was rather evident.'

'I've removed him, with a pension only because of his family's generations of service at Bildenstone. As soon as I complete the rest of the ledgers, I'm going to Newmarket to consult with the stable manager about selling my hunters. I may stop afterward at Holkham Hall to see Thomas Coke and consult with him about the latest in agricultural techniques. Perhaps get a recommendation for a new estate manager.'

Theo searched his expression—which looked resigned, but with none of the despair she'd seen in it before when he talked of selling off his hunters. He seemed…at peace with the decision, and ready to move beyond his loss.

'I'm glad. Letting go isn't easy, but acceptance is the first step in forging ahead.' Then she had to laugh. 'Listen to me, pontificating, when I've never been any good at it myself.'

'Some things, you never want to let go,' he said quietly.

Something in the timbre of his voice pulled her gaze back to his. A shimmering cloud of sensation enveloped them, breathtaking as a thousand dust motes gilded by the sun. But there was sweetness too, empathy, and a deep connection that curled around her heart like a pair of loving hands and made her bones ache with longing.

Ah, Dominic Ransleigh, you are so dangerous to my peace of mind, she thought, struggling to keep from reaching for him. *Good thing you're going away, before I blurt out how much I want you to stay.*

Finally, losing the battle, she let herself take his hand, almost sighing at the jolt that tingled through her. 'Best of luck.'

He held her fingers a few moments longer than was strictly necessary. 'I won't be ready to leave for a week or so. If you'll permit, I'll check with you when I return and let you know how it went.'

'I'd like that,' she said, even as the protective voice within protested she mustn't see him again. 'I shall be interested in your plans for the improvement of the estate,' she answered it back.

Liar, it whispered.

Ignoring it, she said, 'I must get back. I owe the children a story and Miss Andrews a break.'

'What are you offering them? Not Bowdlerised Shakespeare, I hope.'

'Never!' she said with a laugh. 'I was delighted to find in your library an edition of Galland's *Les Milles et Une Nuit.* I'd seen the English *Arabian Nights* translation, but the original French is so much better. What child could resist stories of sorcerers and jins?'

'So you will be their Scheherazade. They will love it.'

'I expect they will clamour for more. Good thing there were one thousand and one nights.' And could there be anything in those Far Eastern stories more outlandish or shocking than the tale she didn't finish telling Ransleigh?

By her omission, she'd managed to retain his good opinion. Keeping it gave her an even more compelling reason to hold him at arm's length.

Two weeks later, Theo sat at the desk in her study at Thornfield Place, looking over the replies to her advertisement for a tutor for Charles. Though he'd continued accompanying her to the school and shared in the lessons, she brought him back to Thornfield Place every night, despite his protests that he'd rather sleep in the dormitory with Georgie and Jemmie. Soon he must start preparing for the more rigorous academics required of the gentlemen who sojourned at Oxford or Cambridge before taking up the management of their acreage. Though, she thought, envious of the men who could pursue study forbidden to women, most of the scions of the aristocracy devoted more of their time at university to entertainment and developing friendships among their peers than pursuing scholarship.

Once the time came, she'd not renew the leases and instead turn several of the properties she'd inherited over to Charles. She was idly wondering how soon they ought to visit the estates to decide which were the most promising, when a knock sounded at the door.

'Miss Branwell, there's a lady to see you,' Franklin said.

'Did she not give her name?' Theo asked, curious. She'd been graciously introduced to several local ladies by Lady Wentworth, but having assured them she was seldom at Thornfield during calling hours, none had ventured out.

'She said you'd not recognise her name, but that she had heard much of you and was very interested to meet you.'

Which told her exactly nothing, Theo thought, a little

uneasily. Had Tremaine managed to drop a few words in some interested ears before he'd taken himself out of Suffolk?

If so, there'd be nothing for it but to face down the rumours. Fortunately, her dress and manner were so far from brazen or seductive, she had a good chance of successfully refuting whatever he'd insinuated.

'I put her in the Green Room, miss,' Franklin recalled her.

Conveying the visitor to the most formal receiving room, with its Wedgwood plasterwork and Adamesque ceiling, told Theo that the butler considered the caller a lady of rank and position. Not that the fact helped her narrow down the identity of her unexpected guest.

Glad she owned no gowns that weren't modest in the extreme, and already thinking about tactics to counter any initial hostility and engage the woman's sympathy, Theo girded herself for the fray and headed for the Green Room.

Normally, she paid little attention to the rituals of greeting, but if this were to be a subtle dance of step and counter-step, she meant to begin with every advantage. 'You'd better announce me,' she told Franklin, to his surprise.

Start from strength, Papa always said. So she'd play Lady of the Manor.

Walking in as the butler intoned, 'Miss Branwell', she sank into a curtsy. Her visitor, a woman some years her senior whose fashionable, obviously expensive gown and dashing bonnet justified the butler's estimation of her status, rose to return it.

'Miss Branwell, I am so delighted to meet you at last.'

Puzzled, Theo gazed down into earnest green eyes that looked vaguely familiar. The visitor was not any of the ladies she'd met after church, nor could she recall Mr Scarsdale informing her about any other family in the county with the wealth and status to dress its matriarch in such prime fashion.

'As am I, I'm sure,' she murmured. 'Although you must excuse my ignorance. My butler did not give me your name.'

'My subterfuge, I'm afraid. Shall we sit? It's a bit of a strain on my neck, looking up.' The woman smiled. 'Marshall wrote me about how tall you were.'

Recognition knifed through her in a stab of horror. Those green eyes—that soft blonde hair waving out from under the stylish bonnet. No wonder they looked so familiar.

This woman had to be Lady Hazlett. Her dead fiancé's mother.

For a moment, Theo thought she might faint, before the primal instinct for self-preservation kicked in and rushed her brain back into action.

Too late to worry about what the woman had gleaned from her initial response. Lady Hazlett might not know anything at all. Her unexpected visit could be just a pleasant coincidence.

Theo could still pull this off, if she went about it cleverly.

Belatedly putting a smile on her face while touching a hand to her heart, Theo said, 'You're Lady Hazlett, of course! I'm sorry, it was such a shock. I'd always hoped to meet you some day…under much happier circumstances.' Trying to make her motions smooth instead of jerky with panic, Theo motioned her guest to a chair and took one herself.

'By the way,' she added belatedly, 'I'm so sorry for your loss. I intended to send you and Lord Hazlett a note. But I was…ill for some time afterwards, and putting anything in writing would make it too…final. It took me a very long time to face the fact that Marshall was gone for ever.'

Grief shadowed Lady Hazlett's face. 'I miss him dreadfully still. Yet, I know that your loss was greater.'

Marshall's mother's words ripped open the lid on the box in which she tried to keep all the anguished memories contained. Hammered by a blow of desolation, Theo couldn't get any words to form, all her energy concentrated on holding back the sobs.

Lady Hazlett poured a cup of tea and handed it to her. Grateful, Theo gulped down a sip, the scalding liquid shocking her back to the present.

'Thank you,' she said after a moment. 'Goodness, where are my manners? *I* should have served *you*. Are you staying long in the area? Not that I'm not delighted to meet you at last, but how did you know I was at Thornfield Place?'

Annihilating Theo's last hope of brazening through, Lady Hazlett said quietly, 'I think you know why I'm here.'

After a moment of agonised silence, Theo said dully, 'Audley Tremaine visited you.'

'Yes. And now, may I see my grandson?'

Chapter Fourteen

Through the roaring in her ears, Theo dimly heard the clatter of her teacup as it dropped back into the saucer. She found herself on her feet, chest so tight she could scarcely breathe, desperately trying to decide what to do next.

She could laugh, look puzzled, tell Lady Hazlett she had no idea what she meant—though her obvious distress would make such a denial rather unbelievable.

She could walk out, order her butler to show Lady Hazlett the door, and hope that was an end to it.

Lady Hazlett had risen, too, and looked up at Theo, an anguished appeal on her face. 'Marshall was my only remaining child, you know. I lost two little boys as infants and one dear daughter, and then, two years ago, our eldest and heir, Edward, died after a hunting fall. When Tremaine told me Marshall had a son, I had to come. Your precious child is all I have left. Surely, you won't be so cruel as to keep him from me!'

'I never set out to hide him,' Theo said softly. 'I didn't know if you and Lord Hazlett would want to acknowledge him, since Marshall and I never married, but I *had* planned to contact you. But then, when I arrived back at the army with him, and everyone assumed he was Alicia and Everly's child whom Everly's family refused to acknowledge, I saw a way of keeping him that would avoid shaming my father. That would avoid having Charles branded a bastard.'

'Good heavens, girl, what were you going to do if the Marquess of Wareton changed his mind and wanted the boy back?'

'I would have told him then about Charles's true parentage. It's all recorded in the register at the convent, so there would be proof. But unless and until that happened, Charles could remain legitimate in the eyes of the world, and free from the true scandal of his birth.'

'As could you,' Lady Hazlett said tartly.

'As could I. For what it's worth, I cared very little what happened to me. I couldn't imagine ever loving anyone again as I had Marshall, so being ruined and unable to marry didn't matter to me. I would have grieved at the loss of my father's respect, but protecting my father from embarrassment and Charles from the stigma of bastardy were my primary motivations. Which you can believe, or not.'

'Oh, child, I didn't come here to harangue you! Only to reclaim a part of myself I thought lost for ever. Blood of my blood, flesh of my flesh.'

Furious determination boiled up from the depths of her soul. 'You can't have him. He's all *I* have left of Marshall, too! I've cherished him and nurtured him since the sisters placed him in my arms after he drew his first breath. Besides, how could you claim him, without the facts of his birth coming out?'

Lady Hazlett shrugged. 'Why could we not continue the fiction you've already promulgated? All my friends know how devastated I was by Marshall's death. We can put it about that, after your return to England, I called on my son's former fiancé, to meet her and commiserate over our common loss. While there, I met this noble orphan whose family didn't wish to claim him. Delighted by the child, I took him up in place of the boy I'd lost. It would make as much sense as the version you've told thus far.'

'He'd be much more visible then. Much more likely that the Marquess would hear about him, and perhaps change his mind about acknowledging him.'

Lady Hazlett laughed. 'That old miser? I've known Wareton since my come-out, and a more selfish, clutch-fisted man would be impossible to find. If he didn't want the boy years ago, he'll not claim him now. If he thought at all about my taking Charles on, he'd look upon it as a fine joke that someone else was paying the bills for one of his son's by-blows. As for the girl's family, I understand they are of slender means, and would doubtless be happy to have the boy recognised by someone of more wealth and influence.'

'Which,' she continued, rounding on Theo, 'is why you should give him up, if it's truly his welfare that concerns you. What can you do for him, compared to what Lord Hazlett and I can offer? Yes, I know you are well funded, but you can't claim to have the influence in society of a viscount, nor can you promote Charles's career through a long association with other landed gentlemen in their colleges, clubs, and Parliament. Would you deny Marshall's son all those advantages? Besides, I understand you've started a school for soldier's orphans. I can't imagine how you can run that and give proper attention to Charles's upbringing, nor is it right that he grow up associating solely with orphans much below his station. How is he to learn to become a gentleman in an orphanage for paupers?'

It didn't help the panic roiling through her that Lady Hazlett was echoing all the arguments Aunt Amelia had always given her about securing Charles's future. And then it came to her.

A battle never went as you'd envisioned, Papa always said, the attack often coming from an unexpected foe or an unforeseen direction. One must fall back into a more defensible position.

And there was only one defensible position in this battle. If she wanted to keep Charles, she would have to find a stepfather for him who could offer the same advantages as his grandfather.

'I can't refute those arguments. I've agonised over them myself from time to time, but never could bring myself to consider marriage. Threatened with Charles's loss, though, I'm prepared to act. So I propose a bargain.'

'A bargain?' Lady Hazlett echoed. 'I don't understand.'

'We're agreed that we both love Charles and want what is best for him. I believe that remaining with me, who has cared for him since birth, is better for him than being sent away with strangers. But I also understand your desire to claim a child who, but for unfortunate circumstances, would have been a grandson you could have loved and acknowledged openly. I propose to marry a gentleman of standing and substance, who can be the mentor, teacher and example your husband would be, while allowing Charles to remain here, with those he knows and loves. But we will also adopt your story of visiting me, being charmed by the orphan, and wanting to take him under your wing. I'll accompany him on visits to you and Lord Hazlett several times a year, and when he's older and knows you better, will let him come alone. It was never my aim to deny him the love of his grandparents.'

Lady Hazlett sat thoughtfully silent. 'Who do you propose to marry?'

'I don't know yet,' Theo said frankly. 'I'll have to consult with my aunt, Lady Coghlane, and see what's possible. I do promise that whoever I agree to wed would be of sufficient stature and wealth to secure Charles's future. In the meantime, you will keep our secret.'

'Will your...potential husband know?'

'I would never deceive a gentleman about something so important. Of course, I would not reveal his true parentage until I was certain of a suitor's esteem, superior character, and willingness to act as Charles's mentor.'

'Finding such a paragon may be difficult,' Lady Hazlett said sceptically. 'And if I do not agree to your terms?'

'I understand there is much fine property available in Belgium, now that the war that killed so many of its owners is finally over. And I have a good deal of ready income.'

The two women faced each other for a long moment.

'I didn't come here to be your enemy,' Lady Hazlett said at last. 'For all I knew, you'd be happy to give up the boy. But I understand only too well what it is like to lose a beloved child; I wouldn't be the means of parting a son from his mother. *If* he can be raised, not in an orphanage, but with a mentor who can offer him all the advantages due his station, and *if* we have assurance Hazlett and I can make him a part of our lives.'

'Then we are agreed?'

Lady Hazlett reached out her hand and Theo shook it.

'Now that that unpleasantness is settled, may I see my grandson?'

'Why don't you follow me up to the nursery?'

A little lightheaded, her hands still trembling in the wake of the confrontation, Theo led Lady Hazlett from the Green Parlour up the stairs. As they got closer to the nursery, she could hear Charles singing a Portuguese folk song with Constancia, his piping voice slightly off-key.

Nausea crawled up her throat and a wave of panic crashed over her. Should she have sent Lady Hazlett away and barred the door? If she mustered her forces poorly, would she lose the person who meant most to her in the world?

Don't concede the field after the first skirmish, she steadied herself. Lady Hazlett wanted what would make

Charles happy, and he wouldn't be happy parted from his friends and the woman who had cared for him his entire life. She needn't figure out every bit of strategy this very moment; she would have time to plan.

Plan to marry.

She swallowed another wave of nausea.

Then Charles heard her footsteps, and rushed to the nursery door. 'Miss Theo!' he cried, popping out. 'Did you hear us? Constancia taught me a new song! Shall I teach it to you?'

'In a minute, Charles. Right now, there's a lady I'd like you to meet. She was a…a good friend of your papa's.'

She led Lady Hazlett into the nursery, where Constancia curtsied and Charles made a fine proper bow. As he looked up, his bright green eyes fixing on a lady whose similar green eyes stared back at him, Lady Hazlett gasped.

'He's so like Marshall at that age,' she whispered. 'May I?' At Theo's nod, she reached out to brush a lock of golden hair off his brow.

Theo felt her heart constrict. How could she deny Marshall's mother the chance to know and love his son?

She couldn't. But that didn't mean she wouldn't fight sword, pistol and whip, take him abroad if necessary, to have him remain with her. He was *her* son, too.

'Why don't you show Lady Hazlett your soldiers before we have some nuncheon?'

'Then can we go to the school?'

'Then we can go to the school.'

'Why can't I stay at the school with my friends? Why do I have to have a—a too door?'

With an anxious glance at Lady Hazlett, Theo said, 'Because you're going to grow up to be a great gentleman, like my father the colonel, and your papa. And to do that, you must go to university. The tutor will help you get ready.'

'I'd rather get ready to teach horses with Jemmie, or plant fields, like Georgie.'

'That's only because you don't know yet how much fun it will be to learn many things and go to university. And afterward, you'll have lots of horses to train and fields to tend.'

'Should you like to have a horse of your own?' Lady Hazlett asked.

Charles's gaze hopped back to his grandmother. 'Oh, I would! Miss Theo said after the school got ready, she would get me a pony.'

'Your papa loved ponies. I think you should have one straight away.'

While Theo absorbed that challenge, Charles subjected Lady Hazlett to a frank stare. 'I like you. Would you like to see my soldiers now?'

'Will you show me?' she asked.

'Of course. I better help you, though. It's awful narrow in the corner for a lady.' He offered his arm.

Theo watched, anguish throbbing in her chest, as the son she could never acknowledge assisted his grandmother to the low eaves in the corner where his lead soldiers were displayed. How she wished Marshall had lived to see this!

But he hadn't, which left her with quite a dilemma.

Now she, who had never wished to marry, needed to find a husband. A *suitable* husband.

And quickly.

A week later, Dom sat in a parlour of the Palladian masterpiece that was Holkham Hall, agricultural tracts spread out on the desk before him. He was immersed in the merits of the Norfolk Four-Crop Rotation system when a footman in gilded livery bowed himself in. 'Mr Ransleigh, there is a…young person to see you.'

'Young person?' he echoed blankly.

'When he arrived first thing this morning, the butler sent him away, thinking it most unlikely a rough sort like that would have any acquaintance with a gentleman. But he stationed himself in the kitchen courtyard, claiming that you do know him and that he will not leave until he's spoken with you.'

The memory of another person a butler had been unable to shoo away popped into his mind—but the footman said this was a 'he,' not a young lady. Besides, he thought with a smile, if contested, Theo would doubtless put her 'colonel's daughter' on and not be put off by a mere butler.

The smile faded as he considered the only other 'young person' he knew whom a butler would not consider receiving—and who had the gumption to refuse to be dislodged from his intent: a boy who'd grown up emulating his sergeant-major father. And Jemmie would never have come looking for him, unaccompanied by Theo, unless something was drastically wrong.

Having gone within an instant from amusement to alarm, Dom said, 'Where is he? I will see him at once!'

The footman shifted uncomfortably. 'I don't think the butler would approve my showing him in here, sir. Perhaps…perhaps I could convey him into the servants' hall?'

'Nonsense!' Dom snapped, agitation lending an edge to his voice. 'I don't intend to conduct my business in front of the servants—or in the kitchen yard. Bring him here at once!'

'Very well, sir,' the footman said, still looking dubious.

Wondering what could have happened at Thornfield or the school that would have prompted Theo to send Jemmie, Dom jumped up to pace the room. He was about to set off and fetch the boy himself when the door opened and an exasperated Jemmie trotted in.

'Think I was tryin' to break a prisoner out of stocks,'

he muttered. 'I was about ready to find an open window and comb the place for ya meself.'

'I'm sorry, Jemmie. I only just learned you were here. But why have you come—and how did you find me? Has something happened to Miss Branwell?'

'Aye, something's happened. Nay, she's not hurt or nothin',' he added quickly at the concern he must have seen in Dom's face. 'Though I can't make any sense of her takin' such a crack-brained notion of a sudden.'

'You'd better tell me the whole.' Dom motioned to a chair, on which, after giving the gold-corded brocade upholstery a dubious glance, Jemmie perched. Seating himself at the sofa, he said, 'Now, what has happened?'

'Everything seemed just fine until about a week ago, when she come to school like she always does, but leaving Master Charles back at Thornfield. And she's all agitated and fidgety-like. I asked her what was wrong—thought mebbe the boy'd taken sick or something, cause she sets great store by the little nipper. She said he was fine, but a lady who knew Charlie's da had come to visit. Then she goes in and has a long talk with Miss Andrews, and after that she talks with Mr and Mrs Blake—that's the cook and her man, what lives with us at the school. And off she goes again, without a word to any of us.'

Jemmie frowned. 'I knew somethin' bad was happenin', cause Miss Theo never left any place, ever, without tellin' me first where she was goin'. She didn't come to the school at all the next day. Then the next day, she comes ridin' up in the carriage with Master Charles and tells us she's goin' off to London, to see her aunt, and mebbe she'd be gone a good while. Then she said goodbye.'

The boy twisted his hands, distress on his face. 'I knew there was somethin' powerful wrong; she ain't looked so broken up since they brought the colonel back after Waterloo, just afore he died.'

'Didn't she explain why she needed to go?' Dom asked, his concern beginning to mirror Jemmie's.

'Nay. I follered her out, cause I weren't goin' to let her go off to London all alone, not til I knew why. She hugged me, and there was tears in her eyes. And she told me she was goin' to London to find a husband! That her aunt would help her, and she might not come back till after she was married. She said she was sorry, and she loved me like her own son, and then she got back into the carriage and drove away.'

Jemmie stared into the distance. 'We been through a lot together, Mr Ransleigh, Miss Theo and me. And it sounded like she was tellin' me goodbye for g-good.'

Tears glittered in Jemmie's eyes before he rubbed them away with a grubby fist. 'Why would she want to get married now, when she's told me for years, after she lost her lieutenant, she'd never marry nobody? And when she knows I'll soon be growed and kin take care of her like her pa did, so she won't never be alone no more?'

Only desperation would ever drive me to the Marriage Mart, he recalled her saying. 'I can't imagine.'

'We need to know what's wrong so we kin do somethin' to help her. She tells me lots, but she prob'ly won't talk to me about marryin'. That's why I lit out to find you straight away. Folks up at Bildenstone told me you was goin' to Newmarket and then here, so's when I didn't find you there, I come to Holkham. But we got to hurry. She'll be in London, with her aunt by now.'

Dom looked at him, astonished at his journey. 'How did you manage to travel all—?' He broke off abruptly. A child who'd scrambled along in the wake of an army probably knew things about transporting and feeding himself Dom would rather not enquire about too closely. 'Never mind. You think Miss Branwell is in London, then?'

'By now, sure as sure. You got to make her tell you

what's wrong. All of us at the school are worried, 'cause we don't want her marryin' so hasty, maybe somebody who don't deserve her and won't treat her right. Then Miss Theo told me a while back if she married, her husband could take everything she owns. Which would mean the school, too, wouldn't it? So if this bloke didn't like us, he could toss us all out on the street.'

'True, a husband normally controls his wife's wealth,' Dom admitted.

'Her aunt's a great lady, so she'll be marrying Miss Theo off to some grand gentleman. I know how the toffs look at us—and I just bet this husband person would want nothin' to do with us, nor let her run the school neither. And even though she's got Charlie, Miss Theo'd be awful sad if she lost all of us. So we got to find her and talk her out of this.'

'I'd certainly like to know what happened,' Dom admitted. Having half-formed an idea of perhaps courting Theo Branwell himself, the notion of her marrying another man didn't sit very well with him, either.

'So you'll go to London and find out what happened?'

He wasn't sure how he was going to justify inserting himself into so private a matter when he had no claim at all upon the lady…but he knew curiosity alone, not to mention a fierce need to protect and shelter her, wouldn't let him rest until he found out.

He was her landlord, after all. If something about the management of the school were going to change, he needed to know that.

And when had Theo Branwell ever hesitated to insert herself into *his* private affairs?

He was smiling at that thought when Jemmie said, 'Mr Ransleigh? I know I ain't always been too friendly-like, and I'm sorry for that,' he said, his freckled face flushing. 'But I know you like us, or you wouldn't've let Miss Theo rent your building. She told me you been askin' around for a trainer to teach me how to manage horses, and someone to help Georgie learn to farm. You like Miss Theo, too—I know you do. And she likes you. She comes back smilin' after she's been with you, happy like I've not seen her since the colonel died. So I think she'll tell you what's wrong— and listen when you talk her out of marryin'.'

Could he talk her out of it? Or should he just suggest a suitable candidate?

He'd already broached to himself the idea of courting her. But he meant to consider it at leisure—not let circumstances rush him into something with such enormous and irreversible consequences.

Delectable consequences, his body whispered.

Ignoring his carnal urgings, he told Jemmie, 'I'll leave for London immediately and see what I can discover.'

Jemmie uttered a sigh of relief. 'I'll be on my way back to the school, then. Can make a good bit afore nightfall, if I get a-goin'.'

'Why don't you go post? I'll spot you the fare. It will be faster than…whatever means you can find on your own.'

'Thank 'ee, Mr Ransleigh. That'd be right nice. But just a loan, now.'

'Just a loan.' Rooting in his waistcoat for some coins, he thought that if Theo Branwell were going to be as independent and resistant to taking help as her protégé, trying to straighten whatever fix she'd got herself into was going to be difficult.

'And, Mr Ransleigh? You will hurry, won't ya?'

'I will.' After ringing for a servant, he handed Jemmie enough blunt to see him safely back to Suffolk. When the footman appeared, Dom instructed him to have one of the grooms carry Jemmie to the nearest posting inn, and ready his own vehicle.

He walked up to his room, to set Henries packing while

he wrote his host a quick note. With luck, he could follow Jemmie's departure with the hour.

Curiosity, unease, and puzzlement kept chasing each other around his brain. He couldn't imagine what catastrophe could have made calm, capable Theo Branwell look 'agitated' and 'fidgety-like'. Nor change overnight the mind of a woman who'd seemed dead set against marriage.

He wanted to find out, though. And he wanted to get to London before his unusually flustered Theo did something precipitous he'd not be able to undo.

Chapter Fifteen

That same afternoon, Theo and Charles arrived at the London residence of her Aunt Amelia in Jermyn Street. After seeing the boy up to a bedchamber with a maid in attendance, she made herself as presentable as was possible after so much time on the road. Having asked the butler not to announce her, she went to knock at the door of her aunt's private sitting room.

Lady Coghlane, wearing a fetching afternoon gown, was dozing on her sofa when Theo walked in. She was halfway across the room when her drowsy aunt, opening one eye, recognised her and sat up with a start.

'My darling Theo! What a delightful surprise!' she cried.

'Please, sit,' Theo said. 'I didn't mean to disturb your rest, only to tell you I'd arrived.'

Her aunt sank back against the cushions, looking befuddled. 'Did I know you were coming? Not that you aren't welcome to visit whenever, and as often, as you like!'

'No, this trip was…rather sudden.' Now that the moment for explanation—and confession—had come, Theo wasn't sure how to begin, the numerous speeches she'd rehearsed in the coach deserting her. Too unsettled to sit, she took a turn about the room.

Inspecting her closely, Lady Coghlane frowned. 'You look distressed, my dear. What is wrong? And how can I help?'

Theo turned to face her aunt, twisting her gloved fingers together. 'The truth is, I'm in a devil of a coil, and I only hope you can help me! Or will still want to, once I've told you the whole.'

'Still want to? Don't be silly! Of course I'll want to, my dearest, darling niece! With Richard gone, you're my nearest blood, save my own children. I'll always love you, regardless of what you've done. Though, with that orphanage you were determined to thrust into the midst of Suffolk gentry…' She paused with a shudder. 'Regardless of what's happened, we'll deal with it!'

The idea of Lady Coghlane swooping up to Suffolk like a fairy godmother, applying the magic wand of her society position to buttress Theo's position, brought Theo a temporary respite from her anxiety.

'It has nothing to do with the orphanage—at least not directly.'

'Whatever it is, let me first ring for some tea. Every situation looks better after a warm, soothing drink.' After tugging at the bell pull, she said, 'Where did you break your journey? Did you get any rest?'

Not sure whether she felt relieved or more anxious at the delay, Theo said, 'We travelled pretty much straight through, except at night, so Charles could have a bed to sleep. I brought him with me.'

'And the others?'

'They're at school. Which is up and running now, by the way. Renovations of the building went splendidly, I found a lovely girl, Miss Andrews, to teach, and an older couple to live in as cook and general handyman. I was in the process of considering applications for a tutor for Charles—before he gets too accustomed to being at the school, too.'

'That wouldn't be wise,' her aunt agreed. 'You can't expect him to act like a gentleman later if he's raised like a foundling. And—what of Mr Ransleigh?'

Theo swallowed hard, Dominic Ransleigh being the one topic she'd forbidden herself to think about since the nightmare of Lady Hazlett's visit.

'He's been an exemplary neighbour. His grandfather amassed quite a magnificent library at Bildenstone, which he is allowing me access to. I…enjoy his company. He's very easy to talk to.' *Oh, and so much more,* Theo thought distractedly.

A knock at the door was followed by the entry of the butler with the tea tray. Once they'd settled themselves in with full cups, Lady Coghlane said, 'So, tell me what's troubling you.'

Her stomach, half-settled by the warming tea, twisted into knots again. 'I suppose it started with me falling in love with Marshall, supremely confident that we would live together the rest of our lives.'

Her aunt gave her a sympathetic glance. 'I'm sure you did believe in for ever…ill advised as that was, with him being a serving officer during a bloody conflict.'

'You'll remember that, almost five years ago now, I was going to accompany Lord Everly's wife back to London for the birth of her child.'

'Of course I remember! You were going to stay with me.'

'Only she became ill on the journey, and we ended up at a convent until after the birth of her child.'

'Yes. Also that she didn't long survive his birth.'

Theo took a deep breath. 'What you didn't know is that she wasn't the only one taken ill. After I learned that Marshall had been killed, I was distraught. Even more so because I'd only just discovered I was…increasing. You see, Alicia wasn't the only one who gave birth at that convent.'

She died in childbed, and her child with her. Charles, the infant I brought back with me, wasn't her son—he is mine.'

Theo waited miserably while her aunt's eyes widened. Dropping her teacup with a clatter, she gasped, '*Your* child? You mean Charles is *your* son?'

Theo nodded. 'Mine and Marshall's. Oh, I was "ill advised" indeed! So confident of our future, I begged Marshall to make me his before I left with Alicia for London. Never dreaming he would not be there that winter to marry me.'

'Oh, my poor dear! What a predicament! Did Richard know?'

'No. I intended to confess the whole to him upon my return, even as I dreaded losing his good opinion—as I dread losing yours, now. But when I arrived back in camp and informed Everly's commander of his wife's death, the colonel assumed the infant I'd brought back with me was their son. Before I could get another word out, he went off into a diatribe about the perfidy of the nobility, with the Marquess of Wareton refusing to acknowledge either the marriage or the child. He asked if I could continue to look after the boy, at least temporarily. I barely had time to agree before he shooed me out to deal with an important dispatch. Then, with the news spreading through camp that Everly's wife had died and I'd brought back her son, it seemed wiser—for Charles's sake and Papa's, more than for my own—to let it be thought he was the legitimate—if unrecognised—grandson of a marquess. Rather than the illegitimate son of a colonel's daughter.'

Theo faced her aunt, the churning in her stomach intensifying. 'I'm so ashamed I let you and Papa down.'

The remorse and guilt she usually suppressed swept through her in a staggering wave. Swamped by it, she needed every bit of strength to hold the sobs at bay, only a single tear escaping to trickle down her cheek.

Her aunt rushed over to embrace her. 'There, now, my poor dear!' she crooned, rubbing Theo's trembling back as she tried to regain control. 'You needn't apologise to me for doing what girls in love have done from time immemorial. If the gods were female, you wouldn't have conceived—or if you had, your beloved would have stayed alive to marry you!'

After a few moments, when Theo regained her composure, Lady Coghlane released her and resumed her seat. 'To tell the truth, of late I'd suspected as much—especially when you were so adamant about keeping Charles, even after Richard's death.'

'You suspected?' Theo cried, horrified. 'Do you think anyone else might?'

'Calm yourself, my dear. I doubt anyone who doesn't know you well would suspect a thing. If the account of Charles's birth was to be challenged, it would have happened when you first brought him back to camp. It's just that I know you truly want the best for him, and knowing that, it seemed…odd for you to hold on to the child after your father's death, when you could no longer ensure he would be raised *by* a gentleman *as* a gentleman. Unless he meant more to you than a chance-met orphan.'

'He does,' Theo acknowledged.

'Why did you feel the need to reveal the secret of Charles's birth now?'

Smiling grimly, Theo recounted her confrontation with Audley Tremaine—and the subsequent visit from Lady Hazlett.

'Wonderful that the viscount and his lady want a relationship with the boy,' her aunt said, after listening thoughtfully. 'But…to take him from you, now, after more than four years? That would be very hard.'

'Impossible. So I proposed a bargain: I marry a well-positioned gentleman, who can provide the advantages of upbringing and access to the gentlemen of society the viscount would, let them develop a relationship with Charles, and I get to keep him with me. Which is why I came: to have you work your magic, and find me someone suitable to marry. Do…do you really think you can find someone?'

Lady Coghlane steepled her fingers, pondering. 'Nothing has changed since we last discussed you marrying. You'd insisted then that you must keep Charles. I assume, if you reached an understanding with a gentleman, you would reveal his parentage?'

'Of course. It's a delicate balancing—I don't want the information to become common knowledge, but I'd never marry anyone who wasn't fully aware of my circumstances.'

Lady Coghlane nodded. 'Wise to proceed that way. As for who you might marry, I must give the matter some thought.'

'Lady Hazlett seemed to think it would be difficult to find someone elevated enough to be suitable who'd also be amenable to marrying me. I'd need a "paragon", she said.'

'I wouldn't have you marry anything else!' Lady Coghlane said roundly. 'Let me put my mind to it and see who I come up with. By the way, I'm promised to dine with the Stauntons tonight. Why don't you come with me? As it happens, I have the gowns my daughter-in-law Lissa commissioned this spring, before she learned she was increasing. You're much of a size; I think my maid could alter them to fit you. She'll certainly be able to do something with that hair!'

'Tonight?' Panic swirled in her stomach. 'I thought I'd have some time to…get acclimated before going into company. I knew you wouldn't let me out of the house in my current wardrobe.'

'Given your circumstances, I don't think you should waste a minute,' her aunt said frankly. 'It's fortunate Lissa's gowns are to hand. It would be best for society to discover you're in town immediately, so I can set my friends listening for the interest it generates. After all, my dear, you *are* an earl's granddaughter, and very rich! After you've had an hour to rest, I'll have Marston bring those gowns to your bedchamber. Choose some you'd like to wear until we can get you to my mantua-maker. Then, after I've spoken with my friends tonight, I'll be better able to advise you on the likely candidates.'

Rising, her aunt came over to give her another hug. 'Don't worry, my dear. We shall find the right gentleman to make you happy—and keep Charles with you.'

'As long as I can keep Charles with me, I will be happy,' Theo said fervently.

As her aunt walked her out, Theo hoped her fairy-godmother aunt could make both circumstances come true.

Though Aunt Amelia had allotted her an hour to rest, Theo found she couldn't. After ten minutes reclining on the bed, her mind ticking fiercely through various scenarios like an overwound clock, she bounced back up.

Driven by the imperative to marry, feeling helpless at knowing the resolution of her dilemma depended on the good will of someone she'd not even met, and writhing with frustration at that helplessness, her stomach churned and head throbbed. How could she attract a potential suitor with the correct qualifications, someone who would be so taken with her that he wouldn't mind the added burden of another man's child?

Until now, the idea of marriage had been only a vague proposition put forward by Aunt Amelia, no more real than a mirage. Since having to make her bow on the censorious stage of the Marriage Mart seemed so unlikely, she'd been able to dismiss the prospect. Now that taking that step was imminent, its outcome so important and the result of failure so disastrous, dread and doubt assailed her like footpads setting on a drunken dandy.

She was too old, she'd never been a beauty, and she was certainly not docile. Aunt Amelia's maid could pretty her up, fix her hair, and dress her in more fashionable gowns. But would it be enough?

Could she learn to hold her tongue, be meek and attentive, defer to the gentlemen? Was it even fair for her to do so, when she'd be unable to sustain such behaviour for the rest of her life?

And what would she converse about, if she dared open her mouth? She knew very little of English politics, nothing of fashion or *ton* gossip. Would she be reduced to murmuring polite 'As you say's, or smiling inanely?

Prepared or not, she had to begin this very night.

Panic bubbled up, adding to the already caustic mix of urgency and uncertainty. She wasn't at all sure she could do this.

But she *had* to do it. Maybe she'd better remind herself of the reason she was doing it.

She'd go see Charles.

Theo walked into the bedchamber to find Charles chatting away to Constancia. As she looked at him, her breath stopped and her chest squeezed painfully.

Now that the toddler roundness of his face had given way to a boy's more sculpted shape, the outline of Marshall's chin and cheekbones was readily apparent. Add to that the curling blond hair and bright green eyes, and for anyone who'd known Marshall well, the resemblance was striking. Much as she resented the dilemma Tremaine had thrust her into, she couldn't fault him for recognising it, especially since Charles's purported parents had both been notably dark.

Dear enough to her in his own right, Charles was also

the living embodiment of a time of hopes and dreams when life awaited, a blank slate for she and Marshall to write upon it whatever they wished, their love a shining beacon lighting the way into their future.

A beacon that had kept her from succumbing to despair after her father's death, that had forced her to move past her loss and plan a future, for all of them.

Despite the anguish of losing Marshall, the anxiety over the shame and scandal she might visit upon her family, the ever-present worry over the secret becoming known, she wouldn't give up a day, even a second of life with Charles. If there was an ache in her heart that he would never call her Mama, as long as she had him with her, she could live with that.

He turned and saw her. 'Miss Theo!' he cried with delight, running over to her.

Theo buried her face in the soft golden locks and hugged him so tightly, he squirmed away in protest.

'London is so big!' he announced. 'I've been looking out the window with Constancia, and the buildings just keep going and going and going! The streets are so skinny, and there's no open fields. Where are you going to ride Firefly? Or me my pony?'

'One doesn't ride very much in the city, except at the park. The streets are so crowded and noisy, horses don't like it.'

'Can we go to the park, then?' Charles asked, picking up immediately on the one place riding was permitted.

'I'll take you tomorrow morning, I promise. It's already too late today; I'm told the fashionable gather to ride and walk in the park in late afternoon.'

'Will we get my pony then?'

Theo laughed ruefully, wishing Lady Hazlett to perdition; once promised such a treat, as tenacious as she—and his father—Charles would keep asking until it appeared.

'We can't get your pony at the park. I'll have to see where we can find one in London. But I will start looking.'

'What are we going to do in London, then? It's too far to go to the school. I miss Jemmie and Georgie.'

Theo felt a pang; her aunt and his grandmother were right. Having had children his own age to play with since birth, now that the excitement of the journey was over, Charles missed their company. He needed to interact with others—particularly those with whom he would continue to associate after he was grown.

Avoiding the question, she said, 'I hope we won't be in London long. Then we can get back to Thornfield and the school. You'll have your pony, and a tutor, so there will be many things to do.'

'But what will we do here?' he persisted, too intelligent to be fobbed off. 'If there's lots of wagons and carriages in the park, there will be lots of horses. I like to look at horses.'

'We can do that. There should be soldiers here, too, and we can go watch them on parade.'

His face lit up. 'I'd love to watch the soldiers march!'

Mad for the military, like his papa, she thought. Marshall had told her how, even as a second son, he'd had to fight for his father's permission to join the army. Recalling the desolated look on Lady Hazlett's face, she could understand why. Praise God, there would be no Napoleon waging war when *her* son grew up!

'There are many activities in London, you need only decide what you'd like to try. Later, I'll have you come to her room and say hello again to my aunt. For now, you can play with your soldiers until dinner.'

'What are you going to do until dinner?'

'I have to try on dresses,' she said in a disgusted tone, making a face.

Charles giggled. 'I'd rather play with my soldiers.'

'So would I. How about you try on dresses and I play with the soldiers?'

'I'm a boy, I can't wear dresses,' he replied in the serious tones of a child not yet old enough to recognise the facetious.

Theo pretended to study him up and down. 'I don't know, I think you'd look lovely in a gown. Don't you, Constancia?'

'Oh, yes, *senhora*, most beautiful in a gown,' the maid agreed, grinning.

'Let's just see, shall we?' Theo said, grabbing him. 'Come, the dressmaker is waiting.'

'No!' he protested, squealing with glee as Theo pulled him towards the door. 'No dresses, no dresses!' he cried between shrieks of laughter.

Laughing herself now, Theo halted at the doorframe. Kneeling down to surround him with her arms, she said, 'No dresses? Are you sure you don't want any?'

He pulled free within the circle of her arms and straightened his shirt. 'No, Miss Theo. You know boys don't wear dresses.'

Theo gave an elaborate sigh. 'I guess you're right. But it's not fair. I'd so much rather play with soldiers.'

'You can come and play later, after you're done with the dresses. I'll let you have General Blücher,' he volunteered, naming his favourite toy soldier.

'What a handsome offer! I shall take you up on it,' she said, rising. 'Now I have to go, before Aunt Amelia comes hunting for me.'

Charles gave her a measuring glance and looked around the room. 'You could hide under my bed.'

Already a tactician, she thought. 'No, when duty calls, one must answer. But I'll remember I have General Blücher to look forward to once I've finished.'

She leaned over to plant a kiss on his head, determination renewed. *There was nothing she would not do to keep him with her.* 'I'll save you some lace.'

Chuckling at his grimace of revulsion, she walked back to her room.

Chapter Sixteen

Later that evening in her bedchamber, Theo gazed at her reflection in the glass, while Marston peered over her shoulder, smiling. 'You look quite a treat, miss, if I do say so myself!'

The figure staring back at her was certainly an improvement, she admitted. Her hair, cut under protest, had been washed and curled and pinned up in a seemingly careless assortment of waves. The gown, in a becoming shade of gold that picked up the shimmer of her brown eyes, was mercifully free of excessive lace and furbelows.

It did, however, feature a form-enhancing silhouette, tiny puffed sleeves, and a bodice cut so low she'd probably contract a congestion of the lungs before the night was out. 'Are you sure you can't add a ruffle of lace here?' she asked, pointing to the low neckline.

'Heavens, no!' the maid replied in scandalised tones. 'Half the girls in London have to pad their corsets to achieve such a full, rounded bosom. You should be proud to display it.'

'It's certainly "displayed",' Theo muttered. 'I feel as naked as an army jolly-bag strutting her wares on a Lisbon street.'

At that moment, Aunt Amelia walked in. 'How lovely!' she exclaimed. 'Marston, you've outdone yourself!'

'So I'll do?' Theo asked, making a pirouette.

'Splendidly! I knew you'd be enchanting, once I got you out of those old gowns and that musty habit!'

'Are you sure it's not an imposition to bring me when I've not been invited?' Theo asked, grasping at the last available straw to delay her inevitable society début.

'I sent a note to Jane Staunton this afternoon, telling her you'd arrived unexpectedly, and asking if she'd mind if you came along. She replied that she'd be delighted—especially since she had an unexpected visitor, too. Her nephew, in from the country.'

'Don't tell me,' Theo said drily. 'He's a bachelor of good reputation and fortune.'

'Quite. A widower, with three children a little older than Charles.'

'On the prowl for a new wife to oversee his brood?'

'Jane wasn't sure, but Lord Sayle isn't fond of London, so she couldn't see any other reason for him making the journey—especially after he told her he planned to stay for some time.'

Theo tried to summon up some enthusiasm. 'Charles would like having other children about. What does Lord Sayle do? What could I talk to him about?'

'Well, he was never in the army.' Theo's hopes of finding a congenial conversationalist faded as her aunt continued, 'He did attend Eton and then Oxford—the New School, not Richard's college. The barony is very old; his estate is in Kent, and I understand he raises some lovely horses.'

'Oxford. Horses,' Theo repeated a bit desperately.

'Besides, you needn't worry about conversing. Ask him about his estate; after that, you'll probably only need to nod and smile.'

Inanely? Theo wondered. *Would there be opportunity to add an 'as you say'?*

Reading the anxiety on Theo's face, her aunt said again, 'You mustn't worry! Just be yourself, and the company can't help but admire you.'

'Spoken like a true loving aunt,' Theo said, giving that lady a kiss. 'But thank you for trying to raise my spirits.'

Lady Coghlane shook her head. 'Silly girl! Why someone who lived between two armies, survived advances and retreats and poor food and sleeping who knows where, could be in such a panic over a simple dinner party, I can't imagine!'

'I knew what to expect in those retreats and advances and billets. I don't know anything about surviving the London *ton*.'

'Just look and listen! You'll soon find how to get on.'

Taking a deep breath, Theo nodded. She certainly hoped she'd 'find how'. The consequences of failing to catch an eligible gentleman's eye were so dire, she couldn't bear to think about them.

A short time later, her aunt's carriage deposited them before a handsome town house in Grosvenor Square. Her heart beat faster as they ascended a wide marble staircase to be announced by the butler to a drawing room full of people.

The room glittered with an array of chattering women whose beautiful gowns in a rainbow of hues were set off against the black coats and pristine white neckcloths of the gentlemen.

How different, the sober attire of civilians, compared to army uniforms in vivid colours with their flashes of gold braid and frogging, she thought, feeling even more out of place.

Then Aunt Amelia was introducing her to her hostess,

Lady Staunton, who in turn introduced her to other guests. One of them, Lord Sayle, was the nephew in question, a distinguished-looking man greying at the temples whom Theo judged to be in his late thirties. After murmuring the proper polite phrases, she followed her aunt to a group by the fireplace. Before any further conversation was necessary, the meal was announced and their hostess led them into the dining room.

Theo dreaded the moment she would lose her aunt's support. As one of the highest-ranking ladies present, Lady Coghlane would be seated beside their host, while the unmarried daughter of an earl's younger son ranked far down the table.

She hoped their hostess would regale them with some of the delicacies for which she'd heard London was famed, so she might apply herself to her dinner and salvage something enjoyable from the evening. Feeling like a rank recruit who'd stumbled into one of General Wellington's staff meetings, she couldn't wait to escape back to Jermyn Street.

Wine was poured, and Theo took a thankful sip, returning the nodded greeting of her dinner partner. Who, wonder of wonders, turned out to be Lord Sayle.

After a few moments of silence, he murmured, 'I won't bite, you know.'

Theo started, then laughed. 'Excuse me, I didn't mean to be uncivil. I suppose I look as awkward as I feel,' she admitted—before remembering that candour was not a virtue prized by society.

Her dinner partner didn't seem offended. 'You look lovely, as I'm sure you know.'

'Oh, d-dear,' she stammered, colouring. 'I really wasn't trolling for a compliment.'

'That's not at all what I thought. But I'm very happy to give one so well deserved. You're Miss Branwell, aren't you? Lady Coghlane's niece?'

'Yes. And you're Lord Sayle, Lady Staunton's nephew.'

'Yes. Now that we've sorted out the family, what shall we discuss?'

How best to safely answer that? 'Why not tell me about your estate?' she answered cautiously.

'Let's not talk about something so ordinary!' He must have read alarm on her face, for he smiled. 'I shouldn't tease you. My aunt told me you've only recently come to England, having lived your entire life abroad, first in India, then following the drum with your father in Spain, Portugal, and Belgium. Also that he fell at Waterloo. My sincere condolences.'

The reminder brought a sharp pang of loss, no matter how many times it was mentioned. 'Thank you. I understand you've recently lost your wife as well. My sincere sympathies.'

He nodded, his expression turning sad. 'It was...very distressing. But one soldiers on, as I'm sure you know.'

'Yes,' she affirmed, liking him the better for this plain evidence of how fond he'd been of his wife.

Though it was nothing to her attachment to Marshall— or he wouldn't be in London looking for a replacement, a mere year after her death.

'Tell me more about your life,' he was saying. 'It's been so much more exciting than mine.'

Dangerous territory, she thought. Struggling for some socially appropriate opening, she finally shrugged. 'My aunt would say there's little about it fit to discuss at a dinner party. I've recently settled at a manor in Suffolk, and have never visited Kent. I understand you raise horses. Won't you tell me about your estate?'

Tacitly accepting her reticence, he nodded. 'Horses, yes. But more cattle and crops.'

'Some of the land at the estate bordering my house has

been much neglected, and the owner is now anxious to improve it.' *Maybe she could learn something of use to Dom.*

Dom. A sudden yearning for him filled her, so strong it almost made her dizzy. How she wished she were back at Bildenstone, riding through the meadows with him! How immensely different, the ease and comfort she felt with him, compared to the stiff awkwardness of this dinner party!

Since her searing conversation with Lady Hazlett, she'd deliberately kept herself from thinking about him—and the fact that her marriage would put an end to the friendship between them for good.

Which, of course, was for the best.

She was only uncomfortable because she was not yet well acquainted with *this* man, she told herself stoutly. Once she got to know Lord Sayle better, it would be easier.

She hoped.

In any event, he seemed pleasant enough as he obligingly described his home and acreage, requiring her only to add that polite nod at intervals.

'I understand you have three children,' she said when, inevitably, he fell silent and looked to her for a conversational contribution.

'Yes. My eldest son is preparing to leave for Eton. I shall sorely miss him, but alas, it's time. My lovely daughter I trust I shall not have to part from any time soon, since I spoil her so thoroughly no suitor will have her,' he admitted with a laugh. 'My younger son is just out of short coats. Rascals all, but I dote on them.'

'I have a little boy, too, that I've cared for since his birth,' she inserted. *If keeping Charles were going to dissuade a prospective suitor, she might as well find out immediately.*

'So my aunt told me,' he replied. 'I think it very noble of you, to insist on supporting the poor orphan, even after your father's death. Infamous that his father's family refused to recognise him!'

Theo smiled fondly. 'Had Lord Wareton ever visited Charles, he would not have been able to turn him away. Since I'm completely attached to him, I'm very glad his grandfather never made the effort.'

'You enjoy children, then.'

Was she being tested? 'Yes. Travelling with the army, there were always some running about. My father and I became attached to several, particularly the son of Father's sergeant-major. Jemmie foraged for us, watched out for Papa's horses, and generally made himself useful.' *A prospective suitor needed to know about Charles, but it was probably best not to fully reveal her connection to the other orphans just yet.*

'It shows broadness of character, to appreciate even children of that class.'

Theo had to keep herself from stiffening. He was, after all, repeating what most of his peers would say. Only someone like Dominic Ransleigh, who'd been with army, could understand what these children had been through and how dear they were to her.

How was she to safeguard them, though, if her eventual husband wanted her to have nothing further to do with them?

Her chest tightened and for a moment, it was difficult to breathe. *One problem at a time,* she told herself. First, she needed to find prospects who'd accept Charles. Whatever happened afterward, she'd make sure her other charges were protected.

Lord Sayle seemed to have cleared that first hurdle.

Smiling determinedly, she prodded him for more details about his land and children, which he willingly supplied. Respecting her reticence, he made no further enquiries about her own upbringing and circumstances.

Unlike herself, who'd stuck her nose immediately into Dominic Ransleigh's affairs.

He'd not slapped her down for it. Would Lord Sayle, were she to let her true 'colonel's daughter' nature show?

She suppressed a sigh. If matters between them progressed, she'd find that out in due time.

Conversation became more general, several other ladies vying to secure Sayle's attention—one of them, a dazzling blonde with a scandalously low *décolletage*, giving her an angry glance for having monopolised it thus far.

So it begins, navigating the ton*'s fields of fire,* Theo realised ruefully.

When, some hours later, she met her aunt to gather their cloaks and depart, she had to admit dinner had not been as dismal as she'd feared.

As soon as they were enclosed within the privacy of their carriage, Aunt Amelia said, 'What did you think of Lord Sayle? He seemed quite attentive.'

'He was...pleasant. When asked, he told me about his estate and fields and his children, just as you assured me. I promise you, though *he* asked, I evaded giving any details about my own upbringing and experiences, so I don't think I shocked him.'

'Thank heavens for that!' Lady Coghlane said with a chuckle. 'I believe you made quite a favourable impression.'

'How could you tell? We talked for a time, it's true, but before long his attention was claimed—almost forcibly—by other ladies, especially the blonde on his right.'

'Lady Serena—Mrs Maxwell,' her aunt said with a sniff. 'Thinks she's entitled to the admiration of any gentleman within sight of her lovely face or dulcet voice.'

Theo grinned at her tone. 'Not a favourite of yours.'

'No. She's a shameless flirt, who may or may not be

collecting lovers while her poor husband languishes in the country. But having already provided him with the requisite heir and two more, he lets her go her own way.'

To be married and yet alone...that would be worse than losing Marshall, she thought. 'Sad.'

'Perhaps, but not uncommon. Few couples find what you and Marshall shared. I'm pleased you liked Sayle, and even more pleased *he* liked *you*, but he's hardly the only champion! I've planned a little tête-à-tête with a friend tomorrow, to examine other possibilities. But you won yourself one suitor tonight, which is useful in making other gentlemen more attentive.'

'What makes you so sure? We hardly spoke after the beginning of dinner, and Lady Serena hung on his arm all during tea, once the gentlemen rejoined us.'

'Perhaps, but though his attention might be drawn away by that annoying Lady Serena or someone else, his gaze always turned back to you.'

Her aunt's words brought to mind the man to whom *her* gaze always returned. *Dom.*

A *frisson* of desire and longing rippled through her. Damnation, that prudence and propriety had forced her to forgo tasting in full measure the bountiful passion that always simmered between them.

Then, as she recalled Lord Sayle's kissing her hand as he bid her goodbye, the observation struck her.

Not once around *him* had she felt that heated anticipation in the pit of the stomach she felt always when she was near Dominic Ransleigh.

The next afternoon, Theo returned to her aunt's house, refreshed after a long walk in Hyde Park with Charles and Constancia. There'd been ducks to feed on the Serpentine, a vendor selling meat pasties, and some beautiful high-stepping bays being exercised by a groom. Trotting back to the waiting carriage after the excursion, her son declared London not so bad a place after all.

After seeing him to his room, Theo returned to her own chamber. She'd just tidied her windblown hair when the butler came up to inform her that Lady Coghlane would like the pleasure of Theo's company for tea.

Knowing her aunt had conferred with a friend earlier that day, Theo returned the expected acceptance and walked to her aunt's sitting room, a sense of dread in her belly.

'Come in, my dear,' her aunt called, her smile brightening as she took in Theo's new gown in Prussian blue, done up with frogged fasteners, *à la* Hussar. 'Very fetching! Marston has done good work—although we must also visit the modiste tomorrow and let you choose some fashionable gowns of your own!'

'I do like the military style of this one. Although, if the evening gown I wore last night is an example of what's "fashionable", I'm going to go about feeling like I've joined the *demi-monde*!'

'Nonsense! Lady Serena's gown was lower in the bust than yours by a good two inches. But I didn't ask you here to discuss gowns, but something more important.'

'More important than gowns? Isn't that statement a sacrilege?'

'Almost,' her aunt agreed with a chuckle. 'But discussing your prospects *is* more important.'

Theo's humour evaporated instantly. Annoyed at the response, she told herself that since marriage was inevitable, she might as well begin looking on it more optimistically.

Think of the prize. A whole childhood's worth of time to walk in the park, skip stones, eat meat pasties and watch high-stepping horses with her son.

'Very well,' she said with determined cheerfulness. 'What do your spies report?'

'I called on an old friend from our come-out days, Sally Jersey. She's one of the patronesses of Almack's, very well connected, and knows everyone. She'd already heard about your appearance at Jane's dinner, and confirmed that Lord Sayle is definitely interested.'

'Really, Aunt, how could she possibly know?'

'Oh, a comment to a friend at his club, overheard by a servant, who mentioned it to one of hers—she has her little informants all over town. Anyway, I think we can include him on the list.'

'There's a list?'

'Of course. I'd already begun compiling one, but wanted to get Sally's opinion.'

Theo shook her head. 'Sounds like preparation for a military campaign.'

'It is a campaign, of a sort. Finding the proper marriage partner always is, for a girl of your station.'

'No one just falls in love?' she asked, only half in jest.

Her aunt looked up, sympathy in her eyes. 'It does happen—but why not carefully cultivate the prospects, so if you *do* fall in love, the gentleman in question is suitable?'

'I suppose you're right,' Theo admitted. Not just anyone would do—she needed a husband with the same power and standing in the polite world as Lord Hazlett, if she hoped to keep Charles out of the hands of his grandparents. 'Very well, who's on the list?'

'Two widowers, Mr James Lloyd, very wealthy and well connected—his father was the Duke of Ingleston's youngest son. Lord Terrington, another baron with extensive property and a large motherless family, and Jeremy Carleton. He's not much older than you, an amusing rattle always welcome in company, much sought after for his charm and wit, but always evasive of marriage.'

'So why would he be interested in me?'

'All the loveliest, most accomplished girls have been

paraded before him—and he's shown not a bit of interest. When she twigged him about his elusiveness, Sally said he replied that all the girls were beautiful, sang and played delightfully—and were as boringly similar as if produced by the same sausage press. Sally thinks he'd be intrigued by someone different and unexpected.'

'I'm certainly that,' Theo said ruefully. 'Though if rather ungraciously comparing young ladies, who were doing their best to be pleasant company, to ground meat is a comment typical of his wit, we might end up at daggers drawn.'

'He probably said it to amuse Sally, that being the sort of naughty comment she likes.'

'Well, I wouldn't,' Theo said flatly.

'I suspect he'd soon figure that out, and accommodate his wit to your tastes.'

'Then I'd have to wonder whether he possessed any strong convictions of his own.'

Lady Coghlane raised an eyebrow. 'You'll certainly charm him if he prefers ladies being difficult.'

Theo blew out a sigh. 'I'm sorry, Aunt Amelia. I shall try to be more accommodating, and look for the positives in each proposed match. So, how do we begin the campaign? Ask them all to dinner and parade me around, like a horse at Tattersall's?'

'Since I know you're only funning, I'll not dignify that with a reply. Sally is giving a musicale tomorrow evening, and they should all be present—no one turns down an invitation from Lady Jersey! Having heard how unusual you are, I suspect she's as eager to meet you—and see how the gentlemen react to you—as I am for you to meet the gentlemen.'

'Wonderful,' Theo muttered. 'Now I get to perform under the eye of one of the most discriminating arbiters of the *ton*. Even in Portugal, everyone had heard of Lady Jersey.'

'Just be yourself, child. She will enjoy your natural wit. We'll have Marston prepare another gown for the musicale, but in the morning, we must definitely call on the modiste. After Sally's party, I expect you'll be engaged for some entertainment every night.'

Theo tried not to shudder at the prospect of spending every evening for the foreseeable future being trailed through the *ton* like a fat minnow on a hook until some acceptable gentleman bit. But Aunt Amelia was doing everything she could to assist her, and much as she yearned to flee back to Thornfield Place and don her well-worn habit, she should be grateful. 'Thank you, Aunt Amelia. My responses may not have reflected it, but I appreciate all your help.'

Lady Coghlane's gaze softened. 'I know it's hard for you, leaving your familiar world for one so foreign to you. I'll try to make entering this one as easy as I can.'

'I know you will,' Theo said, tears pricking at her eyes.

Her aunt patted her hand. 'Don't worry, child. I promise, you'll feel more confident once we get you properly outfitted and gowned.'

The awful vista rose before her of being measured and probed and pinned, then having to look at fabric and trimming and lace until her eyes glazed over. Reminding herself this was all for Charles, Theo swallowed hard and said, 'The dressmaker, tomorrow morning, whenever you are ready.'

She was sipping the last of her tea when the butler came in. 'A gentleman has called, Lady Coghlane. I told him it wasn't your usual day to receive visitors, but he insisted I inform you of his presence.'

Aunt Amelia turned to her with a triumphant expression. 'See! It begins already.' Looking back at the butler, she said, 'Which impatient gentleman has called, Foster?'

'Mr Dominic Ransleigh, my lady.'

Theo gasped, and Aunt Amelia gave her a significant look.

His doubtful gaze going from his mistress to her guest, the butler said, 'I hope I was correct in admitting him.'

'Yes, indeed, Foster,' Lady Coghlane said. 'The gentleman is Miss Branwell's neighbour in Suffolk. Tell him we'll join him directly.'

Chapter Seventeen

Impatient to see Miss Branwell, Dom paced the drawing room. Knowing it was impossible for his still-recovering body to ride as far as London, he'd been forced to hire post chaises, and the longer the trip dragged on, the more concerned and anxious he became. When the last hired carriage cracked a bow, delaying his arrival for hours, he'd been ready to grind his teeth in frustration. He'd finally reached London the previous night, far too late to call.

During the interminable journey, he'd had plenty of time to ponder the conundrum of Miss Branwell's unexpected decision to marry and consider what he might do about it. Though he'd not planned on taking so giant a step this soon, he *had* been toying for some time with the idea of courting her in earnest.

She was lovely, intelligent, unusual, and would never bore him. She'd infused him with a desire to do something important and exhibited total confidence that he would find such a calling—at a time when his own confidence in the future had been at a low ebb. It was thanks in large part to her avid interest in Bildenstone and her probing questions about the land and the estate that he'd started driving out, leading him to the idea of establishing a draught-horse-breeding operation.

And he'd never, ever, desired a woman with the intensity that he wanted her.

After interminable days of waiting, ready to explode with the urgency to discover the truth—and find out whether or not he'd be radically altering his future—Dom hadn't been about to let some starched shirt of a butler deny him entry. He was reasonably sure Miss Branwell, never one to fuss about dress, would join him immediately, even if not properly attired for receiving calls. Though if she didn't appear in the next few minutes, he'd quit the room and go looking for her.

Then he heard the whisper of moving hinges and looked towards the doorway. Miss Branwell entered, stopping him in mid-stride.

She looked radiant in a dark-blue gown with military trim, and she'd done something new to her hair. The glossy brown locks twisted and curled and framed her face in little ringlets that made those luminous brown eyes seem enormous. His mouth dried and for a long moment he could not take his gaze from her face.

She stared back just as fixedly, seeming to drink him in. That ever-present, instantaneous *something* sizzled in the air between them.

'Mr Ransleigh, how nice to see you again.' Lady Coghlane, whom in his total absorption with Miss Branwell, he'd not even noticed, walked over to extend her hand. 'I'm so pleased you decided to take me up on my offer of hospitality, though I didn't expect to see you in London this soon!'

He pulled himself together and retrieved his manners from wherever they'd gone missing. 'I came to town unexpectedly. Thank you for letting me in—even though your butler said you weren't receiving today.'

'We're always available to friends and neighbours, aren't we, my dear? As it happens, though, you've caught me at some correspondence I must finish. Theo, might I impose on you to entertain our guest? Perhaps a walk in the garden? It's such a fair afternoon.'

Throwing Lady Coghlane a look of gratitude, Dom said, 'A walk in the garden would be delightful. If you would indulge me, Miss Branwell?'

'Of c-course,' she stuttered, still looking unsettled.

As soon as he'd bowed Lady Coghlane out, she turned to him. 'What is it? Is something wrong at the school? Are any of the children hurt?'

'No, nothing like that,' he assured her, forgetting until that moment how concerned he'd been about *her* welfare when Jemmie turned up unannounced. 'Shall we walk?'

She exhaled a long breath. 'Now that my heart has commenced beating again, I think I can manage it. I'll even be able to contain my curiosity over what brought you to London until we get outside, out of earshot.'

He offered his arm and she took it. *Ah,* he thought, closing his eyes to savour the delicious thrill that tingled through him at the touch of her hand. She must have felt it, too, for she inhaled sharply and looked up at him, her dark eyes wide.

Realising she was staring, she blushed a little and said, 'It's good to see you again, Mr Ransleigh. Even better, now that I know none of the children are in danger.'

He was the one in danger, Dom thought as he led her to the town-house garden. Thank goodness servants lurked behind every overlooking window, else the minute he got her out the door, he might have succumbed to the ever-present urge to kiss her.

'How was your journey?' she was asking him. 'You didn't ride, did you?'

'Can't quite manage that yet,' he replied. 'I came post.'

'You appear refreshed. Your arm didn't pain you over-much?'

'No more than always. I have to admit, I made rather liberal use of the laudanum last night.'

'Now, since you're well accustomed to my directness, may I skip further pleasantries and ask why you've come to London? You mentioned nothing before you left Bildenstone beyond a trip to Newmarket and a visit to Holkham.'

'I hadn't planned on coming. Until I was told the rather astonishing news that you'd suddenly conceived an urgent desire to marry. So urgent, you abandoned the school and headed for your aunt's house with hardly a word to anyone. Jemmie was most upset.'

'You've visited the school,' she guessed, colouring.

'Why the sudden wish to marry? I've no claim upon you that would make such a personal matter my business, but you are my tenant, a condition which would certainly be altered by your marriage. Besides, I seem to recall when we discussed wedlock, you declared yourself firmly against it, saying something like "only desperation would drive you to it"? Have you just lost your fortune on the 'Change? Do you need me to spot you a loan to secure the school?'

She smiled a little, but her eyes had gone bleak.

'No, my fortune is intact.' She dropped his arm and took a step away, then halted, looking back at him. 'I was going to try to fob you off with some plausible excuse, but I'm a terrible liar. You already know some of the worst about me, so I might as well tell you the rest.'

'I would very much like to know why you've had such a radical change of heart. There's always been honesty between us, which I prize, just as I admire your frankness and ability to face facts as they are, free of wishful imagining. And I think it goes without saying that whatever you tell me will be held in strictest confidence.'

'Only one thing I must insist on before I tell you,' she said, her expression almost...defensive. 'I believe you've developed a fondness for the school and the children. Despite what you may think of me, will you pledge to help safeguard them?'

'Nothing you reveal could alter my regard and admiration—but if you insist, yes, you have my promise.'

'Very well,' she said, and took a deep breath. 'You remember Audley Tremaine, who visited me at the school?'

Distaste and irritation stirred. 'The man you wouldn't let me pummel. How could I forget?'

'After I refused his…disreputable offer, he threatened to reveal something he'd just discovered. I tried to mask my concern by asserting no one ever believed what he said. Well, I was wrong.'

She looked suddenly weary and heartsick. Dom had the strongest urge to wrap his arm around her and enfold her against his chest. Resisting it, he said, 'What had he discovered?'

'Tremaine was acquainted with Lord Everly and his wife, Alicia, and knew them both to be dark-haired and dark-eyed. That day at the school, he got a close look at Charles, who is, obviously, blond and green-eyed. As was my fiancé, Marshall. Putting two and two together, Tremaine concluded that Charles wasn't Lord Everly's son, he was Marshall's. And mine. He must have gone straight from Suffolk to Viscount Hazlett's estate, for the day you left for Newmarket, I had an unexpected visitor. Lady Hazlett arrived, wanting to meet Charles. And telling me she intended to take him away with her.'

Dom felt like he'd just been dealt a roundhouse blow to the chest. 'Charles is…*your* son?'

Miss Branwell lifted her chin and turned back to face him squarely. 'Yes. I had made it known that Alicia became too ill to finish the journey to Lisbon, so we had to stay at the convent until the birth of her child. But I was ill, too, having only just discovered I was increasing when I got the news that Marshall had been killed. We both gave birth there. Her child died; mine survived. When I brought Charles back with me, intending to confess my shame, Everly's commander assumed the infant was Everly's. Seeing a way to keep Charles from being branded a bastard, I didn't correct him.'

Dom shook his head, still trying to wrap his mind around the astounding fact. 'No one else knew, or suspected? Not even your father?'

'Constancia knew, of course. Widowed by the war, she'd taken shelter at the convent with an ailing child who later died. She agreed to accompany me as Charles's nurse. But no one else knew.'

She paced away from the house, away from him, down the small *allée* of trees. As he followed, the full horror of the situation she'd found herself in slowly registered: her fiancé dying…finding herself unwed…increasing…the prospect of the shame, scandal, and the inevitable banishment from polite society she would endure once the truth became known. The child of the man she loved branded a bastard for ever—and nothing she could do to prevent it.

Heaven have mercy, how alone and frightened and desperate she must have been!

Reaching the back garden wall, unable to go further, Miss Branwell halted. Turning to him, anguish in her eyes, she said, 'I wish now that I had followed the dictates of conscience and revealed Charles's true parentage from the first. Papa would have been shamed and embarrassed, but he was a soldier, and had faced worse. Forfeiting his respect and good opinion would have been terribly painful, but my conduct deserved his disdain. Now, unless I take some immediate remedy to prevent it, my irresponsible behaviour threatens me not just with the loss of my son, but the possibility of incurring such censure I might have to close the school, or risk making it impossible for my orphans to find respectable positions when they leave it.

Ruining a number of lives, instead of just two. Only one remedy can prevent all that, Marriage.'

Dom tried to quell the thousand questions running through his head and concentrate only on the important one. 'Why is marriage the remedy?'

'I induced Lady Hazlett to agree that, if I wed a man of substance who can provide the same social advantages for Charles the viscount would—a man of discernment to model himself after, one with the proper connections to introduce Charles at university, in his clubs, and those masculine domains necessary to a gentleman's life—she would allow me keep Charles and uphold the lie that he is Everly's. If the Hazletts support the story of Charles's parentage I have always put forth, Tremaine's version won't be given any credence.'

'What of Lord Everly's father, the Marquess? What if he should change his mind and decide to recognise the boy?'

'Lady Hazlett thinks it unlikely. As do I, at this late date. The Marquess has an heir, several other sons and a number of grandchildren. Lady Hazlett's are the only conditions that matter. And so I must marry. I cannot lose Charles. '

Dom stood silent for a long moment, mulling over what she'd told him. Though Jemmie's alarm had been sincere, he'd discounted the boy's account as over-dramatic, thinking there was probably some more rational explanation for Theo's sudden departure.

But analysing the dilemma after knowing the truth, he had to admit he could not come up with any better remedy than an immediate marriage. 'With the grandparents insisting the boy must be raised as a gentleman *by* a gentleman, there doesn't appear to be any alternative.'

Then he girded himself to ask the only other question that had bedevilled him on the long journey to London.

'Had you someone in mind to marry when you left for London?'

'No. I'm trusting Aunt Amelia to help me find someone suitable. I'll take any gentleman who will accept Charles, serve as his mentor and keep our secret. Most likely some widower needing a new mother for his brood, or an older man wanting a nursemaid.'

Huge relief filled Dom. *So there was no secret admirer waiting in the wings; he could take centre stage himself.* 'Someone who seeks only a governess or a nurse? You'd be bored and miserable within six months.'

'What I feel doesn't matter, as long as I can have Charles and keep the school safe. Which brings me to that favour I mentioned. Even if Aunt Amelia works her miracle and finds a gentleman who'll accept me, it's quite possible he will not allow me to continue running the school. If that happens, would you watch over it for me until I can make other arrangements?'

She gazed imploringly up at him, looking taut as an overstrung bow ready to snap. Incorrectly interpreting his continued silence as disapproval, she continued. 'Think what it would mean if you were threatened with losing one of your cousins—like Will, who nursed you for months after you were wounded. Wouldn't you do whatever you had to, in order to prevent that? What is boredom and dissatisfaction compared to losing someone so dear to you?'

She was trembling, tears hovering in corners of her eyes. 'Please?' she added in a whisper.

No longer able to restrain himself, Dom took her hand and kissed it, the decision already made somewhere on the road to London. 'I can do that, and more. Why not marry me? My family and connections pass muster, you can keep Charles and manage the school. You won't be bored, and—' he ran a finger over her lips '—I can guarantee you won't be miserable. In fact, I think I can quite confidently promise...delight.'

'Oh, Dom,' she whispered, a few tears spilling over to slip down her cheek. To his joy and relief, she closed her eyes and leaned into him. He pulled her against him, wrapping her in his warmth and strength, cradling her as he breathed in her delicate violet scent.

Just as he was about to tell her not to worry, he would always be there to take care of her, she gave a little gasp and pushed him away.

'Oh, no, I couldn't marry you!'

Taken aback, he said, 'Why not? I haven't a title, but I have a large and well-connected family. My uncle's an earl; in fact, I seem to recall that Viscount Hazlett is part of my uncle's coalition in the Lords. I can guarantee to raise Charles as befits a gentleman and assure him entry into whatever career he wants.'

'No, no, it isn't that! Your background is perfect, and I know you care for the children.' She looked up at him, a few more tears dripping down, distress on her face. 'You're—you're too nice, and I like you too much!'

He stared back at her. 'I've heard of unions between parties who cordially detest each other, but I'd never heard of *liking* being a barrier to marriage.'

'It's not that. Oh, I'm making a muddle of this.' She took a deep breath, obviously trying to recover her composure. 'When you like someone, you want the best for them. So I couldn't allow you to be dragged into a marriage, just because I'm caught in a predicament of my own making.'

Relieved, he smiled at her. Dear Theo, trying to 'protect' him as she did her orphans. 'Don't you think I have presence of mind enough to make that decision myself?'

'I think you are brave, and compassionate, and wonderfully generous! But you've only recently ended an engagement—too recently to be pressed into making another. And you yourself admit you haven't yet figured out what you mean to do with your life. How could I let you tie yourself to something and someone who will be of no help to you in whatever endeavour you finally decide to pursue?'

'Just because you will be running the school doesn't mean I can't pursue other options,' he argued. 'In fact, if the breeding operation I'm envisioning comes to fruition, the focus of my business will be in Suffolk, headquartered at Bildenstone Hall. Besides, don't you always quote your father, something about nothing being certain and having to make the best choice as the battle rages? Adapt to conquer?'

She looked at him reprovingly. 'It's not fair to use my father against me.'

He'd not been anticipating resistance—swift and grateful acceptance, really. At the shock of realising she might actually refuse him, feelings of protest and dismay welled up, along with a desire to make her his wife that was much stronger than he'd expected.

'Besides,' she was continuing, 'what if you fall in love? I have loved someone completely, utterly, madly. It's wonderful and magical and I wouldn't want you to miss that.' She grimaced. 'Nor would I want to be your wife when you fell in love with someone else.'

'How long did it take you to recover from losing your fiancé?'

A shadow crossed her eyes. 'One never completely gets over it.'

'Just so.' He nodded. 'My cousin Alastair was completely, utterly, madly in love with a woman who jilted him practically at the altar. Devastated, he joined the army, determined to die gloriously in battle, or some such rot. He survived the war, but he's never truly got over her. So if that's what being madly in love is, I'd just as soon not experience it. Why can we not be *sanely* in love? Isn't friendship and shared interests and compatibility of mind a much sounder basis for a union meant to be happy over a lifetime? And what of this?'

Stepping forward, he drew her to him and feathered kisses from her ear down her throat to the neckline of her gown. 'This,' he murmured as she sagged against him, 'is also unique, this connection between us.'

'C-can't base a marriage on that,' she whispered disjointedly.

'I think it an excellent basis,' he said, gratified that he had to steady her on her feet. 'We've tried to ignore the attraction—but it burns between us whenever we're together. You feel it, too, don't you?'

'Yes,' she admitted.

'I've never experienced anything stronger. I think it will last a long, long time, binding us together. Making us one.'

He kissed her then, a soft, glancing brush of his lips against hers. Then exulted, desire coursing through him, when she immediately opened her mouth, sought his tongue, and wrapped her arms around his neck. Kissing him back with passion and also, he thought, anxiety and fear and relief.

After a few moments, breathing hard, he broke the kiss. 'So marry me, Theo.'

She shook her head dazedly. 'I can't think when you kiss me like that.'

'Thinking is highly overrated.'

'But marriage would be for ever! There'd be no trial period, like I proposed for the school, during which you could reconsider and toss me and the children out. You shouldn't make such an important decision so hastily.'

'I've had time to consider it.'

'How could you? I've only just explained the situation!'

'Jemmie found me at Holkham. In fact,' he added with

a smile, 'he practically ordered me to come to London and sort this out.'

'Jemmie ordered you!' she gasped, her cheeks flaming red. 'Oh, the…the rascal! I'll strangle him for this!'

'It was enlightened self-interest. He knows I like the children and the school, and if you married, a new husband might not.'

'I'm still going to strangle him.'

'He also said he knew I liked you—and that after we'd been together, you seemed happier than he'd seen you since your father died. I'd like to go on making you happy. Won't you let me? Not to mention, we don't want to let Jemmie and the others down.'

The struggle played out over her expressive face. Attraction, affection, and the strong connection that went beyond the physical pulling them together; opposing that, her fierce sense of honour insisting she not allow him to make such an important decision so precipitously, badly as she needed his help.

Had he ever met a woman so brave—or so stubborn? Then a niggle of doubt crept in.

'Am *I* pressing *you* too hard? Would you truly prefer to marry one of the prospects your aunt lines up?'

'There's no one I'd rather marry,' she blurted, sending another flurry of relief through him. 'But,' she added, biting her lip, 'my wishes are not important.'

'Why?' He looked at her curiously. A disquieting notion occurred, and he frowned. 'You don't really think you should marry a man you don't love or even like and be miserable for the rest of life as some sort of penance for the mistake of conceiving a child out of wedlock?' At the slight alteration of her expression, he said, 'Great Heaven, I'm afraid you might! Not that I can speak for the Almighty, but surely God forgave you for that sin long ago. You need to forgive yourself, and think seriously about what would make you, not just stoically endure, not just be content, but happy.' He drew her back against him. 'Delirious, even.'

He kissed her again, harder, deeper this time, until they were both dizzy and gasping for breath.

'Marry me, Theo,' he urged, brushing his mouth over hers.

She nuzzled into him, whimpering.

'Was that a "yes"?'

'I—I don't know! My senses are swimming and my mind doesn't know up from down. C-come back tomorrow, and I'll answer you then.'

He set her on her feet. 'I'll come back tomorrow. And ask you again. And kiss you again. Count on it.' With that, he bowed and walked away, his heart pounding, desire pulsing through his veins.

That he wanted her more than ever was no surprise. That he wanted so badly for her to marry him was.

After that last kiss, however, he was feeling pretty confident that he was going to be satisfied on both counts.

Chapter Eighteen

Theo watched her erstwhile fiancé stride down the garden path until he was lost from sight. Her senses still tingling from his kisses, she tottered to a bench and sat down hard.

She ought to pinch herself. Dominic Ransleigh—'Dandy Dom', formerly society's darling who had snagged a duke's daughter for a bride—couldn't have just asked *her* to marry him.

Could he?

She took long, slow breaths, trying to settle her agitated body and calm her disordered mind. What, exactly, had he told her?

That Jemmie had tracked him down to inform him about her abrupt departure from Thornfield. She really should strangle the boy when she got back, she thought with a sigh.

That Jemmie knew she liked Dom, and Dom liked her. She felt a flush of embarrassment heat her cheeks.

Obviously they hadn't masked their mutual attraction as well as she'd thought.

After the acute discomfort of Lady Staunton's dinner, and with the prospect of a series of equally uncomfortable evenings to come, she'd had to resist the urge to throw herself on Dom and accept him immediately. But she'd paid a high price once for making a decision of enormous consequence without careful reflection, and she'd not do so again.

Still, how great a contrast between the excitement and sense of safety she'd felt, just seeing Dom standing in her aunt's drawing room, and the dread with which she viewed having to entertain other potential suitors—even the accommodating Lord Sayle.

She was far more comfortable around him than she'd been with any other man since Marshall, and had been from their first meeting. Feeling *at home* in the heart of one's home was a valuable thing. Plus, they shared a love of books, horses, and a common interest in the children and their futures.

Marrying him would certainly meet the criteria required by Lady Hazlett. She'd gain an incomparable role model for her son and the support of Dom's well-connected family when it came time for Charles to attend university and choose a vocation.

She could return to the countryside she much preferred, get back to running her school—and have Dominic Ransleigh at her side and in her bed.

Ah, how often had images of heated encounters between them invaded her dreams! Accept him, and she'd no longer have to resist the desire he aroused so effortlessly. After awakening many nights in the dark, afire with longing, she'd be able to follow through on all her erotic imaginings, with the right to explore every glorious inch of his body and discover every possible way to bring them delight.

It was several moments before she could drag her mind from those enticing possibilities back to cold, hard reality.

He didn't love her, and in marrying him, she'd deprive him of the chance to fall in love—or risk turning into the duty wife of a man smitten with another woman. Wincing at the unpleasant possibility, she concluded that boredom or outright misery would be preferable.

Plus, marriage should be an equal bargain. He offered her salvation from an untenable situation, but what did she bring him, save a school full of problems and the possibility that an unsavoury old scandal might one day pop up out of the box into which her lies had crammed it and shock his world, like some evil grinning jack-in-the-box?

Was she, on some unconscious level, pushing herself towards an unhappy marriage as a penance for her sins, as he'd alleged? There might be more truth to that charge than she'd like to admit.

Or was her reluctance, as she hoped, based more on high principle—not allowing him to sacrifice himself in a cause not his own. Though, as he'd argued, he was a man grown, making this choice of his own free will. She had no right to keep him from making it.

Though she had every right to refuse, if after sober analysis she deemed the benefits he offered did not outweigh the risks of marrying a man she could all too easily fall in love with.

For she had to admit—if only to herself—that she more than *liked* Dominic Ransleigh. All the reasons that made it so attractive to accept his hand, made it far too easy to go from liking to *loving* him. Hadn't she promised herself, after the total devastation of Marshall's death, she would never, ever put herself at risk for that kind of desolation again?

The possibilities of loss were more than just having him fall for another woman. True, with the war over, she needn't fear losing him in battle. But there were still fevers and carriage accidents and any manner of dangers that could snatch away one's beloved.

Then she had to laugh at herself. Had the girl who once had been sublimely unconcerned about sending a soldier off to battle now become prey to such alarm she must worry about every ghostie, goblin, and terror that whispered in the dark?

All she knew for sure was she very much wanted to marry Dominic Ransleigh—and that she very much feared doing so would be a huge mistake.

Unable to resolve the matter, she jumped up in disgust and headed back to the house.

Aunt Amelia would want to know what they had discussed, and she'd have to come up with something glib to fob her off. She could not bear revealing her conflicted feelings for Dominic Ransleigh to anyone, even her sympathetic aunt. Who, in any event, would be certain to dismiss any reservations she might have and urge her to get Dom leg-shackled before he changed his mind.

First, she had to make up hers.

Mercifully, she had the rest of the evening and all night to wrestle with it.

Next morning, in the wake of a mostly sleepless night, Theo could hardly recall what tale she'd spun for her aunt or how they'd spent the rest of the evening. Pleading a very real headache, she'd taken herself off to bed early, only to toss and turn as the clock struck through the hours. *Marry or not, marry or not,* its steady tick seemed to taunt her.

It wasn't fair, she thought, sitting in bed in the pale morning light, clutching a cooling cup of chocolate she would gag on if she tried to sip it. Wanting him too much couldn't be good, could it? It would be so easy to fall in love with him—and therein lay disaster.

She knew he'd be here soon, expecting the answer she'd promised. The butterflies in her stomach turned to swallows, swooping and diving against her ribs.

Would she be giving in to her sensual self against her better judgement if she accepted?

Yet, accepting him would solve her problem immediately, making it much less likely that Tremaine could cause any more damage. Thereby safeguarding the school, and giving Charles the most wonderful mentor she could ask for.

Shouldn't protecting herself from the dangers of falling in love be her own task—her peace of mind in avoiding that possibility less important than the security of Charles and her orphans?

Susan arrived with her gown, and had just helped her into it when a knock sounded at the door.

'Mr Ransleigh is here again,' the butler informed her with a frown. 'I told him it was much too early to call upon a lady, but he insisted.'

The swallows swooped through another circuit. Placing a hand on her stomach, she said, 'Yes, I was expecting him.'

His disapproving glance now settling on her for having encouraged such a breach of decorum, he said, 'Very well. I shall inform him you'll be down directly.'

A few minutes later, Theo slipped quietly into the room. Dom stood by the window, gazing into the garden, tapping one booted foot impatiently. She took in the tousled blond locks, the noble profile, the tall, broad-shouldered torso, no longer so thin. *This man may soon be my husband,* she thought with a sense of wonder.

Then he turned and spied her, and every nerve in her body vibrated with awareness. 'Good morning, Mr Ransleigh,' she said, hardly able to get the words out of her tight throat.

He paced over, pulled her against him, and kissed her fiercely. Fuelled by lust and terror, she kissed him back just as hard.

Finally he broke away, still binding her against him with his one good arm. Gazing at her intently, he said, 'Was that a yes?'

She hesitated, still unsure of her answer. She truly hadn't decided before she walked into the room what she was going to do, her thoughts and emotions having yawed wildly back and forth from 'yes' to 'no' since he'd left her yesterday.

His fierce gaze softening, he cupped her cheek with his good hand. 'Do you trust me, Theo? To watch out for you, and protect you, and cherish you?'

That question, she had no trouble answering. 'Yes, I trust you.'

'As I trust you, to watch out for and protect and cherish me. Is there anything else more important than that?'

Her lips trembling, she shook her head.

'Then, Theo, will you marry me?'

With his touch gentle and his voice tender and his bright blue gaze fixed on her face with affection and concern, she said the only thing possible.

'Yes, Dom, I will marry you.'

With a cry of triumph, he hauled her close and kissed her again. Finally releasing her, he said, 'We *will* be happy, Theo, I promise you! Now, shall I go and inform your aunt?'

Having now committed herself, Theo felt a succession of conflicting emotions rush through her—excitement, elation, anticipation, desire, doubt, fear. It was all she could do to say, 'Not now. She'll be abed for hours yet.'

'When and where do you wish to wed? With the need to resolve Charles's position, it's probably best to make it soon. I can ride to Doctors' Commons and procure a special licence, and we could marry whenever you wish. Here, at your aunt's house, or back in Suffolk. Unless you'd prefer to wait to establish residency so we could wed at St George's in Hanover Square?'

'Soon, in this house, would be best,' she confirmed.

'I'll be off, then, and call on your aunt later.' Gently he

took her chin again and angled her head up, his good eye searching her face. 'Are you sure? You won't change your mind later, feeling you were coerced into this?'

She laughed feebly. 'Shouldn't I be asking you that?'

He grinned, the eye patch making him look positively piratical. 'I'm getting what I want. Or I will be soon. Ah, what a wedding night I anticipate!' He drew one finger across her lips.

Yearning ignited in its wake. 'How long do we have to wait?'

His grin broadened. 'I'll try to make it as short as possible.' He gave her another quick kiss. 'I'll see you this afternoon.'

With a purposeful stride, he went out…leaving Theo frozen, a hand to her trembling lips, torn between elation and terror.

Exultant, Dom practically danced out of the parlour. Until the very last minute, he wasn't sure Theo was actually going to accept him—and somewhere over the course of the last few days, it had become terribly important to him that she did. Strangely enough for so important a step, and one he'd not seriously considered until very recently, the idea of marrying her seemed so natural and right, he'd had not a single second thought from the moment he decided to propose.

He'd make sure she never regretted accepting him, either, he vowed. Living with and loving Theo—ah, especially making love to Theo—was going to be an entertaining life's business. He couldn't wait to begin.

Ticking off in his mind all he needed to do to put together a wedding with the least possible delay, Dom paced towards the entry door. He had little doubt Theo's aunt would enthusiastically approve their plans, especially given the delicacy of her niece's position.

Then it suddenly occurred to him that for his marriage with Theo to be a success, one other important person must approve their union. Stopping short so quickly the footman escorting him out nearly ran into him, he turned to the servant and said, 'Before I go, I'd like to speak to Master Charles. Would you show me to his room, please?'

Whatever the footman thought about escorting a visitor who'd arrived far too early up to the room of a person who generally did not receive guests, he merely blinked and motioned Dom to follow him. A few minutes later, he gestured towards the open doorway of a third-floor bedchamber. 'He's in there, sir.'

'Thank you. I can find my own way out.'

As the servant retreated down the hallway, Dom moved to the doorway.

Peeking in, he noted the maid, Constancia, in a wing chair, bent over some sewing, and Charles by the window, sunlight glowing on his fair curls as he repositioned an array of toy soldiers in rows before him.

Dom watched for a moment, curious about this child who meant so much, his mother had been ready to sacrifice her own happiness to keep him. *What would you do if you were threatened with losing one of your cousins...wouldn't you do whatever you had to, in order to prevent that?*

That argument he could understand—losing Will or Max or Alastair would be unthinkable.

Tapping on the doorframe, he said, 'May I come in?'

Charles looked over to the newcomer, his face brightening. 'Mr Ransleigh!' he cried. 'Have you come to take us home?'

Clever boy, Dom thought. Nodding a greeting to the maid as he entered, he replied, 'I thought I might. Would you like that?'

'Oh, yes! London is big and noisy and there are some very nice horses in the park, but I like Thornfield better.

And I miss Georgie and Jemmie and even stupid Maria. Will we go soon?'

Dom walked over and knelt down, so his face was level with the boy's. 'It should be very soon. Before we go, though, Charles, I wish to ask you something. I want to marry Miss Theo.' Ignoring a gasp from the maid, he continued. 'When we get back, you'd both come and live with me at Bildenstone Hall. Would that be all right with you?'

The child paused, considering him. 'Could we still go to the school?'

'Every day, probably.'

'Will I still get my pony?'

Ah, the things of importance to a child. 'Did Miss Theo promise you a pony?'

'After my papa's friend visited us at Thornfield, she did.'

'You mean Lady Hazlett?'

Charles considered the matter for a moment before giving an affirmative shake of the head. 'She said it was time for me to have a pony, like my papa did at my age.'

So the grandmother's blackmail began immediately, he thought. 'Of course you may have a pony. But you will have to learn to ride him properly.'

'Oh, I will!' he exclaimed, his eyes wide with excitement. 'Will you teach me? Jemmie says you are a s'perior horseman. I think it means you ride well.'

'Yes, I'll teach you,' he said, agreeing upon the instant—his first obligation as mentor to Theo's son. Oddly enough, he found himself looking forward to the task. 'Riding well is an important skill for a gentleman.'

Charles nodded. 'Miss Theo says I have to learn to be a proper gentleman, like her papa and mine. They both died in the war.'

'I'm sorry.'

The boy studied him again. 'Jemmie says Miss Theo

likes you, and Jemmie knows everything. Maybe if you marry her, she'll smile more. I like it when she smiles.'

The memory swooped in: Theo after their gallop, laughing in delight, impulsively embracing him. 'I like it, too.'

'Do you like to play soldiers?' the boy asked, gesturing towards the lead figures arranged before him.

'Mr Ransleigh was a soldier,' Constancia inserted. 'He fought in the same war as Miss Theo's papa.'

Charles's interest intensified. 'You were a soldier, too? Will you tell me about it?'

A sudden flurry of images filled his head: smoke, flame, the cacophony of rifle, musket and artillery fire, the yells of the charge, the screams of the wounded. With a shudder, he shook them off. 'Some of it.'

'Can you show me the battles, where the soldiers were? I have General Wellington, General Blücher, and lots of cavalrymen!'

'I could help you arrange the men and explain tactics. Battles are all about tactics, you know.' *As is life,* he thought.

'You can marry Miss Theo, then. Can it be quick? I'm ready to go home.'

'It's a bargain.' Dom held out a hand, and the boy extended his, taking Dom's and shaking it firmly. 'When we get back to Bildenstone, I'll show you the battles. I must go now, but I'll see you later, Charles.'

''Bye, Mr Ransleigh,' the boy said, turning back to his soldiers.

'You are truly to be wed, Senhor Ransleigh?' the maid asked softly as Dom turned to walk out.

'Yes, Constancia. As soon as it can be arranged.'

'Good.' She nodded approvingly. 'You will be kind to Miss Theo, yes? She has suffered much.' She made an oblique glance towards the child. 'She needs a man who will treat her as she deserves.'

'I hope to make her very happy.'

Constancia regarded him steadily. 'See that you do.'

Feeling that he was going to be watched on several fronts, Dom quit the room. How amused his cousins would be, he thought with a smile as he paced down the stairs, when he told them he owed the winning of approval for his suit to his knowledge of the battles they'd fought and his ability to teach riding.

Chapter Nineteen

Four days later, Theo nervously smoothed the skirt of her new Pomona-green gown, watching the clock on the mantel tick closer to the time when she must go down to her aunt's parlour and be married.

Married. The idea still made her stomach clench, sending eddies of trepidation and excitement through her.

She wasn't where she'd expected to be, or feeling how she'd expected to feel when about to plight her troth. It should have been at the English embassy in Lisbon, the wedding breakfast afterwards thronged with army friends and their families who'd relocated to Portugal for the duration of the war. Awaiting her should have been Marshall in his dashing cavalry tunic, attended by his squadron mates, and her father, solemn in full dress uniform, ready to give her away.

All that seemed like a hazy dream from a faraway world. That younger Theo, so completely in love and absolutely confident of the future, was gone too, lost somewhere along the rocky trail from an isolated convent in the Portuguese hills.

The man waiting downstairs, though, was no less worthy of her faith, affection and trust than Marshall. How many women were lucky enough to find two such paragons? If it came to it, she probably knew Dom better than she'd known Marshall, given a whirlwind courtship in the middle of a war. She and Dom had ridden together, walked together, sharing their interests and discussing problems at a length and leisure not possible in an army on the march. Marriage might be the fearful unknown, but she had no doubt whatsoever of the sterling character of the man she was about to marry—even if she still harboured unsettling doubts about the wisdom of marrying him.

Aunt Amelia, though, had been unabashedly delighted when Dom had called, soliciting her permission to wed her niece. He'd set her laughing, telling her he was relieved she'd agreed, else he'd just wasted a great deal of blunt on a special licence.

Her thrilled aunt, insisting Theo must have a new gown of her very own in which to be married, had carried her off to the modiste that very afternoon. A half-finished dress of green shot through with gold caught her eye and was fitted to her immediately. She thought it flattering, and Aunt Amelia, Susan and Constancia all agreed.

She hoped Dom would think so.

Constancia and Charles walked in, startling her out of her reverie. 'Your new dress is pretty, Miss Theo!' Charles said. 'Why did I have to get new nankeens? They're scratchy, and I like my old ones better.'

'A special occasion calls for festive clothes, and the trousers will soften,' Theo said. 'I will only be married once.' *Dear Lord, may this not be a mistake!*

While Charles wandered to the window, eager to inspect the horses traversing the lane, Constancia took her hand. 'Senhor Ransleigh is a good man, Miss Theo. He will take care of you and the boy. This have I prayed for since we left Mary Santo das Montanhas.'

Dom *was* a good man. It made loving him harder to resist, but at the same time quelled that part of her nervousness which stemmed from putting herself in the hands of a man not her father.

A husband held so many rights over a wife, including ownership of all her wealth. Sensitive to that, the day after she accepted his proposal, Dom insisted they consult her father's solicitor and have papers prepared *before* the wedding that would place in trust for Charles all the properties she wanted him to have and set aside a good portion of her inheritance in separate funds for Charles, the school, and her own personal use—all of it untouchable by a husband.

When she protested that made it sound like she didn't trust him, he reminded her that once married, the law gave her no further control over her property—and if anything happened to him, those assets would go to *his* heirs, administered by a solicitor who would look to *their* interests—not those of her or Charles.

Though there wouldn't be time to complete the complicated process before the wedding, he'd also insisted the solicitor begin setting up the jointure and settlement agreements she would receive out of his own funds in the event he predeceased her.

'Not that I have any plans of shuffling off this mortal coil,' he assured her. 'I didn't live through all that pain and suffering to trade this for a halo yet—not when the best part of surviving is about to begin.'

Waggling his eyebrow roguishly, he placed tickling little kisses on her hand that made her laugh and relax, for the moment, the tension within her that coiled tighter and tighter as the wedding approached.

No, she had no qualms about the character of man she was marrying. Just the institution itself—and the difficulties of keeping her emotions in check when living so close to the mesmerising Dominic Ransleigh.

One problem at a time, she told herself. First, she needed to formally settle her arrangement with the Hazletts.

Though too anxious about the school to want to delay their return to Suffolk by taking a wedding journey, she had agreed to remain in London a few days by themselves to settle into their new relationship. The best way not to worry about the ramifications of that relationship, she figured, was to spend that time enjoying the sensual freedom marriage would give them.

Now, *that* prospect she could view with enthusiasm.

After another knock, a beaming Aunt Amelia swept in. 'It's time, Theo, dear. How lovely you look!'

'I'll never be the beauteous daughter of a duke, but I hope I'll do,' she replied ruefully.

'You'll be yourself, and that's what Dominic Ransleigh wanted,' Aunt Amelia assured her.

I hope so, she thought as the small group descended the stairs.

As she entered the parlour, her eyes went immediately to Dom, who stood next to the priest and a gentleman in a Dragoon's uniform she didn't recognise. Dom, too, had the erect bearing of a soldier. But instead of colourful regimentals, he wore a black jacket over a cream waistcoat and black trousers, the jacket perfectly fitted, the sheen of the fabric elegant, and all of it looking spanking new, as if he'd just returned from his tailor. *'Dandy Dom' indeed,* she thought, awe and attraction rippling through her.

Then he saw her. A smile lighting his face, he murmured something to the priest, his gaze never leaving hers as he walked over to take her hand and kiss it. 'How lovely you look! Is that a new gown? I like it.'

'You're looking rather fine yourself. Did you fit in a visit to Bond Street?'

Dom laughed. 'I'm not sure whether my tailor was more gratified to receive a new order or horrified at trying to make a garment for a man with one arm that still fit to his standards of perfection.'

'He succeeded. Though you look equally splendid in an old hunting jacket.'

'You didn't seem so impressed when you met me that first day in the lane.'

'You were thinner then, and tired. Now you're…not.'

'I can't wait to show you how much I'm…not,' he murmured, before turning her towards the soldier who'd followed him. 'Who'd have thought I'd come to such an important day with all my cousins scattered who knows where? Even my uncle, who practically lives at the Lords, is out of town. I had to scour the clubs to find a friend to stand up with me. Miss Branwell, may I present Lieutenant Tom Wetherby, another stout member of the Royals.'

'Delighted, ma'am,' the Dragoon said, bowing. 'I'd kiss your hand, but Dom would skewer me with my sabre.'

Before she could reply, the priest waved to them. 'Time to take our places,' the lieutenant said, and ushered them back to the prelate.

Dom squeezed her suddenly trembling hand in his warm one. 'Trust me, Theo?' he murmured as he led her over.

'Y-yes.'

'Smile, then. You're supposed to be the happy bride—not a prisoner on the way to the guillotine. You'll have our guests think you don't really want to marry me.'

'I must smile, then. I can't have them thinking you anything but the most compassionate, understanding, helpful gentleman I've ever known,' she added, annoyingly close to tears.

'And wise. You could add wise. Witty, well read, liberal-minded.' He lowered his voice to a mock-seductive range and bent to whisper at her ear, 'And devastatingly attractive.'

'Modest, too,' she added with a chuckle, her nerves settling, as surely he'd meant them to. 'And altogether wonderful.'

And he was. She must do all she could to see he never

regretted taking up the cudgels in defence of his too-tall, too-opinionated, problem-encumbered spinster tenant.

Over the next few moments, they intoned the ancient words of the wedding service, Dom placed a plain band on her finger, and the priest pronounced them man and wife. When her perplexed expression afterward protested the kiss of the new bride that was practically chaste, he murmured, 'Wait until later.'

Then it was off to sign the parish register and into the dining room, where Aunt Amelia had assembled a bountiful repast for a small group of family and a few of her closest friends.

One of those turned out to be the formidable Lady Jersey, who cut her from the crowd and drew her away with the expertise of a Lake country sheepdog managing his herd. Leaning close, she murmured, 'I shall congratulate you, even though you cheated me of the amusement of watching you lead the suitors Amelia and I had chosen a merry dance! But I can't complain; you've pulled off a coup. Only a man as high in the instep as the Duke of Dunham would think his daughter could do better than a Ransleigh. No matter; I've invited the duke and the daughter to dine next week. I can't wait to share the details of your nuptials.'

She swept away to attach herself to the Dragoon, leaving Theo immensely relieved she'd got herself married before she was pulled into that lady's web of intrigue.

Still, as the afternoon wore on, she became increasingly anxious for the party to end. Her cheeks ached from smiling, her head ached from giving polite replies to congratulations and turning evasive answers to those brash enough to enquire about the brevity of their courtship. Dom had abandoned her to play the perfect bridegroom, circulating among the society ladies Aunt Amelia had invited, parcelling out attention equally, keeping them all nodding and laughing with his wit. It was the first time Theo had seen him work his charm in public, and his skill was impressive.

When he finally came back to claim her arm, she said, 'Now I'm sure the wedding was a mistake.'

His smile faded instantly. 'What do you mean?'

'The way you've bedazzled all Aunt Amelia's friends, you should have been a politician. I can see you now on the hustings, charming the masses.'

'All the Ransleigh men are bedazzling,' he tossed back. 'And I think we've been sociable long enough. Shall we leave? The staff at Alastair's town house has a cold supper ready for us whenever we like. If we get to it. I anticipate the meal we share first may last a very long time. I'm ravenous, and I've been waiting for it for ever.'

Desire spiralled though her. 'No more ravenous than I.' As he clasped her hand and led her over to Aunt Amelia to say their farewells, Theo hid a secret smile.

Oh, was she ravenous! And she couldn't wait to start proving it.

Less than an hour later, the carriage deposited them a short distance away at Dom's cousin Alastair's town house in Upper Brook Street. The travelling case with some of her clothes and toiletries had been sent over earlier, and Susan waited to attend her.

As Dom took her arm and walked her up the entry stairs, she was finally able to cast aside all her fears and embrace the one thing about this marriage she knew would be an unqualified success.

'You're trembling,' Dom murmured as they reached the floor where the bedchambers were located. 'You're not afraid, are you?'

Now, when the time had finally come to make all her imaginings real? 'Oh, no! I'm eager.'

She halted, making him stop beside her in the hallway.

She ran a finger over his lips, then slid it down his shirt to draw a line from his waistcoat down his trouser front, increasing the pressure as she descended. She smiled when she felt his member leap under her tracing finger. 'I think you're eager, too.'

After an inarticulate response, he kissed her. Joyously she tangled tongues with him, laving and retreating, teasing and withdrawing. Dom fumbled behind him for the door handle, walked them in and banged it closed, and kissing still, wrapped his arm around her and backed her towards the bed. When her legs touched the edge, he finally broke the kiss, panting. 'Wine, before I snuff out the candles?' he asked, gesturing towards the decanter on the night stand.

'You needn't snuff out the candles. I'd like to see… everything.'

'Certainly I would,' he said with a wry grin. 'I'm not so sure *you* should, though. Wouldn't want for my bride to faint with horror before I can even make her mine.'

Her teasing smile fading, she wanted nothing so much as to reassure him. 'Oh, Dom,' she said softly, 'don't you know I will see nothing but honour in your scars? And *be* honoured, that you've given me the right to touch them?'

He stood beside her, still looking uncertain. 'If you're sure.'

Snagging his cravat, she untied it and used the freed lengths to pull him down to the bed. Then, still in hat, gloves, gown and pelisse, she went down on her knees before him and wrenched open the buttons of his trouser flap.

His erection sprang free and he groaned as she took him in her gloved hands, smoothing the soft kidskin up and down his hard length before guiding him into her mouth.

She sampled the smooth slick head, nibbled at the ridge, slid him fully into her mouth.

'Theo—no—can't stand much more,' Dom gasped.

She paused, sliding him slowly, slowly, slowly free. 'You want me to stop?' she asked, and drew her tongue by infinitesimal millimetres across the head of his erection. 'Stop this?' She took him within and suckled gently. Withdrawing again, she said, 'Or this?' before plunging him deep.

Since by then he appeared to be beyond words, she took that as permission to begin a rhythmic pattern of sliding him deep, pulling him free then sliding him deep again.

Writhing against her, he tugged off her hat with one frantic hand, raked the pins from her hair and wrapped his fingers in the curly strands. A short time later, the tension in his body released as he reached his peak.

Afterward, he pulled her head against his torso and leaned over, embracing her, while his gasping breath and thundering heartbeat filled her ears.

A few moments later, when he'd regathered strength enough, he levered her up on the bed beside him. She tilted his head down for a long kiss. 'Much better than wine.'

He wrapped his arm around her, kissing the top of her head. 'Theo...merciful heavens...I never dreamed...'

She chuckled. 'I know. You see, I'm wonderfully inventive—' he groaned '—and I have a vivid imagination. Oh, so vivid! The nights I lay awake, dreaming of doing that...'

He smiled then. 'I could tell you something about nights and dreaming and imagining. But I'd rather show you.'

Positioning her at the edge of the bed, he knelt before her. He drew her face down for a soft, sweet kiss, and slipped his hand under her skirts to toy with her ankle.

Already thoroughly aroused by her ravishment of his body, she licked at his lips, seeking entry. He refused to open for her, kissing closed-mouthed as she laved and nuzzled.

Meanwhile, his stroking fingers slowly ascended her

leg, kneading and caressing the muscle of her calf, then cupping and fondling her knee. She gasped when he broke the kiss for a moment to lick his finger and apply its soft wet pressure to the sensitive skin behind her knee.

As he slowly worked his hand higher, her knees fell apart, her legs a boneless conduit of sensation from his stroking fingers down to her toes, up to where her centre throbbed. When he reached the velvety skin of her inner thighs, he finally, finally opened his mouth to her, and she surged within in a frantic slash of tongue and teeth.

By the time his fingers reached the crease where her thigh joined the soft curls of her mound, she was beyond kissing, her breath in gasps, her hands clutching his shoulders. She cried out when at last, at last, he glided one probing finger up and across the flesh of her centre, and moaned when he slid the finger within.

But before she could move her hips against it, desperate to reach completion, he pulled the hand away. She'd barely gasped out an inarticulate protest when he swept her skirts back and let his tongue take the path his fingers had just traced.

A few quick strokes of his tongue, and the tension that had been building through her peaked in an eruption of such intensity that for a moment, there was nothing but blinding light and heat and sensation.

When the cataclysm receded, she sagged and would have fallen flat back on to the bed, had Dom not supported her. Gently he held her up and eased her back against the pillows, then seated himself beside her. 'You're right. Much better than wine. But if we're going to talk about dreams and imaginings…' He grinned at her. 'I haven't yet begun.'

Theo lay her limp head upon his shoulder. 'This has already been the most erotic night of my life—and I'm not even undressed yet.'

With a tender look, Dom pressed a kiss in the centre of her forehead. 'Fear not, dear wife. The night has only begun.'

Some time in the early dawn hours, Dom awoke. In the moonlight drifting in from the window, he looked down at Theo, snuggled by his side, her hair a tangle of curls on the pillow, her bare shoulders showing above the bed linen she'd pulled up over her breasts.

Ah, her glorious breasts! Tasting and nibbling and teasing them had been one fantasy he'd been able to turn into reality this night. Also, the one of slowly undressing her, one piece of clothing at a time—and for this game, ladies had such a delightfully large number of garments to remove— tasting each bit of skin as he revealed it. Then another, of having them both naked and slick, kissing slowly as they explored each other with hands and mouths before she pulled him over her and urged him within and wrapped her legs around him to draw him deeper as he thrust again and again.

He'd expected Theo to be passionate, and the reality more than lived up to the dream.

Thank heavens for Jemmie! He must hire the best trainer in England to school the lad. But for the sergeant-major's son, he might have been halfway across England when Theo had been driven to marry in haste to secure her son and her orphans. Some other gentleman might have seen her, appreciated her, felt called to save and protect her.

The very idea of any other man marrying her, holding her, touching any bit of her, even to solve her problems, brought a fierce indignation welling up.

Theo was *his*.

He must be the luckiest man in England.

How wise he'd been on that journey to London, deciding to marry her straight away, with no delays for courting or manoeuvring around other gentlemen or second and third thinking. Marrying her felt right then, and felt even more absolutely right now.

The realisation settled over him then, not in a *coup de foudre* or a lightning strike, but with a calm sense of absolutely certainty.

He was *in love* with Theo Branwell. That was why deciding to marry her had been so easy and done with such confidence in its absolute rightness.

He looked down at her, shaken by the revelation, but filled with the sweetest sense of peace and delight. He wasn't sure when love had begun to curl its tendrils around his heart, growing so quietly he hadn't noticed, until now, when the mature length and strength of it covered his heart and soul completely.

He only knew, with same certainty he'd felt when he decided to marry her, that he loved her, and always would.

And she…liked him?

He frowned and shook his head. No, that would never do. He was almost certain she felt more strongly than that. But for some reason, she was afraid. He'd seen that nervous anxiety on her face a number of times since she accepted his proposal.

Why? Surely she knew he'd never hurt her, that he meant to cherish her. She'd several times affirmed that she trusted him.

Then he recalled the off-hand remark he'd made about marrying someone she did not love to 'punish' herself. Did she still think some sort of retribution for her mistake meant she had no right to be happy? Or, having been devastated by loss before, was she afraid of claiming a happiness she might lose again?

The death of a fiancé that placed her in such horrific circumstances would make anyone afraid to chance loving again. As for any lingering notion of punishment, constant affirmation of her worthiness from someone who knew of her past, and admired her for surviving it, might finally free her from any lingering hold it had upon her.

He should woo her, until she was assured of his love and secure enough to let go of the past and love again without fear. Until she believed in the depths of her soul that she was deserving of happiness. That he would always support her. That she would never again be left alone and desperate and in danger.

How best to reach her?

Beside him, Theo stirred. Opening groggy eyes to smile at him, she slid a hand up over his bare leg. As his member leapt in response, Dom knew he had his answer.

His Theo had no fear at all of love*making*. If he wooed her with words and bedazzled her with kisses, until she trusted the affection they shared was as deep and unending as their passion, he could bring her to acknowledge and eventually revel in loving him.

Then he truly would be the luckiest man in England.

He'd just have to think of ways to seduce her.

Ah, now *that* was a challenge he could embrace with enthusiasm!

Chapter Twenty

Two days later, Theo sat at the table in the breakfast room sharing a light repast with her husband.

Her *husband*…the fact of being wed still amazed her every time she thought of it.

Though they'd spent so much of their marriage thus far in the bedchamber, she felt her face flush every time one of the servants looked at her, as a footman did now before refilling her cup.

'That's all, Thomas, you may go,' Dom said. Grinning as he looked at her no doubt rosy cheeks, after the footman left the room, he said, 'It's all right, Theo, we're married now.'

'I could scarcely face Susan when I finally got back to my room yesterday at noon, when we'd arrived so early the previous evening! I apologised for having her wait so long to help me change. And I still feel…odd, knowing they all know what we've been doing. '

'They expect it. Maybe not so much of it…'

She felt her face heat further, and his grin turned into a chuckle before he took her hand and kissed it. 'My Theo. So calm and matter of fact in public—and such a siren in the bedchamber. Who dreamed I would be lucky enough to marry every man's secret fantasy? I'd be the envy of London, did anyone suspect.'

'Well, I trust you're not going to go announcing it in your clubs,' she said tartly, still feeling embarrassed.

'Certainly not! It's my secret—and my good fortune. I hope the last two days have made you as happy as they've made me.'

She smiled and squeezed his fingers before releasing them. 'I've been wonderfully…content.'

His smile wavered, as if that wasn't the answer he'd hoped for. Before she could figure out what else to say, he said, 'This will be our last day before we rejoin the others at your aunt's and prepare to leave London. Lady Coghlane urged me, and I think it wise, to complete purchasing a wardrobe for you before we go back to the country.'

'"Dandy Dom's" wife, after all, should look the part?' She made a face. 'Must we? I thought you didn't mind me riding about in my comfortable old habit.'

He laughed. 'I've wanted to have the dressing of you since the day we met. And the *un*dressing. Since I've managed that last several times, quite skilfully I thought, it's time to proceed to the former.'

'My old habit being a challenge—or an affront, as it is to Aunt Amelia?'

'A bit of both.'

'Sure you don't want to do more of the "undressing" first?' she asked, leaning over to give him a lingering kiss.

He reached up to hold her chin, prolonging the kiss, which now lacked the urgency of passion long denied, but was sweeter for the promise of passion to come—wherever and as often as they chose.

When he finally broke the kiss, Theo noted with gratification that Dom looked as flushed as she felt.

'Now, where were we?' he asked unsteadily. 'Ah, yes. Commissioning some new gowns and a new habit.'

Theo groaned. 'You *do* have a mind like a poacher's trap.'

'Did you think to distract me? Remember, I have a reputation to maintain.'

'Very well. But only if you promise me a ride in the park this afternoon.'

'It will have to be tomorrow. I've already made an important appointment for today—visiting Tattersall's to find a pony for a little boy.'

She drew back a little, surprised. 'A pony? When did Charles ask you about that?'

'The day I proposed, I asked his permission to marry you, and he said he would agree, as long as he got his pony—and I showed him how to arrange his soldiers in line of battle.'

Something softened and twisted in her heart as Theo realised Dom had thought to include her son in his vision for their marriage. *He really would be the protector and champion she and Charles both needed.* 'That was so kind of you. Even if he did take shameless advantage of the opportunity, the little rascal.'

'Enlightened self-interest, like Jemmie. I've got no suitable ponies at Bildenstone, so it would be best to find one for him here. We'll have a groom bring it back, while we take the carriage.'

Impulsively, she rose and went to hug him, gratitude and affection intensifying the connection she'd always felt to him. 'Thank you for accepting my son,' she whispered.

He caught one hand and kissed it. 'You and your son are one blood. I could no more marry one without embracing the other than you could marry me without inheriting my cousins as well—though, to your relief, none of them are yet near enough to irritate you. But be warned! Eventually, Max, Will and Alastair will be tripping over our threshold and taking over our sitting room.'

'I shall love to welcome them.'

'So, before Tattersall's—which, sadly, admits gentlemen only—we shall visit the modiste.'

'Very well—but I can't imagine anything more of a dead bore.'

'Oh, no, it will be tantalising. I can imagine you in—and out—of each gown. Then there are chemises, and stays, and stockings, and garters…'

'Chemises and stays and garters!' she echoed, scandalised. 'You cannot accompany me to buy those!'

'Why not? Because I'll be looking at you lasciviously the whole time?' he asked, grinning again—obviously enjoying her discomfort.

'It would be too intimate to view such apparel together, in front of total strangers,' she said stiffly, her face heating again at the thought.

'Very well.' He relented. 'Gowns only.'

'That *will* be a dead bore,' she muttered.

He caught her chin again. 'What will be the forfeit, if I prove you wrong?'

'You can have your wicked way with me—when we return, of course, not in the modiste's dressing room.'

'And here I thought you had imagination.' He sighed. 'I'll take your bargain, though. Did you bring with you the gown of Prussian blue *à la* Hussar?'

She looked at him blankly for a moment. 'You mean the dark-blue one with the double buttons and frogging on the front? Yes, Susan packed it.'

'Wear that one,' he said drily. 'While you're changing at the modiste's, I can imagine undoing all those little buttons.'

Chafing at having to waste their last morning together at a dressmaker's, Theo dutifully presented herself a half-hour later in the requested gown, and a short time after that, the hackney deposited them before the elegant shop of 'Madame Emilie'.

To Theo's chagrin, the shop girl who greeted them must have recognised Dom, for a moment later, the modiste herself hurried over in a flurry of curtsies. Welcoming him by name, she enquired about his injuries, expressed her joy at his recovery and her delight to see him back in her shop. After telling her what they were seeking—Theo mute through the whole exchange—Madame Emilie hurried off in pursuit of the latest copies of *La Belle Assemblée* and the materials Dom had requested.

'She greeted you like an unexpected bequest from a distant relation,' Theo murmured. 'Just how many mistresses have you dressed here?'

Dom laughed. 'Just one former fiancée—even wealthier than you, and much more interested in acquiring a wardrobe.'

'Madame must have been devastated when she heard you'd broken the engagement and gone off into the country.'

Merriment in his eye, Dom nodded. 'Probably saw half her projected yearly earnings disappear in the dust of my departing coach. We'll have to make it up to her.'

At that moment, the modiste returned. '*Eh, bien*, so we begin, yes? First, I must take your lady's measure.'

To Theo's embarrassment, Dom accompanied them to the dressing room, despite her motioning him out when the shopkeeper's back was turned.

Settling himself in the corner, he watched avidly as the dressmaker's assistant removed her garments, until she was standing before him clad only in chemise and stays. Her body grew tight and prickly as Dom's gaze followed every movement of the tape being drawn against her body, his eye darkening with desire.

It was almost as if it were his own fingers tracing over her skin, rather than a strip of numbered cloth.

By the time the measuring was completed, she was feeling hot and shaky. But there was more.

Seated again with Madame to discuss style, he *did* touch her. Sliding his hand over her shoulder and down her arm to demonstrate a desired cut and length of sleeve…sweeping a palm over her hip to indicate a fit of skirt… And when his fingers made a leisurely transit across her chest, the tips almost but not quite grazing her nipples as he outlined the depth and cut of the *décolletage*, it was all she could do to hold back a gasp.

Desire pulsing through her, relieved to be almost done, she was envisioning what she would do to him once she got him back to the town house when he announced it was time to choose the materials.

Bolts of fabrics were dutifully bought in.

First, he talked of colours—peach, apricot, honey. His voice and the heavy-lidded gaze he fixed on her made her picture biting into rich, ripe fruit, its perfume filling her senses, its juice sweet against her tongue.

Her eyes fixed on his mouth, she jumped when he took her hand and ran it across the subtle texture of the lute string. He unrolled some of the honey silk from its bolt and draped the material over her neck, slowly rubbing its sensual softness against her bare skin, from her chin to the tops of her breasts.

Her nipples hardened, and a moist, urgent throbbing started between her legs.

He moved to a velvet and then a lace, her intensely sensitised skin feeling every nuance of difference between softness and texture, weight and lightness as he drew them across her—as if he were making love to her with fabric.

She thought she would go mad with frustration and impatience.

When at last the assistant finished getting her back into her garments and the modiste left them, looking immensely pleased at the number of gowns they'd commissioned, Theo leaned over to whisper, 'What must she be thinking!?'

Dom shrugged, his heated gaze on her lips. 'She's French. She'll think I was seducing you.'

Her face burned with chagrin—but the idea of him practically making love to her in public was so immensely arousing, her mouth felt dry. 'If you ever shopped like this with anyone else, I'll murder you,' she finally managed to get out.

He grinned at her. 'Only with you. Most females require no assistance to enjoy shopping.'

By the time she was released from the torture of the shop to find a hackney, Theo was almost beyond speech. She scarcely knew what she replied to the idle chat he made during their short drive back to Upper Brook Street.

When they arrived, before Dom could say anything else, Theo took his hand and marched him straight upstairs to their bedchamber, where bright afternoon sun blazed through the windows.

Good; he'd be able to see everything clearly.

Time for the boot to go on the other foot.

'I never thought shopping would take so long,' she said as she closed the door behind them. 'Did you really find this garment so offensive?'

'It's not offensive. I rather like it.'

'But at the shop, you said you preferred something lower cut. To better display my breasts?'

He nuzzled her neck. 'Seeing more of those breasts is always a good thing.'

'Perhaps I should remove the gown, then. Will you help me?'

'Willingly.' To her satisfaction, his breath caught, his fingers fumbling with ties and laces as he freed her from the gown. When he'd helped her out of it, she swept a hand towards her stays. 'Are these too plain, do you think?'

'Absolutely,' he said promptly, obviously catching on to the game.

'Take them off as well.'

He swept a bow. 'As my lady commands.'

He undid them and Theo shrugged them off.

'What of this chemise? You'd prefer a new one, of finest linen, so fine you can see my body beneath it? These—?' She cupped her breasts, thumbing the nipples until they peaked. 'And this?' She slid a hand down to stroke over the dark curls at her mound.

'Yes,' he breathed, his gaze locked on her.

Theo untied the laces, pulled the garment over her head and let it drift to the floor beside her.

Sitting abruptly on the edge of the bed, Dom watched her intently, his chest rising and falling, his lips moist and parted.

Feeling triumphant, powerful, and oh-so-female, Theo kicked off her slippers and walked over to him, naked but for her stockings and garters.

She stopped before him and put one foot up on his knee, opening her most intimate area to his view. She took his limp hand and stroked it over the embroidery of the garter on her unbent leg.

'These, I think are pretty enough. Don't you agree?'

A garbled sound issued from his lips.

Tightening her grip on his hand, she drew it straight up her inner thigh, across the tight curls of her mound, and dipped his index finger into the slickness between her legs. Shuddering as his guided touch further heightened her arousal, she moved his finger to stroke her there, again and again through the increasing wetness.

'You see what you do to me?' she whispered.

Apparently beyond speech, he made no answer.

Guiding his now moist finger, she traced a wet path down the inner thigh of the bent leg until it reached her other garter. 'This, too, I think is…adequate.'

With a growl, Dom grabbed her waist and levered her on to the bed. Sliding her feet up so both legs were fully bent, he parted her knees to open her to him completely, then laved with his tongue where his finger had just been.

Theo gripped the bedclothes, her heartbeat stampeding as he licked and nuzzled. She twisted under him, trying to angle him deeper, inside her, and he murmured at her to be still.

Nibbling and laving gently, he inched closer, until finally, when she thought she could stand it no longer, moving to her pulsing centre. By the time he thrust his tongue deeper, moving in long, hard strokes within, then without to caress the little nub, she was gasping. It took only a few more strokes to bring her to shattering climax.

Afterward, as she lay panting, scarcely conscious, she dimly heard the rustle of him loosening his shirt, unbuttoning his trouser flap. Uttering a long moan of pleasure, she felt the smooth head of his manhood against her slickness. So limp, she was unable to tease him further, she closed her eyes, the waves of pleasure building again as he caressed with his hardness the damp flesh his tongue had just pleasured.

Finally, as she breathed his name, he entered her. She thought he intended to be gradual and slow, but he must have been as transported as she, for after two short strokes, he thrust deep. She wrapped her legs around his back to urge him on, harder, faster, until he cried out and the hot press of his seed spilling deep inside her brought her over the edge again with him.

A long time later, after drifting on a languid cloud of satiation, she came to earth to find herself tucked against his good shoulder.

'I'll never think of shopping the same way again,' she murmured.

'If that is how you pay a forfeit, we should make wagers daily.' After kissing her forehead, he said, 'I thought we should make a short detour before we return to Suffolk.'

She shifted to look up at him. 'I don't really need a wedding trip. Nor do I want to leave the school on its own much longer. I still have some apprenticeships for the boys to set up with the local craftsmen.'

'It would be a brief stop. Before we go back to Bilden-stone, we should take Charles to Hazlett Hall to meet the viscount and his lady.'

When Theo gasped, he said, 'Confront the ogres in their den. Or, less melodramatically, forge the agreement for how we mean to go on. You were prepared to bind yourself to a stranger with no hope of future happiness to safeguard your relationship with your son. I think it's important that we hammer out a formal arrangement with the Hazletts now, so you can be easy about his future—and ours.'

'You…you would deal with the viscount for me?'

'Of course. I'm your husband, Theo. I have that right now. And didn't I promise to defend you? I can't think of anything you are more eager to protect than your relation-ship with your son. So let's accomplish that now.'

She'd known she would have to confront Charles's grandparents again, probably soon. But that Dom would suggest it, and offer to take her there and stand as her champion in dealing with the only people who could threaten to take Charles from her—that, she had never envisioned.

'I don't mean to meddle in what you see as your business,' he continued when she didn't immediately reply, 'but wouldn't settling this now put your mind at ease?'

Relief and gratitude filled her. 'Oh, yes! It would mean a great deal to have it settled. And please, "meddle" all you like!'

He smiled at her, the look so tender her chest grew tight and she had to hold back tears, the affection she struggled against threatening to engulf her.

'Plan on it, then. I don't want you to worry about losing Charles ever again. I promise, I'll make sure that never happens. Trust me, Theo?'

'I trust you,' she whispered. *And I'm very much afraid I love you, too.*

Chapter Twenty-One

A week later, their carriage approached the pastoral vista before the old Tudor manor of Hazlett Hall. Dom watched Theo closely, a curious mixture of jealousy and concern warring in his chest.

For one, he'd like to put to an end for good and all any lingering connection to the man she'd loved so deeply. On the other, he knew that as long as Charles remained of primary concern—and that would be for ever—he would have to deal with her memories of the man who'd sired him. And for her to truly be open to finding happiness again, she would have to be assured of keeping her son.

He'd already displaced Marshall Hazlett in her arms. Though he really didn't begrudge her fond memories of her child's father, he hoped to soon rival the man in her affections. But securing the boy's future he could and would settle today.

Clasping and unclasping her hands, she gazed out the window at the manor house, Charles dozing by her side. Attuned now to signs of her nervousness, he captured one of her restless fingers.

'Steady, Theo. Everything will work out as you wish. I promise you.'

She nodded. 'I'm so very grateful you offered to accompany me. It seems so…strange, coming here, seeing the place where Marshall grew up, where I once thought I'd return as his bride.'

'Forgive me for preferring that you're coming here as mine.'

She smiled, a little forlornly. 'Forgive *me* for letting myself be dragged into the past. I'm not sorry that he was so large a part of it—and I am very, very glad that you are my future.'

'Glad' wasn't exactly what he was hoping for, but under the circumstances, he would have to settle for it. Giving her a kiss to signify his approval of that sentiment, he leaned her back. 'What do you know of Viscount Hazlett's feelings about Charles? I suspect his opinion will have more impact as to how we resolve this than his wife's.'

'I really don't know anything. Lady Hazlett spoke of her own longing to reclaim a part of her blood, but she gave me no sense of how enthusiastic, or resistant, her husband was to that desire.'

Dom could see apprehension in the furrow of her brow. 'We shall soon see. And don't worry, sweeting, regardless of his position, we will agree to nothing that does not guarantee Charles remains with you.'

A few minutes later, the carriage drew up before the entrance, and Dom gave Theo's hand a reassuring squeeze. He'd sent a note ahead to Viscount Hazlett, so he wasn't surprised when the butler, who escorted them through a timbered great hall into a wainscoted withdrawing room, informed him that Lord and Lady Hazlett would receive them shortly.

While Charles delightedly examined the carvings of griffins and gargoyles on the roof beams, Theo paced before the fire. Dom watched her, wishing there was more he could do to ease her anxiety—about the interview to come, and for the heartache she must inevitably feel at knowing her son, but for his father's early death the viscount's rightful heir, had no legal right to the home whose sculptures so fascinated him.

The door opened, admitting a tall, balding man whose grey hair might once have been fair, and a slender, still lovely lady—who had eyes for no one but the boy.

Hearing them enter, Charles halted his inspection and looked over as Lady Hazlett walked towards him, a tremulous smile on her face. 'Welcome to our home, my dear!'

Dom had to admire the lad's manners, for he gave her a proper bow before saying, 'You came to visit us at Thornfield, didn't you?'

'I did,' she affirmed.

'I have my pony now. When you visit again, I'll be able to ride ever so well.'

'I'm sure you shall,' Lady Hazlett said. Holding out her hand, she said, 'May I introduce you to someone? My husband, Lord Hazlett.'

Charles didn't look impressed, but he took her hand and let her walk him over to the gentleman who'd stopped abruptly just inside the room, his gaze locked on his wife and the boy.

The viscount was scrutinising the child as avidly as Charles was inspecting him. Dom watched his face as scepticism gave way to surprise, and as the boy drew closer, he paled and shuddered visibly.

'Lord Hazlett, may I present Charles,' his wife said.

Charles made another bow. 'Pleased to meet you, my lord,' he piped.

Dom turned his attention to Theo, who had been observing the proceedings with anxious eyes. Nothing the highest stickler could find to fault in the boy's manners so far, Dom thought—he was the picture of a well-brought-up gentleman's son.

First hand to Theo.

Lady Hazlett looked back over her shoulder at Dom and Theo. 'Mr and Mrs Ransleigh, forgive my lack of manners. I wished Lord Hazlett to see Charles before we proceeded any further. You both are also very welcome in our home. Now, if you will permit, Mrs Ransleigh, I'd like to take Charles up to the nursery while you speak with Lord Hazlett.'

Getting the child out of the way so he couldn't over-hear anything he shouldn't, Dom thought approvingly. It seemed Lady Hazlett had the boy's welfare at heart, then.

Turning back to Charles, Lady Hazlett said, 'We have some very fine toy soldiers in the nursery. And some balls and games and a toy horse that your f—that other children enjoyed very much.'

'Soldiers?' Charles echoed. 'Oh, I would like to see them. May I go, Miss Theo?'

'Of course, Charles. Mind your manners, now.'

'I always do. You know that,' he said calmly before trotting out with Lady Hazlett.

Lord Hazlett stared out the open door until the pair was out of sight. Still pale, he started when he turned back to them, as if surprised there was still someone in the room.

'I'm Hazlett, of course,' he said belatedly, bowing to Theo and holding out a hand to Dom. 'You're Swynford's nephew, aren't you?' Turning to Theo, he said, 'So you're the woman my son meant to wed?' Glancing towards the door through which Charles had just exited, he said, 'A pity you didn't bother to get your marriage lines before you proceeded to that.'

Theo's chin jerked up and her eyes turned cold. 'Yes, isn't it? But since that guarantees the child has no claim on you, we will just collect him and take our leave.'

Before Dom, in a fury, could utter something blighting and lead her away, the viscount held up a hand. 'I'm sorry, that was unkind. I must ask you to forgive an old man's shock…and pain.' He sighed. 'But for a Frenchman's bullet, or a few weeks' delay, I'd not be facing the prospect of turning the home of my ancestors over to a cousin, instead of the son of my son.'

'There's nothing anyone can do to change the laws that prevent Charles from inheriting,' Dom said. 'But if you'd like to salvage some relationship with the son of your son, we're prepared to discuss it—as long as you treat my wife with respect.'

'My apologies, Mrs Ransleigh,' the viscount said. 'There will be no living with my wife if we don't reach some agreement. Won't you take a seat? I'll have Sanders bring wine.'

Giving Theo a reassuring look, Dom led her to the sofa, their host seating himself in the wing chair opposite. 'I have to admit, I didn't really believe all that nonsense Tremaine spouted when he visited here. A nasty piece of work, that one, and his father before him. It angered me to have him lead Emily on—she's never stopped mourning the loss of all her chicks, and to have him setting her up for more heartache! Which is what I thought you'd done, too, young lady, when she visited you. But she's right; the boy is the image of Marshall at that age.'

'Why would I lead her on? Since having anyone question the already accepted story of Charles's parentage would put him at risk, I should probably, by rights, have denied the story and turned her away. But I could see how much it would ease the pain of Marshall's loss for her to know his son—and I couldn't.'

'It's hard for me to forgive you for spinning such a yarn about the boy's father, keeping us in ignorance of his existence for so long. True, I can't pretend to understand what you faced when you found yourself increasing, with Marshall dead and you not yet married. But how convenient for your reputation, to have a dead man's dead son's name to claim for my grandson.'

As Theo flinched under the harsh words, Dom stood up, a hand on her arm. 'Another speech like that,' he said with cold fury, 'and I'll take my wife and the boy and you'll never see or hear from him again.'

The fire died out in the viscount's eyes. 'I beg your pardon—again, Mrs Ransleigh.'

Theo gave a short nod, and Dom sat back down.

'What I did, I did to protect Charles,' Theo said, her eyes going distant, as if she were reliving the events. 'If all I'd cared about was my own good name, I could have left him at the convent, as the sisters urged. I'd confessed my sins and received absolution, they said, but if I took the child back with me, my shame would become known, and society would never forgive it. But right from birth, Charles was so fair. Even if some Portuguese peasant wanting a sturdy son took him in, he'd always look like a foreigner. Always be an outsider. I thought, even as a bastard, he would fare better in his homeland. Stumbling upon an identity as Everely's dead son was never what I'd planned. And he was my *son*, mine and Marshall's! How could I abandon him in a foreign land?'

'Well, that coil can't be unspooled now. But even as a bastard, we would have accepted him, loved him, found a place for him.'

'How could I have known that? I couldn't risk exposing him, only to be rejected—and then have him grow up with a taint on his name.'

'You have your chance now, Lord Hazlett,' Dom interrupted. 'Learning about him today, or four and a half years ago, wouldn't have made any difference; under law, he could never inherit the title or the entailed portion of your estate. You can still leave him whatever you wish that isn't entailed, and when he's old enough, he'll be told of his true lineage. If you do want him, why not just enjoy sharing that?'

'Aye, that's what my wife counselled. Loving him should be easy enough. He's the image of my dear b-boy,' he said, his voice breaking.

'He was dear to me, too,' Theo said, tears glittering in her eyes.

Dom put his hand on her shoulder, wanting her to feel his silent support. 'They are both under my protection now,' he said evenly, but with a warning in his voice. 'Unlike your son, I managed to get a ring on her finger. I'd appreciate your support of the plan my wife and yours agree upon, but if you attempt to harass her, we'll raise the boy without you. You have no legal claim to either of them.'

The viscount met his steady gaze. 'Do you mean to dictate terms to me?'

'Not at all. I'm merely reminding you of our respective positions. Treat my wife with the courtesy and respect owed to her as the woman your son loved and the mother of your grandson. As part of my duty to secure her happiness, I'm prepared to respect her wishes about letting you and your wife see the boy and draw him into your lives. As long as you never attempt to cut Theo out of this. Or disparage her in any way.'

Lord Hazlett looked back at Theo. 'You seem to have found a champion.'

She gave Dom a look of affection and gratitude. 'I have.'

'About time she had one,' Dom muttered.

'Very well. Why don't you stay a few days,' the viscount said, addressing himself once again to Dom, 'while my wife and yours work out the details of sharing Charles? If that is agreeable to you, Mrs Ransleigh?'

Dom looked over at Theo.

'Anxious as I am to get back to Suffolk, I suppose we could spare two days,' she said. 'For Charles.'

She couldn't be more anxious than he was, Dom thought. Anxious to get her away from things that mired her in the past, unable to move into the future. *Their* future. He couldn't wait to get her back to Bildenstone Hall, where he could continue wooing—and seducing—his new wife. Every day he spent with her, it grew more important to him to persuade her to let go of fear and pain and embrace the future, loving only him.

'I should like to join Lady Hazlett and Charles now,' Theo said, breaking into his abstraction.

'I'll have Henry show you up,' Lord Hazlett said. Turning to Dom, he said, 'Would you like a stroll about the grounds? There's a fair vista from the back terrace. I seem to recall you breed hunters. I'd invite you to the stables, but I sold off all mine after…after Edward died.'

His eldest son and heir had been killed in a hunting fall, Dom knew. 'Having been cooped up for hours in a coach, I would enjoy a walk. Perhaps you could tell me about selling your hunters. I have some to dispose of as well.'

As they walked out, Dom felt confident the two ladies who loved Charles the most would quickly come to terms over the logistics of sharing his life.

Then came Bildenhall, and the final conquest of his bride's heart.

Chapter Twenty-Two

A week later, the carriage came to a stop outside the school—Theo, in her eagerness, having begged Dom to let her visit the children before returning to Thornfield.

Smiling, he watched as she sprang out the carriage door almost before the wheels had stopped.

Nor was she the only anxious one. As soon as she descended, Jemmie ran out of the building, followed by the others.

The air rang with choruses of 'Miss Theo! Miss Theo!' Maria, ever silent, raced over and threw her arms around Theo's waist. Soon she was surrounded by a laughing, chattering group of children.

'Yes, I'm back. No, I'll not be leaving again,' she replied to the questions being peppered at her.

'Did you come back married?' Jemmie asked.

Blushing a little, she said, 'Yes, I did.'

Seeing that as his cue, Dom came over to take her hand. 'I asked Miss Theo to marry me, and she did me the honour of accepting my suit. We were wed in London, about two weeks ago now.'

'We had a big party,' Charles inserted.

'Oh, I like parties! Why didn't we get to come?' Anna asked.

'It's a very long coach ride,' Theo explained. 'I thought you'd prefer having a party here. Miss Andrews, could you grant a short holiday, so I may get reacquainted with the children?'

'Of course, Miss—Mrs Ransleigh. My heartiest congratulations to you both!'

While the children closed in around her again, Jemmie approached Dom and held out his hand, which Dom shook solemnly.

'Thank you for helpin' her out.'

'It was my pleasure.' *Oh, if you only knew how much!*

'Guess she don't need to wait for me to grow up no more,' he said wistfully, his eyes on Theo.

The teacher walked up to them. 'Jemmie, could you help me carry some of the books to the cupboard?'

Eagerly, the boy turned to the blonde, blue-eyed, apple-cheeked Miss Andrews—who was only a handful of years older than Jemmie. 'Sure can, miss.' From the flush on his face as he took the books, Dom speculated the lad might soon find another candidate to replace Theo as the lady he wanted to protect and care for.

Before the teacher could lead him inside, Charles came trotting up. 'Can I help, too? I missed you, Jemmie!'

The older boy smiled and tousled his hair. 'Sure, scamp. I missed you, too.'

With the girls still clustered around Theo, Georgie came over to tug at her skirt.

'Farmer Jamison came to the school, Miss Theo. He said I can come work with him. Will you talk with him tomorrow? He said I can help him put wheat seeds in the meadow!'

'Of course, Georgie. I'll ride over tomorrow. Today, I'll be getting resettled at home.'

'Ready?' Dom asked, holding out his hand.

She looked fondly at the children, whom Miss Andrews was calling back into the building. 'Ready.'

He helped her into the coach. Charles having begged to remain at the school with his friends, with Mr Blake to drive him home later, they set off for Thornfield Place.

'I know it sounds ridiculous,' Theo said after she'd snuggled on to the seat beside him, 'but while we were still in London, I was so caught up in the wedding…and what came after, and then completely occupied by the task of settling things with the Hazletts about Charles, and then thinking about the school and the children on the way back to Suffolk, I've only just begun considering what to do about Thornfield. I imagine you'll want your wife to reside at your home.'

Dom smiled. 'That's generally how it's done.'

'I'd thought to keep the staff at Thornfield for the duration of the lease, even though, after the first week or so, we will no longer be living there. Just because my circumstances changed so suddenly, it's not fair to deprive them of jobs they expected to sustain them for at least the next year—'

She halted with a frown. 'Though I suppose you now control any lease written in my name?'

'Under the law, probably. But I assured you from the beginning you were to have a free hand with the school and any of your properties you wish to control, as well as the funds set aside for you.' He grinned. 'Only now, you can spend my funds, too.'

'Careful what you offer,' she warned, her expression teasing. 'I might decide the school needs a stable for Jemmie to train in, or a forge for the boys to learn blacksmithing.'

Dom groaned. 'Which would doubtless prove more expensive than jewellery or gowns. I knew a wife was going to cost me, one way or another.'

'This one will try to cost you as little as possible,' she said, suddenly serious.

He tipped up her chin to give her a kiss. 'This one is worth whatever she costs.'

'I hope you'll always think so,' she said, her voice gruff.

'I will,' he assured her. 'Once we pick up some things at Thornfield, you will join me at Bildenstone tonight, I hope? If you absolutely insist, we can stay at Thornfield, but I'd much prefer to carry my bride across the threshold of her room in the house that will be her home for the rest of her life.'

She nodded. 'I did plan on that, though I think I'll let Charles stay at Thornfield with Constancia for a few days. All his things are there, and it will be less disrupting for him to take the move in stages.'

'He won't stay there long when he realises his pony is in the stables at Bildenstone.'

'You're probably right,' Theo said with a smile. 'I also thought you might like us to have our first few nights in your home to ourselves.'

He gave her a quick kiss. 'I definitely like the sound of that!'

They stopped briefly at Thornfield. While a maid ran up to collect some of her things, Theo spoke with the butler and the housekeeper, who passed along their congratulations and the staff's—with rather anxious looks, Dom thought, until Theo assured them their positions were secure for the duration of the lease. Expressing their relief at that, and their disappointment that they'd no longer be able to personally serve so kind and understanding a mistress, they sent the bridal couple off with their good wishes.

A short time later, the coach finally reached their destination. As Dom gave Theo his arm up the steps, she halted, looking wide-eyed at the ivy-covered brick front. 'I know I've been here before, but it's different, somehow—coming here as if I belong.'

'You do belong now. Here, and with me. Always,' he assured her.

Then Wilton opened the door, his worn face breaking into a rare smile as he ushered them in. 'Welcome back, Mr Ransleigh—and Mrs Ransleigh. Congratulations, sir, on acquiring so lovely and accomplished a bride!'

Mrs Greenlow rushed up then, making Dom suspect the household had been lying in wait for them. 'Welcome back, master and mistress! Mr Blake sent one of the farm boys to let us know you'd returned. I took the liberty of arranging a small feast in honour of your homecoming. And, Mistress, if it pleases you, I'd like to suggest that Nancy, our senior housemaid, act as your lady's maid.'

'With the new wardrobe you commissioned soon to arrive, you'll be needing a maid to keep it in order,' Dom said, eyeing Theo, who made a face at him behind the housekeeper's back.

'Thank you for your thoughtfulness, Mrs Greenlow,' she said to the housekeeper. 'I'm sure Nancy will be exemplary.'

'Shall you proceed to the small dining room?' Wilton asked. 'I believe Cook had the meal ready to serve whenever you returned.'

Dom exchanged a look with Theo. Though he would rather show his wife up to her new rooms and make her at home in the most intimate way possible, he knew they couldn't disappoint their excited retainers.

'A feast?' Theo whispered to him as she took his arm.

'Eat quickly,' he replied with a rueful look.

And so they did, trying to do justice to the multiple courses Cook presented, complete to wine and wedding cake.

* * *

At last they finished, thanked the staff and bid them goodnight, and Dom was able to escort Theo upstairs.

'The wedding celebration they prepared for us was thoughtful, but we'll want to host a larger gathering for all the staff—and the neighbourhood,' he told her as they climbed the stairs.

Theo groaned. 'I hadn't thought of that, but I suppose you're right. At least I'll be able to employ the talents of the Thornfield staff in the preparations. We can make it a large enough affair that the children from the school can attend, too.'

'You can introduce them to Lady Wentworth,' Dom said with a chuckle. 'Now, that's an event I'll look forward to!'

A moment later, they reached his chamber. Dom paused outside his door. 'This will be a little more awkward than it would have been a year ago, but if you wrap your arms around my neck, I think we can manage.'

Smiling tremulously, she obligingly reached up and clasped her hands behind him. Going up on tiptoe to kiss him, she said, 'You've guaranteed my respectability by making me the wife of the most important man in the county, secured the future of my son, and protected my orphans. I'd do anything for you.'

Let yourself love me, then, Dom thought.

Inside the door, he carried her to the bed. Undressing her tenderly, he kissed each bit of flesh revealed, making that erotic journey more slowly than he had the first time, wanting her to feel to the marrow of her bones how much she was cherished.

In the aftermath of loving, he clasped her to his side, both of them panting and spent. His whole heart expanding with peace and joy, he couldn't imagine life without her; couldn't imagine any other woman in her place.

He ached to say the words, but he knew, when he reached the point of confessing his love, she needed to be nearly there, too, or he'd frighten her off, like trying to loop a halter over a colt not yet ready to be led.

Not yet. But soon.

Easing her against the pillows, he said, 'I shall have to rustle out Mother's jewels from whatever vault they were put in after my parents' death. There's a ring that's always given to Ransleigh brides, and then there are the Ransleigh rubies. A magnificent set, Mama always wore them for special occasions.'

Theo shook her head. 'Coming to Bildenstone, a wedding feast, carrying me over the threshold, now your mama's ring and jewels... Somehow, being married seems more real and *permanent* here.'

'It is real and permanent,' he said with a grin. 'No trial period, remember? We're yoked in harness for life now.'

'I hope you'll never regret it. I know I'll never stop being grateful.'

Dom tried not to wince. He wanted so much more than *gratitude* from Theo. 'I won't regret it.'

'Would you like to come with me when I call on Farmer Jamison tomorrow?'

'I would. His holding is known to be so prosperous and it's one of the few farms I haven't yet visited.'

Yawning, she sank back against the pillows. He followed her down to give her a kiss. 'Don't think you're going to sleep just yet.'

'Oh, Dom! It was a very long carriage ride today.'

'I'm thinking of another ride.' He moved his fingers to caress one breast, then the other, while she stirred and murmured under his hand. 'This one's just beginning.'

And it was...the seduction would continue, until he won his heart's desire—all of *her* heart.

* * *

The next morning, Dom sat at ease in the saddle outside the stables at Bildenstone, waiting for Theo to join him. A feeling of joy and well-being suffused him, a contentment that went far beyond the peace of last night's lovemaking. He had a fine home, a lovely wife, good land that, with the projects for improvement he'd read about at Holkham, he looked forward to making better. And an exciting new endeavour to begin, as soon as he completed the sale of his hunters.

For a man who, a few short months ago, wasn't sure he was going to survive, he was surrounded with blessings.

Theo exited the stable and rode up. 'Thank you for having Firefly brought over.'

'I thought you'd prefer your own mount to anything left in my stables—which is not much, now.'

'I see Charles's pony arrived safely, too.' She chuckled. 'You're right, once Charles learns the pony is here, he'll have Constancia hustled out of Thornfield's nursery and on the road to Bildenstone in a flash.'

'Mrs Greenlow already has their rooms prepared.'

'Will you visit any other farms after we meet with Mr Jamison?'

'Just him today. I'm looking forward to meeting with the tenants, seeing if I can persuade them to implement some of the techniques I saw and read about at Holkham. I'll also ask around to see who's best suited to take over Winniston's duties as steward. Though if I can't find anyone, Thomas Coke said he knew of several young men he could recommend. I'll probably consult my cousin Alastair, too. He has a fine estate in Devonshire. I'll have to take you there; it's a beautiful part of England.'

'I'd like that, once the school is fully settled. Which is where I'd like to ride first, to see Charles and check on the children, if you're agreeable.'

'I'm agreeable to anything that pleases my wife.'

She gave him a naughty grin. 'Careful, now! I shall recall that phrase and use it against you.'

They rode in companionable silence, Dom taking the opportunity to admire Theo on horseback. He loved watching her, the smooth line of her figure leaning over her mount, the soft tones as she crooned to her mare, her hands stroking its neck. The horse obviously liked it—and Dom couldn't blame her; he loved that soft voice and those hands touching him, too.

He caught himself before he could drift into reliving their latest love-play—an exercise that would tempt him to abandon plans to meet farmers and look instead for a secluded dell. A sudden memory recurred, and he grinned.

There might be occasion today to fit in both.

Theo looked up then, saw him staring, and coloured. 'What?' she asked, patting at her hat. 'Have I a curl coming loose? A leaf on my skirt?'

'No, your habit is perfection. I just like looking at you.'

Her eyes softened. 'Not half so much as I enjoy looking at you.'

He raised his eyebrow. 'All of me?'

Her look turned wicked. 'Oh, especially *all* of you.'

'I shall keep that in mind for later. You mentioned you wanted to explore the possibility of setting up other apprenticeships? We could ride to see the masters together.'

Her face brightened. 'I'd like that! You provide excellent counsel and advice.'

For the rest of the ride, they discussed which craftsman's skills might enhance the learning experience for the children. Arriving at the school, mindful of the disruption their arrival caused yesterday, they waited quietly until they heard Miss Andrews dismiss the children for a break.

They came running out, exclaiming as they saw their mentor.

While Theo chatted with the girls, Jemmie came up to Dom.

'Mr Jeffers talked with me when he come to school the other day. He told me you might be lookin' into breeding some draught horses. If'n you do, could you let me help you?'

'You'd rather do that than apprentice at a racing stud?' Dom asked curiously.

Jemmie shrugged. 'What do the likes of me have to do with them fast horses and the toffs that own 'em? Some fancy gentlemen winnin' or losin' more blunt than I'll see my whole life on which one comes across a line first! Naw, I'd rather know the horses I bred ploughed Jamison's field faster, or let the neighbours finish their ploughin' with the horses still havin' stamina enough left to do Widow Blackthorn's fields, too.'

'I haven't completed purchasing all the stock yet, but when I do, yes, I'll let you help.'

'Thank you, Mr Ransleigh.' Jemmie grinned. 'I knew I done the right thing when I sent you after Miss Theo.'

After Theo finished her conversation and gave Charles a hug, they remounted and headed through the Home Wood to the northern boundary of Bildenstone estate, where Jamison's fields were located.

They received a warm welcome from the farmer's wife, who invited them to sit and have some cool cider while she sent one of her daughters to tell her husband, out ploughing in the furthest field, that visitors had arrived. The farmer himself hurried up a few minutes later.

'First, may I offer my congratulations to you and your lady,' Jamison said.

'Thank you. We were wed in town, at the home of my

wife's aunt, but we plan a grand party soon so that all of Bildenstone's tenants can celebrate with us.' Dom kissed Theo's hand, making her blush. 'I'm a very lucky gentleman.'

'Aye, so folks say! They admire what you've done fixing up the old barn as a school, Mrs Ransleigh, and offering jobs to the many that need them. Now me, I've the opposite problem—fields to work, and all daughters but for my newborn. So I'd be right pleased to hire young Georgie to help me. Doesn't know a turnip seed from a carrot yet, but he's eager, and he'll learn.'

'He'll continue lessons at the school in the afternoons,' Theo said, 'but I'd see he was driven out to help you in the mornings first. Shall we have him begin next week? Good!' she said as the farmer nodded. 'Thank you, Mr Jamison, for giving him a chance.'

'Be my pleasure, Mrs Ransleigh.'

'Our thanks to your wife for the cider. It was delicious!' Theo said.

'Honoured to have you stop by, ma'am.'

They walked back to collect their horses, grazing in the nearby meadow, and a few minutes later, waved goodbye and set off towards Bildenstone Hall.

'Pleased to have the business with Georgie settled?' Dom asked.

'Yes. If I can find places for the others at positions that interest them, doing useful things, I'll be even more pleased. As Papa would be, too.' She gave him a mischievous look. 'Even if establishing a school for the orphans wasn't exactly his dying wish.'

'He'd be proud of you, Theo. I'm proud of you.'

She flushed at his praise. 'As I am proud of you. I heard you mention to Jemmie that you might start breeding farm horses. Do you think that would hold your interest?'

'The fascination of breeding is in studying characteristics, seeing which will transfer, which will not. If I ended up with an animal that would help more farmers feed themselves and their neighbours, that would be not so bad a result.

'I think it would be a wonderful one!'

'It is good to be well thought of by one's wife.' *Even better to be loved,* he thought. But with admiration, gratitude, and trust, love should soon follow…shouldn't it?

'You said you'll have to go to Newmarket?'

'Yes. On my last trip, I arranged the details of the sale with the stable manager; he'll begin setting it up as soon as the horses arrive from Upton Park. I'll need to go to supervise it—and purchase the sorrels and trotters to start the breeding project.'

'Will you be away long?'

'Perhaps a week or so. Will you miss me?'

'Very much.'

'Maybe we should get ahead while we can, then.' *And maybe it was time for another try at seduction…*

Halfway through the Home Woods, Dom pulled up his mount near a small stream that ambled along the east side of the road. 'Shall we let the horses have a drink? We could sit there under one of those trees you so admire.'

She chuckled. 'I'd like that.'

Dismounting under a large oak, they let the horses go to the water. Dom leaned back against the tree trunk, pulling Theo to him for a long, slow kiss.

'Maybe it's time to fetch the horses and get back to Bildenstone,' she suggested, heat in her eyes as she trailed fingers down his chest to his breeches. He groaned when she touched him, already hard and ready. 'It appears you're definitely eager to return.'

'Or we could stay. Isn't there something erotic about the sibilant trickle of water over stone?' he asked, reaching under the jacket of her habit to caress her breasts as he kissed her again.

For a moment, Theo responded, opening her mouth to him. But as he started on the buttons of her jacket, she pulled away.

'No, Dom, not here.' She pushed away from him and crossed her arms over her breasts, creating a distance between them that was like a sudden slap after the intimacy of the previous moment.

'Loving under the stars was what started all the misery. That and Tremaine spying on us,' she whispered.

Dom put out a hand to steady her. 'You're safe here, Theo. Not on foreign soil with threats all around. We're on my land. It's private. No army of reprobates to spy on us.

'There might be a gamekeeper. If he saw me naked, he'd be so shocked, he might shoot himself.'

'No, he'd think he'd seen a vision. A forest nymph. *My* forest nymph. I'll not try to persuade you into this, if it makes you uncomfortable. But it's not just that. These last few weeks, since our wedding, I've seen you smiling, as if almost brimming with happiness, and then you…stop yourself. The smile fades and you…turn inward. As if you think you don't deserve to be happy. Life, love, is a *gift*, Theo. It's too rare and precious to turn away from.'

'I'm…frightened to trust it, Dom,' she whispered. 'If I let myself go and lost again, I'd be desolated. I can't go through that.'

'We can't keep ourselves safe from whatever lies ahead,' he argued. 'Ponsonby was standing right next to Wellington at Waterloo when that cannonball took off his leg—and not a hair on Old Hookey's head was even ruffled. Life is random, unpredictable—and never safe. Isn't it preferable to embrace every joy while you have it, than to shut yourself off for fear of losing it? You're the bravest girl I know. Don't hold yourself back!'

When she shook her head and pulled away, exasperated and driven by need, Dom cried, 'I love you, Theo! Can't you see that? I know you care for me. Why won't you let yourself love me back?'

'Because I...I can't! Not now! Not yet!'

'I seem to remember a girl in a lane telling me "You could if you wanted to".' Angry, frustrated—why did she have to be so stubborn?—Dom continued. 'You told me to look past my limitations, to all that I could still be. I can't believe you don't have the courage to try, after all you've suffered and survived!'

'That's right,' she snapped back, 'I *have* suffered and survived. By protecting myself—and carrying only the burdens I could handle!'

Stung, he said, 'Well, thank you very much. I shall try very hard not to be one more "burden" you are forced to handle.'

Furious, Dom stalked off and threw himself on to his horse. He knew he'd said too much, but her ridiculous resistance made him so angry! And he loved her so much, he'd better take himself away before he said anything more.

Chapter Twenty-Three

Hands on her hips, furious too, Theo watched Dom ride off.

They'd only just settled the matter with Charles. Why did he have to push her to examine her feelings, looking for a declaration she was not yet ready to give?

Then, with a shock, she realised—he'd said he loved her. *Loved her.*

And what did she do after that heartfelt declaration, but push him away!

Idiot.

He'd offered her his heart—shouldn't she have the courage to accept it? She knew she trusted him not to hurt her, and as he'd said, nothing in life was sure. So why was she still so afraid?

Losing Marshall, finding herself alone, pregnant, unwed, had been a horror that had haunted her for years. But she'd faced other difficult situations since then—the loss of her father, the loss of her familiar place in the army, coming to an unknown land where she knew almost no one—without falling to pieces. Wasn't it time for her to move beyond the trauma of that past?

Let it go, and embrace Dom fully?

Still, when she thought of saying words of love out

loud—irrevocable words that couldn't be taken back—a sudden panic made it hard to breathe.

She couldn't do it, not yet. He had to give her a little more time.

She sighed. In any event, she needed to apologise. He'd professed his love, and she, basically, had rebuffed him. It took only a moment's reflection to realise how she would feel, had she confessed *her* love for *him*, and he'd pushed her away, claiming he wasn't prepared to take the risk of loving her.

She felt like she'd been punched in the stomach.

Sick and shaky, she collected her grazing horse and looked around for somewhere to mount.

Once again, she found nothing at all she might use as a mounting block.

It looked like she'd face another long trudge home.

Nearly two hours later, she arrived back at Bildenstone, hot, disgruntled, and more than a little annoyed with herself. She'd call for a bath and refresh herself before she went looking for Dom. Maybe put on something cut low in the bosom, to distract him, while she apologised and before she showed her contrition in a way he would most appreciate.

Maybe if she kept him too exhausted and satiated from lovemaking to think, he'd be content enough not to press her about the other.

Feeling better, she gave her horse to a groom outside the stables and proceeded on to the Hall.

'Wilton, where is your master?' she asked as he opened the door for her.

'I expect he's halfway to Hadwell by now, mistress.'

Theo stopped short. 'Hadwell?' she echoed.

'Yes, he told me he hoped to be well on the way to Bury

St Edmunds by nightfall, and from thence to Newmarket soon after.'

'He…he already left for Newmarket?'

'Yes, ma'am. He did tell me to beg your pardon on his behalf for leaving so suddenly. A messenger came from his stable manager at Newmarket this afternoon, saying all the stock had arrived and requesting his presence there as soon as he could manage it.'

'I see,' she replied, her recently revived spirits taking a sharp downward spiral.

'Shall I send Nancy up to you?'

'Yes, please,' she murmured distractedly.

Up in her room, she stood, looking out the window. Towards Newmarket.

She knew he was angry when he'd left her by the stream. But she still couldn't believe he'd left without waiting to speak with her, or attempting to repair their quarrel.

She must have wounded him even more than she'd thought.

She never thought she *could* wound him that badly. He must care very deeply.

She'd wanted to bathe, apologise, and make it all up to him.

It appeared all she'd be getting was a bath.

Five days later, Theo still had no word from Dom. She busied herself completing the transfer of her belongings from Thornfield, and checking in at the school, but always with a sense of looking over her shoulder, listening for hoofbeats.

She'd thought she was self-sufficient, but suddenly there seemed to be a tremendous gap yawning around her where, a very little time ago, there'd been none. She'd expected to miss Dom, especially after parting on such an ill note, but she found herself missing him much more than she'd dreamed possible.

When had he become so important to her well-being?

Wilton wanted to know when she wished to schedule the party for the tenants—and she wanted to consult him. She needed to set up a training program with the blacksmith for Jemmie—and she wished to ask his advice. Miss Andrews had a question about some stories she might read to the children—and she automatically thought about asking him for recommendations.

Dinners, sitting at the small formal table alone, were wretched, and even evenings spent exploring the magnificent library didn't cheer her.

Nights, of course, were the worst. A few weeks of anticipating the unparallelled bliss she'd found in his embrace quickly made her entirely resentful of having to sleep alone. Nor had she ever slept as well as she did after his sweet and thorough loving.

After not resting well at night and missing him continually by day, she soon became short-tempered even with Charles.

To travel as far as Newmarket, he'd be gone at least a week, she thought disconsolately.

All she knew for sure, was when he got home, she meant to give him a welcome, and an apology, he would never forget.

Later that same day, Dom rode towards Bildenstone. He should have remained at Newmarket another day or two; there were still horses from Upton Park not yet disposed of, but once he set up the purchase of several Norfolk trotters and Suffolk sorrels, so anxious was he to return to Bildenstone, he turned the rest of the hunters over to his stable manager and set out.

He'd hated to leave Bildenstone without speaking with

Theo—who delayed so long coming home after their quarrel by the brook, Dom knew she must have been even angrier than he'd thought.

His fault, all of it. He'd pushed her too hard, too soon. So what if it took another month, or two, or a year, until she trusted him and trusted their life together enough to admit she loved him? He *knew* she did, on a deep level that connected them in spirit as passionately as the union they made between their bodies.

He shouldn't yearn so much to hear her say the words, when her tender touch showed how much she cherished him every time they came together. And in the meantime, he should be thankful for the blessing of having claimed her as his wife, when, but for divine intervention in the form of Jemmie, he might have lost her to someone else before he could begin to woo her.

He hoped, despite his abrupt departure, that she'd not still be angry when he returned.

He *was* bringing her a gift, which might help him redeem himself. He smiled. At the least, it would give her a new project to work on.

Never again, he promised himself, would he be impatient with her.

It was mid-afternoon by the time he turned down the lane to Bildenstone. Finally reaching the manor, he left the horse to find its own way to the stables, too impatient to wait any longer.

'Wilton, where is your mistress?' he asked as the butler admitted him.

'Welcome home, sir! The mistress rode over to the school today.'

'Is Master Charles with her?'

'He and his nurse were going to Thornfield to gather

up the rest of the young master's things. Shall I bring you some refreshment?'

'Later,' he said. He'd go clean up a bit, then ride out to meet Theo. 'Would you tell Cook I'd like something special for dinner tonight?'

''I'll let her know, sir,' Wilton said, bowing.

Though nearly writhing with impatience to see Theo again, he thought it best not to meet her all covered in mud. Trotting up the stairs, he called for a footman to bring him hot water.

A half-hour later, cleaned and changed, Dom had a fresh horse brought round and rode off towards the school. It would be better to meet her in private to apologise, so he might gauge her mood, he thought as he urged his gelding to a canter, but he was too impatient to wait until she returned and they could have some guarantee of privacy.

Then, with a leap in his heart, he heard the clip-clop of approaching hoofbeats. As he looked over the next rise, he saw the familiar bay mare in the distance. Thrilled beyond measure that it was Theo, he pulled up, waiting for her to meet him.

'Dom!' she cried, making his heart exult at the unmistakable joy on her face. 'I'm so glad to see you! Was your Newmarket trip successful? If you'd let me know you were coming back today, I would have been at Bildenhall to meet you!'

'When we finished early, I came at once; I didn't want to wait long enough to send a note. It was bad enough that I had to ride off without seeing you after my hasty and ill-advised speech by the brook!'

Her face flushed. 'I thought I'd made you angry, and I was heartsick, for the quarrel was just as much my fault as yours.'

'No, I pushed too hard, Theo. I love you, will always love you, and I'm willing to take whatever you can give me. Having you as my wife is the most important thing to me.'

With a huff of frustration, she said, 'How dare you declare all that to me on horseback, where there is nothing I can do about it! We're not far from the stream. Shall we ride there and let the horses drink while we finish this conversation?'

'Lead on.' He gestured.

Continuing without further speech, they soon reached the old oak. Dom dismounted and hurried over to catch Theo as she slid from the saddle. He pulled her to him, their kiss of greeting long, slow and sweet.

Dom held her against him, savouring her violet scent, her warmth and nearness, the reassuring thud of her heartbeat against his chest. 'How I missed you, Theo. I'm so sorry we parted after angry words. Will you forgive me?'

'Of course. I missed you too, oh, so much! Your absence showed me how vital you've become to me, for I felt I'd lost a piece of myself with you gone. I suppose it crept upon me so slowly, I didn't notice—until you weren't there beside me. The man who makes me laugh and understands how important my orphans and my son are to me and stimulates my mind and eases my anxieties and has supported me through every obstacle I've faced since we met. Who gives me the most exquisite pleasure I've ever known or dreamed of. What an empty shell my life would be without you!'

After that stirring speech, he just had to kiss her again. 'My darling Theo, how could I exist without you? The girl who challenged me in the lane to be more than I thought I could be, who sat on my wall in the rain until I was forced to deal with her, who believed I could accomplish whatever I chose to do, even as I now am—and is making me believe it, too. I thank God every night that my father built a stone barn in the south pasture.'

Then her mouth was on his, demanding, her hands at his chest, untying his neckcloth, seeking skin beneath, her torso rubbing against his erection. She broke the kiss to ease him out of his jacket, free the buttons of his trouser flap, and moved his hand to tug at the jacket of her riding habit.

He stopped her fingers and broke the kiss. 'Are you sure, Theo? I don't want to force you into anything you don't want.'

'I want this now.' She breathed against his lips. 'This land belongs to you. I belong to you. I know you won't let either of us come to harm.'

She could do it, Theo told herself. The episode beside the dry creek in Portugal had led to shame, and the threat of losing her good name and being cast out of polite society that had hung over her for years. But like one of those storms that blew up over those dusty plains, sudden, furious and violent, it had spent itself and moved on. It was over now, over for ever. She could dare believe in a future—with the ardent man beside her.

Fingers hot, shaky, he helped strip off her habit, stays and chemise, laughing as his hand tangled with hers trying to wrest him out of his garments. He laid her down on their jackets, and she pulled him down over her, his skin warming hers, a sense of peace and coming home sweeping through her as he slid into her. After being apart for days, their lovemaking was fast, urgent, and just a short time later, she found bliss in his embrace.

Afterwards, they lay panting, listening to the rush and gurgle of the stream, the breeze ruffling the oak leaves above them. Through layers of contentment, Theo felt a subtle shift as the wind picked up, then a sprinkle of droplets.

'I think it's beginning to rain,' she said, eying the clouds.

Dom rolled to her side and drew her to him. 'I believe you're right.'

As the wind increased in speed and volume, the sprinkle turned into a shower. Laughing, Dom sprang up, then grabbed her hand to pull her to her feet.

'Dance with me!' he cried, his face joyous. 'We'll waltz in the rain.'

'Here?' she asked, half-amused, half-incredulous.

He gestured around them. 'We have a strip of mossy ground as a ballroom floor, the swaying candelabra of oak branches above us, the music of the wind through the trees, and a heart full of melody because you're back in my embrace again. How can I not want to dance, and shout my happiness to the world?'

'Madman!' she laughed. 'Someone might see.'

'They shouldn't look. Come, let's dance.'

He stood gazing down at her, such unrestrained joy on his face, she couldn't help smiling back. He was so uninhibited, so comfortable in himself. She wanted that assurance, that sense of liberation. She wanted *him*.

An answering joy bubbling up, she threw her arms around him and let him waltz her around the bank, while the wind whistled and the stream burbled a melody. The precipitation increased, and she threw her head back, letting warm summer rain course down her face, washing away the dust of the ride.

As she danced with him, drawing on his unconditional support and boundless optimism, Theo felt the burden she'd carried within for so many years rinsing away like that dust before the rain, until she felt so light, buoyed by his love, she thought she might float right up into the clouds.

Dom had given her this, the gift of seeing herself through his eyes: without shame, without guilt, no longer waiting for a reckoning that was surely coming to punish her someday. Freeing her from fear of loss, bringing her to believe in a future.

Marshall would always be dear to her, but the man who'd helped her do all that deserved her love, given unreservedly, just as she'd given him her body.

Finally, laughing again, he halted, mopping his wet hair off his forehead. 'I suppose we need to stop and dress.' He bowed. 'Thank you for the dance, my lady.'

'Thank *you* for the dance, though it's only just begun, my lord. My life. My love.'

Bent halfway over, retrieving his jacket, he halted abruptly and looked back over his shoulder at her. 'What did you say?'

'I love you, Dom. I've known it a long time, but been too frightened to admit it. Until you freed me of that fear, as our marriage has freed me from the past. I only wish I'd struggled out of it sooner.'

Dropping the jacket, he came to her and drew her close. Trailing his fingers down her cheek in a caress, his gaze tender, he said, 'It's all right, beloved. We have the rest of our lives. Which, I promise you, will be a long, long time.'

He placed a kiss on her forehead. 'Now, we'd better get my bride dressed and home before we both contract an inflammation of the lungs. Besides, I brought you a gift which, by now, should be waiting at Bildenstone for you.'

'A gift? You shouldn't have! What is it?'

'You'll see soon enough. Now, help me with these wet ties.'

She assisted him into his soggy garments and he helped

her. Finished haphazardly dressing each other, she stood back to examine him and burst out laughing.

'I can't imagine what Wilton will think when we get back! We look like we've been kidnapped by gypsies, rolled through a hay meadow and then dunked in a stream.'

'Or making love in the rain on a mossy bank?'

She would be brave, as he was. 'Or making love in the rain on your mossy bank beside your stream. My fearless lord.'

Almost giddy with happiness, Dom rode beside Theo back to Bildenstone, where they turned their horses over at the entrance and walked hand in hand up the stairs.

Wilton opened the door to usher them inside. 'The, ah… item you sent from Newmarket has arrived, sir, and has for the time being been installed—under much protest— in the small blue bedchamber.'

'Very good. And don't worry, Wilton. It won't be there long.'

'That is my present?' she asked as they mounted stairs.

'Yes. Let me show it to you before we wash and change. Ordinarily, for a lovely lady, I'd think of gems. But my Theo is hardly ordinary, and if the prospect of wearing the Ransleigh rubies didn't tempt you, I knew no paltry diamonds would. But this—this I thought you might truly appreciate.'

They reached the blue bedchamber, Dom opened the door and waved her in.

The small figure standing by the window whirled to face them. Thin and grimy, his bony shoulders were encased in a ragged jacket that dwarfed his frame, the garment so old and dirty only the frogging and the few remaining buttons identified it as having once graced the back of a Ninety-Fifth Rifleman. Apparently awed and intimidated by his surroundings, he stared at them, fear and defiance in his eyes.

'Theo, meet Tommy of No-Last-Name. He came out of the shadows of the stables in Newmarket, offering to hold my horse for a penny. Before I knew you, I might have tossed him a coin and passed him by with barely a glance. But one lucky day, I met a girl who showed me every one of God's creatures is precious, even the abandoned and the maimed. That every one of us should have a chance to become more.'

Blinking back tears, Theo pressed his hand. 'You were right. This is the best present you could give me.'

Smiling, Dom watched her walk over to kneel in front of the boy. 'Hello, Tommy. Was your father a rifleman?'

'Yes'm,' the boy spoke at last. 'No matter what summun said, he were me da. Me mum give me his jacket afore she died. I never stole it.'

'I'm sure you didn't. How did you get to Newmarket?'

As Theo talked with the child, the trepidation on his face gradually faded, his defensive posture relaxed, and he took her hand.

'Ring the bell, Dom, would you?' she asked a few minutes later. 'Tommy's agreed to let Mrs Greenlow give him a bath before we drive him over to the school to meet the other children.'

'Letting Mrs Greenlow do it? Wise woman,' he teased. 'Looks like he could bite and scratch.'

'Nonsense. He'll enjoy a bath. Won't you, Tommy?'

The boy looked up dubiously, leaving Dom confident he had no notion of what a bath actually entailed. But, with more reassurances from Theo that she would rejoin him as soon as she found him a shirt and breeches, he trotted off with the footman who answered Dom's summons.

She came dancing over to him, gratitude and delight

on her face. 'Thank you for my present! You are the handsomest, kindest, wisest man I've ever met!'

'And I'm your dearest love, for ever,' he said, hungry to hear the words again from her lips.

She looked up, her eyes tender, her expression radiating affection and joy. 'You are my dearest love, and I will love you for ever.'

With that, she leaned up into his kiss.

* * * * *

MILLS & BOON
A ROMANCE FOR EVERY READER

- **FREE** delivery direct to your door

- **EXCLUSIVE** offers every month

- **SAVE** up to 25% on pre-paid subscriptions

SUBSCRIBE AND SAVE

millsandboon.co.uk/Subscribe

MILLS & BOON

THE HEART OF ROMANCE

A ROMANCE FOR EVERY READER

MODERN

Prepare to be swept off your feet by sophisticated, sexy and seductive heroes, in some of the world's most glamourous and romantic locations, where power and passion collide.

HISTORICAL

Escape with historical heroes from time gone by. Whether your passion is for wicked Regency Rakes, muscled Vikings or rugged Highlanders, awaken the romance of the past.

MEDICAL

Set your pulse racing with dedicated, delectable doctors in the high-pressure world of medicine, where emotions run high and passion, comfort and love are the best medicine.

True Love

Celebrate true love with tender stories of heartfelt romance, from the rush of falling in love to the joy a new baby can bring, and a focus on the emotional heart of a relationship.

Desire

Indulge in secrets and scandal, intense drama and plenty of sizzling hot action with powerful and passionate heroes who have it all: wealth, status, good looks…everything but the right woman.

HEROES

Experience all the excitement of a gripping thriller, with an intense romance at its heart. Resourceful, true-to-life women and strong, fearless men face danger and desire - a killer combination!

To see which titles are coming soon, please visit

millsandboon.co.uk/nextmonth

JOIN US ON SOCIAL MEDIA!

Stay up to date with our latest releases, author news and gossip, special offers and discounts, and all the behind-the-scenes action from Mills & Boon...

 millsandboon

 millsandboonuk

millsandboon

It might just be true love...

MILLS & BOON

MODERN

Power and Passion

Prepare to be swept off your feet by sophisticated, sexy and seductive heroes, in some of the world's most glamourous and romantic locations, where power and passion collide.

Eight Modern stories published every month, find them all at:

millsandboon.co.uk/Modern